Millie Rafferty – Th

A Victorian Saga

Val Clamp

Copyright ©2019 Val Clamp

All rights reserved.

ISBN 9781672712774

Dedication.

To my husband Brian for his patience as I sat for hours over my computer, and to my sister Pat who had to suffer reading all my attempts before I found the style I was happy with.
Also to my parents and younger sister Sue who sadly are no longer with us to see the finished product.

Acknowledgements

To my nephew Richard for his help and patience in launching my books with Amazon kindle and to all my friends who encouraged me to take my writing from a pastime to try and reach a wider audience, Doreen, Barbara, Jane, Josie, Karen, Michelle and Pat.

Prologue.

March 1850.

I lay upon my back in the cramped bunk which I shared with two other girls, in the sliver of moonlight shining in through the tiny windows set high up in the wall I could just about make out the shape of some of the other girls who shared this overcrowded room with me. I hadn't counted them, but there must have been upwards of eighty sharing that space, some were asleep, some were crying softly in the night, others like me were awake watching the vapour of their warm breath rise up into the cold air, but we all had one thing in common, the desperation which had brought us to that place.

The thin grey blanket which did little to keep the cold at bay was rough and scratched at my skin, the thin mattress offering poor protection from the wooden slats of the bed, my skin itched and my back was sore but all that discomfort was bearable compared to the loneliness I felt after having spent another day apart from the family I loved.

I sensed rather than saw that Irene, the small chatty girl who was laid on my right side, her feet alongside my shoulder as three of us lay top to tail in the bunk, was also awake and studying me with her dark eyes.

'Can't you sleep?' she whispered.

'No, I don't think I will ever get used to not seeing my family every day, we have never been apart before and I am worried how they are faring.'

'I know what you mean, I am lucky that I see my two sisters every day but I miss my brothers so much.'

'How many brothers do you have?' I asked hoping to prolong the conversation as it made me feel less alone.

'Three.'

'Have you been here long?'

'Since the end of the summer, I'm not sure how long. I did try and keep a count of it but I lost track after a while.'

'Are your parents here?'

'No, they died just after we came in, 'her voice catching as she choked back a sob. I could feel her body begin to tremble next to me and I reached down under the blanket to find her hand and take it in mine. I knew that this action was as much for me as for her and a part of me felt guilty that I was using her grief in order to feel some human contact.

After a few moments her trembling subsided and she rolled onto her side, the conversation over. As the darkness and silence enveloped me once more I tried to take my mind back to happier times with my family back on the farm in Ireland before fate intervened and brought me to the place I now called home. Life had always been tough, but in 1845 things took a dramatic change for the worse, a change which would eventually affect just about every Irish person.

Eventually the faint light of dawn crept in through the window signalling the beginning of another day, the door to the room was pushed open by a large woman, loudly ringing a hand bell which was our command to get up and go for a breakfast of gruel before we started the day's work. Although the work could be hard, I didn't mind it too much because it took me closer to the time I would be allowed to see my family for the first time since coming here. Climbing off the bunk, slipping on my shoes and dragging my fingers through my long black hair I joined the others in forming the long queue to the kitchen. My fifth day began.

Chapter 1.

Ireland, June 1847.

Tommy and I had been walking for nearly two hours and were just approaching the town. I would normally have enjoyed going into town, a place which always held a fascination for me whenever I visited with my father on the odd occasion he had something to trade at market. I used to love the hustle and bustle of people going about their daily lives, street sellers shouting out their wares, horses pulling carts loaded with goods from the farms and children and dogs running through the streets. The town was situated in a small valley about twenty miles west of Dublin, it was home to about one hundred and fifty people, although now with its transient population as folk passed through on their way to the port, the numbers rose and fell.

As I looked around, the town seemed to have lost all that energy, the features of the men and women drawn and grey, a look I now saw on the faces of my own parents. Children trailed alongside their parents, tear stained faces and ragged clothes, some holding out their tiny hands towards me, begging me to take away their misery.

I turned to look over at Tommy and gave him a weak smile knowing that he hated being there as much as I did. Aged eight Tommy was three and a half years younger than me; his ninth birthday was later this month, with deep brown eyes set in a broad face topped off with unruly dark brown hair, already his hands were larger than mine and he loved nothing more than to take mine in his and squeeze until I begged him to release me. Mama said he was going to take after our father who was of average height with broad shoulders and a muscular body due to the physical nature of his work. I took his hand in mine and we walked over to join the queue as it slowly shuffled forward to receive the ration of corn meal that would keep my family alive for another day.

At last we reached the head of the queue.

'Card,' said the man.

I reached into my pocket to retrieve the card and handed it over to be checked.

'Name?'

'Rafferty,' I replied.

'Bowl.'

Tommy handed over the bowl and it was filled with the corn meal. The man handed me back the card and we turned away. I placed a cloth over the bowl so that we didn't lose any of the precious cargo and we made our way out of the town and back to the cabin.

On the journey back, with the town now behind us for another day, I could feel my mood beginning to lighten. The sun had burnt off the early morning mist and the cloudless sky was a deep blue, birds were flitting along the hedgerows and with the song of the skylark high above, I hoped that today we would turn a corner and things would start to improve for us. We had been making this daily trek for the last two weeks, once the last of the potato crops we had left were gone. Like most families in Ireland potatoes were the main part of our diet and it was always a struggle between June and July when the old crops were finished and the new ones were not yet ready to harvest. This year was even worse due to the blight which had begun two years before, ruining about a third of the national crop; the following year about three quarters of the crop were devastated. This led to food shortages and many people had left these shores to try and make a better life elsewhere. Others had died, not due to starvation but malnutrition which left them susceptible to illness and disease. Our family had survived the devastation of 1845 which was mainly on the west coast but it was reported to be spreading at about fifty miles per week by the summer of '46 and our yield last year was down by about half.

At last the cabin came into view and I could see my mother and youngest brother Danny bent over the small plot of land in which we grew our crop, my mother lifted her head at the sound of our approach and slowly straightened up, her hands massaging the small of her back. Danny ran over, his cheeks pink from the combination of the sun and his efforts tending to the garden.

'I can see lots of leaves Tommy,' he said, 'come and look.' He grabbed Tommy by the hand and dragged him over to the plot chattering as they went.

I followed my mother into the kitchen and placed the bowl on the table. It took a while for my eyes to adjust to the gloom inside. The kitchen was cool and dim, the light struggling to reach the farthest corners of the room. Home was a two roomed cabin made from mud, the only light coming in from the doorway and a small opening cut into the side wall of the kitchen. The room was partitioned off by a mud wall which divided our sleeping quarters from that of the kitchen and the floors were covered with peat. There was a table with a wooden bench either side for our meals with a cook pot in the corner nearest the window, the kitchen floor was below the level of the yard outside as the cabins were not allowed to be above a certain height and this gave added headroom.

As my mother set about preparing the family meal I went outside to join my brothers and began the daily chores required. That day my father was working on the farm, the cabin and land we had belonged to the landowner and in return my father had to work three days for him each week. Time was when Tommy would have joined him but now due to the problems with the harvest there wasn't enough work for him as well.

As the sun was dipping down behind the tree line I saw my father appear at the end of the lane. 'Here comes Papa, Danny,' I said and without further prompting Danny was up and running to meet him as fast as his skinny five year old legs would carry him. I watched as my father crouched down; his arms outstretched to snatch up my younger brother and hoist him onto his shoulders. As Papa reached the cabin he lifted Danny from his shoulders, ruffled Tommy's hair and placed a kiss on the top of my head, before walking inside and gently pecking my mother on the cheek.

'How has your day been?' my mother asked.

'Not bad, but the main crop on the farm looks like it's going to be down a great deal to normal, the plants look healthy enough, there just aren't going to be enough. I don't know how much longer he can afford to employ us all.' My father drew his hands over his face, rubbing at his eyes. I knew he was tired, as work on the farm was long and hard but there was something else in his blue eyes that I couldn't quite read.

'I'm sure it will improve,' replied my mother, spooning the supper into the bowls and passing them round the table. 'Our crop seems to be doing well; Danny is very pleased with it.'

'Is that right?' Papa asked Danny.

'Yes Papa, I have been checking it every day and I know it's going to be a good one this year,' Danny replied. I could see in his face how proud he was in his contribution to the welfare of the family. Normally at five years of age he would have been doing some work on the main farm, Tommy started at five, but again due to the blight, work had been reduced and Danny had been disappointed to still be at home.

'That's good son, we need a good one because we will have to lay extra aside for the next planting to bring the new crop up to the normal level. Still with the cornmeal ration as well we should just about get through.'

Once the meal was finished, I along with my brothers cleared and washed the dishes. My father lit his pipe and sat on the old stool outside the kitchen door enjoying the last of the evening; my mother lit a candle, placing it on the table and took up her sewing basket. This was the best time of the day, my family was complete again and after a hard day's work we were content to sit quietly enjoying the company of those we loved whilst listening to the sounds of the countryside as the creatures that occupied the dark came out and began their task of surviving another day.

Chapter 2.

The following week passed in much the same way, Tommy and I making the daily trek into town, my mother and Danny tending the smallholding and my father working the two crops. Summer was getting well into its stride and the potatoes were coming on well. Everything seemed to be going to plan and that morning as we approached the town I felt optimistic that we had survived.

Once again we joined the queue which seemed to grow each day we came, more people having to admit defeat and seek out help to feed their families.

We reached the head of the queue.

'Card.'

I duly passed over the card.

'Name?'

'Rafferty.'

'Bowl.'

Tommy handed the bowl to the man as I stuffed the card back into my apron pocket.

'There's not as much as normal, 'said Tommy looking first at the bowl and then at the man who was doling out the rations. 'Where is the rest?'

'That's it,' he replied already taking the bowl from the woman behind us in the queue.

'But that's not enough, there are five of us and my mother can only just make it stretch as it is,' I said.

'Sorry, but supplies are running low and what with all the extra people who keep turning up that's all we are allowed to give out.'

'But what will we do? What will I tell Mama?' my voice was shaking and I felt myself on the verge of tears fearing I had let my family down.

'Come on love,' said the woman behind us, 'I need to get back to my kids.'

The walk back to the cabin was a quiet one, neither Tommy nor I wanting to talk. We knew that this was going to upset our mother and as each step took us nearer our destination the slower we seemed to walk. Eventually we reached the end of the lane and upon seeing my mother's welcoming smile I ran to her and wrapped my arms around her.

'Whatever is the matter Millie?' she asked pushing me back to look into my eyes. 'Are you hurt?'

'No Mama but we weren't given as much cornmeal as normal and it's my fault,' the tears flowed freely down my face now as all the worries of the past few months, the setbacks and the seemingly dashed hopes overwhelmed me.

'It's not her fault,' said Tommy, 'they haven't got enough left to give us.' He passed the bowl to mother and I watched her face drop as she lifted the cover.

'That's alright, I can manage with this, take Danny with you to the bottom meadow, I think you may find some nettles there, that will help. Millie come inside with me and we will get started on this.'

My mother and I spent the next hour or so grinding the cornmeal whilst we waited for my brother's return from foraging in the hedgerows and talked about any trivial thing that came to mind to take our thoughts off the matter. My mother was doing her best to put on a brave face and by the time the harvesters returned with a basket brimming with the green stinging plants I had begun to believe again that we would get through this. I could see that the nettles had not surrendered easily and both Tommy and Danny were covered in red rashes from the leaves, their legs stained green from the dock leaves they had used to alleviate their stings.

As the rain began to fall lightly, the grey clouds pushing back the blue sky, my father appeared at the end of our lane, Danny was off as usual but today my father merely removed his cap and placed it on the head of my brother, took his hand and walked the rest of the way home. As he drew nearer I saw that look again, the one from last week and this week I could place it, it was the look of a man who had no more left to give, no more energy to fight and a proud man who was admitting defeat.

'Just give me a moment to talk to your mother alone children, I'll call you shortly.'

As I watched his retreating back, the three of us sat down on the old log under the lean to where we used to store the crops, my stomach was churning and subconsciously I clenched my fists digging my nails into my palms, a nervous habit I have always had which I did whenever I was frightened or worried.

After what seemed ages my father called to us to go in, my mother was stood with her back to us but when she turned I could see she had been crying, her green eyes red rimmed and puffy.

'Sit down children,' my father said taking the bench opposite. My mother joined him and slipped her hand in his; trying to give him the strength he undoubtedly needed to break whatever bad news we knew was coming.

'I know you know a lot of the problems we are all suffering at the moment, not just here on our farm but all over the country. Well it seems things are going to be some time before they get any better. Today the landlord has told us all there will be no more work to be had on his farm until things improve, the crop that he does have can be managed by him and his sons. Our crop is not yet ready for harvest and your mother says that the corn meal ration was halved today. More and more people are in need and the demands are too high.'

'What can we do?' I asked.

'Well your mother and I have been talking and there are only about two options. There is talk that they are opening a soup kitchen in town and we can all go there once a day to receive a meal. That should hopefully see us through until the crop is ready. '

'Is that as well as the corn meal?' Tommy asked.

'No son, the corn meal has run out, it will just be the one meal a day.'

'Can we find food out in the hedgerows like we did today Papa?' enquired Danny.

'No I don't think we can rely on that, everyone else will be doing the same thing.'

Suddenly I remembered a possible answer, 'What about the hiring fair, don't they normally come around this time of year?' Hiring fairs were held twice a year where labourers would offer their services to work on farms, this was a way to reach further afield than normal.

'Yes that's true,' said my mother a look of hope lighting up her face.

'Yes Papa, Millie and I can go with you while Mama and Danny tend the crop.' added Tommy grabbing onto this idea also.

'I had forgotten that for the moment, yes they should be here next week.'

'Was that the other option Papa?' I asked tentatively not sure whether I wanted to hear the answer.

'No Millie, the other option is to follow the others and leave.'

'Leave home?'

'Yes, leave home and this country,' my father's voice faltered. 'I know it's a big step but I don't know how else we can survive and stay together.'

'I don't want to leave here,' said Danny tears spilling down his cheeks.

'None of us do but we want to all be together don't we?' my mother answered going round the table and taking Danny in her arms, she rocked him gently, her hand wiping the wet tears away. 'Anyway who knows they might have some work at the fair.'

'Can't we wait until the potatoes are harvested?' Tommy enquired. I could see he was also nervous about the prospect of leaving here.

'No lad, if I am not working on the farm we will have to pay rent and we have no money. Any harvest we get will be used for food and seed for the next planting. We could be evicted,' was my father's reply.

That seemed to be the end of the discussion, supper was eaten and cleared away and it was agreed tomorrow we would all make the journey into town and see what the prospects were. The earlier light rain gave way to a steady downpour, the dark clouds matching the mood of the occupants in the cabin. As I laid on my back on the straw mattress in the family room listening to the sounds of the night I knew my life was about to change dramatically but I just didn't know in what way.

Chapter 3.

Sleep did not come easily to me last night and the next morning I woke up feeling tired, the weather seemed to reflect my mood. Although the rain from the previous evening had moved on the sky was still grey and the yard awash with deep puddles. I looked out of the doorway to where my father and Tommy were inspecting the potato plants. Even from where I stood I could see that many of the previously erect green leaves were now laid flat to the ground, in some areas the soil had been washed away leaving the tubers exposed. I watched as they painstakingly tended to the plants, raking the soil back into place and doing what they could to ensure they had the best chance of survival. The constant damp weather did little to aid the crops as it allowed the fungus to spread more rapidly. Although this year had been slightly better than the previous two the combination of heavy rain and damp was hitting hard.

My mother walked over to me and placed her arms around my shoulders saying, 'Millie go and wake Danny up, we need to be setting off to the soup kitchen and we don't know how many people will be there.'

I turned to my mother, 'We will be alright won't we?'

She smiled at me, but the smile didn't reach her eyes. Not knowing what to say I turned and went to rouse Danny.

'Danny, wake up we are ready to go to town, get your shoes and hurry up.'

Danny sat up slowly and rubbed the sleep from his eyes, 'Are we having breakfast before we go?'

'No, we have to get off now or we'll be late,' I couldn't bring myself to tell him that we didn't have anything to eat that morning.

At last we were ready and we set off for town, it was a long time since the whole family had been together on this journey but the joy I would normally have had under those circumstances was missing. Upon nearing the town we were joined by tens of people also making their way to the soup kitchen. Some of the faces I recognised from my previous visits with Tommy over the last fortnight but many were strangers and those I did know had been joined by other members of their family who like us now had no option but to all attend in order to receive a meal.

The queue for the kitchen stretched the full length of the square, men, women and children, the sick and infirm also. I had never felt as wretched as I did at that moment; I looked up into the face of my father and saw the last shred of his pride disappear as he acknowledged he could no longer provide for his family. Finally we reached the head of the queue and each of us received a bowl of watery soup which was tasteless and did little to stave off the growing pangs of hunger. Before returning home my father went to enquire about the hiring fair due here next week.

'I doubt it will be here Daniel,' stated the small man with a whiskery grey beard and watery blue eyes. 'There is so little work around I don't see the point in it, even if they are hiring just imagine how many will be here seeking work. It's hopeless, there's no work, no food and yet we still keep selling oats and maize to England because they get the best price. Pure greed watching their fellow countrymen starve just to line their pockets.'

'Thank you Patrick, what are you going to do?' asked my father.

'The thing I should have done last year 'was his reply. 'Get out while I still have my health. You should think about it too, you owe it to them bairns of yours.'

'Well good luck to you Patrick, come on Maria let's get these children home.' With that my father turned and headed off home, a quiet air of determination settling upon him. All the way home he was deep in thought.

As they walked home Daniel looked around at each member of his family, his wife Maria the woman who had been beside him since their marriage thirteen years ago, who had worked tirelessly at his side supporting him and caring for their children. She had a strong will and nothing had ever got her down for long before, but he could see the look in her eyes now as she struggled to come to terms with the situation they found themselves in. Millie his daughter who never complained no matter what she had to do, bravely taking it upon herself to make the journey into town these last weeks with her brother to fetch the rations leaving her parents free in order to carry on working where they could. Tommy his eldest son who worked alongside him in the fields when times were easier, determined not to let his father see when he was tired, trying so hard to become a man to his parents and earn his keep. Then he looked at Danny, his youngest son who didn't fully understand the implications of the current situation but would follow his father to the ends of the earth trusting he would never let them down. With this thought in mind Daniel came to a decision, one that his head was telling him must be done although his heart was very much against it. The time for further delay was over; too much time had been wasted waiting for the turn of fortune which he was now convinced would not come without more suffering. He was not looking forward to the conversation he must have when they got home but knew there was no other way.

'Come in and sit down all of you,' he said. 'I have been thinking on the way home and I have come to a decision. I will tell you of it and I don't want any interruptions until I have finished, then you may ask questions but unless any of you can come up with a strong argument for not doing this then it will happen.'

His family took their seats around the table and waited for him to begin.

Daniel cleared his throat before beginning,' we all went to town today and saw with our own eyes the situation we are all in. It's not isolated anymore, it's affecting everyone. People are suffering, there is no work or prospect of such, disease is spreading, people are dying, and soon they will be starving too. That soup is not worth the walk to town, it alone won't keep us alive not on its own. The landlord hasn't any work and without it we cannot pay rent, we will lose our home. The hiring fair won't be coming and if it does there won't be any work locally, I will have to go where they need me and I can't go, not knowing what is happening to you back here without me. You heard what Patrick said, we are growing wheat and maize and it is being sold to the English as they are the only ones who can afford it. So my decision is we go to England and find work there.'

The room was quiet and Daniel waited as his family came to terms with what he had said.

'I suppose you are right,' said Maria, 'I can't see any alternative; we must leave to protect the children.'

'Does anybody have any questions?' said Daniel expecting some resistance.

'When will we go?' asked Tommy.

'Tomorrow, there is no reason to delay if we are going to do it, we will have to walk to the port to find a ship and I don't know how often they sail but waiting won't make it any better. Millie, anything you want to say?'

'No Papa, I trust you and Mama to make the right decision.'

Daniel looked at his wife wondering what they had done to deserve such faith.

That was it then, we had decided we were going to England, I had never been further than the town and the prospect of the forthcoming journey filled me with both excitement and fear.

Suddenly my mother put her head in her hands and asked of my father, 'What about Frances?'

'I am afraid we will have to say goodbye to Frances before we go.'

At that my mother burst into tears and my father took her gently in his arms and held her until her sobbing subsided.

Frances was my younger sister who would have been two years old now had she lived. My mother miscarried at six months, narrowly escaping with her own life and as a result was now barren. I knew the loss of my sister was a constant source of grief to my parents and the thought of leaving her here alone in her small plot was tearing them up again.

After a while my mother left the kitchen and walked down to the edge of the meadow where the trees stood vigil over my sister.

'Shall I go with her?' I asked.

'No, leave her be, we will all say our goodbyes before we leave but for now your mother needs to be alone.'

As night came and we retired to bed I could not help but feel apprehensive, although I knew it was not a decision my parents would take lightly, I would miss this way of life to which I had become accustomed.

Chapter 4.

The next morning broke with a promise of better weather as we made our way down the meadow to pay our respects to Frances and bid her a final farewell. As we stood heads bowed and silent I could not help but wonder what my sister would have looked like. Would she have had the dark colouring of my father, Tommy and me or the auburn hair of my mother, which had given Danny a dark blond colouring? Part of me envied her that she would not have to undergo the trauma of leaving the country of her birth; I immediately regretted that thought knowing the circumstances that led to her being left behind.

Danny wandered to the edge of the tree line, disappearing into the trees for a few moments. When he reappeared he was clutching a small bunch of flowers which he offered to my mother. Bending down to take the flowers from him, she pulled him to her and hugged him tightly, the tears falling freely now. Then she kissed him and rising, walked over and placed the posy on the grave then turned and walked back to the cabin not looking back. We took our cue from her and also returned.

We were ready to leave, all we owned we were wearing; we had no money and no food heading into town for a meal at the soup kitchen before setting off to walk to Dublin to catch the ship that would take us from all we had ever known to a new life in Liverpool.

The sun came out and as we walked past the small patch of land that held our potato crop Tommy ran over and began pulling at the plants.

'They are small Papa but it's a shame to leave them behind to rot.'

'Well done, son. I hadn't given them a thought, I know they wouldn't go to waste as someone would have taken them but they are ours and they will make a meal or two.'

The next half an hour was spent pulling the small tubers from the ground and placing them in a pail. Feeling that things were improving we set off into town. When we reached the outskirts of town my mother stopped us.

'Do you think we should go in separately? If they see we have some food we may be turned away and we will need the potatoes for our journey.'

'That's a good point,' Papa replied, 'you go in with Danny while we wait here and then the three of us will go upon your return.'

'What do you think Liverpool will be like?' asked Tommy while we settled in to wait our turn to go to the soup kitchen.

'I have no idea son; I only know that many Irish have gone there already. Some have stayed and others have gone on further to America and Australia.'

'Are we staying there or going further?' I asked. I had only just come to terms with going to England and didn't think I could cope with having to move on.

'I don't really know Millie, it depends what we find when we get there. All I know is we don't have money for the sailing so I would think it would be best to find work and get some money together, then we can decide if we want to move on or not. The first priority is finding work and somewhere to live.'

'Do you know anyone there Papa?' I enquired.

'Well I know a lot of people who have left before us but where they are now I have no idea.'

'How far is it to Dublin?' said Tommy lying on his back with his hands behind his head, chewing on a small grass shoot.

About twenty miles, we won't get all the way today, hopefully if we get an early start tomorrow we should be there by noon.'

My mother and brother returned a short while later and then Papa, Tommy and I set off into town. The ranks of those waiting in line for their meal seemed to have swelled in the space of a day and I knew then that my father was right in his decision to leave, who knew how long it would be before this lifeline was exhausted. Also the mood seemed to have changed as people grew irritable waiting in line, grumbling and worrying whether the soup would be gone before they got to the front. This underlying tension frightened me and it was with some relief that after having received our meagre meal we were once again heading back to join the others.

'Right then, are we ready for this?' my father asked.

'Yes let's go,' replied mother, 'The sun is high now and it's going to be warm.'

Picking up the pail of potatoes we set off.

The road was dusty and we were not alone as we made the journey, families, couples, old and young all with the same goal were making their way to the town of Dublin. I made sure to take in all the sights and sounds of the countryside I was seeing for the first and also my last time. All my life had been spent on the land we rented with the odd excursion into town or the weekly visit to chapel. The scenery was quite breath taking and I marvelled at the expanse of it, green pastures all around, fields of potato crops and the occasional farm dwellings dotting the vista. I just wished I were seeing it under different circumstances. After walking for some three hours, having made many rest stops along the way, we came across a small stream and took the opportunity to take a drink and rest for a while. Danny laid his head on my mother's lap and within a few minutes his breathing changed to a shallow rhythm as he drifted off to sleep.

Maria stroked her son's face as he slept in her lap; his cheeks were ruddy and his legs dusty. He had not complained once during their journey and even offered to take his turn carrying the pail of potatoes which was not taken up.
'How much further do we have to go Daniel?' she asked.
'We are nearly half way I think, probably eleven miles to go,' replied her husband although he knew their progress hadn't been as good as he had hoped for and they were only about seven miles into their journey but he didn't want to dishearten them.
'Shall we rest here for the night? The children are tired,' Maria said turning to her husband who she could tell was eager to continue on their way. Daniel had always been this way, once his mind was made up he saw no reason to delay, but she was concerned for the children.
'I would like to make the most of the light while we have it. The earlier we get into Dublin the better; we don't know how long we will have to wait for a sailing. I will carry Danny for a while. It's only about three o'clock. If we walk another three hours we will only have a few miles tomorrow.'
'Daniel,' Maria said quietly, 'the children are not used to walking this far and don't forget they have only had one bowl of weak soup to eat.'
'You are right,' was Daniel's reply, 'if we rest now we can be up with the sun tomorrow and should reach Dublin by ten at the latest. We have water here so it makes sense.'

I emptied the pail and went down to the stream to fill it with water, Tommy and my father went to find some kindling for a fire and laying Danny gently on the ground my mother began to prepare some of the potatoes for supper.
'Tommy and I spotted a small copse a little further on which I think we should use to spend the night, it will give us some protection from the

weather and is off the road,' Papa told us. 'After supper we will set up there.'

I couldn't remember the last time I felt so hungry and hoped that we would make Dublin before we used all the food. I hadn't even given thought to how we were to survive once we were in Liverpool, I just clung to the hope that our fortunes would change once we reached England, also trusting in my parents to make the right decisions.

The meal, which was small and barely enough to take away the hunger pangs, was eaten in silence as we all gave thanks to Tommy for his forethought. Once finished we set off again for the copse in order to find a place to sleep for the night. The sky had now made way to cloud and the temperature began to drop quite quickly, so as we reached the edge of the trees and began to search for a suitable resting place I could feel my skin begin to cool. I had never spent a night outdoors before and the prospect filled me with dread, I had no idea what creatures may be out there and had no wish to find out.

Eventually we found a small hollow which would give us some shelter from the breeze that was starting to make itself felt. My father and brothers went to find more fuel for a fire which would not only keep us a little warmer but help to fend off the insects and animals. By the time they returned and the fire was burning it was fully dark, with dark clouds threatening rain either that night or tomorrow. We all hunkered down in the dip and huddled together for warmth with my parents on the outside of the group as we settled down for our first night away from the cabin.

I closed my eyes and tried to block out the strange noises as the wood came alive to the night. Mysterious rustlings and snuffling could be heard and it took me all my time to not jump up and bolt off into the night. I think the only thing that made me stay was the fear of what I may be running to. I felt I had only just drifted off to sleep when I felt the first drops of rain begin to fall, they began lightly enough but after about ten minutes turned into a relentless downpour which dowsed our fire and soaked us through. We were all fully awake now and thoroughly miserable, picking up the pail we ventured further into the trees hoping to find better shelter. Progress was slow as we could not see much further than arm's length and the floor was littered with roots and hollows waiting to trip the unwary traveller. At last we reached a group of sturdy trees whose leaf canopy kept off the worst of the rain, but some drops penetrated the foliage. Sitting underneath the dripping branches I thought we all accepted there would be no more sleep tonight as we sat shivering, wet and hungry waiting for dawn. How I longed to be back in the safety and relative warmth of our cabin, snuggled alongside my brothers and parents under the thin blankets, the light from the fire flickering shadows across the mud ceiling. I could feel Danny's body trembling as he shivered next to me, I pulled him closer into me hoping to have some body heat to share with him although I doubted I was much comfort to him. I also doubted that this was the last time I would suffer discomfort on this journey from all we knew and loved to the new life overseas.

Chapter 5.

I sat with my back against the tree trunk, watching as the day slowly replaced the night, the rain still falling. My hair and clothes were damp and clung to my shivering frame. Since we had moved under the protection of the tree canopy I don't think any of us had managed more than a few minutes sleep at a time. I looked at the faces of my family and saw reflected in them the way I was feeling.

'Maria, how many meals will we be able to stretch the potatoes to?' asked my father.

'If we are careful, two maybe three at a push,' was her reply.

'Right well I think we should try and find some dry tinder and make a fire, we can have some breakfast and hopefully dry out a little. We have a full day if we want to reach the port today,' said my father as he got to his feet, stretching and scratching at the stubble on his chin.

Tommy and I set off in search of kindling whilst Danny and my father walked the short distance back to the stream for water. We found a small handful of twigs enough to get a small fire going and took these back to the others. After a while the damp wood succumbed and gave way to a smoky light. We huddled around the weak flame whilst the potatoes cooked and hung our outer garments over the low branches in an effort to dry out the worst of the wet. Once the meal was finished we shrugged back into the still damp clothes and made our way out of the wood back to the road. Although it was not raining at present the sky was laden with heavy black clouds which threatened to release their contents at any moment.

The road was muddy and filled with puddles, and it wasn't long before the heavy walking conditions were taking their toll on us all, Danny especially. Progress was slow, the deep mud clawing at our feet making each step more effort than normal, but we plodded on knowing that we had to make it to the port today if our food was to last us. After about two hours we found a small hand cart at the side of the road, one of the wheels had snapped in half and it had been abandoned where it fell, but it provided a somewhat drier option than the wet and muddy track and we sat there to rest a while.

'Do you think we will reach Dublin soon Papa?' I asked removing my shoes and wringing out my socks. My skin was rubbing against the damp socks and chafing my heels.

'It will be a fair while yet I am afraid, this mud is slowing us down. How are you feeling Danny?' my father asked looking across to my young brother who was hunched, elbows on knees and chin in hands.

Danny looked up at our father and answered, 'I am hungry Papa and my legs ache.' I looked at my brother with his legs caked in mud, his red rimmed eyes from lack of sleep. He looked so different from the boy he was only a few days ago before we left the safety of our cabin, he was a small skinny boy who was slow to wake in the morning but once he had eaten he was constantly on the move. He had a gentle nature and was a keen animal lover and was happiest when he managed to find some creature he thought was in need of his care. Many a time he had startled Mama when he opened his hand to show her his latest capture. My heart went out to him and it hurt me to know there was no physical or mental comfort I could offer him to make the situation better. Then wiping his eyes against the back of his sleeve he added, 'but I will be ok.'

Mother took his hand in hers and stroked his hair. 'I am so proud of you Danny,'

Father pulled himself to his feet saying, 'We must be going now, the rain has kept off so far but looking at those clouds I don't think our luck will last much longer.'

He was right, we had only been walking for around ten minutes when the first of the drops began to fall, and all too soon the drizzle turned to a steady downpour drenching us once again. As I walked with my head down to keep the rain from my eyes I wondered how much longer we could keep this up. The rain was running down the back of my neck and I was shivering, my hair clung to my face and my hands were numb. I looked around in the hope of seeing some shelter somewhere but there was nothing in sight but the muddy road stretching on before us dotted with fellow travellers. Suddenly I spotted something that made me cry out.

'Mama, Papa look over there!' I called stopping everyone in their tracks.

At the side of the road just across from a small ditch was a blackberry bush, it was not laden with fruit as I was sure all who passed this place before us would have also taken advantage of the free fare but there were some small berries to be seen, some ripe enough to eat. The five of us staggered down the bank, through the small gulley and began to pick the fruit. The fruit that was ripe was soft and juicy and at that moment I couldn't think of anything that had tasted so good, unfortunately it didn't take long before we had stripped the bush of all the edible berries. All that were left were the unripened fruit, and I wondered who would be the next weary family to find this unexpected gift in such a time of need.

As we struck out again there seemed to be an upturn of mood and even the rain had lessened to a steady drizzle. We passed a couple with a young baby sitting at the side of the road whilst the mother nursed the child and the man held his jacket over the pair to keep the rain off. It brought a timely reminder that we were not the only ones suffering and making this journey in hope of salvation.

'Papa, 'asked Tommy, 'how many others will be waiting for the boat?'

'I don't know son, I have heard that hundreds are leaving each day.'

Danny was concerned at this answer and asked, 'Will we all be on the same ship?'

'Of course, that's why we are making this journey so we will not be separated,' my mother answered for him.' 'We won't leave you for one minute.'

This reassured him and he smiled up at her taking hold of her hand.

Another couple of hours into our trek we took another rest, the rain had stopped now and a watery sun appeared in the sky, a gentle breeze making the clouds disperse and generally lifting the spirits.

'We are not going to reach Dublin today I am sorry to say but the berries saved us from using some of the potatoes so I think we should walk for another two hours, then stop for the night. That means we will have enough food for supper and breakfast tomorrow. We will definitely reach port tomorrow,' my father announced.

No one disagreed and the thought of being within striking distance of our goal tonight was a welcome one. We walked on but after about ten minutes we saw an old cabin sitting at the end of a rutted track, it was obvious that it had been abandoned and deciding that this would make a good place to spend the night, and although we hadn't walked as far as originally planned, we turned off the main road and made our way to the building. Secretly I think we were all grateful to be stopping as we were all weary. As we got nearer we saw that we were not the only ones to have this idea and could see that the cabin was already occupied.

'Come Daniel, let's go and leave them to it, they were here before us,' said my mother taking his arm. My delight at the thought of a dry night under cover was dashed and I turned to continue on hoping we may be more fortunate later on.

We turned and began the walk back when a woman called to us from the doorway, 'Come back, there is room for you inside, you look like you need a rest, especially the bairn.'

'Thank you so much,' mama replied.

I followed my family into the gloom of the cabin and once my eyes adjusted I could see at least two adults and five children in the kitchen area and discovered there were another two adults and four children in the sleeping room. I sat down and leant my back against the wall; I couldn't remember having felt so tired in a long time, my legs ached from the walking and my stomach ached from the hunger. Even though it was still only late afternoon I could happily fall asleep there and then, I looked over at Danny and saw he had beaten me to it, eyes closed, his small chest rising and falling as he slept.

Maria looked round at the gathering of people in the small cabin and felt grateful that they were willing to share their space with her family. She worried for a few moments about how she would cook for her family while these people most likely had nothing. Then making up her mind she said,' we don't have much but we do have a small amount of potatoes that you are welcome to share.'

Daniel looked at his wife knowing that this would deprive them of their morning meal but also knowing that's the way his wife was, she could not eat if these people had nothing.

The woman who had called them back answered,' that is so kind; we have a little bread we can put to the meal.'

Having heard the conversation between the two women, the man from the sleeping area came through and said, 'I am very sorry but we have nothing we can offer towards your meal.'

Maria looked at the man, his tattered clothes hanging off his skinny frame, dark circles under his eyes, beard and hair matted, 'It's alright; you can still share what we have.'

She looked across to the woman who had supplied the bread who nodded in agreement.

'No, that's very generous of you but we can't do that.'

Maria was about to say something else to persuade the man to change his mind when a small girl of about six squeezed past him into the kitchen and looking up at her father held her hands out to him. 'Daddy, I have these. I saved them from this morning.'

Her father looked down as she tipped four blackberries into his hand and then slipped back into the next room; I smiled thinking of the family standing in the same spot as we were earlier feasting on the berries.

'That's settled then,' Maria said.

The man handed the berries to Maria and went back to join his family in the other room.

Soon the meal was ready and although there was not much everyone received a small portion, the bread was rather hard but once it was dunked in the potato water it became edible. Once finished we settled down to rest, it had been a long and tiring two days. The adults swapped tales of their hardships, where they were from, what had driven them to this, where they are going, and what their hopes were.

The family from the sleeping area had been walking for eight days now, surviving on anything they could find along the way, today was the first hot meal they had had in that time, and they were evicted for non-payment of rent and had decided to sail to England to find work. The kitchen family had been on the road for four days, they left after the death of the husband's mother due to illness caused by the lack of food, and they too were going to England but wished to continue on to America once they could afford the additional fare.

The thing that struck me most was the measures all these folk were prepared to go to in order to provide for their kin and the fact that despite that they were willing to help others if they could, none more so than my mother.

The evening was turning to night as the light faded, plunging the inside of the cabin into near darkness. I adjusted my position against the wall sat in between Tommy and my father in order to try to get as comfortable as I could as I prepared to spend my second night away from the home I had known for twelve years. At least it had stopped raining.

Daniel sat in the gloom and contemplated the precarious situation his family were in. The journey was taking longer than he anticipated, he was hoping to be nearer their final destination by now, but he hadn't taken into account just how tired they would be through lack of food and sleep and also the energy sapping effect of the road conditions and the constant rain. He estimated they had covered about twelve miles in total, leaving them eight to go. Today it had taken them an hour longer to cover the distance they had made yesterday and now they were completely out of food. He knew there was no way they would be able to complete the journey tomorrow. His concerns threatened to overwhelm him and just as he could feel the tears gathering in his eyes he felt a small hand take his. The hand was cool to the touch but the strength it gave him was immense. He knew he could not let a single one of them down and he would fight to his last breath to protect them.

'Papa, I was frightened at first when you said we were leaving home, but now I know you were right. We would have starved if not for you, I love you Papa.'

'I love you too Millie,' he said, 'but we still have a long way to go with no food and although he doesn't complain I know Danny is struggling.'

'Don't worry, something will turn up tomorrow, I just know it. Goodnight Papa.'

'Goodnight Millie.'

I knew my father was worried, he felt he was responsible for the situation but I knew he was right in what we were doing. I hoped my words would help ease his conscience, I also hoped my words would come true. Surely we must be due a change of fortune soon.

Chapter 6.

The new morning broke and the various families sharing the cabin started to get themselves ready for the next part of their journey. It was strange but even though we all ate and slept together last night, today we were all strangers and I thought we all would feel more comfortable walking in our family units. Without having had any discussion about the matter, it seemed to be mutually decided that each group would set off at different intervals. We all bade each other farewell and good luck and set off.

As we reached the main road once more the conditions had improved slightly from yesterday, although there were still some puddles around, the road was nowhere near as bad as it was and walking was easier. The rain had passed over and the sun was trying to make an appearance. The sky was a pale blue with a scattering of light wispy clouds. I began to dare to think that maybe things would turn for the better. The only thing detracting from this feeling was the dull ache in my stomach.

After walking for an hour or so we turned a corner in the road and could see a little further along that the road met the canal which then ran alongside each other towards Dublin. The canal was about ten feet wide and carried produce to and from the town by horse drawn barge. On the opposite side of the canal to the road was the path where the horses walked pulling their loads. Although the canal was empty at the moment I hoped to see a barge before we reached the port. I realised there was so much of my native country that I had never and now may never see. My life existed around the farm and the odd trip to town, I never worried about missing out, but just then I somehow felt a little cheated and vowed if I ever got the chance to return I would.

We passed a mile marker at the side of the road which told us we still had another six miles to go.

'How long will it take us to walk the six miles Papa?' asked Tommy.

'Well if we can keep this pace up and with a few short rests I think we will be there early afternoon,' my father replied.

'How will we find the ship?' asked Danny.

'Just head for the port,' was the reply.

Up ahead we could see a small group of travellers resting at the side of the road. They consisted of three young men, a young woman and a child along with a small dog. As we reached the group the dog suddenly jumped up and began to bark at us, Danny was walking nearest to the dog and startled by this he leapt to one side, accidently crashing into Tommy and knocking him to the ground. As Tommy fell he automatically put his hands out to stop his descent but struck his knee against a large stone at the side of the path.

'Are you alright?' asked my mother rushing to his side.

'Yes I think so,' said Tommy trying to struggle to his feet.

'Sit where you are a minute son,' instructed my father, 'that was a nasty tumble you took, let your mother look at you first.'

Tommy got up into a sitting position and looked down to check on the damage. His left knee which took the impact with the rock was bleeding quite fast and already starting to swell. My mother took her scarf off and wrapped it around the wound.

'That should help to stop the bleeding but I think we should sit here a while before you try to walk on it.'

'I will be fine,' Tommy replied through gritted teeth, the pain showing in his face, tears gathering in his eyes and threatening to spill down his cheeks.

On seeing the damage Danny did begin to cry, 'I didn't mean it Tommy, I am sorry.'

'It wasn't your fault, it was just an accident,' I said trying to console him, wondering when we would ever get a break in fortune.

Daniel looked down at his son, blood seeping through the makeshift bandage and like his daughter was wondering if anything would go right for them.

'Can you stand on it?' he asked.

'I'll try Papa,' Tommy stoically replied taking the hand offered by his father and pulling himself up. As soon as he put his weight on it his face was contorted with pain and fresh blood appeared on the bandage.

'He can't walk on that,' said Maria.

'Right, Maria help Tommy onto my shoulders,' said Daniel squatting down.

'You can't carry me all that way Papa, it's a long way and you are tired too.'

'Well you can't stay here, so let's go.'

Maria helped Tommy onto her husband's shoulders and the party set off again.

After walking another two miles Daniel realised he must rest, the lack of food taking its toll. Normally he could have borne his son for longer than this but not today. He gently lowered Tommy to the ground and walked over to the canal taking a handful of the water.

'Right then, this is what we will do,' said Daniel. 'It's four miles to Dublin. If I go on my own I can get there and back in about three hours. I will go in and see if I can find any food, they should have a soup kitchen and maybe I can get enough to bring back. That will see us through today hopefully and then maybe tomorrow Tommy will be well enough to walk.'

'Do you think they will give you extra?' asked Maria.

'I don't know but I have to try. We have eaten nothing today and Dublin is the only hope. '

'I will go with you Papa,' I said, 'maybe if there are two of us we will get more.'

'No stay here with the others, there is no point wasting energy Millie,' he replied.

'I am going with you and that's it, two of us will make the journey seem quicker, it's always better to walk with company.'

'Let's go then I know how stubborn you can be so there's no point trying to argue.'

Leaving my mother and brothers behind we set off for Dublin. About a mile further on the road came to a crossroads and there was now a notable increase in the number of travellers. Previously there were odd groups of people we could see ahead and behind us but now the steady stream of people coming down from the north was incredible. I had no idea where they were all coming from but I knew one thing and that was they were all in a poor condition, thin bodies, ragged clothes, dark eyes sunk into their gaunt faces, some were coughing badly. I had never seen so many people together suffering so badly.

Maria watched as her husband and daughter disappeared from view and tended to Tommy's knee. Carefully removing the scarf she walked over to the canal and soaking the cloth in the water went back to begin cleaning the wound. Once done she ripped the hem of her skirt and rebound the knee, the bleeding had stopped but the knee was now swollen and purple with the bruising.

'Mama, I can try and walk a little,' said Tommy, 'that way they won't have so far to walk back.'

'Well alright, but if you are in too much pain you must say so and we will stop.'

Tommy rose to his feet and keeping the weight off his damaged leg by leaning on his mother they began to make their way forward. He managed to keep this up for around thirty minutes and then wincing with the pain asked to stop. As he sat at the side of the road he saw a barge come into view being pulled by two large horses. 'Look Danny, a barge is coming.'

Danny stood up and walked to the edge of the canal, waving at the man on the stern as the craft drew nearer. The man at the tiller waved back and then noticed the woman sitting at the side of the road with another boy whose leg was heavily strapped.

'Are you alright?' he called out to Maria.

'Yes thank you, my son has fallen and cut his knee, we are waiting here for my husband to return.'

'Where is he?'

'He has gone into Dublin with my daughter to see if they can find something to eat. We haven't eaten today and still have some way to go.'

'Well we are going into Dublin, we can take you in if it would help your son,' the man replied.

'Thank you for your kindness but we had better wait here for my husband, he will be worried if we are not here when he returns.'

'Look I travel this canal all the time and from now into Dublin the canal and road run alongside each other. If you sit up top you will be able to spot them. Your son looks about done in.'

Seeing the pain in Tommy's face Maria made up her mind. 'Well if you are sure we won't miss them, that would be wonderful, thank you so much.'

The man called to his companion leading the horses to stop; he then lifted a long pole from the deck of the barge and began to push the craft to the bank where Maria and her two sons were waiting. He passed the end of a rope to Maria and asked her to hold it tight, once she had the barge held fast against the bank he stepped off and picked up Tommy taking him aboard and setting him down carefully on the deck, he repeated this for Danny, he then held his hand out to Maria so she could also climb aboard. Once all were safely settled he pushed the boat back to the centre of the canal, called to his friend and then they were off.

'I can't thank you enough for your kindness,' said Maria, 'I must admit to not being comfortable sitting there with the two boys without the protection of my husband. No one has actually done anything but some of the people who passed us looked so desperate I was worried what they may do.'

'Yes these are bad times indeed and I can't see any end in sight. I am lucky to have this barge to work, if I were relying on the crops I think I would be doing the same as you and your family. I assume you are going to Dublin to catch a boat across the sea.'

'Yes, my husband was a tenant farmer but the landlord has no use for him at the moment and our small crop would not have sustained us.'

'Did you say you have not eaten yet today?'

'Yes I did,'

'Well I have some bread and cheese you and your sons are welcome to.'

'No I couldn't possibly; you are doing enough for us as it is.'

'Look even if you won't take any please at least let the children have something.'

'Very well, thank you once again Mr?'

'Sullivan, Mr Sullivan but my name is Royston. Most folk call me Roy and I would be pleased if you would do the same.'

'Pleased to meet you Roy, my name is Maria Rafferty and these are my sons Tommy and Danny.'

'Danny,' said Roy pointing to a small cloth covered basket in the corner, 'there is some bread and cheese in there, take some for yourself and your brother.'

Danny stood up and looked at his mother to make sure that this was alright and receiving a nod from her he went over and took a slice of bread and a piece of cheese for them both, then went back to sit next to his brother and share the gift.

'Thank you sir,' said Tommy prompting Danny to follow suit.

'You're welcome, I am sorry it's not much.'

As they made their way slowly along the canal Maria told her sons to keep a look out for their father and sister.

'Once we reach the edge of Dublin we will stop, 'said Roy. 'We don't travel much faster than walking speed and if they had a head start on us I doubt we will catch them before they get there. Then there is a danger we may miss them so it is best if we wait for them starting the return journey,' he explained.

My father and I had been walking for about an hour now and could see the outskirts of Dublin. The road was now filled with throngs of people all heading the same way. Some were barely moving forward, each step painful, many had bare feet which were cut and bleeding, children were crying, their tears making clean tracks down their dirty cheeks. Some were sitting on the side of the road, the effort of continuing just too much for them at present. Up ahead were two people sleeping in the middle of the road, most were just passing by them as if they didn't exist. Then one man stopped and bending down began to rummage through their pockets.

'Papa, that man is robbing those people, we must stop him and wake them up,' I said pointing ahead.

'Millie, I am sorry but those people are either dead already or very near dead. As bad as it sounds it is each for them self now.'

As we drew level with the couple I could not help but look, it was a man and woman. Both were just skin and bone, their cheeks hollow and sunken, dark circles under their closed eyes. I couldn't tell how old they were before their deaths. Their hair was matted and their skin dirty, clothes ragged and torn, both were barefoot and the man had blood around his mouth which had run down his chin before congealing on his cold skin. They were so close and yet still so far. This just served to remind me how desperate things were and I gave thanks we were still alive and prayed it would remain so.

Chapter 7.

'Millie, take my hand and don't let go. We cannot get separated here,' said my father as we entered the town. Everywhere I looked there were people; it didn't look as if there was room for another soul on these streets. The mass of human suffering shuffled slowly forward, all seemed to be going to the same destination. We joined the crowd and my father asked a woman in front of us where we were headed.

'To the ship,' she replied.

'Do you know where the soup kitchen is?' he asked.

'Down that street there, you will see the queue.'

'Come Millie,' and we turned down the street indicated by the woman. If anything this street appeared even more densely packed and I gripped onto my father's hand. People were pushing against each other as those trying to reach the front of the queue grew impatient and those already served were trying to get back to the main road and the ship.

Eventually we reached the front, and were confronted with the fact that we didn't have any bowls.

'We don't have any bowls, 'said my father.

'Well I can't help you, we don't keep bowls,' said the man. 'Move on.'

'Look I need soup for my family, my wife and two sons are waiting up the road for us. My son is injured and cannot walk.'

'I can't help that, even if you had a bowl I can only feed the people here. How do I know you aren't lying just to get extra?'

'He's not lying; he wouldn't do that,' I said jumping to my father's defence.

'Sorry miss, but rules is rules.'

'Come Millie, we will just have to go back to find the others.'

'But Papa, what will we do?' I asked and tears began to fall from my eyes. The thought of letting down those depending on us was too much for me to bear.

'Here take this lovey,' said a small woman with grey hair pushing a bowl towards me. 'I have more at home and I have eaten today.'

'Thank you Mam,' I said taking the bowl from her skinny hand and offering it up to the man. 'Please can you give us enough for five?' I begged.

'Look I can only give you enough for two, that's the rule,' he said but he lowered his voice saying, 'I will fill it as much as I can, good luck miss.'

Taking the full bowl from him and thanking him for his generosity I handed it to my father terrified someone would rob me of it; it didn't look any better than the soup we had previously received but it was food of some sort. Edging out of the crowd we made our way back to the road that would take us back to our waiting family.

The stream of people entering the city was unrelenting, some not even appearing to see us as we made our way against the tide of humanity fleeing the country in order to stay alive. Our path was frequently blocked with people and we had to keep stepping off the road so that we didn't spill the precious contents of the soup bowl. At last we reached the outskirts of the town and there was more room to walk and so avoid the worst of the crowds.

'Right Millie let's go and find the others and then depending on how Tommy's leg is we can decide what we will do,' said my father carrying the bowl as if it contained the most precious thing in the world, which at the moment, to us, it did.

Part of me was regretting my decision to walk into town and back as my legs were tired and I was so hungry I was feeling quite light headed but I was determined to do whatever it took to help where I could. Then I heard it, such a welcome sound I don't remember hearing before.

Maria sat on the bow of the barge with her sons as they kept watch for the return of Daniel and Millie, the constant procession of people walking to the port was concerning her that they may not see them go past and worse still may have already missed them. She could not bear to think of the anguish they would be caused upon reaching the place where they had left them only to find it deserted. She was just considering alighting and walking back when Danny jumped up and pointing shouted, 'Mama there they are, I can see them.' Maria followed his gaze and then she saw them, walking to the side of the road, Millie head down, slowly plodding alongside her father who was clutching a bowl.

'Daniel, Millie over here,' she called. They did not respond and she realised they could not hear her. 'Boys, shout make as much noise as you can or they won't see us.'

'Don't worry Mam,' said Roy, 'I can get their attention.' With that he reached under a sack which was thrown in the corner and pulled out a bucket which was used to feed the horses and began to beat it with a hammer, the clanging sound carried across the canal and along with the calls of the passengers reached the two travellers.

Looking up Millie saw the barge with the man in the stern loudly beating a bucket and waving apparently at her, and then she saw her mother and brothers frantically waving their arms and shouting.

'Papa, look they are on that barge,' I said. I could not believe my eyes and gave thanks that they were safe and I wouldn't have to make the long walk back. Looking up into the face of my father I could see he was also relieved to find them so soon.

The man pushed the barge over to the bank and told us to step aboard, which we gratefully did. I hugged my mother and then joined my brothers at the front of the boat. As my mother introduced the boatman, who was apparently called Roy, to my father and told him how he had helped them I listened as Danny and Tommy told me about their trip down the canal. In turn I told them of our experience in the town, I did not mention the two dead people I had seen in the road.

'I can't thank you enough for helping my family Roy,' I heard my father say shaking the man's hand.

'Don't mention it; I just couldn't pass them by.'

'How is your leg son?' he asked Tommy.

'It's stopped bleeding Papa, it's just sore now,' was his reply. 'I should be able to walk into port.'

'Nonsense,' said Roy, 'as I said to your wife we are going right into the town so you can ride in with us. We only stopped here so we wouldn't miss you. First we will eat and Ronald will see to the horses and then we will go.'

'Can I help with the horses?' Danny asked excitedly. He had always loved animals and used to constantly tell Papa that he was not going to work on the potato farms instead he was going to farm all kinds of animals.

'No son, I don't think that's a good idea.'

Roy looked down at the disappointment on the small boys face and said, 'He can help with Bess, she is friendly enough. Ronald will look after him, but I suggest he stays away from Sergeant, he can be a bit temperamental.'

He called Ronald over saying, 'take the lad with you when you feed the horses, he wants to help.'

Ronald was a boy of about seventeen with a deeply tanned face and thick sinewy arms; he took Danny by the hand and led him over to where the horses were standing patiently waiting for their food. Danny filled a bucket with oats and held it out to the large brown and white mare; she lowered her head to feed from the pail. Danny was beaming and I could see how happy he was in carrying out this simple task. Ronald left him in charge of Bess and turned his attention to Sergeant. He was huge, his coat was a glossy jet black with a white blaze on his face, his mane and tail were thick and the mane fell over his left eye. All the time he was eating he was watching Danny with Bess, his front hooves pawing in the dust on the ground. Suddenly Danny in his excitement ran over to Ronald calling out, 'She has finished eating, what can I do now?' Sergeant pulled away from the bucket and tossed his head from side to side, snorting loudly, his tail lashing up and down.

Mama cried out,' Oh Danny stop, don't frighten him.'

Danny stopped dead in his tracks, looked over to us on the barge and then walked calmly up to where Ronald had dropped the bucket in the confusion, shovelled some of the spilled oats back in and walked up to Sergeant saying,' Hey big fella, I am sorry I frightened you, come and finish your meal.'

The horse dropped his head and ambled over to my brother; he nuzzled him on the shoulder and started eating.

'Well I'll be,' said Roy, 'I have never seen that before, I can't even do that, he only lets Ronald touch him. Your young son must have the gift.'

After the shared meal of cold soup, bread and cheese we made our way along the water into the heart of the town. The sights and sounds of the people seemed less frightening to me, as I sat with my legs dangling over the edge of the barge, separated as we were by the water of the canal along which we slowly made our way. For the first time since we had left home I felt sure we were going to make it, the change in fortune I was hoping for had arrived at last. As we passed the straggling lines of people walking to the port I studied them, all looked weary, desperate and defeated. They were eerily quiet, energy not being wasted on talking; the only sounds were the forlorn cries of children as they struggled to keep up with their parents.

Eventually the grass banks of the canal gave way to the bricked walls of the goods yard, Roy edged the barge slowly to the mooring posts, and Ronald took the ropes and secured the vessel, then took the halters from the horses and led them away, tying them to a post and giving them food and water. Ronald then placed planks from the landing to the side of the barge ready to begin unloading the cargo.

Slowly we got to our feet and went to thank Roy once more for his generosity.

'Mr Sullivan,' said my father shaking the man's hand, 'once again I thank you for all the help you have given me and my family. I wish I could repay you in some way but I have nothing to give.'

'Your thanks are enough Mr Rafferty; however I have a further proposition for you if you are interested, 'replied the man.

'Anything I can do for you, I am in your debt.'

'Well, from what you have just said about having nothing to repay me I presume you have no money for the sailing fares. I usually pay casual workers to help the lad and I unload but if you are willing I can use you for a small return,' Roy said holding out six pennies towards my father.

'Tell me what you want of me and you have it,' replied my father removing his jacket and rolling up his shirt sleeves.

'Daniel, I think as we cannot help with the unloading I will take Millie in to town and find out about sailing times and prices if you agree,' said my mother.

'That's a good idea, the boys can stay here with me, take care and hold onto Millie's hand at all times as the crowds are dense and it will be easy to lose sight of each other,' said my father making sure we both understood the situation. He needn't worry; I would make sure we stuck together after my experience of being there earlier.

My mother walked over to Mr Sullivan and standing up on her tiptoes she kissed him tenderly on the cheek. 'As my husband says we will be forever in your debt, you are one of the kindest men I have met and I wish you and your family well and hope you survive this terrible disaster.'

As we headed into town I turned and waved to the big man who as far as I was concerned was a saint, and received a wave in return along with a doff of the cap. We left the relative sanctuary of the canal and walked into the town, the sights and sounds assaulting me again as we walked down to the quayside. There were small boats dotted at anchor in the harbour but no sign of any sailing ships. My mother spotted an old woman sitting on a stool, her hands working on repairing a fishing net, walking over to her she asked,' Do you know when the next ship will be sailing to England?'

The woman did not stop working but answered without hesitation, 'Tomorrow evening at six o'clock, leaves from that mooring over there,' with that she pointed a skinny hand towards a large rusty metal ring set into the harbour wall, above it the letters SS Elise were painted. 'Best be here early though if you want to get on, lot's of folk asking the same thing.'

'Thank you, do you know how much it costs?' my mother enquired.

'No, go ask him, he works on the ships sometimes,' she said indicating a man leaning on the harbour wall smoking a pipe.

'Excuse me sir,' said my mother,' can you tell me how much the fare to England is?'

The man turned to look at us,' Just the two of you is it?'

'No, there is my husband and I and our three children.'

As he looked at us I noticed that he had a scar running from the corner of his left eye to his jaw line, the left eye was a milky white colour and it took me all my time not to gasp out in horror.

'Well, it's three pence for each adult and a penny for each child.'

We thanked him and left the harbour to return to the others. When we arrived we found that the barge had gone and my father, Tommy and Danny were sitting at the edge of a jetty.

'The ship will sail tomorrow at six o'clock in the evening and it will cost us nine pence,' my mother told them. 'We were also told if we want to get aboard we must get there early.'

'We only have six pence though, 'replied my father frustrated at yet another obstacle being placed in our way.

'Look Papa,' said Tommy pointing down the canal, 'another barge is coming. Maybe we can earn some money helping them. While you were helping Roy unload I watched other men helping as the barges came in and they were all paid.' Tommy got to his feet but Papa told him to rest his leg a while longer. 'Papa, I want to help you, I am well enough now,' replied Tommy, pulling at the bandage.

'Tommy let your mother look at your leg and we will see, and while you are doing that I will see if I can earn some more money.' So as the barge edged into the unloading bay my father joined the other men and managed to secure some work for which he received a further six pence. Now it did seem our luck was turning.

My mother gently removed the bandage from Tommy's knee causing a small trickle of blood to appear where the scab had adhered to the cloth; Tommy winced but did not make a sound eager to prove he was indeed healed. His knee was still slightly swollen and vivid colours of yellow and purple but he could flex it gently and it would bear his weight. 'Tommy, I don't think you should work today, we have to walk into the port tomorrow and will have to stand around waiting, then there is the journey the other side, 'said my mother, 'you don't have to prove yourself to us remember we are your family.'

I could see Tommy was disappointed and so I went to sit by him, 'Tommy don't be so down on yourself, who was it who remembered to take the potatoes, who was it who thought to work the barges?' and giving him a playful dig in the ribs I added,' and without you falling over we would never have had Roy's bread and cheese.'

Tommy smiled and answered, 'That's true, and you found the berries so we have all played our part in getting here.'

On hearing this conversation Danny looked downcast,' 'I haven't done anything,' his bottom lip trembled and tears formed in his eyes threatening to fall.

'You have carried wood, fetched water,' said my mother trying to console my brother.

'So have they,' he retorted not satisfied with his contribution.

'Ah, Danny,' Tommy said laughing, 'if you hadn't knocked me down in the first place none of this would have happened.'

The rest of us joined in the laughter and Danny relaxed.

'Although wait for a while before you do it again,' Tommy said smiling at his brother.

Daniel walked back to join his family and was delighted to see them in such good spirits after all they had endured the past couple of days. 'We need to find some shelter for the night and we have one shilling. After the fare tomorrow we will have three pence left, I think we should save that for England as there won't be a soup kitchen there. We will get a meal at the kitchen here before we go in the morning. There are some sheds at the back of the yard I noticed earlier, let's try there.'

Sure enough at the back of the yard were three small sheds in which tools, ropes and such were stored. The inside was cramped but dry and out of the weather, there were even a few sacks covering the ropes which the family used for bedding. The evening sky was turning a dark red as the sun set in the west promising a fine day tomorrow.

'Papa, just through that fence there are some fields, can I go and see if there is any food to be found?' asked Tommy.

'Yes alright but don't go out of sight of the shed and don't go on your own,' Daniel answered. He would normally have gone with him but the fatigue of the work and walking had taken its toll on him.

'We'll go with him won't we Millie?' was Danny's reply.

With that the three children left the sanctuary of the shed, climbed over the fence and walked off into the field, as Daniel let his eyes close he drifted off to sleep.

He awakened to Maria gently shaking his shoulder, 'Daniel, look what the children have found.'

Daniel pulled himself upright and saw set on a bucket lid a dozen small apples, they were slightly soft but edible.

'Where did you get these?' he asked.

'There is a tree right over on the far side, all the apples have been taken but Danny spotted these lying at the bottom of a ditch, they must have been missed,' Millie answered.

'Well done lad,' said Daniel, 'we will have half tonight and save the rest.' Danny beamed as he received the praise from his father, another contribution to the family effort.

The Rafferty family felt the optimism that came with having some food, money and the means to leave these shores tomorrow within reach.

Chapter 8.

The early morning sun crept in through the open doorway and warmed my cheek, waking me gently and for a moment I forgot that I was not at home in the cabin. As I opened my eyes I was brought back to the present casting an eye around the gloom of the shed. My eyes settled on a cobweb high up in the corner of the roof and I watched as a fly brushed against it, the tremor bringing out the eight legged occupant, only to find its prey had got away. It returned to its lair to patiently wait for the next unsuspecting visitor.

My mother and brothers were still asleep and so I pushed back the sacking and crept quietly outside where I saw my father standing near the fence at the back of the yard. He was standing side on to the shed and I could see his features in profile against the light rising in the east, the thick mass of curly hair topping a high forehead, his sharp nose and chin accentuated as the sun cast one side of his face in shadow. I stood for a moment watching him; he leant on the fence and bowed his head, bringing his hands together in front of him. It was only when I saw his mouth moving silently that I realised that he was praying, praying for the safe passage of his family as we made the journey across the sea to our new life. I slipped back into the doorway and after a few moments noisily exited into the yard. My father stood and turned towards me, a smile lifting the corners of his mouth, he looked tired and drawn as he approached asking,' Are the others awake yet?'

'Not yet Papa,' I answered.

'Well we had better wake them, we need to go into town, find some food and then make our way to the harbour.'

'I'll fetch them Papa,' I turned to enter the shed but remembering my father's prayers I said, 'tomorrow we will be in England and things will be good for us again, don't worry.'

'God bless you Millie, sometimes I forget you are only twelve, you always seem to know just what to say to lift someone's spirits.'

'Just as you always know what is best for us Papa.'

At that moment my mother appeared followed closely by my brothers. 'Morning Daniel, Millie,' she said, 'did you both sleep well?'

'Yes thank you Mama,' I replied.

'We need to get moving if we want to get to the soup kitchen early,' stated my father. 'How is your leg today son?'

Tommy flexed his leg and said,' A lot better thank you Papa.' It was still a vivid purple and yellow colour but the swelling had diminished and the cut had begun to heal.

'Are we eating the apples now?' asked Danny, more in hope than actually expecting to do so.

'No, we can save those for later, we will have soup this morning and can eat those while we wait for the ship,' answered our mother.

As we started out on the mile walk into the town centre I turned to look back along the road we had travelled the past few days and also offer up a silent prayer for having got this far. Already the road was filling with travellers seeming to increase by the minute as they emerged from various overnight shelters and headed into Dublin.

We joined the queue for the kitchen and offering the bowl we still had from the other day received a large portion of the anaemic looking liquid, at least it was warm. The meal shared, we made our way to the harbour where we were told to wait for the ship yesterday. There were already around fifty people waiting, some looked as though they had spent the night here in order to secure their place on the boat. All were thin and ragged, some were old and could barely stand, the children all seemed to have a wretched look in their eyes that told of the suffering they had endured just to arrive this far.

I thought we had fared quite well compared to these poor people until I actually took the time to study my family whilst we waited. My father who always prided himself on being tidy and presentable even when going to work now had thick dark stubble on his chin, grey hairs mixed in here and there. His hair was dishevelled and greasy, his bright blue eyes were red rimmed and the whites were yellow with dark circles underneath, his normally tanned skin had a grey tinge to it.

My mother also had a grey complexion, her red hair which was always pinned up neatly catching the light was now falling around her face, her hands and face were grimy from the dust of the road and her dress ripped and torn where she had used it for a bandage and the unstitched hem had caught as she walked the uneven road.

Tommy had ripped his shorts where he had fallen on the road, his eyes showing dark against his pale skin, his hair sticking up at all angles and his lips were cracking due to lack of water over the past few days.

Danny stood against my father, his tiny frame covered in dust and dirt, the toes of his shoes were scuffed and as I gazed upon him I wondered how much more he could survive. I also knew that Danny housed a determined streak in him sometimes to the extent of stubbornness and thought he would take all that came at him provided he had his father at his side.

I wondered how I looked but decided I was better off not knowing.

At noon the sun was high in the sky and as we sat on the quayside the effects of sitting out there were beginning to take effect. We dare not seek shade for we would lose our place in the waiting line which grew ever by the minute. We took out the last of the apples and shared them, the juice helping to quench our thirst a little as well as our hunger. Others looked on as we ate and although I felt guilty I remembered the words of my father, 'It's each for themselves now Millie.'

'Tommy take the bowl and go and fetch some water from that horse trough,' said my father pointing to a large iron container at the edge of the harbour.

'What happens if they don't let him back in the queue?' asked my mother, concern showing in her face.

'They will let a child return to his family but they may not let an adult back,' reasoned my father.

Tommy left and returned a short while later, the bowl full of the slightly warm water but it was refreshing all the same. As we were drinking I noticed a small girl watching me each time I lifted the bowl to my lips, I still had the words of my father ringing in my head but thought this was different and rising to my feet walked over to the trough and returning handed the bowl to her mother. As I retook my position next to my mother she smiled and nodded at me approvingly. I watched as the bowl passed down the line a few times before being returned by a young boy who hugged me before scampering back to his parents.

We watched as a steam ship laden with passengers bound for England left the port, their journey would only take them around three hours but the cost of two shillings each was far more than we could afford and so we had to wait for the slower sail ship.

Around three o'clock a ship appeared on the horizon and made its way into the harbour mooring just below us. We watched as some sacks were unloaded and a few crew members alighted and made their way to the tavern, everyone in the waiting queue was now on their feet in anticipation and those at the back began to press forward, this had an adverse effect on those of us towards the front of the line and I was worried that someone would plunge over the wall. I held tightly onto Danny's hand and closed my eyes.

The Captain looked at the line of people waiting to board his ship, there must have been at least three hundred or more. His vessel was only allowed to take around one hundred and eighty but he calculated if he filled the hold and the deck he could take the lot. As he thought of the additional profit he decided it was worth the risk. Just at that moment the crowd started pushing forward in an attempt to board, worried that he may lose some of these paying customers he made the decision to start loading now even though they would not sail for another three hours.

'Davey,' he called down to the deck hand who was currently overseeing the loading of food and water for the passengers for the voyage, 'as soon as you have done that come to see me. I have new instructions.'

'Aye sir,' Davey replied wondering what the old man was up to now. Davey did not like the man at all and in his three months of working for him had witnessed many incidents that he did not approve of, but work was hard to come by and until he could find something else he was stuck here. He had always wanted to go to sea but the twice weekly return sailing from Ireland to England was not what he had in mind. The loading complete he made his way to the Captain's cabin, knocking on the door and entering upon hearing the gruff 'Come.'

'Sir, you asked for me.'

The Captain was sat in his chair, a bottle of whiskey in his large gnarled hand. He raised it to his mouth and took a large slug. Davey watched in disgust as the amber liquid trickled from the side of his mouth and into his bushy grey beard. 'Yes, I have decided that we will start loading the passengers now.'

'Sir, we don't sail for another two hours, it will be chaos with all those people on board for that long, besides the crew are not back from the tavern yet.'

'Well you had best go and find them then, the crowd are getting restless and I am concerned for their safety if there is a stampede. You know how desperate these folk are getting.'

Davey thought to himself, you aren't bothered about their safety; you are bothered at losing precious customers. 'Sir, are you sure about this?'

'Confound you man, do as I say and when you have found the crew send Bill to me.'

'Sir.' Davey left the cabin and did has he was told.

Bill walked into the Captain's cabin, 'Sir, Davey says you wish to load the passengers now.'

'Yes and also I want you to take as many as we can, use the holds and the decks.'

'Aye sir, but we will .....,'

'Stop there man and don't question me, just get it done,' interrupted the Captain.

Bill turned and after passing on the Captain's orders began the loading of the passengers.

It was around four thirty now when we heard the call that we were to begin to board the ship. At once the crowd became alert and the jostling began again. As we edged to the side of the harbour wall I looked down into the water which was lapping against the side of the ship, it looked dark and unforgiving and I began to worry about whether I could manage to cross the gangway without slipping in. My father handed over the fare and we were allowed to proceed.

'Millie, take my hand,' said my mother. I unclenched my fists and took hold of her, maybe a little too tightly, my father had taken hold of my two brothers and we followed them across. It wasn't until we were all safely on the deck that I realised I had been holding my breath. My respite was short lived however for as I stood looking out towards the open sea I felt a push in my back. I turned to see a man of around forty with narrow eyes in a weathered face pointing downwards.

'You don't have time to gawp love,' he said, 'down the ladder.'

I cautiously made my way down the ladder into the hold and took my place with my family. The space was warm and stuffy and already filled with around sixty people, but as I watched more and more made their way down to join us. Eventually a face appeared at the hatch above and looking down seemed satisfied, retreating out of sight calling,' No more room down there, it's full.' I felt trapped as I pressed up against my mother and a man I had never set eyes on before.

'It's alright Millie, we will soon be in England and then we can put all this behind us,' my mother whispered to me wrapping her arm across my shoulders.

Davey stood horrified as he watched the people boarding the ship, they had never taken this many before and he knew they did not have near enough food and water aboard. He looked over to where the Captain was standing chatting and laughing with Sam, his first mate. He could not help himself and marched over to where they stood, 'Sir, we can't take anymore and we don't have enough provisions for those already on board, we need to load more.'

'Did you hear that Sam?' mocked the Captain, 'this lad thinks we don't know what we are doing.'

'Well he has been here for three months now Sir,' Sam answered sarcastically, laughing at his own wit.

'Well if he wants to be here another three months he had best do as he is told, I can find someone else to replace him.' With that the Captain turned and walked away.

'You heard lad, either get on with it or get off the boat,' Sam ordered.

Davey opened his mouth to answer but then remembered his mother and sisters at home depending on him and walked back to his station.

At last we began to move, I could feel the slight motion as we slipped out of the harbour. We had been squashed down here for over an hour whilst others were packed on to the decks and the temperature down here was hot and sticky, there was barely room to move but we managed to sit down in a small huddle with Danny at the centre. The light above began to fade as night approached, the boat started to move more as we reached the open waters. The rise and fall increased as the wind outside picked up, I wondered if it was in our favour or against us. The sooner we arrived the better. The sights, sounds and smells of this journey would live with me forever of that I was sure, human suffering had never been more on show to me than as it was at that moment. Old and young cramped in a hot, tiny space. Children were crying from hunger and their distraught mother's had no means to alleviate their suffering, some people were coughing uncontrollably, blood staining their hands when they took them away from their mouths. Others were vomiting from the motion of the boat and some of those with empty stomachs were dry heaving, the noise was terrible.

This was not the way I had envisioned leaving the country of my birth, trapped in an enclosed damp space with hundreds of sick and starved strangers, barely enough room to sit and an empty stomach.

The ship was halfway across the Irish Sea and it was at this point in the journey that the passengers were normally given their ration of food and water. As no one had made a move to do so yet Davey took it upon himself to see to it. He walked over to the area where the rations were stowed but was halted by a shout from above. 'What are you doing lad?' it was Sam.

'The passengers need feeding Sam.'

'I thought you said we didn't have enough aboard,' he snarled walking over to stand eye to eye with Davey.

'We don't but we will just have to give each one less.'

'And how is that going to work?' He was so close Davey could smell the rum on his breath as the warmth of it hit his face.

'Well we have to do something,' Davey protested.

'You might, I don't. I guarantee you will have a riot on your hands if you give them half a cup of water each.'

'So what do you suggest then Sam, you are first mate after all?'

'Either give nothing or just give to those on the deck, the ones in the hold will never know and if they do what can they do about it?' Sam replied casting a look over to the darkened hold.

'You can't do that, it's inhuman!' exclaimed Davey.

'Look do whatever you want, I am having nothing to do with it, just don't come moaning to me when it all goes wrong.' Sam turned to walk away and then turned back to face Davey, 'I bet you'll still be happy to take your wages though won't you? '

'At least I have a conscience! 'Davey shouted to the retreating back.

'Conscience or money, you choose, you can't afford both.' With that remark Sam disappeared to join the Captain in his cabin.

Davey decided he could not possibly feed and water all aboard and so shared out the rations to those on deck. He felt sick to his stomach but Sam was right that trying to do otherwise would cause more trouble.

We had been sailing now for some time but how long I could not tell, it was still dark above me and I could see neither stars nor moon through the opening in the ceiling, the sky appeared to be clouded over. The last time we had either eaten or drank anything was whilst waiting for the ship at around three o'clock. My throat felt dry and I could feel the dull ache behind my eyes signalling the onset of a headache. I wondered how the rest were feeling but in the pitch dark I could not see any one's faces. Not wishing to wake a soul if they were lucky enough to have found temporary sanctuary in sleep I whispered, 'Is anyone awake?'

'I am,' Tommy answered quietly.

'How are you feeling?'

'Hungry, thirsty and my knee hurts again being bent up all the time, how about you?'

'Apart from the knee exactly the same.'

'I wonder how near we are to England; I hope it's not much longer, I don't like it down here. Some of the people look really ill and I'm afraid of what they might have.'

I considered his words, he was quite right; some of those sharing this space looked more than just starved. I closed my eyes in the hope of sleeping the rest of the way.

Suddenly I was jolted awake by screaming, I could not see who this was but the noise cut through me. I heard a voice I took to be that of a woman saying,' Arthur it's alright I'm here, I'm here.' This was followed by someone mumbling over and over, the words incomprehensible. I was reminded of when mother had lost Frances and she had a high fever with bouts of delirium, she would wake at night screaming and then mumble to herself before slipping back into a restless sleep.

At last dawn began to arrive, and the faces of my fellow travellers became clearer. This told me we must have been at sea for at least twelve hours, without food or water. My head was throbbing now, my mouth parched and my stomach rumbling. There was still no sign of anyone bringing us any nourishment. As people woke up, an air of discontent began to grow as they realised we appeared to have been forgotten down here. Some began to cry out to those above, 'We need food and water.' Still no response, a man nearest to the bottom of the ladder began to climb; as he neared the top we heard a voice shout, 'Where do you think you're going?'

'We need food and water please.'

Then I saw a foot push against the man's chest and losing his grip he fell back into the hold, his fall broken by the packed ranks below. Then the hatch to the hold was dragged back over the opening and I knew we were all going to die. After all we had been through; this seemed a cruel twist of fate. As the sun rose in the sky above, the temperature in the closed in hold began to soar making the need for water even worse. I could feel the sweat trickling down my back and plastering my hair to my scalp.

Davey could stand it no longer, he walked over to join Bill, a man who he thought held his views on the way the Captain ran his ship.

'Bill, those people in the hold have had no provisions and now the hatch has been shut, they will surely all die if nothing is done.'

'What do you suggest?'

'Well we can at least open the hatch to give them air.'

'And if we get caught?'

'I don't think I care anymore, I'm going to do it.' Davey walked over to the hatch and began to lift it.

'Higgins, who said you could open the hatch?' It was Sam who had seen the exchange between the two men and sensing what was about to happen had followed Davey as he made his way aft.

'Sam they will all surely die.'

'So?' Sam sneered, 'they have already paid us.'

Davey knew the only way to get any sort of agreement from the greedy man was to appeal to his kind of logic. 'Well there are two problems to that as I see it. One we will have to dispose of over one hundred bodies, some of which clearly have some sort of sickness, and two when word gets round as it will, no one will board this boat again.' Davey knew he had hit the man's weak spot, greed.

'Very well, open the hatch but that's all.'

Davey slid the hatch open and called down, 'You must all promise not to try to climb out again or the hatch will be sealed for the rest of the journey.'

No one moved; the message was clear enough, if they wanted fresh air they were to put up without sustenance.

The draught of cooler air hit me and I watched as the young man who had opened the hatch looked down at us, his face showing his compassion before he turned and walked out of sight. The time in the hold stretched out before us and the only way we knew of time passing was when the light began to fade once again. The noise in the hold was becoming unbearable as children cried and adults moaned and coughed. Suddenly another scream rose amongst us, I thought at first it was the feverish man from before, but it was his wife. 'Arthur nooooooo, Arthur. He's dead, he's dead, somebody help me he's dead.'

But of course nobody could help her or him.

Night fell and I slept, my body could not take any more, I was running on empty.

I was woken by my father shaking me, 'Millie we have stopped moving. We haven't moved for a while now, I think we may be there.'

I listened and could hear the sound of many feet moving across the deck above, the top passengers must be disembarking. We had indeed made it into England. I wondered what this new land had in store for us.

Chapter 9

As knowledge of our imminent escape from the cramped, smelly claustrophobic hold spread through my fellow passengers, an excited chattering began. Even the children temporarily stopped their crying. People began to get to their feet and tried to stretch their aching limbs. As I stood up I suddenly felt dizzy and grabbed onto my mother to save myself from falling, my head was throbbing and my lips were dry.

A face appeared through the darkness at the opening to the hatch and called down, 'Keep quiet for a while longer down there, the deck passengers have to get off first and then you can go. Get any belongings together now.' It was the face of the young man who had managed to get the hatch reopened for us. The sky above was still a deep black and I could see bright stars twinkling in the heavens, I had no idea of the time, but it must be either late night or early morning.

'Maria, Millie,' whispered my father, 'take this and hide it in your shoe.' He passed each of us a single penny. 'Just in case they search us, after the way they have treated us I wouldn't be surprised. At least this way we may manage to keep some of our money.'

We took the money and did as we were asked.

The people were now becoming restless, anxious to be off. Some started to mutter about the lack of food and water and a few of the men said they are going to find out what had happened. Anger started to build as people agreed and I just wished we could get out of here now and avoid any trouble.

The young man appeared once more and instructed us to climb the ladder and disembark.

'Captain, I think we should be careful when they come out of the hold, most are too weak to do anything but some may feel they have been treated unfairly.'

'I agree Sam, get all the men together and form a line from the hold to the gangway. That should put any ideas from their minds. Let me know when the ship is clear.' The Captain then retreated to the safety of his cabin.

'All hands to the hatch, form a line and make sure no one tries anything,' Sam called to the crew and they promptly fell in line.

Gradually people began to climb up the ladder, some struggled to climb unassisted due to weakness and fatigue. The people below pushed impatiently at those taking too long to scale the ladder and on a couple of occasions they were pulled down and left to wait until others had taken their turn. We began to move slowly forwards and I prayed we would all be able to make it up to safety. As we neared the opening I noticed that there were some people who had not moved at all, they lay still and silent on the floor of the hold. They had made it to England but their journey was now at an end.

One woman lay with her eyes wide open appearing to stare up at me; I had to physically turn my head away in order to break free of her gaze. I reached the bottom of the ladder and placed my foot upon the first rung, grabbing either side and hauling myself up step by step until my head was above the deck and I was hit by a sudden rush of sweet fresh air. As I stood on the deck waiting for my family I gulped in lung full's of the salty night air. My father appeared next with Danny on his back, arms clinging tightly around his neck, and then Tommy's head rose from the black hole followed by my mother. I looked at the faces of the men lined up on the deck and as we walked past them the young man who had helped us cast his gaze to the floor as if ashamed by his actions, the only one with no need to be. The others appeared not at all bothered by the state of their passengers.

We walked to the gangway and at last stepped foot on English soil, we had made it, we were all still together. I had never been as relieved as I was to leave the ship and I was so glad we were not going further. I knew many people were determined to travel to America, Canada and Australia and I hoped my father did not decide to take this course of action. I learnt later that these ships were named 'coffin ships' due to the high numbers who died aboard due to starvation and disease.

'Is that the lot?' Sam asked.
'I think so,' one of the men replied.
'Well check it out; we don't want any stowaways when we set sail for Ireland.'
The man descended into the hold and shouted up, 'Sam we have some dead ones down here.'
'How many?' Sam asked not at all concerned for the dead themselves only for the inconvenience to himself.
'About twenty,' came the reply.

'Right men, get the boat hooks and pull them out, don't touch them; you don't know what they died of. Then weight them down, wrap them and we will put them over when we are out at sea.'

Chapter 10

We followed the others as they slowly shuffled along the darkened quayside. There were literally hundreds of people making their way forward towards the faint lights of the gas lamps burning through the darkness. They were heading for the town in the hope of finding shelter and sustenance. Others had just decided to rest where they were and sat around looking forlorn. The fresh air had helped a little to relieve the pressure in my head but I still felt dizzy and my thirst was raging now.

I looked down at Danny and could see tears spilling from his hazel eyes, as he clung to Papa's hand.

'Daniel, we must find food and water for the children and somewhere they can rest,' my mother said.

'I know, I just don't know where to find either. I would go on ahead and look but I don't want to risk leaving you here alone.'

'Papa, I feel sick,' Danny said in a voice barely above a whisper.

My father picked him up and made a decision, 'we will walk on a little further and if see what there is to offer.'

As we rounded a corner we came upon a boat hanging above the dockside, it was covered with a tarpaulin and smelt of fresh tar. There were some crates against the wall and my father passed Danny to my mother to hold and then piled the crates so he could climb up and look inside. 'It's empty and dry,' he said, 'right everyone climb in here.'

Danny was passed up and set in the bottom and then we all made our way up, then my father pulled the tarpaulin back into place over us saying,' keep quiet and stay here, I will go and see what I can find.'

Daniel covered the boat and moved the crates away so as not to draw attention to the hiding place of his family. He walked towards the town and clung to the shadows in order to go unnoticed. He passed many people sleeping on the streets, who he assumed had been his fellow passengers. He saw nowhere that would make a better temporary shelter than the boat but he was desperate to find some water at least for his family. He was feeling dizzy himself and his heart felt as if it would burst from his chest at any moment. He stopped and waited for his heart to return to normal and as he did so he saw a movement in the shadows ahead, he quietly stepped further into the darkness and watched as five men appeared and moved over to a group of people sleeping on the street about a hundred yards from where he stood. The men began kicking at the prone figures, and as they woke terrified, they demanded anything of value they may have, the women were crying as they told the attackers they had nothing. This did not please the men who dragged one of the men up by his hair and shouted at him, 'Is that true?' The man nodded vigorously and was knocked back to the floor and received a further kicking as they vented their frustrations on him. They moved on to seek out their next victims hoping for better pickings, moving towards Daniel.

   Daniel quietly crept down the alley he had been watching from and rounded the corner to the back of a building. He let out a short sigh of relief as the men passed by the alley but it was short lived as he realised they were heading towards the docks. He was contemplating what to do when he spotted a barrel in the corner of the small yard. Crossing over he found it to be a water barrel which was three quarters full of cool clear liquid. Daniel drank his fill and then looked around for some sort of container in order to carry his treasure back to his waiting family. After much searching he found a small pail and filling this crept back to the street.

Danny was laid with his head in my mother's lap, his eyes were closed and his breathing came in rapid gasps, his skin was very dry to the touch and he was complaining of a headache and feeling sick and dizzy.
   'He needs water,' said my mother stroking his face, 'where is your father?'
   At that moment Danny's eyes opened briefly and then closed as he fell limp against the bottom of the boat.
   'He's fainted,' cried my mother gently patting my brother's cheeks.
   'Shush,' whispered Tommy, 'someone is coming.'
   'It must be Papa,' I said hopefully, 'I wonder if he has found any water?'
   The relief was soon replaced by concern as we realised there were more than one set of foot steps outside. They walked nearer to the boat and stopped; they must be right outside now. Tommy made a slight move towards the opening through which Papa had left a short while ago. I caught his arm and shook my head, he sat down quietly and we listened hard to try and make out what was happening outside. I dared not move for the risk of drawing attention to our hiding place. My heart was pounding in my chest; it was beating so hard I feared we would be discovered, they must surely be able to hear it. My mouth was dry and I

was finding it hard to swallow, my nails dug into the palms of my hands as I tightly clenched my fists. I had no idea what we would do if we were discovered. Then I heard the familiar sound of a match being struck, after a few moments the smell of tobacco drifted into the boat.

Danny had begun to come round although as he regained consciousness his breathing remained fast, coming in short gasps, his little body shaking. Mama clamped her hand over his mouth in case he made a sound, his eyes opened wide with fright, and his arms thrashing wildly as he tried to remove my mother's hand. Tommy grabbed at his arms and pinned them to his sides trying to quieten him. Then as he came round more he was able to focus better and as his eyes locked onto mine I held my finger to my lips to signal he must keep quiet and still. He relaxed enough for Mama to feel confident enough to take her hand from his mouth. My mother pulled him to her chest and hugged him tightly, she bent her head to his and whispered to him to try to soothe him and also warn him of the danger just feet from us. I was starting to shake slightly and had to ignore the fact that my brain was telling me to run as fast as I could. In the faint light I saw Danny was clinging to Mama and tears were falling freely down his cheeks. Tommy had found a small length of wood in the bottom of the boat and was gripping it so tightly that his knuckles had turned white.

Daniel crept to the entrance to the docks and stood for a few moments as his eyes adjusted to the light, he scoured the dock side and was horrified to see three men standing right outside the boat where his family were hiding, smoking. He hoped they had the sense to remain quiet, he watched as they passed the cigar from man to man, then after about ten minutes one of them pointed to a spot further along and after saying something that made the others laugh, they moved away. Daniel waited and watched as they neared a small group of people and began to harass them as they had done to the others earlier. Once they were fully engaged in their pursuit he crept to the boat hoping his family were still safe inside.

Then suddenly we heard one of the men outside say, 'look over there, there are some more of them. Let's go and give them a proper welcome to Liverpool.' We heard laughter and then the sound of receding footsteps. I let my breath out as I relaxed slightly, my heart rate slowing, I began to shake uncontrollably, my mouth felt so dry and my hands were hurting where I had been clenching them and I could feel the impressions in my palms where my nails had dug into my skin.

Then just as I felt we were safe I heard footsteps outside once again, this time there appeared to be only one person, had one of them come back to search the boat? Again we all froze, but the tarpaulin was gently pulled to one side and a small pail of water was handed to me by my father. He climbed quietly in to join us.

'I could not find anywhere better to rest tonight and no food but I did find this water and know where we can get more. It's dangerous out there at the moment though, there are men wandering around robbing folk and beating them if they don't have anything to give. We must stay here until it is light.'

'Yes Papa, we heard them outside just before you returned,' Tommy told him.

Mother took the pail and held it to Danny's parched lips. Danny's natural reaction was to try and gulp the water as fast as he could but my mother made him take small sips saying he would be sick otherwise. We all drank and as the cool liquid slipped down my throat I noticed Danny's breathing had improved slightly. Papa made two more trips to the water supply before the early light of dawn appeared and we climbed from our refuge.

On our way into the heart of the town we passed people sleeping in alleys, rough on the streets and on benches. Some were emerging from dark cellars and even dog kennels, others were cut and bruised and I wondered if they had received 'the Liverpool welcome' we had heard discussed last night.

Even though it was still very early, the sun only just risen, the town was busy, stall holders setting up for the day, men heading to the docks and women to factories. The houses were brick built and their doors opened straight onto the cobbled streets. After the wide open space of the farm back in Ireland I felt hemmed in by dwellings and the amount of people all bustling about.

We came upon a stall selling freshly baked bread and the smell was delicious, my mouth began to water and the deep pangs of hunger presented themselves once again.

'We have to find some food and then we can think about shelter and employment,' said my father. He approached the woman on the stall and asked if she could tell him where we might find some inexpensive food.

'Well they used to hand out food at the mission every day,' she told him,' but that was before so many of you came here. I think they may have stopped it but you could try there.' She gave us directions and we set off in hope of a meal. We found the place easily enough and although it was closed there were many people waiting in line. We waited for around an hour and were just about to give up when the doors opened and a voice called out, 'You can come in, no pushing, get your food quickly and leave so others can come in.'

My parents suggested that as we only had the bowl and pail it was best we children waited outside for them to return in order to avoid the worst of the crush inside. After some fifteen minutes they reappeared carrying the bowl and pail filled with steaming hot broth and five slices of bread, I found myself salivating at the thought of the meal as we walked away from the mission to find a quieter place to eat.

The food was hot and nourishing, far better than we had received back in Ireland, the bread still warm and I could feel my spirits rising. I looked at my brothers who were enjoying the fare as much as the rest of us, Danny's cheeks bulging as he chewed on his bread. Once we had finished we decided to see if we could find employment of any sort.

'We need to secure work before we can think of lodgings,' stated my father,' they will want money for rooms and we don't have it at the moment.' We turned and headed back towards the docks, the noise assaulted my senses as we approached, men shouting, hammers striking, boat horns blasting and stall holders calling out to the passersby, the pungent smell of fish being unloaded and the smoke from the braziers all foreign to me.

'Excuse me,' my father said to a man pushing a barrow loaded with sacks of grain, sweat running down his face, 'where do I go to ask for work?'

The man stopped and dropped his barrow, wiping his brow on a neckerchief he pulled from his pocket and pointed across to a small office building at the edge of the yard near the wrought iron entrance gates, 'Over there mate, foreman's name is Frank Sanders.'

Thanking him we walked to the office, father went inside and returned within minutes saying,' they take casual labourers on a daily basis but I need to be here when the gates open at six each day as places are filled very quickly. The wage is seven pence ha'penny a day. So I will come back tomorrow early.'

'What about me?' said Tommy, 'Will they take me?'

'I don't know, I will ask tomorrow, I don't want to bother the man again today.'

'I need to find something as well,' said my mother, 'the cabin back home was part of your wage but we will need money for food and lodgings now. A lot of women were walking up behind that warehouse earlier; shall we go and look there?'

As we had nothing further to do we walked on until we found the factory but there was no work to be had there, so we made our way back into the centre keeping an eye open for suitable shelter for the night. We passed a house with a notice in the window offering a bed within a shared room for one penny per day but with only three pence decided to keep that in case we could not find work tomorrow. Our second night in England was spent in a damp cellar with two other families. The date was 20th June 1847.

Chapter 11.

The day broke with a mist clinging to the streets of the town as Daniel walked down to the dock gates, it was five o'clock and as he turned the corner he saw with despair that there were already over one hundred men in front of him waiting for the gates to open. Then he reasoned that many of these must be employees with a permanent situation so in a yard this large it wasn't so bad. He was desperate to secure some work today and provide for his family once more. The night in the cellar had been damp and uncomfortable but one that was now behind them. The unfamiliar sounds of the town at night and the noises of the others sharing the shelter made it a long night with little sleep. He was hungry and somewhat weary as he joined the back of the queue. The man in front of him turned and nodded his head in greeting.

'Thought I would get here early to be in with a chance, looks like everyone else had the same idea,' he said to Daniel. 'My first day here, what do you think to our chances of getting in today?'

'I don't really know, it's my first day also,' Daniel replied, 'but some of these must be employees already surely.'

'No I don't think so, see that small gate off to the left, I was told that's the one the normal workers use, casual wait here for the main gates to open and then they hire based on what ships need loading and unloading.'

As they stood and waited Daniel watched as others entered through the small gate, the line behind him growing longer by the minute. At six o'clock the main gates opened and Daniel followed the rest as they filed to the office where two men were standing holding clipboards with details of the ships timetables and cargoes. They divided the men between them allocating jobs to each in turn and directing them on where to report and to whom. Today was a busy day and Daniel was relieved when he was told to report to Mr Lane at the far berthing.

My father had left early for the docks in the hope of some work and we were all pleased to note that some two hours later he had not returned. We took that to mean he had been successful.

'Come children, let's get ready and walk to the mission to get some food. If we are lucky we may be able to get some to take to your father. If he is working he will need something to keep him going. After that we will see what other employment is available,' my mother said anxious to get out of the damp cellar.

After a meal at the mission, in which we managed to get something for my father once we explained where he was, we walked down to the dockyard, if possible it seemed busier than yesterday, there was a small line of men stood by the main gate in the hope of work but their chances seemed slim. We stood at the gate searching in vain for a sight of our father but in such a crowd it was impossible to locate him. Watching the comings and goings for a few minutes I noticed the two men standing by the small office. Men were constantly approaching them and after they had consulted their paperwork were directed to some area of the dock; I decided to take a chance and ran over to them.

'Excuse me sir, I am looking for my father, I have some food for him,' I said to the older of the two.

'Well now miss you shouldn't be here, you had better go back home,' he replied.

'Please sir, I won't get in the way, I just want to give him this food, he left early and hasn't eaten today,' I pleaded.

'Does he work here?' the younger man asked me.

'No, I mean yes, I mean I think so,' I stammered.

'I take it you mean he is casual,' the older man stated.

'Yes sir.'

'Well he could be anywhere, so I think you are wasting yours and our time.'

I decided if I was going to get anywhere my best chance lay with the younger of the two, turning to him I asked, 'could you check if he is here please?'

He smiled, 'I don't think she is going to take no for an answer Alf, if we want to get rid of her and get on I think we should help her.'

The older man sighed, 'very well, what's his name?'

'Daniel Rafferty,' I told him pleased with myself that my persistence appeared to have paid off.

They both consulted their lists, the younger one saying, 'I've got him, and he's with Lane. Follow me; it's not safe around here on your own.'

We walked down to the far end of the dock and I saw my father, sleeves rolled up, jacket off loading sacks onto a hand barrow. 'There he is,' I said to my escort pointing him out.

'Give me the food,' he said holding out his hand.

I handed him the parcel and watched as he walked up to my father, spoke to him and then turned and pointed to where I was stood. My father took the parcel, waved at me and then said something to the man which made him laugh and nod his head before returning to my side and taking me back to my family.

'What did he say to you?' I asked curious.

'He said I was right to bring you in because you could be stubborn once you had your mind set and would probably have still been here when we closed otherwise.'

I was still smiling at this when I re-joined the rest.

'Did you see him?' Danny asked of me.

'Yes he is busy, but he looked alright.'

'Well done Millie,' my mother said. 'Right let's go and see what I can find.'

The rest of the day was spent walking the town in the vain hope of finding work. We found nothing and returned to the cellar to await Papa coming back. After a while we found the cramped conditions so bad we decided to sit outside to wait for him. The cellar was about forty feet square with a low ceiling that made the taller of the adults have to stoop, the floor was just bare earth and the water dripped from the ceiling forming puddles on the uneven surface. The only opening was the hatch way set in the far corner and so the air was stale and fetid. The two other families sharing this space with us were made up of three adults and five children so space was limited but we all kept to our own areas and unlike the sharing of the cabin on our journey back in Ireland here no one spoke to anyone outside their family group, it was an uncomfortable situation.

Some two hundred and twenty miles away the place was in uproar.

'Order, order,' cried out the speaker, banging his gavel on the bench. 'Please keep calm, we need to bring this matter to a conclusion and vote on the proposed law.'

Slowly the men took to their seats and eventually peace was restored to the house.

'I think it is obvious what must be done. Liverpool is besieged with these people and whilst we have compassion to the circumstances back in Ireland that has brought them to these shores we can no longer fund it all. The financial burden of feeding all those mouths has brought the town to the brink of ruin. Then there is the housing problem, people are sleeping in cellars, dog kennels and on the streets. All the extra people are putting a strain on the sanitation system and disease is rife. We must do something to placate the tax payers and relieve the situation.'

'Gentlemen, 'said the speaker, 'it is time to vote.'

The vote was cast and counted and the new law allowing local authorities to deport the homeless Irish back to Ireland was passed on 21st June 1847.

Chapter 12

At four o'clock the horn sounded signalling the end of the day's work. Daniel shrugged into his jacket following the casual workers to the small office and received his pay for the day. Seven pence ha'penny was given to him and he made his mark on the slip, making his way to the gates and the cellar doors. Outside he found his family waiting for him. Danny ran towards him, a smile on his face that Daniel hadn't seen since they had arrived here.

'Papa, did you get work, did you eat the food Millie bought you, are you going tomorrow, how much did you get?'

'If you will stop asking questions for one second I might get a word in to answer you,' he replied as he joined his family and sat down wearily.

'How are you dear?' Maria asked of him.

'Tired, the work on the farm was hard but this is ever more so, nonstop for ten hours, carrying, loading, dragging but the main thing is we have some money. Did you find anything?'

'No I am afraid not yet, we will try again tomorrow. Are you going back tomorrow?'

'Yes but I shall go earlier to guarantee getting in, it's worth the wait.' He answered passing the money to his wife. 'I think we should save this money today to get some food tomorrow. I know the cellar is not an ideal place to sleep but whilst the nights are mild I think we should use it. Accommodation will take a big part of any money we get and eating is far more important. What is your view?'

Maria took his hand in hers and nodded in reply, 'Yes I agree, food is our priority. The children must eat.'

Daniel looked at his daughter and smiling said, 'thank you so much for bringing me the food today, I would really have struggled without it. I think you impressed the foreman with your tenacity.'

Millie smiled and blushed slightly at this praise coming from her father.

'Papa did you ask about me?' Tommy asked.

'Not yet son, there are only men working there at the moment and still they did not all get work. I think we should wait a while.'

'But I always helped you on the farm,' he answered.

'I know son and I would love to have you alongside me once more but the dock is no place for a young boy especially while men cannot get work. Some of them may have families like I do. Would you want to take food from their mouths?'

'No but I want to help us too,' he snapped.

'Tommy,' coaxed his mother, 'we have only been here three days. Your turn will come, please just be patient.'

Without reply Tommy rose and walked to the far side of the yard in which the cellar was located.

I watched as Tommy walked off, I knew how much he wanted to help and he was hurting. I joined him as he sat on the wall trailing a stick through the dust of the yard making swirling patterns in the dirt.

'Tommy, we all know you want to work but Papa is right, we have to let the men find work first,' I said. I received no reply from my brother as he continued to draw with the stick. 'If Papa could not work because there was a man and his son working instead of him would you think that fair? Two wages for one family and none for another.' Still no answer, then he raised his head to look at me and I could see the tears building in his eyes. I took this as my cue that he was willing to let me in on his hurt, and I walked across and sat by him.

'It's just not fair Millie, first they stopped me working with him on the farm, then I couldn't do anything because of this stupid knee,' with those words he slapped at his remaining bruises, ' and now this. I feel so helpless.'

I put my arms around his shoulders and pulled him to me, 'Tommy the time will come for us all to play our part in helping our family get through this, in the meantime we must do as Mama and Papa ask without question. They only want what is best for us and are living day to day at the moment, we can't cause them any more concern, and we need to be strong for them.'

Tommy laid his head on my chest and I felt his silent sobs as he wept as much in frustration as sorrow. All the pain and uncertainty of the last few days breaking down his last defences. At last he lifted his head and wiped his hands across his face saying, 'Thanks Millie, you are the best sister,' then as the meaning of those words hit him he wept again, as did I.

Eventually we returned to the rest of the family, dusk was giving way to night and reluctantly we descended into the darkness of the cellar. Mother kissed us both and seeing whatever the issue had been was now resolved, wished us goodnight.

Chapter 13

I heard Papa as he crept out of the cellar early to go to the dock; it was just beginning to get light. I followed him outside and when he heard my footsteps on the wooden steps he turned to face me.

His face looked tired and drawn due to lack of food and sleep, 'Millie what are you doing up?'

'I heard you leave and thought I would walk to the dock with you so you didn't have to wait alone.'

Papas face broke into a tired smile and he rested his hand on my shoulder, 'Millie that is very kind and thoughtful of you, but it is not safe out there on your own in the hours of darkness. There are some very unsavoury characters around waiting to rob vulnerable folk.'

'But Papa, I don't have anything to give them,' I answered.

'But they will only find that out when it's too late, please go back inside. I will see you tonight.' He kissed me on the top of my head and left alone. I had still not grown used to this place we now lived in, back in Ireland I had no fears of walking down the country lane on my own, but here things were very different. As I stood watching him until he disappeared round the corner I realised how much I owed to the sacrifice of my parents and vowed I would always be there for them as they were for me. I returned to sit on the top step of the cellar stairs and watched as the sun rose above the mission roof, shortly after which my mother and brothers appeared ready for the challenge of another day.

'Ah there you are Millie,' greeted my mother coming over to kiss me. 'I think after we have been to the mission this morning before we go looking for work we should buy some food. It's not right that your father goes to work without anything for the day, and although you managed to get something to him yesterday, you may not always be so fortunate.'

'What are we buying Mama?' asked Danny excited at the prospect of actually choosing what we ate for a change.

'I don't know yet, we will have to see what we can afford. We have ten pence ha'penny and can't use it all in case your father doesn't get work today.'

Tommy was eager to join in these plans after his frustration yesterday, 'Well Mama, surely after the mission we could go to the docks and take him something, that way we would also know if he is working today. It won't take us long to do that before we look for work.'

'That's a good idea Tommy, let's go,' replied my mother receiving a beaming smile from my brother.

As we were making our way to the mission Danny asked,' Mama do those people in the cellar with us go out?'

Once he had said this I realised I had never seen some of them move, they were always in the same place whatever time of day it was.

'I don't know Danny, 'she answered, 'I think some of them are poorly.'

The rest of the day followed much the same pattern as the day before, we took food from the mission to Papa at the dock, and this time he was working in a different area loading horse drawn carts. I insisted Tommy take his lunch to him today, hoping to make him feel more useful. With our money we managed to buy a loaf of bread and some apples, leaving us a penny ha'penny.

Then we wandered the town looking for work, I could see my mother was becoming desperate. The story was the same as before, there was nothing to be found. We were a despondent group as we returned to the yard to await Papa's return. We sat outside in the warmth of the day; we always stayed outside as long as possible not wishing to go underground any sooner than we had to.

My mother was sat at the edge of the yard, elbows on knees, and her head in hands. I felt a lump in my throat as I walked over to sit next to her. Words did not come readily to me as I tried to think of what I could say to make her feel better, but something that she could believe in and hold on to.

'Mama, I know it's hard but I also know we will overcome this. We are Rafferty's and Rafferty's never give in. We will find something I know. Maybe tomorrow you could take Danny and I could take Tommy, that way we could cover more places at the same time. Today we were told twice that we were just too late. What do you think?'

'I don't know Millie.'

Tommy was keen on this idea and came over taking Mama's hand in his, ' Mama Millie's right, we can cover opposite sides of the town, we could even be on the same street.'

'We'll speak to your father when he gets back.'

When Papa returned he looked happier than when he went out this morning. He kissed my mother and lifted Danny into his arms hugging him closely. 'Maria, today they told me they like the way I work and although I will still be casual I am guaranteed work for the rest of the week. I can go in at six with the others.'

'Oh Daniel, that's wonderful,' she kissed him and added, 'I still haven't found anything and we could only afford some bread and apples but that is good news.'

She then told him of my plan and when she had finished he looked at me and Tommy,' If I say yes to this you must promise to stay together and also to stay on the main streets. You must not stray from this or you cannot go.'

We both promised to do as instructed and when we finally descended into our temporary home I hoped Tommy felt as optimistic as I did at that moment.

The light was fading but I could see the family we had spoken of earlier were still sitting quietly in the back of the room, one woman had her head in the lap of an older woman and I had to stare hard to see the movement of her chest as she took in shallow breaths.

Chapter 14

The next morning broke with a heavy mist shrouding the streets, the temperature had dropped and the damp air clung to my clothing. As I passed the family to follow my father outside to bid him goodbye for the day I cast a quick sideways glance towards the young woman from last evening. To my horror I saw she was laid off to one side and her face was covered with a scarf. The rest of the family remained in the same places as before, no words were exchanged and they did not even seem to acknowledge our presence.

Before he left he took me to one side and bent down to whisper in my ear, 'Millie do your best to get your brothers out of there without them seeing that poor woman. Also tell your mother I want you all to meet me at the dock yard gates tonight when I finish work. We are not going back to that cellar again.'

'I will see to it Papa,' I promised as he left. I shuddered at the thought of re-entering the cellar but if I was to keep my promise to my father I had to go and help my mother with my brothers. Taking a deep breath I descended the stairs and kept my eyes straight ahead as I went to join my mother. She was just stirring and so I waited until she was fully awake before passing on the news of the woman's death and the wishes of Papa.

My mother looked over to where the woman's body lay, turning to me she said, ' Right we will wake the boys and when we leave I will walk that side in order to block their view and you talk to them about our work hunting plans today so they look your way. Hopefully that will work.'

We did indeed manage to leave the cellar for the last time without Tommy or Danny seeing what had happened during the night.

After a meal at the mission we decided to split up in order to seek work for my mother. Tommy and I were to take the north of the town and Danny and my mother the south.

'Millie, Tommy I want you to remember what your father said, stay on the main streets and do not stray from them. Meet us back here at noon and we will discuss what to do next. Good luck.'

'Same to you Mama,' and with that Tommy and I strode off purposefully along the cobbled road.

At ten o'clock the local authority met in order to discuss the latest word from the government.

'Attention everyone,' began the spokesman, 'we have received word from London that in order to deal with the problem of the housing shortages due to the immigrating Irish an extraordinary law has been passed saying we can deport these people back to Ireland. We must discuss how we propose to carry this out.'

'That is going to be a momentous task, there are thousands of them,' one portly gentleman said.

'Exactly, that is why we need to make plans today, the sooner we start the better for all of us,' the spokesman responded.

Ideas were bandied about and by noon a plan had been drawn up that a special committee be formed who were responsible for this task. This consisted of six of the most respected businessmen in the town. Each would recruit teams of people who would hit the cellars and lodging houses taking the people from these properties and sending them back to Ireland by boat. Boats would have to be sourced and ready to take the immigrants once they were delivered to the docks. There could be no risk of people fleeing whilst waiting to board. Co-ordination was the key to the success of this task. After more deliberations they agreed to meet again in four days to ensure all was in place for the operation to begin.

'Gentlemen unless you have any other pressing issues I recommend we bring this meeting to a close and begin putting our plans into operation.'

'One more thing I would like to raise is the issue of the missions giving out free food to these people. I think because of this some are not even bothering to seek employment,' the portly man opined.

A further murmuring went round the room agreeing with the man, 'Yes the tax payer is having to bear the brunt of these costs with no benefit to themselves.'

So it was also agreed that the missions would be closed with immediate effect.

I must admit to feeling slightly nervous being in the town with my brother, neither of us were familiar with the place and it was far busier than anything we had been used to. Even the way they spoke was different, of course there were plenty of Irish people here but mostly they were working in the docks and factories.

'I think we should start on this side of the street and work our way to the top, then cross over and back down,' I said to Tommy.

We had completed the first side of the street stopping at each shop, stall and business. Each time the answer was the same; there was either no work or we were not what they were looking for. Approaching the first of the stalls on the opposite side Tommy took the lead and walked up to the man behind the wooden counter, 'Do you know where we may be able to find any work sir?'

The man looked at us, a smile crossing his face,' yes actually I do.'

'Where?' we both chorused in unison.

'Right here, 'the man replied,' I need someone to help me on the stall. I can only take one of you so you had better decide between you. It would mean being here first thing in the morning to help me set up and then keeping stocked up and running errands.'

'How much does it pay?' Tommy asked.

'Penny a day, six days.'

Tommy dragged me to one side saying, 'It's not what we were looking for, but I think one of us should take it.'

'I agree, which one of us you do think should take it?' I replied although looking at the excited face of my brother I already knew the answer to that question.

'I will let you decide,' he replied generously.

'Well I am the eldest,' I started to say, teasing him, but the look of disappointment on his face was more than I could take, 'although you did ask and so I think you should take it.'

Tommy beamed as he went back to the man and shook his hand saying 'I will take the job sir.'

'Be here tomorrow at five thirty son, my name is Stan. What's yours?'

'Tommy Rafferty and this is my sister Millie. We were actually trying to find work for my mother, do you know of anything she could do?'

'You have a certain amount of cheek I'll give you that lad,' Stan said pushing his cap back on his head and wiping at his brow. 'Has she tried the cotton mill?'

'No sir, where is that?'

Stan gave us directions and we said our goodbyes, Tommy promising to be there tomorrow and went back towards the mission to meet up with the other two. We were a little early and sat down of the edge of the pavement to wait. Tommy was so pleased to have some good news for our mother and he could not keep still, he was up and pacing every few moments looking up the road for their return. At last they appeared, Danny looking tired as he plonked himself down next to me.

'Any luck Mama?' I asked although I thought I knew the answer by her demeanour, she looked weary.

'No darlings, I am afraid not. Did you?'

I looked to my brother, letting him deliver the good news.

'I have got a job helping on a stall and I start tomorrow, it's sixpence a week,' he said his face splitting into a grin,' and we have been told about a cotton mill that might have work for you.'

'That's wonderful, well done Tommy,' my mother said hugging us both.

It was with a spring in our step that the four of us set off towards the cotton mill. The mill was about a three mile walk away from the town centre and Danny was beginning to drag his feet a little after having walked all morning. We could see the imposing red brick building looming ahead of us, it was three storeys high and the front was made up of many windows, with three tall chimney stacks reaching up into the sky like red smoking fingers.

Mama looked down at Danny and said to us, 'I think it is safe enough here for you to wait while I walk to the factory, you can rest for a while until I get back.'

'Do you want any company Mama?' Tommy asked.

'No it's alright, you need to save your energy for tomorrow, I won't be too long.' With that she walked on towards the mill, the road was straight and we could follow her progress from where we sat.

'If Mama gets some work then there will only be two of us not earning,' I said feeling a little disappointed with myself.

'You will find something I am sure, 'Tommy said trying to cheer me up and failing.

'What do you think I can do?' Danny asked, as he watched Mama walk ever further down the road.

'I don't know, this place is far bigger than I expected and I don't think we have covered all of it yet,' I answered him knowing he was still hurting from having done no work at all yet.

After around an hour and a half we saw Mama walking back towards us, as she approached us I could see the expression on her face and knew that she had been successful.

'I can start tomorrow,' she said, 'your father is going to be so pleased when he gets back. Let's go and buy some food for tonight. Things are looking up and I think we can afford to celebrate.'

As we walked back to the town we chatted excitedly about the change of fortune and what we might buy for tonight's meal. Then I remembered we had nowhere to sleep, 'Mama, where are we staying tonight?'

'Aren't we going to our cellar?' Danny asked.

'No darling, Papa doesn't like it there, 'Mama said not wishing to tell my brothers the truth about the death of the young woman.

'Neither do I,' Tommy stated, 'some of those people looked quite ill.'

'We will find somewhere once your father returns,' Mama answered.

We bought bread and fruit and went to meet Papa at the dock gates.

At four o'clock the horn sounded and the workers poured out of the docks into the street. There were hundreds of men, various ages, shapes and sizes but all with one common intent, to go home and relax. Papa came out of the office and walked over to join us, I could see in his face that there was something he wanted to tell us but before he could Danny burst out,' Papa, Mama and Tommy have found work.'

'Is that right?' Papa asked, looking at the smiles on their faces he knew this to be true.

'Yes Daniel,' my mother replied before Danny could take over, 'I have work at the cotton mill starting tomorrow. Tommy, tell your father your news.'

'I am going to work on a street stall, I also start tomorrow.'

'That's wonderful news, well done both of you, I too have some news,' he said smiling, 'Mr Johnson likes the way in which I work and has asked for me to stay on until this work is finished. The job will take at least another six weeks.'

'Okay let's go and find somewhere to stay tonight and then we can work out how much money we will have and what we are going to do next,' my mother said.

'Millie,' Danny said taking my hand as we walked a little behind the others,' what are we going to do when the others are working? We don't have any job to go to.'

I looked at Danny and knew how he was feeling, back in Ireland I had always helped my mother around the cabin, cleaning, baking, and tending the crop. Now we had no cabin and my mother would be gone all day.

'I don't know, I am sure we will find something,' this was meant to allay his worries but did little to quell mine.

After a short walk in the opposite direction to that of the cellar we had spent the previous nights in we came across a plot of waste land, at first there were no obvious buildings to be seen but on closer inspection there was an old shed hidden behind a thick tangle of shrubs and bushes.

'I'll go and check to see what its like,' Papa said pushing aside some of the branches and crouching down to duck underneath the foliage. We waited for a few moments and then he suddenly appeared behind us.

'It's perfect,' he said,' dry, empty and you can get in from the back so we won't have to trample the bushes at the front down, that way it will stay hidden from the road.'

We followed him round through the shrubbery and came up on the rear of the medium sized shed. The wooden building showed signs of being deserted for a long time, cobwebs around the doorway and hanging down from the roof, inside weeds had squeezed their way in from outside through the wooden slatted walls, but the roof was intact and the place completely dry. Also it showed no signs of occupancy.

'I claim this building in the name of the Rafferty family,' Tommy squealed dancing around like a mad thing. Suddenly he grabbed hold of Danny and me and we swung round madly before collapsing on the grassy patch in front of the shed, breathless.

As we ate some of the bread and fruit, some being saved for the other three to take with them to work the next day, Papa asked to know more about the work Tommy and Mama had secured. It was decided that Papa would walk Tommy and Mama as far as the stall before heading the opposite way to the docks, Mama would travel the rest of the way with the other women who all started work at six o'clock. The combined wage would be seven shillings and three pence per week. I had been put in charge of food shopping, looking after Danny and looking for accommodation. This made me feel a lot better about playing my part and knowing how much my little brother was feeling left out I delegated him the job of keeping the barricade of bushes in place and so hiding our temporary new home. Today was a good day and I slept well for the first time since we had arrived in England.

Chapter 15

A light rain was falling when my parents and Tommy left our shed at five o'clock to go out to work. I could tell Tommy was slightly apprehensive about being on his own with a complete stranger today, so whilst Mama was sorting out the food for their lunches I went to the doorway where he stood watching the drizzle.

'How are you feeling Tommy?' I asked hoping he would tell me the truth and not try to hide his true feelings from me. Tommy and I had always been close in that way and we had never hidden our feelings from each other. When Frances died two years ago even though Tommy was only six we used to sit at the bottom of the meadow side by side and talk about our grief for the sister we were looking forward to helping to raise and our worries for Mama when she was ill. We wanted to be strong for Papa and so took that time to work out our emotions away from him so that when we returned to the cabin he could lean on us for a change. Tommy and I grew up a lot in that short time.

'Truthfully Millie?' he asked turning to face me.

'No other way.' I replied.

'I am a bit scared, I have never been on my own like this before. When I worked on the farm I was with Papa and even if I was on another job I knew he was close by. I am also excited at the same time.'

'I know you will be fine, as soon as you start working you will forget your worries and he seems like a kindly man. Mama and Papa have faith in you otherwise they wouldn't let you go on your own. Make sure you take notice of everything he tells you and you can't go wrong. And I will want to hear every single detail when you get back.' I leant over and planted a kiss on his cheek and hugged him to me, as he hugged me back I thought to myself, 'my little brother is becoming a man.'

'Millie, don't forget now, you and Danny are to go to the mission for your breakfast and then buy the things I have told you to,' Mama said.

'Yes Mama, I will,' I answered smiling. This was not the first time we had had this conversation.

'Are you sure you and Danny will be alright?' she asked.

Papa came to my rescue, 'Maria, I am sure her answer will be the same as it was the last ten times you asked her, they will be fine and if there is a problem, which there won't be,' he quickly added before she could say anything,' they know where I am. It will be us who have worries if we don't hurry up and get off to work.'

I watched as they walked off around the back of the shed to reach the road into the town, Danny was still sleeping and I suddenly felt very alone. The grey sky and the lightly falling rain added to my feeling of isolation, even the birds were quiet at the moment waiting for the weather to improve before they emerged into the morning. I checked my pocket again to make sure I had the money I was entrusted with last night from Papa when I became house keeper. I had seven pence ha'penny in order to buy food for tonight and tomorrow's lunches. It was tight but once Mama and Tommy received their wages on Saturday we should be able to get a little in hand and not have to live day to day as we were at the moment.

This was the first time since we arrived in England that I had been left alone with my thoughts; I tried to imagine how things would work out for us, where we would live, what work I might eventually find. I failed to come to any conclusions on these matters and so turned my mind back to the life we had left behind, the cabin which was not much more than a mud hut but it was all I had ever known. With the opening cut into the wall for a doorway and a window it was cold and draughty and in the winter if the wind changed direction the snow would blow in and pile up in the corners. Those days we would retreat to the sleeping area where there were no window openings so the snow could not get in but neither could the light, those nights used to stretch out before us as we tried to keep warm by snuggling together and my parents would take it in turns to tell us stories. Papa had such a vivid imagination and held us enthralled with his tales of dragons, giants, and pirates. I was brought out of my daydreaming when I heard a small voice behind me call out.

'Morning Danny,' I said as I walked in to see my brother sitting up rubbing his eyes and yawning, 'how are you?'

'Hungry,' he answered, 'have they gone to work already?'

'Yes, they went a while ago but you were still asleep.'

'Why didn't you wake me up? I wanted to say goodbye to them,' he said looking slightly sad.

'I am sorry Danny but we thought it would be better to let you sleep if you were tired, we have a lot to do today. We are in charge now remember?'

His face brightened a little at this thought, 'can we go and find breakfast now do you think?' he asked hopefully.

'Danny,' I said, 'today we can do whatever we want whenever we want, providing we are back here when they get back from work with the food for supper.'

The rain fell heavier as we walked into the town towards the mission, the air was cool and soon we were both quite cold. I did consider turning back and waiting for better weather but there was no guarantee of that and I knew we needed to eat and so we plodded on. As we turned the corner to the mission I was surprised to see a large crowd of people milling around outside, the normally orderly queue was gone and the doors were still closed. I did not like the look of this. We drew closer and noticed there was a hand written notice pinned to the door. My mother had taught us to read a little and I walked closer in the hope I could make out what it said. My heart sank when I saw what was written, the pleasure I would normally have felt by the fact that I could read the words outweighed by their meaning.

The mission will no longer be serving free food.
24 June 1847.

'What is it Millie?' Danny asked, sensing something was wrong.

'They aren't going to give us any food today Danny, or any other day,' I told him.

'But I am hungry,' he said, 'what are we going to do?'

'I don't know Danny,' I answered, 'I think we will have to buy some but that will leave us short of money for the other shopping Mama wanted.'

Why did this have to happen today, my first day in charge of the family budget and I was faced with this. What would my mother do?

I looked down at my brother as he stood holding onto my hand, he was soaked through and shivering, hungry and depending on me.

'Shall we go and find Papa?' he asked as the rain trickled down his face.

'No I don't want to worry him so early; we will go and see what we can find in the market. Don't worry I will find something for us,' I said trying to sound more confident than I felt.

Daniel and Maria left their son in the care of Stan and went their separate ways to work.

'Morning lad, you are early that's good to see.'

'Yes sir,' Tommy replied.

'Have you ever worked on a stall before?'

'No sir,'

'Well I will tell you what needs doing and when and I am sure you will soon get the hang of it,' Stan told him.

'Yes sir,' was all Tommy could say. He looked up at the man he had pledged to work for. He stood taller than his father and had a wild head of curly grey hair with bushy side whiskers. His eyes were a deep blue with deep creases around them as if he smiled a lot. Everything about him seemed huge to Tommy, the man's hands were the size of dinner plates, his arms were thick and his trousers were held up by a pair of bright red braces over his large belly.

Stan sensed the boy's nerves and tried to break the ice by tossing him an apple out of the box he had just unloaded from the handcart. 'Tommy if you can help me get all these boxes off this cart and onto the stall by six you can eat that apple.'

'Yes sir, thank you sir.'

'And another thing, please call me Stan.'

'Yes sir,' Tommy replied,' I mean Stan.'

The ice was broken and man and boy worked well together loading the stall and unwrapping the fruits and vegetables and before long the stall was ready for business. Tommy sat on an upturned crate eating his apple and watching as Stan called out to the people walking by to try and entice them over to buy his wares.

Tommy was surprised at how many people were buying the produce and was kept busy restocking the displays. It was obvious to him that a lot of the customers were regulars by the way they spoke to Stan, some even spoke to him as if they had known him for some time. He began to relax a little in the presence of the big man and thought that his sister was right and he was indeed a kindly man.

I was beginning to get quite desperate about the situation I found myself in. The only good thing was that the rain had finally stopped. Danny and I had been walking around the market for around an hour and I had been checking out the prices of the things Mama had asked me to buy with the money I had been entrusted with. If I bought everything now there would be no money left to buy any food for my brother and me to eat now. I wondered whether to risk waiting until later in the day when I remembered that the market holders back in Ireland would sometimes drop the prices of some of the goods if they looked like they would not last another day. I was tempted but my worries of missing out altogether were outweighing this idea. I was deep in thought when suddenly Danny tugged on my hand and pointing said, 'Millie there's Tommy, can we go and say hello?'

Without waiting for my consent Danny broke free from me and dashed across the square to the stall where Tommy was busy stacking empty crates onto a barrow.

'Hi Tommy,' shouted Danny as he approached his brother.

Tommy turned in time to see the missile that was his younger brother hurtling towards him.

'Hey Shorty what are you doing here?' Tommy asked Danny, smiling at me as I joined them.

'We are shopping for Mama,' I replied. I was embarrassed to admit defeat on my first day in charge. Although I had forgotten to take into account the fact that my youngest sibling could not keep anything quiet.

'Yes and we haven't had any breakfast yet because they have closed the mission,' Danny blurted out loudly.

Stan looked over at us and afraid we had got Tommy into trouble for stopping work I grabbed Danny by the hand and tried to walk away before we were seen.

'What's going on here then?' Stan asked Tommy.

'Sorry sir I was just talking to my sister and brother, I didn't mean to stop working,' Tommy answered picking up another crate.

'Don't worry about that son, 'Stan said, 'I don't mind you speaking to your family, as long as it doesn't take up the whole day. Now I know Millie but who is this young man?' he asked looking down upon Danny.

'My younger brother Danny sir,' Tommy told him.

'Pleased to meet you young sir,' Stan said addressing Danny and bending down to shake his hand. 'Now did I hear you say you had not eaten yet this morning?'

Danny nodded taking his small hand back from the man and looking up into his face. 'Yes sir that's right, we were going to the mission but they have closed it.'

'Well let's see what we can find for you both eh,' Stan said and went to the back of the stall coming back with a handful of grapes and two rosy apples, passing them over he turned to Tommy and said,' You have worked hard this morning, why don't you take a break and go and sit with these two over by the back of the stall and eat your lunch.'

'Are you sure sir, I mean Stan?' Tommy asked, remembering what he had been told about using the man's given name.

'Tommy, believe me if I didn't mean something I wouldn't waste my breath in saying it, now go and eat,' Stan instructed him holding his arms out and shooing us to the area he had pointed out.

We all took a seat on the wooden crates and began to eat the fruits we had been given, Tommy sharing the bread he had taken with him this morning.

'How are you getting on?' I asked wiping the grape juice from my mouth.

'You were right Millie, I am really enjoying myself and Stan is really nice.' Tommy replied before taking a bite out of the apple he had also been given.

'And he's kind too,' Danny chipped in.

'That's true,' Tommy added, 'this morning this old lady wanted to buy some potatoes but didn't have quite enough money and Stan let her have them anyway.'

'Why would he do that, he is losing money surely?' I said not sure of the logic of this.

'I asked him that,' Tommy told me, 'and he said that the lady would feel obliged to come back here again because of his generosity instead of going to a competitor.'

'That's clever,' I said. By this time we had finished our meal and got up to go, making sure we once again thanked Stan for his kindness.

'You are welcome children,' he answered, 'and please call by again.'

'We will sir,' I said before turning to Tommy,' do you know what time you will be finishing because we will meet you and walk you home?'

Tommy looked at his employer who said, 'I expect to be finished by three o'clock.'

'Bye then, we will go and buy Mama's shopping and see you later.' I said.

Danny and I had collected the items as we were told and were passing the mission on the way back to meet Tommy when I glanced once again at the notice pinned to the door. Since leaving home, crossing the Irish sea and settling here in England I knew I had lost all track of the days as I am sure the rest of my family had, but looking at the date on the poster reminded me of something very important and I knew I would have to speak to my parents to ensure they were aware.

Once the three of us were back at the shed and I had prepared the food ready for the evening's meal, as Mama would not finish work until six o'clock, I told my brothers I was going to meet Papa from the docks.

'I want to come too,' Danny said jumping to his feet.

'No you stay here and keep Tommy company, he has been working all day and needs to rest,' I told him in the hope of getting Papa alone.

'It's alright Millie, take Danny with you I think I am going to have a nap,' Tommy said.

I looked at him and could see he was tired and so decided it was probably best to take Danny with me. So my brother and I waited at the docks for Papa to arrive, after a wait of around ten minutes he appeared from the office after collecting his pay. Smiling as he saw us I thought I could begin to see some of the familiar Papa I was used to beginning to return. His complexion from working outside again was beginning to return, replacing the grey from the last few days in Ireland, his arms were a lightly tanned brown which I knew would soon deepen once exposed to the elements for much longer.

'Papa,' I asked after receiving my usual kiss,' do you know what the date is today?'

'Millie, I am not entirely sure I know who I am at the moment, why do you ask,' Papa answered me.

'Because today is the twenty fourth of June,' I told him.

It took a few seconds for the relevance of this information to sink in and then he said,' It's Tommy's birthday tomorrow.'

'That's right,' I said, 'he's nine tomorrow.'

'Papa, 'Danny asked, 'what can we surprise him with?'

'Son, I really don't know, maybe your mother will be able to think of something.'

When we lived back in Ireland we always received a homemade present from either one of my parents depending whether it was a carved wooden toy or a hand sewn handkerchief. Here they had neither materials nor tools to make anything and certainly no time.

Back in the shed we called home I put the vegetables on to cook and waited for my mother's return, at last she arrived. She looked really tired and her hair and clothing was covered in a fine dust from the cotton machines.

'Oh Millie, thank you so much for preparing the supper, I really don't think I could have found the strength to do it,' she said to me from outside the hut where she was trying to dust herself off.

'You have no need to worry any further about that, I will be doing all the meals whilst you are working,' I said to her. 'Here let me help you,' I joined her outside and began brushing the back of her clothes. When we were satisfied we could do no more we went inside to eat our supper but not before I whispered in her ear about Tommy's birthday tomorrow.

'Oh my,' she said covering her mouth with her hands, 'how on earth can I have forgotten that?'

'Well since being on the ship for however long we were, we have all just lost track of the date', I told her trying to make her feel better. 'I am afraid other things took priority.'

'Yes you are right of course but what are we going to do for him?'

'I don't know, maybe we will think of something later Mama, come let's eat.'

'I am nearly too tired to eat,' she said but once I placed the meal in front of her she did so.

'Maria,' my father said looking my mother,' you certainly did a good job of teaching our daughter how to cook.'

After supper we all settled down to sleep, exhaustion creeping up on us all. Although my mind was filled with Tommy's birthday surprise as I drifted off.

Chapter 16

I was awakened by the early morning sun streaming in through the window, the heat warming my face. Only Danny was still asleep as the others were readying themselves for work. I shook my younger brother knowing he would be upset if he hadn't seen them off especially as it was Tommy's birthday today.

'Danny, wake up, they are all leaving shortly, and I thought you might want to see them off today.'

Danny leapt up and before I could remind him that we didn't know what we were going to do for Tommy yet, he had shot outside and hugging Tommy shouted wildly, 'Happy birthday Tommy!'

Tommy looked at us all, bewilderment on his face, then realisation sank in. 'Oh is it really my birthday today?'

'Yes happy birthday,' we all chorused and surrounded him, kissing him.

'I am sorry Tommy but we don't have a gift for you,' Mama said.

'Mama, don't worry about it, I wouldn't have even known if you hadn't said. My gift is being here with you all and starting our new lives.'

I looked at him and realised that after all we had been through the last few weeks since leaving home; mentally we were no longer children. He was working independently from my father and I was in charge of my brother, money and meals. I felt a twinge of sadness knowing that no matter how much things may improve for us in the future our childhood and the relatively carefree days on the farm were over. Only Danny was fortunate enough to still have the innocence and trust of a child, how I envied him. I was not feeling sorry for myself and I was so very grateful for all my parents had done to get us away from almost certain starvation and who knew what else, but I knew there would be no return to those days, where Danny still existed, for us, days where he knew no real worries, days where any problems he had he could rely on my parents to tell him it would be alright and it would.

'Millie, is it right that the mission has closed?' Mama asked me concern showing on her face.

'Yes, we found it closed when we went there yesterday, how did you know?' I answered.

'I saw the notice when I passed on the way home last evening, what did you do for breakfast?'

'Stan gave them something,' Tommy told her.

'Well I must thank him this morning when we see him, do you have anything for today?' she asked of me.

'Yes Mama, I saved a little from last night, don't worry.' I answered.

Papa clapped his hands loudly saying, 'come along or we will all be late.' With that the three of them left and Danny and I sat down and ate what I had saved us from last night's supper.

The remainder of the morning was much the same as the previous one, we walked in to town and bought the food shopping, called to see Tommy and after Danny had blurted out to Stan that it was his brother's birthday we once again shared some fruit with him.

'Sir, 'I said to Stan, 'please don't think badly of us. We didn't come here to get free food from you, we just have such a long day on our own and seeing Tommy makes us feel less lonely.'

Stan looked at me and took my hand in his saying, 'Millie I don't think badly of you at all. If I didn't want to give you the fruit I wouldn't. You haven't asked me for anything but I want to help you and your brothers. My wife and I never had our own children and even though I have only known your family for two days I can say if we had I would be proud if they were like you three.'

Blushing I took my hand back, promised to meet Tommy from work and collecting Danny decided we will explore a little more of the town.

Tommy called us back, 'Millie, Stan says you may as well leave the shopping here and collect it when you come to meet me, there is no point carrying it round all day.' Gratefully I handed him the shopping and set off once more.

We turned off the main street behind the market square and after a walk of around fifteen minutes we came upon a set of iron railings that surrounded a vast area of luscious green grass, tall trees, bushes and winding pathways. We approached carefully and peered through the railings; we could see women pushing babies in prams and others sitting on benches talking whilst their charges slept.

'Millie, can we go in?' Danny said already looking for a way to get through the narrow railings.

'I don't know,' I answered honestly. I had never seen such a place before but I must admit to desperately wanting to go inside.

As we stood a woman passed us pushing a small child in a pram, 'Millie let's follow her and see if she goes inside,' Danny suggested already tugging my arm in an effort to keep her in view.

She walked turning a corner and entered through a large iron gate which was standing open, we followed and as we drew closer I saw a large sign, a lot of the words I was unsure of, but the main ones I could read and understood that this was a public park.

'Danny, it's a park and we are allowed in, come on let's go and explore it.'

We followed the path around the edge of the grass, passing the women we spied from the street earlier, on rounding a bend in the path we were confronted by a large pond with ducks and geese idly floating on the water which was sparkling in the summer sunshine. Small children were throwing food for the fowl and they were pecking wildly at the food, their long necks stretching out, sometimes squabbling between themselves as they tried to get as much as they could.

Danny and I spent the next two hours walking through the park, running on the grass, watching ladies feeding the ducks on the lake, playing tag around the trees and hiding from each other in the bushes before making our way back to the park entrance to go and meet our brother. I paused and looked at the sign once more trying to work out the rest of the words, but there seemed so many of them I was lost. An elderly couple were walking towards us and I plucked up the courage to speak to them.

'Excuse me please, could you help me with some of the words on this sign?' I was embarrassed to ask them but I had had an idea and needed to know whether it could work.

'Certainly dear,' the woman replied, 'what exactly do you want to know?'

'Are there any rules about who can use the park?' I asked.

'Well dear, there are many rules about what you can and can't do but mainly it says that you must not swim in the lake, leave any litter, pick the flowers or dig up the grass. It also says that the park is open from eight o'clock in the morning until nine o'clock at night and then the gates are locked. Does that help you?'

'Oh yes thank you so much ma'am, 'I replied.

The couple walked on and I tried to decide whether I could trust Danny to keep a secret for a few hours, deciding to do so I swore him to secrecy before outlining my plan. 'Millie that's a wonderful idea, and I promise I will not say anything,' Danny swore to me and I trusted he could keep his word. When we arrived at the stall Tommy was just loading the last of the empty crates on to the barrow so I took the opportunity to speak quietly to Stan. He was happy to help and so all was in place as I collected the shopping and we returned to our shed. Leaving my brothers I walked to meet Papa from the dock and shared the secret with him.

'That's ideal, well done Millie,' he said taking my hand as we walked the rest of the way home.

When we got back both Tommy and Danny were asleep, Danny's cheeks still pink from the afternoon spent in the summer sun. As the afternoon wore on Papa suggested we walk to meet Mama from work as a surprise.

'What about the supper Millie?' asked Tommy, 'Mama will be hungry when she gets back.'

'It's alright son, Millie has something that won't take long and so she can do it when we get back,' Papa said, rescuing me from having to think of an answer. He gathered up the basket we had prepared whilst my brothers slept without Tommy noticing and we were off. We waited at the corner of the market square and before long Mama appeared walking with two other women, upon seeing us she said goodbye to her companions and came over to us.

'This is a pleasant surprise, 'she said smiling at us, 'is everything alright?'

'Everything is fine Maria,' Papa told her lightly kissing her cheek and taking her hand in his. 'Come Millie and Danny have a surprise for both you and Tommy.'

Danny could barely contain himself and looked at me asking, 'can I say now?'

'Not just yet, we are nearly there and then they will see for themselves,' I replied smiling at his impatience. As we came to the park he could not last any longer and the words come rushing out,' it's a public park and we are going to have our supper there. Come on hurry, we get in round this corner.' With that he grabbed Tommy's hand and ran on ahead dragging his brother along before disappearing round the corner suddenly reappearing on the other side of the railings inside the park.

I led my parents round to the gate and as we entered Mama said, 'oh Millie it's beautiful.'

As we sat on a bench near the lake eating the food we had bought with us I explained how we discovered the park earlier in the day and after finding out when it closed decided to have our supper outdoors in the warm evening air to celebrate Tommy's birthday. I also said that I had asked Stan if he would let me swap some of the vegetables I had originally bought for our meal for some things we could eat outdoors. As usual he had given me some fruits and even managed to get us some bread from the stall next to his once he had explained what it was for, and would not hear of swapping so we still had a meal left. He said the fruit and bread would not be saleable tomorrow and that we were doing them a favour.

'I think he did us the favour darling,' Mama said, 'there is nothing wrong with any of this food; they could have sold it tomorrow.'

I made myself a mental note to thank Stan when I next saw him.

We spent the rest of the evening enjoying the fresh air of the park, strolling along the winding pathways until it was time to return to our home. The evening light was turning to dusk as we entered through the back way to our shed. As we settled down ready for sleep Tommy yawned and said to me and Danny, 'thank you both so much for the birthday surprise, it was wonderful. I know I will never forget my ninth birthday.'

'Who would have thought there could be such a beautiful place right in the middle of the town like that,' Mama added. 'If the weather is good we must go again on Sunday, Tommy and I will get paid tomorrow with it being Saturday.'

I laid back on the old sacking we had managed to find for bedding and for the first time in a while felt truly happy; we had been a family again.

Chapter 17

Sunday 27th June 1847

The follow up meeting four days later convened at twelve noon after they had all returned from their church services.

'Well, is everything in place?' asked the chairman.

One of the six business men assigned to the task stood up replying, 'Yes sir, we have each recruited a team of twenty men and designated areas of the town to each group. They will all strike at the same time and remove all the homeless starting with the cellars, kennels and those on the streets. All those found will be taken to the docks, put on ships and deported straight away. They are to carry out the first strikes today at three o'clock to coincide with the best tides. These will continue until we have found and deported all the homeless. This afternoon is ideal because any of them who may have found temporary employment will not be working on a Sunday. I suggest we meet again next Friday for an update on the situation.'

'That sounds satisfactory, carry on.'

With that the meeting was concluded and the business men returned to their homes to sit down to their Sunday roast dinners with their families.

At three o'clock precisely twelve groups' ten men strong stormed into the temporary dwellings of the immigrants dragging them out into the streets and down to the docks. Here they were loaded onto the waiting ships, old, young, sick or healthy it made no difference to the men at all. By the end of the day some five hundred people had set sail back to the poverty they thought they had escaped. This action would continue and by the end of the exercise some 15000 would be deported in total.

The day began with a promise of fine weather to come for the rest of the day, the sun was already up and casting shadows from the tall trees across the shed. We had made our plans to go to the park again today and were all excited about the prospect of another chance to be together enjoying the fresh air and each other's company.

Mama was right and both she and Tommy had received their pay for the part week they had worked. Even though Papa was being kept on for at least six weeks he was still being paid daily as were all the casual workers, so last night we had two shillings and four pence ha'penny in cash come into the house. We still could not afford any living accommodation and our meals were mainly vegetables, fruit and bread, a joint of meat would cost around four shillings, but back in Ireland our diet had been eighty percent potatoes so we did not feel the need to waste money on meat at present, but we were eating regularly now and were beginning to feel better health wise. Papa and Tommy were losing the pale sallow complexion they had when we first arrived here due to being outdoors all day, and both myself and Danny were also looking healthier. The only one who wasn't was Mama, she was indoors for twelve hours a day, working in dusty conditions and, impossible as I thought it could be, she looked paler than when we landed. She was eating regularly like the rest of us, but the long walk to and from the mill each day meant she was expending more energy. Papa had tried to get her to eat more at suppertime but she insisted on only taking her share. I was concerned that after only three days at the mill she seemed to have been affected so much. Still she insisted she was alright and that given another week she would have got used to the conditions and the walking and would settle down. I vowed to keep a watch over her and let Papa know if I had any concerns.

So after a quick breakfast of an apple and a slice of bread each we made our way to the park, when we reached the market square the clock was showing nine o'clock and the normally busy streets were relatively quiet.

'I expect many people are at church,' Mama explained, 'maybe when things settle down a bit we should find a place of worship we can attend.'

As we turned the corner and entered the park gate it seemed to me that those who weren't at worship were here. The park was full of families and couples strolling along the pathways or sitting on the grass enjoying the summer sunshine. We walked around to the far side of the lake and found an empty space under a willow tree. Immediately my brothers were off playing hide and seek and tag.

'Aren't you going to play with them?' Papa asked me.

'If it's alright with you and Mama I would just like to sit here with you both a while, I seem to have seen so little of you lately,' I replied.

'Of course Millie,' Mama said smiling at me.

I lay on my back in the soft grass and listened to the sounds of the birds singing off in the trees and the gentle buzzing of bees as they visited the flowers in search of pollen, the squeals of children playing and thought I could stay there forever.

After a lunch of bread I went and joined my brothers exploring deeper into the shrubbery at the far side of the park, we discovered an ant's nest and spent some time watching as the creatures scurried about to and fro, fascinated when some returned carrying leaves or the bodies of their fallen comrades. Danny tried to pick one up and received a bite for his efforts, 'Ouch I only wanted to see what they looked like close up,' he said rubbing at the red mark on his wrist.

'Well how would you like to be picked up when you were just minding your own business looking for food?' Tommy laughed.

'Mmm I suppose you're right, let's go and show Papa my bite,' Danny said jumping up and running back to where our parents were dozing in the sun. We didn't have the heart to wake them and so sat quietly watching two small boys playing sword fights with two sticks. A group of adults were standing talking a little further away from us, they were pointing towards the town and at times they raised their voices. When they did I caught snatches of their conversation, although I missed much of it.

'They just dragged ......from ...., and then they took them.........., some of them looked half dead,' one man said waving his arms to emphasise what he was saying.

'Well it's not before time, I ....' replied a woman standing next to him.

'But surely the ill ones aren't fit to make the journey,' a second woman said.

'Come,' the first man said,' let's go and see ....'

With that they all turned and headed for the park gate.

'Papa, Mama, wake up,' I said shaking Mama gently by the shoulder.

'What is it Millie?' Papa asked hearing the concern in my voice.

'I don't know, but some people were over there talking about something going on and although I don't know what it's about I am worried.'

Tommy added, 'I heard them mention the docks,'

As we left the park we saw a crowd of people headed towards the docks, all seemed in a hurry to get there. As two men passed us one said to the other, 'I tell you Albie, they are deporting the Irish. Some passed me earlier being dragged by some men. The women and kids were crying but they took them all the same.'

That stopped us all dead in our tracks, we had just enjoyed a family day in the sunshine and now were on the verge of being dragged to the docks and deported, sent back to a certain prolonged death.

Mama clutched at Papa's arm, 'Daniel what is happening, are they really sending us back to Ireland?'

'I don't know Maria,' he replied, 'if what those people said is true then it sounds like it, but I have no idea which ones they are taking.'

'Daniel we can't go back there, 'Mama said, 'we have nothing to return to.'

'Look, take the children back,' Papa said, his voice just above a whisper in case we were overheard, 'I will go and see if I can find out anything further.'

'We need to keep together, Daniel,' my mother answered, 'how will I know what is happening to you?' Tears were slipping down her cheeks and she was holding tightly onto the hands of my brothers.

'I will be alright but you need to go now, I will meet you back there,' Papa said. 'I will just go down to the docks and follow you after that.'

'What happens if someone comes to get us?' Tommy asked my father, he looked more frightened than I had ever seen him.

'They won't I promise you, you must all go now, keep walking, don't stop for anyone and don't talk to anyone either, now go please.'

With that he kissed us all and turned walking in the direction of the docks. We had no option but to do as instructed and started back towards the shed. Word had spread about the deportments and more and more people followed my father towards the dock. We did not speak a single word all the way back, I was fearful that if I spoke someone would recognise my accent to be Irish and drag me away. Mama had stopped crying now that she knew she had to get us to safety. Tommy was frowning and constantly casting quick glances behind us convinced that any moment we would be caught. Danny clung to Mama's hand and mine and gave out small sobs every so often.

At last we reached our shed, stopping in the front of the shrubbery which hid it from view from the road. I was terrified that men were waiting inside for us and looked back down the road in the hope of seeing Papa coming, but the road was totally deserted. I took a deep breath and said,' I will go in first and make sure it is safe.'

'Millie, no don't do that, let's wait for your father,' Mama said.

'Mama, we can be seen out here, we need to get off the road at once,' I replied not believing where I had found this sudden burst of courage.

'I will come with you,' Tommy said, 'if there is anyone there they will have difficulty catching us both.'

'Ok, let's go.'

Tommy and I walked around the bushes to the back of the shed and stood for some minutes, our ears and eyes straining for any sound or movement. Satisfied we crept ever closer to the door and waited again. I could hear nothing and grabbed Tommy's hand and edged to the side of the open doorway and peered around the corner. The shed was exactly as we had left it the morning and totally empty, even our small amount of food was still in the wooden crate we had raised off the floor in order to keep it from being eaten by any animals that may find it.

Tommy let out an audible sigh and said, 'I will go and get them, you wait here just in case.' With that he was gone. It was moments before they all came back but I stood in the open doorway, not daring to move and held my breath, my nails digging into my palms. We sat quietly and waited, talking in whispers, afraid of being discovered, after about twenty minutes we heard a noise outside. It was someone walking slowly across the grass in our direction, then Papa's face appeared at the opening and we were united once more.

'Did you learn anything?' Mama asked him.

'Well I didn't stay long in case anyone recognised me but it would appear that this afternoon groups of men have raided cellars and taken all the homeless they can find down to the docks where they have been loaded onto waiting ships which are taking them back to Ireland,' Papa told us.

'Oh my God, what are we to do?' Mama wailed, pulling Danny into her arms.

'I think we should stay here tonight, if they are searching the cellars in the town they will not find us here.'

'But surely they will check everywhere?' my mother said.

'Yes they probably will but I think they will concentrate on the town today, that way they can find the most people in the quickest length of time. Also there were no ships in the docks when I was there so I think they won't be able to take any more today. Tomorrow we will see what else we can find out. '

This seemed logical to me but it was also terrifying, but I trusted my father and so I helped my mother prepare the supper. I don't think any of us were particularly hungry but forced down the food in an effort to keep our strength up. Once darkness fell Papa moved to the doorway and sat in the entrance saying,' I will keep guard tonight so you all get some sleep, we will be up with the sun tomorrow and go into the town first thing.'

'Are we going to work Papa?' Tommy asked.

'Yes I think we are probably safer there than anywhere else.'

'What about Millie and Danny?' my mother said concern etched on her face.

'Well when we take Tommy to Stan's we can ask him if he will look after them, if not we will have to think of something else. He seems a kind man and I think he will help the children if he can.'

I drifted into a restless sleep; I dreamt I was being dragged through the town streets and people were pointing at me and shouting,' Go back to where you belong.' In my dream I shouted that I belonged here with my family but they wouldn't listen and I was thrown onto a ship and put in a small crate. A man nailed the lid shut and as I peered through the slats I saw the rest of my family standing on the dock waving goodbye to me.

Chapter 18

We were all awake early; Mama was sat in the open doorway next to Papa, their arms interlocked. She was resting her head on my father's shoulder and turned to face me as I moved towards the door. Her face had taken on the haunted look I saw back in Ireland and she had dark smudges under her eyes, I doubted either of my parents slept last night and once again I realised just how much they were willing to sacrifice to make sure we were all safe.

'Right children,' Papa said to us once we were all ready to leave the shed,' we must take anything with us that may show the searchers that this shed is occupied. We can't risk it being discovered and have anyone laying in wait for our return.'

'What about the sack bedding, Papa? Shall we take that?' Tommy asked.

'No leave that son, but make sure it is not laid out as it is now, just throw it in the corner.'

We gathered up the little food we had left and the bowls and pans and crept out into the morning. The road was deserted as we walked into the town, my nerves were jangling and I couldn't help thinking that any moment I would be grabbed and dragged off, the dream from last night still vivid in my mind. A short distance down the road we passed an old timber plank which had been placed over a small ditch to make a bridge, Papa took the pots from us and scrambled down the steep sides, hiding them out of sight. 'If people see us carrying these around with us it will be obvious we are homeless, but we can't afford to lose them. Hopefully they will still be here when we return,' he explained.

Reaching the market square the bustle of people setting up for the day was as normal, I began to feel a little less nervous, nevertheless looking down I could see the impressions of my nails on my palms where I had been clenching them. Stan looked up and his face broke out into a huge smile, 'I wasn't sure I would see you today,' he said quietly as we drew closer. 'I have heard all sorts of rumours about people being dragged from their homes and being sent back to Ireland.'

'That's what we heard, it's true then?' Mama asked.

'It would seem so if the tales are true, and there are so many folk telling the same tale there has to be some truth in it.' Stan replied.

'Stan, can we ask you a huge favour?' Papa said.

'Of course, anything I can do to help you all.' Stan answered.

'Would you mind if Danny and Millie stay here with you today whilst Maria and I go to work? We would stay with them but we desperately need our wages and are afraid to leave them on their own.'

'Of course not, they can help on the stall that way people will think they are with me. I cannot afford to pay them all though I'm afraid.'

'Stan, you have been so kind to our family, you certainly have no need to apologise for anything.' Mama told him.

My parents gave us all a hug and kiss goodbye and left for their places of work. My mother was reluctant to leave but eventually did so.

Daniel walked towards the dock gates, walking in through the small gate the employees used. His first impression was the fact that there were only a small group of men waiting outside for temporary work. Whether this was due to the deportations or the fact that people were afraid to come out onto the streets he was not sure. He walked to the office to clock in for the day and check where he was required.

'Morning Rafferty, 'the foreman said as Daniel wheeled the barrow to the far end of the dock to begin unloading the sacks of grain, 'you survived the raids then I see?'

'What raids?' Daniel replied, hoping to learn more and not to give too much information away. At the moment he was unsure whom he could fully trust.

'Don't you know?' the foreman asked him. 'Yesterday there were gangs of men authorised by the local authorities taking the homeless off the streets, bringing them here, putting them on waiting ships and sending them back to Ireland. '

'No I didn't hear anything about that,' Daniel lied, picking up another sack and tossing it on to the mounting pile. He walked over to the waiting horse and cart, leaving his barrow to be unloaded and stacked before going back to begin the task again. Everywhere he passed a group of workers the conversation was the same, he listened carefully where he could without trying to arouse any suspicion. People knew he was Irish of course but as far as he knew no-one knew where he was staying and he was desperate to keep it that way. It wasn't until the horn sounded for the men to take a quick break for lunch that Daniel learned anymore.

He sat with his back against the wall of a storage warehouse, alongside part of the gang he had been working with since he had been made a permanent casual labourer. They were a good group, friendly enough and extremely hard working.

'So did any of you come down here yesterday?' Jack asked the others.

There were shakes of heads from most but one young man of around twenty five answered, 'I did, but I wish I hadn't.'

'Oh why's that, Harry?' Jack asked.

Harry took a bite of his pie, chewing it slowly before answering. 'Well, I am sure you have heard that men were instructed to find and deport as many homeless Irish as they could. Rumour has it that they were paid by the person, so the more they found the more they were paid. 'He took a drink of water before continuing, 'they didn't care about the folk themselves, and they took old and young alike, sick and healthy. I saw one woman carrying an infant of about three. She was begging the men to stop, she kept saying,' please let me go; I need to find my husband.' The men paid no attention to her and put her and the child aboard the boat. She continued calling out to them, 'I promise we will come back to the ship when I find him but if we go now I may never see him again.' The men just ignored her, it was awful. That woman and child have now been sent back to Ireland and God knows where her husband is, he must be going out of his mind.'

'I don't think that's going to be the last of it,' Norman said, 'my wife said she heard someone say that they are going to round more of them up tonight.' Then he suddenly looked over at Daniel,' I'm sorry Daniel, I didn't mean anything by that.'

Daniel held up his hand saying, 'That's alright Norman.' He rose to his feet and walked back to his barrow and began stacking the sacks once more, he felt too ill to eat further. He had no idea whether it would be safe to return to the shed tonight or not.

Harry turned to Norman, 'you can be such a fool sometimes Norman.'

'I didn't mean him any harm, I forgot he was there,' Norman answered.

'Daniel's a good man and a hard worker, I wouldn't want to lose him,' Harry said turning his gaze in the direction of Daniel who was pushing another loaded barrow towards the waiting cart.

Norman realised that he had said too much saying, 'neither would I but I don't see what we can do. I don't even know if he is at risk, I have no idea how they are selecting the ones they take or where the man is living,' with that he returned to his work.

Harry also packed up his lunch bag and walked over to where Daniel was. 'Don't take any notice of Norman, he doesn't mean any harm he just speaks before he thinks.'

Daniel raised his head to look Harry in the eyes, 'Can I ask you something Harry?'

Harry looked wary, wondering what the man was going to say but once he looked at the concern etched into the face of his fellow worker he replied,' of course you can, what's bothering you?'

Daniel hesitated before continuing not sure whether he should voice his concerns. 'Do you resent my being here?'

'What do you mean by that?'

'Well do you think we should have all stayed in Ireland?' Daniel persisted. 'Do you think we are taking jobs off the English?'

'Look Daniel, every year hundreds of Irish come over in the season to find work and we are grateful for the help because we need the extra hands. The only issue at the moment is that many have stayed instead of returning home and they have brought their families with them this time. I have nothing against anyone who pulls their weight and I am sorry to hear about the conditions back in Ireland that drove you all here. You are not taking jobs off the English but the problem is there is not enough food, housing or sanitation to support so many people. Many of those who came over were too ill to work and disease has been spreading. The authorities see the deportation as the only answer and although I don't agree with the way they appear to be handling it, something has to be done or the town with be ruined.' Harry cast his eyes down feeling guilty to have said what he did to a man whom he knew was just trying to feed and provide for himself and his family.

'Thank you for being honest Harry,' said Daniel.

'Do you have family?' Harry asked realising he knew very little about the man he had been working alongside the last few weeks.

Daniel thought hard before deciding whether he felt he could trust this man enough to tell the truth. 'I have a wife and three children here.'

'Are they safe?' Harry enquired.

'They were this morning when we parted and I pray to God they still are,' Daniel replied.

I was watching Stan and Tommy as they unpacked the fresh produce and piled it high on the stall. Tommy did not have to ask what was required of him as he worked alongside his kindly employer. He was already familiar with the workings of the stall and I could see he liked Stan, a feeling that was reciprocated.

'Please sir,' I said, 'is there anything Danny and I can do to help? You are kind to look after us but we don't wish to be a burden or get in your way.'

Stan looked at me from under his bushy eyebrows, his blue eyes reminding me of Papa's. 'No lass, thank you not at the moment. When it gets busier there will be things you can help with, but just sit tight behind the stall for now until we can find out more about what is happening to the homeless.'

As the morning wore on the stall along with the market square became busier as people went about their daily tasks of buying provisions. Stan was very clever in the way he spoke to his regular customers, seeming to know exactly which ones had both the time and which enjoyed passing on any gossip, true or not, they had.

'Tommy, here comes Mrs Waters, she will take 3 apples and 4 large potatoes, have them ready.'

'Yes Stan,' Tommy replied, picking out the best he could find and passing them to Stan.

'Morning Mrs Waters, a mighty fine one it is, we have your usual, is there anything else I can tempt you with?' Stan asked as a stooped woman approached the stall, her hair was pure white and her skin was deeply lined but the sparkle in her deep brown eyes showed she was mentally alert.

'No thank you Stan,' she answered, 'you would pick my pocket bare if I let you.'

Stan laughed and placed the produce in her basket, took her money and rather nonchalantly asked her, 'Any news I should know about Mrs Waters?'

'Well, I presume you have heard all the shenanigans at the dock yesterday,' she answered and without waiting for a reply launched into her tale. 'They are deporting all the homeless Irish and putting them on ships and sending them home. They were taking them from cellars, off the streets and out of the lodging houses. It doesn't matter where they find them, they are taking the lot.'

'What, all of them?' Stan asked.

'I heard this morning that they are not going to stop until they have got them all, they started yesterday afternoon because that way they would catch most of them at home, but they know there are more to be found. Mr Berry told me they are going to wait until dark the next time for the same reason, in the week days some of them will be working.'

'But surely if they are able to work they are not a problem,' Stan ventured.

Mrs Waters was fully into her story now and seemed to be enjoying the telling of it. 'Yes but even if some of them are working, they all have large families, many of which are not able to work because they are so diseased. You mark my words; if they stay here much longer we will all be infected. You should make sure your young 'uns stay away from them. They should have done this a long time ago if you ask me. Well I can't stand here gossiping all day I have to get Mr Waters' dinner on.' With that she plucked her basket from the counter and swept off down the street, stopping a little further on to engage a younger woman in an animated conversation.

I just couldn't believe that after all we had suffered to get here, just as things seemed to be improving we were now in real danger of being caught and sent back to Ireland. I just didn't know what was going to become of us, for the first time that I could remember it would seem our fate was not in our own hands. I wished my parents were here at this moment to allay my fears, but they had placed me in charge of my younger brothers and I would make sure nothing happened to them. I felt a presence at my shoulder and turned to see Stan standing by my side, his normally jovial expression replaced by one of concern.

'Millie,' he began, 'I don't know how much of that you heard?'

'Enough to know we are not safe here anymore,' I replied.

'You are safe whilst you are here with me, even Mrs Waters thinks that you are mine, and if she thinks so, then everyone else will. Once your parents return from work I cannot say what will happen. Still there is nothing we can do until they return this evening so come and help us on the stall; it will take your mind off things for a while.'

Stan was right, the day passed fairly quickly as the four of us spent the rest of the day serving the customers and keeping the displays full.

However as the afternoon wore on and Stan began packing up for the day my thoughts turned to our situation once again. Normally Danny and I would meet Tommy when Stan packed away and then walk down to meet Papa at the docks. Today I dared not go there for fear of being taken by the gangs. Once all was stowed away Stan once again came to our rescue, 'Right children I want you to come with me, your father is not due to finish work yet and I dare not leave you on your own. So I have decided you are to come to my house and wait for him there. I will leave you with my wife and go and meet him and bring him back here. Then we can see what he wants to do.'

So trusting in him once again we walked the short distance to where Stan and his wife lived. It was a large house of red brick with a black painted door. The paint was flaking but the brass door knocker and handle gleamed in the late afternoon sun. We stepped into a long narrow hallway with bare wooden floors and a staircase on the left going up to the second floor. Off from the hallway there were three doors, all closed, from behind the one off to the right I could hear a small child crying and a woman's voice as she tried to calm it. I was confused by this as Stan had said they had no children. Suddenly for some inexplicable reason I believed this was all a plot to steal us from our parents and keep us for themselves as they had clearly already done with others, or worse still report us to the men who were deporting our countrymen.

I backed away and took my brothers by the hand, saying 'I don't think this is a good idea, we will take our chance on the street.'

Danny immediately began to cry saying, 'Millie I am frightened, I don't want to go out there. There are bad men waiting to get us.'

'Whatever is wrong Millie?' Stan asked me.

'You said you didn't have any children, but there is one in there,' I answered accusingly.

'Yes, there are other families living in this house, my wife and I live in a room upstairs. Come on I will take you to meet her.'

Suddenly I felt rather stupid and followed him up the staircase and onto a small landing. The door at the far end was ajar and I could see a small woman with her back to the door, she was humming softly to herself and turned as Stan pushed the door open.

'Susan, my dear we have some guests to meet you.'

She turned to face us and her hands went up to her mouth, then she broke into a beaming smile and came over to us. 'Stan, who are these little angels?' No let me guess, Tommy, Danny and Millie!'

'That's right love; I brought them here to wait for their father.' He then went on to tell her of the happenings at the docks yesterday and the worries he had for our safety.

'You did the right thing Stan,' she answered, 'they will be safe here with me while you go and fetch their father.'

Daniel walked slowly to the gates as the horn sounded the conclusion of the day's work, he stopped briefly to mark the paper and take his money. His heart appeared to stop beating when he looked to the gate seeing Stan waiting for him and no sign of his children, he pushed past the men slowly making their way home and raced to join the man.

'What's happened, where are my children?'

'It's alright, they are at my house. I didn't feel it was safe to leave them alone, come with me and I will take you to them,' Stan answered.

'Oh thank goodness, I have been so worried all day. I can't thank you enough, you are a true friend.' Daniel said, relief flooding through him.

Once he had seen his children he walked to meet Maria, filling her in on the details of the day, 'It doesn't sound like this is going to stop until they have cleared the town of all the homeless.'

'Yes that is what everyone at the mill was saying, we are not safe anywhere. What are we going to do Daniel, I am so scared?'

Reunited with my parents at last I listened as the adults discussed what may happen.

'I would love to help you,' Stan said, 'but we just don't have the room here for you to stay.'

My mother looked at him and said,' Stan you have done everything you can do for us, I cannot thank you and Susan enough. You have no obligations to us at all but you have helped us so much.'

Stan looked bashful and tussled Danny's hair for want of something to do. He was a big man not used to showing emotions and yet I felt he really cared for us all.

My mother and Susan pooled the food they had and produced supper and then as the darkness of night drew in we once again thanked our hosts and made our way to our sanctuary for the night.

Chapter 19

The men met at the back of the mission hall and formed into their groups making their plans for the night. During the raids they had carried out since they began on Sunday they had rounded up and deported at least two thousand people and they knew there were still many left to be found.

'I think we should spread the search wider, we have found most of the ones in the town now,' one of the men said.

'Yes that's true enough but they are like rats, as soon as we clear the cellars, others move in. I have no idea where they are coming from,' another replied.

'Here's what we will do, four groups do the cellars and alleys as usual, one group go north out of town and search all the buildings you find, the other group do the same south.

The plan agreed the men split up; the night was soon filled with screams as people were once again dragged from their resting places, out onto the streets and down to the waiting vessels.

The southern group worked their way steadily out of the town, searching cellars, kennels and alleyways. After a while the dwellings become less and less and they were left with a choice of either going back or venturing further into the outskirts.

'I think we should continue down this road awhile, none of us have searched this part yet and I bet some of them have scattered out here to wait until things calm down,' the gang leader said. He could not believe how much he was actually enjoying this job, when he was first approached to do this he took it on because the pay was better than he could earn elsewhere. Now he looked forward to pitting his wits against the Irish, they had taken jobs, food and accommodation from his fellow English and it was time they were shown it would no longer be tolerated. If they wanted to come here they should be prepared to work. He did not understand the circumstances which had brought these wretched people to his town and if he did he may have felt more compassion, but as it was he enjoyed the hunt and the feeling of satisfaction as he watched them loaded on to the ships. He was even beginning to enjoy the feeling of power he had over them as they begged him to let them go, they promised to give him everything they had if he will just release them. He had begun to play with their emotions, he waited until they are about to be put on the boat, then he said to them in a conspiratorial voice, 'well what do you have to trade for your family's safety?' they usually offered him some pathetic amount of money or some food, when he took it, they would smile at him and some fell to their knees thanking him. That was just before he pushed them into the waiting arms of the sailors.

We spread the sacks on the floor and huddled together, more for security than anything else. I was so very tired; the worries of the day catching up with me, but sleep would not come. I found myself lying as still as I could listening in the darkness for the danger that must surely come. Danny was lying next to me and I could feel his warm breath on my face and wished I could just scoop him up and make him safe. But this was something even my parents could not guarantee at the moment so I knew I was helpless. There was a new moon tonight, its beams shining down making the corners of our dwelling feel dark and sinister. I imagined there were men waiting for us to go to sleep before making their move, their rough hands grabbing at us and pulling us down to the ships. I woke with a start and realised it was a dream, as I turned to try and return to sleep I caught my breath. I was sure I had heard something outside; I listened, my ears straining to make out the slightest noise. There it was again, a rustling as someone walked quietly over the soft damp grass.

'Over here, Will,' one of the men called, as the others joined him, he pointed to where the bushes had been pulled over the small opening in an attempt to obscure it from the road. 'They don't look quite normal to me.'
'Let's see what we have got then.'
The men squeezed through the narrow gap and stood in a small clearing, by the light from the moon they could make out a shed in the far corner. Signalling to each other they made their way across the damp grass towards the door way. One man held his hand up, the others all stopped; he listened for any sound he could make out. Then he signalled to two men to cover the back of the shed in case anyone tried to run for it. Once they were positioned he waved the others on toward the doorway. The men raised their sticks and began to beat them on the sides of the shed, there was more sport to be had if the occupants were woken and tried to flee in panic than if they were taken from their slumbers.

Then there was a loud banging on the side of the shed, I leapt terrified from the floor and screamed out loud, 'Wake up, we have been found!' I clutched Danny by the arm and held him close to me, hoping I would be strong enough to save him from whoever was outside. His eyes opened wide with fright and he stared at the doorway in fear.

Papa ran to the door way and looked outside, then he returned inside saying, 'It's alright its only Stan.'

Stan appeared in the entrance, his huge bulk filling the gap, he offered an embarrassed smile as he explained to us,' I am sorry if I have frightened you all, I came to wake you ready for work but I tripped over a root and fell against the side of the shed.'

'Well you certainly gave us all a scare, but I thank you for letting us use this shed last night,' Papa answered. 'I would not have felt safe otherwise; I don't think they are searching out buildings where people are living, just the unoccupied ones.'

Nothing moved in the shed and as the men moved in they only saw an old pile of sacks thrown in a corner, the disappointment on the face of the gang leader was obvious, but as he kicked at the ground outside in frustration he uncovered a small pile of ashes. 'Well boys, we may have come up empty tonight but I think if we return at a later date we may be in luck.'

With that they made their way back to the docks to check on the progress of the night's activities.

Chapter 20

September 1847

Thousands of folk had been deported and whilst my heart went out to them, I praised to God that we appeared to have been spared, mostly due to the generosity of a complete stranger who took it upon himself to help a family in need. We spent the intervening weeks helping Stan on his stall, reuniting with our parents at the end of the working day, pooling food for supper with Stan and Susan and then creeping out under cover of darkness to spend the night in the shed on the common land adjoining the land to the back of their house. The housing shortage seemed to have abated and the gangs that were to be found roaming the streets looking for the homeless had been reduced to one group of men that just went out at night making sure there were no people sleeping rough on the streets. Ironically emigrants were still arriving from Ireland but not in the numbers that had descended on the town previously.

Last night when Mama returned from the mill, she was very pale and had a hacking cough. She did not eat any of the supper Susan and I had prepared and dozed in the corner of the room. When the time came for us to retire to the outhouse Susan took one look at her and stated,' Maria is in no condition to spend the night outside, I will make up a blanket on the floor and she can sleep there.'

'Nonsense woman,' Stan said,' she can sleep in the bed with you, I will take the floor.'

And so for the first time since arriving in England we left Mama and went out into the night.

I woke this morning and looked over to the sleeping forms of my brothers; neither of my parents was there. I wondered where they could be at this early hour and then I remembered that Mama was not well last night and had slept in Stan's house. Suddenly I was gripped by an irrational fear that something may have happened during the night and my father had been called to be at her side. I was torn between rushing into the house and staying with my brothers so they did not wake alone. I crept to the doorway and stared out across the patch of greenery between our dwelling and the house; all was quiet with no sign of movement at the windows. The early morning sun was just rising above the horizon, its weak light giving no warmth at the moment, the ground was covered in fine dew and it shimmered in the light, there was a visible trail leading from the shed to the house. It did not look wide enough for two people to have been walking side by side, so unless they were walking in single file then only one person had made the journey. That was something of a relief to me as it made me think that Papa had gone to see how Mama was when he awoke as opposed to someone coming to find him due to a down turn in Mama's condition. As I continued to watch the window of the house for some clue as to the situation my father appeared at the glass. He was sideways on to me and was talking to someone in the room, he turned to look out and saw me standing in the doorway, I raised my hand to wave and he beckoned me to come in. I cast a glance back into the shed to see if my brothers were showing any signs are waking yet, but they were both still fast asleep. I turned back to signal to Papa but he was now striding across the grass towards me. I tried to read his face as he approached but all I could tell was that he was not upset.

'How is Mama?' I asked of him as he neared me.

'Susan says she cannot lay flat otherwise she starts coughing again, so sleep has not been easy. She is sleeping at the moment, but she has had a troubled night. She doesn't have a fever which is good news. If you want to go and see her I will watch the boys, make sure not to wake her.'

Relieved I walked back the way my father had come and quietly entered the room. Stan and Susan were sat in the hard wooden chairs at the kitchen table, they both look tired and I realised they wouldn't have had an easy night either. Mama was laid propped up against the white pillows, her breathing was laboured and there was a slight wheeze as she exhaled. My mind went back to the last time I saw my mother ill two years ago, she had been feverish for over four days and at night she used to wake herself up screaming and then would mumble to herself for minutes at a time before falling into a restless sleep, her bed sheets would be saturated as she sweated away the infection she had contracted at the loss of my sister. I prayed she would not suffer that badly again.

'When she wakes up I will try to get her to drink something, she hasn't been able to keep any fluids down yet and I am worried about her becoming dehydrated,' Susan said to me.

'What do you think is wrong with her?' I asked.

'If looks like a chest infection, I think. I know many of the mill workers suffer from them. The best thing for her is lots of fluids, rest and steam bowls. Luckily it is Sunday today so she won't have to worry about missing a day at work.'

'Thank you so much for all you are doing for her,' I said. 'I will go and help my father with my brothers; once I have seen to them I will come back and help you. If she wakes up before I return please come and fetch me.'

'Of course we will, there is nothing you can do at the moment until she wakes so go and feed your family,' Susan told me.

We spent the day tending to Mama; she drifted in and out of sleep and did manage to keep some water down but not a lot. The cough had developed into a deep hacking one which often ended in her bringing up green coloured phlegm. We were trying to get her to inhale the steam from a bowl of hot water covered with a cloth but the moment she leant her body over it another spasm began.

By the late evening it was obvious she would not be well by tomorrow and so would not be able to attend work. There had been no improvement whatsoever in her condition. As she slept we tried to decide what we could do in order to care for her and continue to earn money.

'Well I can go out and collect my laundry first thing and bring it back here and watch her,' Susan said. Susan earned money by doing laundry and mending jobs for people from her house.

Papa said, 'Susan, you and your husband are already doing far more for our family than we could expect. I don't have any guaranteed work at present so I will stay with Maria tomorrow so you can carry on with your work. Then when you return I will go to the docks to see what is available.' Papa was back to being a casual labourer now that the six week project had been completed, and had returned to queuing up daily, so far he had remained lucky and had procured work most days.

'Well that seems settled then, 'said Stan. 'I suggest we get some rest while we can.'

I looked about the room at all the people who were all working so hard to ensure the welfare of my family, my father and brother included, and I was so grateful to each and every one of them. Even Tommy had been playing his part in earning money and I felt ashamed that I had fallen into a complacency that was unlike me. Whilst the raids were taking place it was safe for Danny and me to be with either Stan or his wife whilst my parents were working. Now that the immediate danger seemed to have past I had been content to carry on with this way of life without making any effort to look for further work which would help to ease the burden on the others. I was even beginning to accept that Stan and Susan were there to help with protecting us. I looked at my mother laid in the bed; pale faced and couldn't believe how selfish I had become. It was then that I decided I would pull my weight along with the rest of them and contribute to our welfare.

Chapter 21

Monday morning began at five o'clock, Papa, Tommy, Danny and I walked over to the house and joined Stan and Susan for a meal of leftovers from yesterday. Mama was awake; her auburn hair contrasting with her pale skin, when we entered Danny rushed over to the bed and threw himself into her arms.

'Careful lad,' Susan told him, 'your mother is not up to wrestling just yet.'

Mama smiled and took him into a hug, then she held out her arms to us and Tommy and I rushed over showering her in kisses.

'How are you feeling Mama?' I asked.

'A little better, thanks to you all but......' she then began coughing again, her face turning pink as she tried to catch her breath. Susan passed her a cup of water and she sipped it carefully the spasm subsiding.

'Right you three, let's get off to the stall and leave your mother to get some rest,' Stan said.

'I want to stay here with Mama,' Danny said holding tightly onto her hand.

'Very well,' Papa said, 'if that's alright with you both?'

'Of course,' Susan answered for them both,' if he's happiest here I think that's a good idea. Then even when I am outside doing the laundry Maria will have some company.'

I kissed Mama goodbye and left with Stan and Tommy; once we got to the stall and began setting up I made my announcement. 'I won't be helping you today I'm afraid, I am going to take my mother's place at the mill. That way she won't lose her position.'

'What happens if they don't let you in?' Tommy asked me.

'I will make sure they do,' was my reply, determination taking over me.

'Good luck Millie, that is a brave thing to do and I know your parents will be proud of you,' Stan said. He passed me an apple and a pear, 'for your lunch,' he explained.

I reached up and placed a small kiss on his cheek, then blushing I turned and took the road out of the town to join the women on their journey to the cotton mill. I had never been close up to the mill and as we neared I saw just how large it was. The red brick building dominated the landscape, its three storeys pushing up into the sky, the chimneys seeming to touch the clouds themselves. I could count at least twenty large windows on each level and the closer we got the drier my mouth became.

'I wonder what has happened to Maria today?' a large plump woman of about fifty said. 'Has anyone seen her?'

'Not since Saturday when we left work, 'another answered, 'she was coughing really badly though, I'll be surprised if she comes in today.'

Nobody seemed to have noticed me, if they had they hadn't commented on the fact and I was grateful for that, it meant I could listen to the chatter and see if I could learn anything about the job I was about to undertake.

'Well that's a shame, I like Maria, she is a good worker, but if she doesn't turn up today she could lose her job, there are usually plenty waiting to take over,' a third said.

Finally we reached the imposing building and lined up to go in, each woman gave her name, collected an apron from the hooks inside the door and went off to various areas of the factory, each one knew where they were meant to be and here I realised was my first problem. I was not sure whether naively, I just expected to be able to pass for my mother and carry on as such, or whether I expected everyone to be so grateful I had come that they would make allowances for the fact that I knew nothing. Finally I reached the front of the line, a tall man with white hair and a thin face peered down at me, 'and who are you?' he asked,' we haven't taken on any new workers and if you are looking for work you need to wait outside until called.'

I swallowed hard, my voice deserting me came out as a squeak,' please sir,' I coughed and tried again.' Please sir I am here instead of my mother, she is really poorly today and so I am hoping I can take her place.'

'What is your mother's name?'

'Maria Rafferty, sir,' I answered.

'Have you worked here before?'

'No sir.'

'Well I'm sorry, your mother has been here a while now and is a very good worker, you can't possibly take her place if you don't know what you are doing.' With that he dismissed me and addressed the woman behind me, asking her name to check her against his register.

I had no idea what to do next, I did not wish to accept defeat so easily and return home having failed. So instead I stood my ground and did not move, the women having to walk around me to enter the mill.

'Miss, you need to go home, I am sorry about your mother but tell her when she is better to come back and hopefully there will be something for her,' the man said to me.

A woman who was standing off to one side listening to this exchange whilst putting on her apron walked over to me,' Did you say you are Maria's daughter?'

'Yes, mam, she is sick in bed and I was hoping to take her place today so she won't lose her position.'

'Wait there,' she walked over to the man at the desk and said to him,' Mr Althorpe, if you let Maria Rafferty's daughter take her place today, I promise that if she falls short I will make up the difference.'

Mr Althorpe looked between me and the woman, stroking his chin as he did so.' Very well, but I will hold you to that, any shortage must be made up before you leave tonight at no extra cost to me.'

'Thank you Mr Althorpe, don't worry I will look after her,' turning to me she said, 'my name's Pamela, what's yours?'

'Millie,' I answered, 'thank you so much for your help. I promise to work hard.' If I had known what was waiting for me on the other side of the large double doors I might not have been quite so grateful.

'Millie eh?' Mr Althorpe said, 'that's handy I can put you down as M. Rafferty as normal.'

Pamela passed me an apron and I followed her through the doors. The first thing that hit me was the noise; never had I encountered such a racket. Pamela took my arm and led me to a machine on the far side of the room, there were two vacant spaces in front of it and I took one of these to be that normally occupied by my mother. As we walked across the room I found it hard to keep my balance, the floor was covered in water and machine oil and was treacherous. When we reached the machines Pamela pointed down to my feet, I looked down wondering what was wrong. Then she removed her shoes and nodded to me to do the same. She said something to me, possibly explaining why we were doing this but I could not hear a word above the noise of the machinery. Instead I removed my shoes and placed them at my side and waited for further instructions. She then moved forward and took the shuttle in her hand and began work. The shuttle rushed to the far end and when it returned to the end I was standing it did so with such a crash I literally jumped with fright. This continued and as I watched I began to understand what was expected of me. I nervously approached the terrifying apparatus; I found that walking in bare feet, it was slightly easier to keep my balance. As I loaded the shuttle Pamela watched intently, ready to step in if I faltered but after a moment's hesitation I copied her and received a smile and a nod of the head. The vibrations coming up through the floor as the machines thundered on were sending shudders up my legs and body. The air was thick and humid and the temperature was overwhelming, very soon I was sweating profusely. The air was also full of cotton fluff and this was irritating my eyes and settling at the back of my throat making me dry and sending me into coughing fits. Suddenly something bumped against my ankles and I looked down to see a small boy not much older than Danny crawl underneath the machine I was using, after a moment he came out clutching a shuttle and scampered off back across the room.

    This monotony continued all morning and when the bell sounded for a break for lunch I felt about to drop. The machines were stopped but not switched off in order to keep them warm, so although the noise abated it was not totally silent. We did not have enough time to go anywhere else to eat and so we leant against our looms in order to do so. A group of three other women came over to join us and I found out these were all friends of my mothers and that they walked to and from work together each day. They enquired after her health and then we started eating, knowing there was little time for chat.

    As I reached into my pocket to retrieve my fruit I noticed that the ends of my fingers were red raw and the thumb on my right hand had the beginnings of a blister. How I felt for Mama, she had been working here for three months now and had never once complained about the conditions she was subjected to daily. I took a bite out of the pear and as the juice slipped down my parched throat I also gave thanks to Stan, there was no way I could have managed to eat either dry bread or vegetables. I was about to bite into my apple when the bell sounded, and we resumed work once again. As I became a little more practised I risked a look around the room, the parts I could see, the air was so thick that I could not see fully across the space. I marvelled to see that Pamela and one of the women who joined us previously appeared to be having a conversation, I was stood next to Pamela and even I couldn't hear what was being said, but when the other woman began to laugh and my neighbour joined in it was obvious they understood each other.

    Suddenly the shuttle I was working with flew off, I instinctively reached out to try and catch it but I missed. What I succeeded in doing was trapping my hand in the wooden slats, just managing to drag it free before they slammed down on my fingers. Shaking I looked down to assess the damage and was grateful to see only grazed knuckles, it could have been a lot worse. Then a little girl appeared at my side and handed me my missing shuttle, I thanked her even though I knew she couldn't hear me and returned to work.

Finally the bell sounded and the machines were switched off, a sudden silence descending on the room.

'Did I do alright?' I asked Pamela, eager to not have let my mother down.

She answered me but I could not really hear what she said as even though the machines were quiet the noise had been replaced by a loud ringing in my ears, but I took the smile she gave me as a positive sign.

Removing our aprons we stepped outside to begin the walk home, after the humid air inside the chill of the autumn evening made me catch my breath and I began to shiver uncontrollably.

Pamela linked her arm through mine and said, 'can you hear me yet?' She was a short slender woman of about thirty with blond hair pinned up on the top of her head, and a ready smile.

'Yes I can now.'

'You did well today love, Maria would be proud of you.'

'I didn't know it was that bad, Mama never talks about it to us.'

Pamela smiled and replied, 'I don't tell my husband how bad it is either, I am worried if I do he will make me stop and we need the money.'

Realising this was the same reason Mama kept quiet I changed the subject. 'How were you two talking to each other earlier?' I asked of the two women.

'We lip read,' the other woman told me, 'it's the only way to pass the time. You ask your mother to show you how, she is good at it.'

We reached the point in the road where we separated to return to our homes and I agreed to meet them again tomorrow if Mama had not fully recovered. There was no way I was going to let her return until she was.

Before stepping inside to see Mama, I brushed myself off as best I could. She was awake and looking a little brighter than this morning. 'Millie,' she said reaching out her hand for me to take, 'come and sit by me.'

I sat on the edge of the bed holding onto her hand, the hand of the woman who I was reminded would suffer anything for us. I could feel the tears threatening to spill down my cheeks. I could not speak for fear my voice would give me away. As she looked into my eyes I knew she understood and she nodded at me and kissed me on the cheek. 'I know darling,' was all she said.

That evening we all ate together, my mother managed some broth and water before drifting off to sleep once again.

Papa said to me, 'Millie what you did today for your mother was very thoughtful and you are to be proud of yourself, I know we are proud of you.'

'It's only right I help in any way I can,' I answered trying to steer the conversation away from myself in case I was asked how I fared. 'Did you get any work today Papa?'

'Yes, I did. Susan wasn't back too late and so I was alright. You look tired though, I think we should all go to bed.'

I kissed Mama goodnight and as soon as my head was laid down fell into a deep sleep, not stirring until I was shaken in the morning by Tommy.

Chapter 22

It took me a while to fully wake up; I had slept so deeply last night that I was still drowsy as I walked over to the house with rest of the family. Susan and Stan were eating their breakfast and as I walked in I saw that Mama was awake and eating some broth, her cheeks had a slight colour to them this morning which had been missing for the past three days. Danny ran over and sat next to her on the edge of the bed, 'Can I stay with you again today Mama?' he asked looking up into her face.

'As long as Susan doesn't mind darling,' Mama answered.

Susan looked up from her meal and said,' Of course I don't mind.'

I was filled with dread at the thought of returning to the mill again today, but I knew if I was to help my mother return to full health then I needed to do it.

Once we had all eaten, we left the house and made our way to our various places of work. I left Danny snuggled up in the crook of my mother's arm, not for the first time recently I wished I were once again five years old.

After leaving Tommy setting up the stall with Stan I walked to the edge of the town and met up with the other mill workers to begin the long walk to the factory. The women were friendly enough and asked after the health of Mama, they chattered incessantly knowing that once inside unless they could make eye contact they would have no further opportunity to converse. Each step forward I made took me closer to the source of my apprehension. Once again I found myself admiring these women, who along with my mother, were prepared to endure these conditions to provide for their families. I wished I could step inside their minds and find out if they were actually feeling the same way as I was at this moment or whether they were so used to it that it no longer affected them, I couldn't believe it was the latter.

Finally we reached the large double doors and I found that my mouth was dry and it took me all my courage not to turn and flee, back to the safety of my mother's arms, away from the dust, the noise and the vibrations of the machinery.

Mr Althorpe looked at me and said, 'Well if it isn't Rafferty junior back again, is your mother any better?'

'Yes she is recovering but is not fully fit enough to return yet.'

'Well, I hear you did alright yesterday so go on in.'

'Thank you sir,' I replied and donning an apron, followed Pamela over to our places at the far side of the room.

Once again the noise assaulted my ears and it was not long before I was sweating profusely in the hot humid air, the shuttle slid back and forth relentlessly and the floor beneath my feet shook. The small children ran in and out of the machines diving underneath to retrieve the tools. My eye was drawn to a small boy of about four who had just popped up in the aisle between where I was working and the woman at the next machine. As he jumped up with the mule in his hand about to run back to return it to its owner he lost his footing on the greasy floor. The next few seconds in time seemed to slow down as I watched the boy as he started to slip back underneath the machine, instinctively he reached out with his other hand to try and stop himself from falling, his hand moving towards the wooden slats and the hot mule as it moved rapidly to and fro. Without thinking I rushed forward and leant down to grab his arm before he became trapped, catching his wrist and pulling him clear. Relief at saving him was soon replaced by terror and pain, my hair had become entangled in the moving parts and I was dragged nearer to the clanking beast. The pain was indescribable and my eyes were watering, I began to try to pull away, my hair was pulling me back down and as I tried to move forward it came away at the roots. Then suddenly I was freed and fell forward as my momentum at being released from the jaws threw me to the ground.

Shakily I got back to my feet and turned to see Pamela standing at my side with a large pair of scissors in her hand, I realised that she had cut me free. As I stood up straight I was hit by a bout of nausea and my head began to spin, I sank back to the floor in a state of shock. Pamela knelt beside me and put an arm around my shoulder; she looked me in the eye and raised her eyebrows questioningly as if to enquire if I was alright. I nodded slowly careful not to make the nausea worse; lifting my hand I gently touched the top of my head. I could feel a bald patch where my hair had been torn out, and when I inspected my fingers I saw they had signs of blood upon them. Gradually I began to feel better, the shaking had subsided and I no longer felt sick. Tentatively I stood up and returned to my station, then stood horrified as I saw dark hair woven into the fabric of the cotton. I grabbed Pamela by the arm and pointed to the issue, I had no idea what to do about this as the machine continued and my hair was completely woven into the cotton. Pamela rushed from the room and came back seconds later with a harassed looking Mr Althorpe, he blew a whistle hanging around his neck and the machine slowed and stopped.

'What the hell happened here?' he asked me.

'I slipped and trapped my hair,' I replied.

'Well young lady you have ruined this whole sheet of fabric. This will come out of your wages at the end of the week.'

The woman who was stationed on the other side of the aisle from me stepped forward, 'She was trying to stop the boy from falling into the machine, she did so but her hair got caught. If not for her, you might have had a boy without a hand.'

'Hmm,' was all he said. Turning to Pamela he told her, 'You are vouching for her so you had better get this problem sorted out and quickly. Anything over ten minutes and you too will lose money, and both of you will work later to make up the lost time.'

'Yes sir,' Pamela answered and began to help me to cut the spoiled material and rethread the mule in order to continue weaving. We managed to reset and were ready in under the time constraints applied. The rest of the day continued as normal and I was so relieved when the whistle blew and we were allowed to start on our way home.

Pamela linked her arm through mine, 'how are you feeling?' she asked me.

'I am ok,' I lied. My scalp still hurt where the hair was torn out, 'but I must thank you for coming to my assistance in there. I hate to think what would have happened if you hadn't thought to cut me free.' I could feel tears pricking at the back of my eyes as I relived the incident in my mind.

'You aren't the first and you won't be the last to do it, that's why we tie ours back, I feel badly about it, I should have told you the risks earlier.'

At last I was back at the house and threw myself into the task of helping Susan prepare the evening meal after enquiring about the health of my mother.

Chapter 23

Maria laid back against the bed pillows as yet another coughing fit subsided, she was hoping desperately to be able to return to the mill this morning, but when she tried to raise herself from the bed she knew there was no way she would even be fit enough to make the walk let alone spend a full day in the machine shop. The door into Stan and Susan's room opened and her family walked in to share a breakfast before leaving for their various work. Danny leapt onto the bed and asked if he could stay with her today, she knew he had been missing his parents as they both worked long hours six days a week, but if they were to survive and accrue enough money to be able to move from the shed into some proper accommodation, it was necessary. It was now September and the weather would only get worse as the year came to an end. As Millie walked into the room last, Maria reached her hand out for her to come over to join her, yesterday she had taken it upon herself to make the walk to the cotton mill and actually managed to convince the foreman to let her step in for her mother, thereby ensuring no loss of money and more importantly no loss of position.

Maria had never told any of her family of the appalling conditions she endured each day, she knew if she did they would try to convince her to leave and find something else. Employment was difficult to find and whilst she would love to leave, her husband was still being used as casual labour at the docks and though he had been lucky so far in as much as he had secured a wage since starting there, nothing was guaranteed. Between them and Tommy they were bringing in seven shillings and three pence each week. Bed and breakfast would cost them three shillings a week, leaving four shillings and three pence for food, and a bed in a shared room would cost four pence weekly, the room Stan and Susan lived in took seven shillings from their weekly earnings, something they could not afford yet. Their weekly diet of fruit, vegetables, bread and milk amounted to seven shillings and two pence, leaving one penny a week. Maria had been saving this penny each week just in case Daniel did not secure work at any time. She had eleven pence saved, nearly enough for one pound of butter or eighteen pounds of vegetables, certainly not enough for a room.

Millie walked over and took her mother's hand, Maria looked at her twelve year old daughter and felt a lump form in her throat, such was her pride for her. Not only had she helped secure money coming in for the family, she had not complained about the conditions she had experienced yesterday , and she was here again today ready to take it on once more.

'Millie,' Maria whispered to her daughter so no one else could overhear them,' I am so proud of you. I know what you experienced yesterday must have terrified you and I wish you didn't have to go back today. If you can't face it no one will blame you, least of all me.'

'Mama, if I have ever taken you and Papa for granted then I apologise now. I will go to the ends of the earth for both of you and my little brothers,' Millie answered laying a kiss on her cheek.

All too soon her family left her and with Danny nestled in her arms she once again drifted off to sleep. At one point she wakened to find the spot on the bed empty, then she heard voices drifting up from the back yard and realised Danny was helping Susan with the laundry. She thought back to their time in Ireland, a time that was hard but she was able to spend the day working with Millie and Danny for company as they helped her with the daily chores, Daniel and Tommy used to work long hours but they returned to their hut and spent happy evenings together. When the crops were healthy they always knew they had plenty of food to rely on. Now she, Daniel and Tommy were working long hours six days a week, time for the family was scarce, their Sundays in the park were cherished and every moment they could stay outdoors in such idyllic settings were stretched as far as possible. But the days were shortening now and soon it would be too cold to spend long there, they needed to find lodgings soon. As she heard Danny's laughter she once again thought of the child she had had to leave behind and began to weep, Millie and Tommy had needed to mature quickly and she felt that she had lost her children too soon. She was determined to ensure Danny did not have to grow up just yet, although she also knew he wanted nothing more than to take his place alongside the others in providing for the family.

Gradually the family were coming back together as they returned from work, Tommy and Stan were always the first to get home followed by Daniel an hour later. Millie would not be back for another two hours yet, this was a further source of guilt for Maria knowing she was leaving the shopping, cooking and sitting for Danny with her daughter when she was fit enough to work. She was caught between earning a wage and being a mother in the true sense of the word. That evening as Millie entered the room Maria could see something terrible had happened to her, her face was deathly white and as she beckoned her over and Millie sat beside her, her arms enfolding her she could feel her slim body shaking against her.

'Darling whatever is the matter?' Maria asked.

Millie just shook her head and said nothing, holding on to her tightly.

Maria lifted her hand to stroke the head of her daughter, Millie winced and she let out a small gasp of pain. Maria guessed at once what had happened and taking her daughters head gently in her two hands tilted it to see the damage. An area about the size of a penny piece was totally bald, the hair having been dragged out by the roots and the scalp dotted with dried blood. She lifted Millie's face to hers and kissed her on the cheeks, drying her tears as she did so. Seeing her daughter so upset made Maria's mind up there and then she would be returning to work tomorrow come what may.

Chapter 24

This morning when I awoke I felt physically sick at the prospect of the mill but I walked over to the house to join the others anyway. I was surprised to find Mama was up and dressed ready to leave for work. She looked better than she had but I was sure she was not yet up to it, Papa had obviously tried to convince her of the same, as she was saying to him,' I am fine now Daniel, do not fret so.'

'I don't think you are capable of doing the walk no matter a full day's work,' he answered her.

My parent's very rarely disagreed but when they did neither one was happy to back down. I tried to ease the tension by saying,' Papa, I will go with Mama this morning and if she is not up to it when we get there I will send her home and take her place.'

'Very well then,' he said looking at me, 'but you must promise to do so or neither of you are going.'

'Papa I promise you.'

We all made ready to leave the house; Danny had opted for staying with Susan and helping her with the laundry. I thought this made him feel happier than the alien environment of the market stall, after all this was how he used to help Mama and me at home.

While we waited at the corner for the other women I took a quick glance at Mama, she looked a little pale but so far hadn't had any coughing fits, she saw me and said,' I am alright Millie, I want to thank you properly now that we are alone. I know it can't have been easy for you especially after your accident yesterday. The fact that you are willing to return today is very brave of you and I am so proud of you.'

'Mama, you are the brave one, you have been working there for two and a half months now and never once mentioned how bad it was.'

When the others arrived we were locked in an embrace.

'Maria, how are you?' Pamela asked rushing up to Mama and linking her arm.

'A lot better thanks to my daughter.'

'Yes she is a good one,' then turning to me she asked,' how is your head?'

'Sore,' I replied.

When we reached the mill doors I asked my mother if she felt well enough to work.

'Yes Millie, you go home. I will see you tonight as normal.'

I had walked no more than a few steps homeward, my emotions mixed, relief at not having to go in, guilt at leaving Mama to that place, when I heard Pamela calling my name.

'Millie, stop a minute.'

I ran back to join her, fearing something had happened to Mama.

'Mr Althorpe says one of the women hasn't come in today, there is work for you if you want it.'

I would be a hypocrite if I were to abandon my mother to this work if I was not prepared to pull my weight when the opportunity arose. I needed to help toward the provision for our family, I just hoped it would not be here, but I nodded and answered, 'Yes of course I will do it.'

My fate sealed I entered the forbidding building but felt relieved I had my mother by my side; I knew she would protect me. Before entering the machine shop I secured my hair away from my face and then followed Mama into the hot humid room. I was not standing next to her but I could see her from where I was and began to slowly pick up the skill of lip reading, she started off by talking very slowly and exaggerating each word, but at least we could communicate and I didn't feel so isolated.

I managed to secure employment for the rest of the week and this brought an extra two shillings in to the house which Mama put with the other savings, we now had three shillings in total that was not required for our weekly food.

On Sunday we all went to the park for a small celebration, it was Papa's birthday yesterday and we were blessed with a warm sunny autumn day. For the first time since arriving here we actually had some savings and were not living hand to mouth. Although we still needed to find a place to live, I was sure that providing I could carry on working at the mill, it wouldn't be long before we had a roof over our heads. Susan had even taken to giving Danny a ha'penny a day for helping her with the laundry, with his help she had been able to take on some more customers.

Chapter 25

December 1847

The winter wind was biting and I pulled my shawl around me tighter as I walked with my mother and the other women to the mill. The woman whose position I took earlier never returned to work and I was now employed permanently. It was still dark but the full moon overhead was lighting our way as it reflected off the laying snow. It had been snowing now for three days and the going was difficult, my feet were wet and cold. The wind had whipped the snow into large drifts at the sides of the road and we had to keep to the well trodden path in order to avoid sinking down to our knees in the freezing conditions. The falling snow was whipping across my face and coating my eyelashes, my breath freezing at the back of my throat as I trudged wearily along.

Although I was not happy to be working there still, it had meant a turn for the better in our fortunes as we were now bringing home ten shillings and sixpence per week. We were also able to eat better than we were and Mama was managing to save some money each week. Papa had been made permanent and did not have to queue for work each day. Danny had turned six on the fifth of October and was becoming quite an experienced hand at the laundry, as was I at lip reading. We moved into a shared room at a lodging house in late October and although far from ideal because there were three other families in with us, at least we were inside out of the winter weather. The room held seven beds between us all, the adults taking a double bed for each couple and the other three beds were for all the children, of which there were eleven including me and my brothers. I was so pleased to be out of the shed, although our hut in Ireland was open to the elements, the sleeping room had a dividing wall and with no windows it at least cut out some of the draughts. The shed with its thin wooden slatted walls was no barrier against the wind blowing in from the west coast. Sleeping was only possible by huddling together for warmth, the hard floor also felt damp and cold even through the old sacking we had scavenged from various places.

Stan and Susan had become like family to us all and I would forever be grateful to them both for all the help they had given us during the past six months. If Tommy had not approached Stan and enquired as to a position I had no doubt we would have been a lot worse off. We still returned to their room in order to cook supper together before returning to our lodgings to sleep. We could move into bed and breakfast but this extra cost would mean using nearly all of our weekly income and my parents were afraid of committing to this at the moment, so we endured this for a while longer.

Finally we arrived at the mill and stepped in through the double doors, the relief I felt in getting out of the cold was immense. I was even looking forward to entering the machine room with its hot temperature; I knew this would be short lived because as soon I had thawed out the humidity would once again become almost unbearable. The work was still hard and the conditions sapped your energy quickly but I had become fond of the women I shared my working day with, they were kind, friendly and at times funny. We didn't have much to laugh about so when one of them came out with some witty remark, often involving their husband, we could spend minutes giggling like children. I must admit I didn't always understand what it was they were laughing so hard about but I could not help but get caught up in the jollity. Once when a lady called Thora told a tale about an incident from the previous night I found my mother looking over at me with some concern, I had no idea what Thora meant but I joined in the laughter anyway. That night when we were walking home after leaving the others Mama put her arm through mine and began asking me questions as to what they were talking about earlier, I had to confess I didn't know. Mama seemed relieved and told me she would speak to me about these things later but I was not to worry about them at the moment. I thought later meant after supper or tomorrow but the subject was not addressed further.

Next Friday I would turn thirteen, I was looking forward to my birthday but I was also looking forward to two full days off work to spend with my family. My birthday was the twenty fourth of December which meant Saturday would be Christmas Day; this was not something we had heard much of in Ireland but here in England everyone took the day off. The richer people had huge feasts and gave each other presents; they also decorated their houses with holly, mistletoe and trees. I was not worried about any of that, although a present would be nice, I just wanted the time with my loved ones. Mama and Susan had spent hours each evening chatting quietly about their plans for the big day, no one else was allowed anywhere near these discussions.

Chapter 26

Christmas 1847

I was woken up with a start as a small missile known as Danny landed squarely on my chest knocking all the breath from my body,' Millie wake up, it's Christmas Day,' he squealed.

'Happy Christmas Danny,' I gasped.

He climbed off me and ran over to where my parents lay still blissfully asleep, not for long though.

It was not long before the five of us were up and walking the mile journey to join Stan and Susan for the day. The morning was crisp and bright, the night had brought another fall of fresh snow and everywhere looked white and clean. I could see my breath each time I breathed out and my nose was already beginning to freeze as we continued on our way. We met other families journeying to and fro and all called out a seasons greeting as they passed. Tommy and Danny were running ahead, sliding in the snow, scooping up handfuls and moulding into balls before throwing them at each other. It was not long before they were both red faced, panting and their clothes and hair were damp.

'That's enough boys,' Mama called to them, 'whatever will our hosts think if you turn up dripping wet all over their room?'

'Sorry Mama, we were just having fun,' Tommy answered, looking slightly disheartened that his fun may cause others some inconvenience.

I could tell Mama felt bad for having upset him and in an effort to make him feel better she turned to Papa nodding and tilting her head in their direction. Papa took his queue and picked up the biggest handful of snow and threw it at Tommy. I found I could not resist it and before too long we were all dusting ourselves off and laughing uncontrollably, passersby smiled at us and recovering our composure we finally arrived at our destination.

We let ourselves into the hallway and at once my sense of smell was overpowered by the most delicious aromas I could ever imagine. From behind the closed doors of the downstairs rooms we could hear voices, some singing, others squealing and laughing. Climbing the stairs the atmosphere was no different, the sounds of jollity carrying to us.

On the approach to Stan and Susan's door I noticed a large holly wreath was hanging on the outside, but what awaited me inside I could never have imagined.

There was a huge fire roaring in the grate and on top of the range stood a large lidded pot which was bubbling and clattering away. The furniture had all been pushed back to the side of the room apart from the table which was laid with a pure white linen cloth, seven places had been set, and at each place was a small orange, there were glasses at each setting with a deep red liquid in. In the middle of the table were some sprigs of mistletoe and holly in a long slender bottle. Chairs of various shapes and sizes were arranged around the table, and the most delicious smell pervaded the air. Stan was dressed in his Sunday best, his hair and side whiskers neatly trimmed and brushed, Susan was wearing a deep red dress over which she wore an apron, her face was flushed and her freshly washed hair was crafted into a neat pile on the top of her head held in place by a multitude of pins.

A chorus of Happy Christmas rose from everyone's lips and hugs and kisses were passed around, even my brothers readily took part in this. Mama and I took no time in removing our outer garments and going over to assist in the cooking of the dinner.

Whilst the dinner was cooking, Stan entertained us with tales from his days on the market stall as a lad working for his father. At last the meal was ready and we all took our places around the table, I was sitting between my two brothers opposite Susan and Mama, Stan and Papa occupied the ends of the table. Susan placed on the table dishes containing mashed potatoes, carrots, turnips, green beans and deep rich brown gravy, then she placed a large serving dish on which rested a goose, when Stan carved into it the juices ran down the sides and the skin crunched as the knife sliced through. Each of us received a slice of white and dark meat and once the meat was served the vegetables were passed around. As we linked hands and said grace I found I was salivating at the anticipation of the delights to come, I was not disappointed as I took my first mouthful of the succulent bird. A silence descended upon the room apart from the sound of knife and fork against the china plates and moans of appreciation from all. Once the course had been finished and cleared away Stan asked us all to raise our glasses in a toast to the day and each and everyone's good health in the year to come. We all stood and held our glasses high, the contents being a red port that Stan had mixed with water for us three children. As I swallowed I could feel the port as it warmed the back of my throat, Danny gulped his down in one go and wiped the back of his hand across his mouth, Mama smiled and said to Papa,' we may have to watch that one as he grows up,'

Then just when I thought it could not be bested by anything Susan and Mama served up a slice of sticky fruit pudding topped with a creamy custard, as we plunged our spoons in Susan said,' make sure you look carefully before you eat, you may find some treasure. Sure enough each portion had a shiny sixpenny piece inside. Once the dishes had been cleared and the table set against the wall we spent the afternoon playing parlour games of which we knew nothing but thoroughly enjoyed.

Then just before we were set to return home my parents gave us all a small handmade gift, I received a felt bonnet, Tommy a wooden boat and Danny a small toy soldier.

'Thank you so much for the most wonderful day,' Papa said to our hosts, 'the meal was amazing.'

'Maria has helped to pay for it,' Susan said, not wishing to take all the glory herself.

Papa turned to Mama, who smiled bashfully and said,' I have been saving hard, and although I felt bad keeping it from you I feel it was worth it.'

We took our leave and walked back to our room, I had never felt as happy in my life as I did that night, and the knowledge that we had another day to spend together tomorrow as it was Sunday lifted my spirits further, Danny was sleeping in Papa's arms as we climbed the stairs.

Chapter 27

April 1848

Life seemed to have settled down into a routine at last, we all had employment and were bringing money into the home. We actually had some left over at the end of each week despite having improved our standard of eating. We remained in the shared room because we only returned there to sleep each night, when we were not at work we were either with Stan and Susan in their room or on Sunday's when the weather was fine we would all go to the park. Mama was saving a little each week in case we fell on hard times due to ill health. I overheard her speaking with Papa one evening when she told him she never wanted to go through a time again when she didn't know where the next meal was coming from or where we would be living.

'Do you have any regrets about leaving Ireland?' he had asked her.

'Only the one,' she answered, remembering the daughter they had left behind,' Daniel I want you to know that I had every faith in you and I knew you would protect our family. We had some hardships along the way but here we are, all together, all healthy and happy. That is down to you, you had the foresight to know what we needed to do to survive, I don't think I would have ever had the courage to make that decision.'

'You would my darling, I know how strong you can be, you have proved that time over. I also know that you endure the conditions at the mill in order to help with the income.'

'What conditions?'

'I don't know the full extent but I could see it in your face when you came home those first few weeks you worked there, a look I also saw in that of our daughter when she took your place. I will not interfere, I trust you enough to know you would not be foolish in any way just to prove a point, but I also wish you to know that if ever it becomes too much for either or both of you, you have my blessing to do what may be necessary.'

'Thank you Daniel, you are a truly good man, you know me better than I thought possible.'

'The children have also done more than I could have hoped for, Millie and Tommy have had to grow up quickly and have done so without complaint, even Danny is finally earning a wage,' he laughed.

'Daniel, I have an idea, I have some money saved, we can spare a little without suffering. I have seen there is to be a travelling fair here in May, let's take the children for a day.'

Papa kissed her tenderly on the lips and then said goodnight to her.

As I lay in the bed I shared with my brother's I found sleep hard to come by, I was so excited of the prospect of a day at the fair. I had no idea how I would manage to keep this a secret from them for three weeks.

Chapter 28

May 1848

I don't think I slept at all last night; I was so excited that the day of the fair was actually here. It was difficult enough to keep a secret from my brothers, but also to not let my parents know that I knew of the surprise was even more taxing, I knew they would be disappointed that I had known in advance.

So I lay in bed with my eyes closed trying to keep as still as possible hoping they would believe me to be asleep. Finally I felt a gentle hand shaking my shoulder and heard Mama's voice saying, 'come on children, time to get up, we have somewhere to be today.'

Danny stretched and yawned asking, 'aren't we going to the park today, it's Sunday?'

'No dear, not today.'

Danny's face dropped, I could see he was upset, 'but we always go unless it is raining. Is it raining?'

'No it's not raining, now hurry and get dressed, we have to meet Stan and Susan at the market square soon.'

'Why aren't we going to their room for breakfast?' Danny asked, not moving from his place in the bed.

'Because we don't have time for breakfast if we are to get there in time.'

'Where?'

I tried to help by saying to my brother without giving myself away, 'well the only way to find out is to get up and go and see.'

'I don't want to; I want to go to the park.'

'Well, you go to the park then and I will go with Mama and Papa, if it was any fun I will let you know all about it when we return.'

I knew that would work, Danny loved the park but the off chance of something better being on offer was too much for him to risk. He threw the covers off and jumped down, urging his brother to follow, pulling his shoes on he asked, 'will we be eating breakfast when we get there?'

'Don't worry son, you won't go hungry today I promise,' Papa told him, helping him on with his jacket.

As we left the lodging house and began to walk to the edge of the square I was surprised by the amount of people already crowding the streets, they were all heading the same way as us. The sun was already beginning to warm the early morning and it promised to be a lovely day. We met up with the others and continued on towards the common on the edge of the town. As we got nearer the sound of music came across the air, Tommy suddenly realised what it was.

'Papa, Mama, are we going to the fair?'

'Yes we are,' Papa told us. 'We want to give you all a treat for being so good since we left home; we are both very proud of you all.'

Danny squealed with delight, eager to be off, Mama grabbed him by the hand just before he could escape. 'One rule for today is you must stay with us at all times, there will be lots of people here and we cannot risk losing you. Do you all understand?'

We all nodded vigorously; keen to be on our way, I think we would have agreed to anything at that moment in time.

We spent the day watching jugglers and clowns, throwing balls at coconuts, hoops over poles and looking at the animals in the cages. We ate sticky sweets and bitter toffee; we sat on the grass and watched children chasing each other around the tents as we ate a lunch that Susan had packed for us all. We queued to go into a tent to see a freak show, losing sight of Danny for a moment, we were just about to go and search for him when he appeared at our side, his eyes wide as he told us, 'I have just seen a woman who has a beard.'

'Where is she?' Tommy asked.

'In there,' he answered pointing to the tent. 'I crept underneath.'

'Danny, you shouldn't have done that,' Mama told him, but she couldn't be too cross with him as she looked at his face and saw how alarmed he was by what he saw.

Once inside we stared at a giant of a man standing next to a dwarf, there was a man with skin as black as night, his eyes shining white against his skin. In the next tent was the lady with a beard down to her waist, there were two ladies who were joined together at their hips and a man who was so fat I was sure he must surely burst.

After that we rode on a carousel which whirled us around at a tremendous speed whilst also going up and down, music blaring from an organ at the side of the ride. The man turned the handle relentlessly, he was dressed in black trousers, a striped top and a small red hat, sitting on his shoulder attached by a lead which looped through the man's waist belt was a small brown monkey, dressed identically. He chattered incessantly and occasionally bared his teeth which looked like he was grinning at us.

We ended the day by each riding on the back on a small pony round a fenced ring, before returning home. We all said our thanks to the adults for a wonderful day and fell exhausted into bed, sleep coming easily, dreams full of the sights and sounds of the day.

Chapter 29

On the way to work all Tommy and I could talk about were the things we did and saw yesterday, those memories would last a lifetime of that I had no doubt. Tommy was telling Stan all about the people in the freak show tent, and even though Stan had been there with us he was gracious enough not to say anything and made the right responses to Tommy's vivid descriptions. Stan certainly looked upon us as his family as we did him and his wife.

The day passed in a world of humid temperatures, clattering machines and cotton filled air. Mama and I bade the women goodbye and joined the others at Susan and Stan's; as soon as we entered the room I could sense something was wrong.

Mama's eyes quickly swept the room to make sure everyone was accounted for and they were well before asking, 'what's wrong?'

Susan wrung her hands and looked down at the floor, tears spilling from her eyes; she opened her mouth to speak but shook her head, the words sticking in her throat.

Stan rose to his feet, 'it is Susan's mother, she was been taken very ill and we must go to her to look after her.'

Mama rushed over to Susan and took her in her arms, 'Susan I am so sorry, is there anything we can do to help at all?'

Susan buried her head in my mother's embrace and sobbed, shaking her head.

Then Papa gave us the rest of the bad news, 'Susan's mother lives away and they must move in order to care for her.'

'Of course, that is to be understood,' Mama said. Then I could see she had realised something that had so far not struck me. 'Oh you are leaving for good.'

Susan still cried and Stan said, 'if there could be any other way you know we would take it but Susan needs to be there and I cannot let her go alone.'

'When do you have to leave?' Mama asked.

'Well Susan is going tomorrow and I will leave just as soon as I can sell the stall.'

I walked over to my brothers who were both devastated, we were not only losing truly good friends, they were losing their employment and we were losing vital income.

I wondered, just when would our fortunes change for the better and stay that way?

The evening meal was a sombre affair and we said our farewells to Susan, wishing her and her mother good health before going home.

Chapter 30

When we woke up we all walked across to the house to have our last shared breakfast with our friends, no one was in the mood for talking. Arriving at the house Mama stopped us before we went in, 'listen I know we are all devastated about the news we received last night but I have been thinking about Stan and Susan on the way over, especially Susan. Her mother is very ill and she has to leave everything she has, to go and care for her. Remember how we felt when we left to come here, well that's how they are feeling now. What I don't want us to do is make her feel any worse by letting her think she is letting us down too. They have done more for us since we arrived here than anyone else, if not for them we may be back in Ireland now facing who knows what, so when we go inside make sure we don't moan about our circumstances and give them some support and comfort.'

'Your mother is right,' Papa added, 'we will sort something out but we must think of our friends first. Does everyone understand?'

'Yes Papa,' Tommy and I answered.

'Danny do you understand that we must be nice to Stan and Susan?' Papa asked my brother.

'Yes Papa, but can we still have breakfast?' Danny asked.

'Yes of course darling,' Mama said.

We entered the room determined to put on a brave face but were surprised when Susan rushed over to Mama. 'I have had an idea Maria that will help us all I think.'

Mama smiled as Susan began to explain, 'Stan and I were talking long into the night last night and have a proposition for you. We have both spent a long time building up our trade and are worried about how we will manage without the money we make from it. Obviously we will have the money when Stan sells his stall but we don't know how long that will last, Stan will have to find a job when he gets there but I will have to look after mother all the time. We know she won't get better so it's just a matter of time, so when ....' she brushed away tears as her voice broke.

Mama put an arm around her and gently rubbed Susan's back, giving her the support to continue. I marvelled once again what a strong, kind and thoughtful person my mama was.

Susan took my mother's hand in hers and continued, 'we hope to be able to come back here. This is where we belong and where all our friends are,' she said looking at us all, 'so I would like it very much if you would take over my laundry customers Maria. It would bring you more money than you are earning at the mill, then when we return we could both work it together and hopefully take on more work. Also it would mean you wouldn't have to take Danny and Tommy to the mill or lose money by staying at home to look after them. What do you think?'

Mama looked at Papa and then at the couple who once again despite their problems were prepared to help us. I could see she was tempted but needed the approval from Papa.

Stan stepped in to help, 'Susan will take Maria round with her and Danny this morning and explain to them all that Maria will be taking over and that nothing will change, they all know Danny already so that will help. We are both hoping you will agree but don't feel obliged, also I must say without trying to put you all under any pressure that if you are going to do this it must be this morning as Susan has to leave this afternoon.'

'What shall I tell the mill?' Mama worried.

'Millie can tell them when she goes in this morning,' Papa said, thereby endorsing the decision.

It was then that it dawned on me that I would be going to the mill on my own from now on. I smiled my encouragement and said, 'of course I can Mama, take it.'

Mama walked over and hugged me and whispered to me, 'we will talk tonight about this I promise but it is too good an opportunity to miss.'

After our meal we all left for our respective work, Papa went to the docks, Tommy and Stan to the market, Mama and Danny with Susan, and I left to meet the women on the walk to the mill. I tried to remain positive as I knew it would mean more money for the family but I hated the work at the mill and it was only the fact that Mama was there that made it bearable for me. Then I remembered all that my parents had done for us and I found myself feeling both guilty and selfish for just thinking about how this was affecting me. I determined there and then that I would support her and leave my misery locked away, the way she had done all the time she had been working there.

Once through the mill doors I lined up with the others to register my attendance for the day, 'M Rafferty sir,' I said.

'Which one?' Mr Althorpe asked as he did every day since the two of us began working together.

'Millie, sir.'

'Where is your mother today?'

'She isn't coming in today sir.'

'Is she ill again?'

'No sir, she has some different work now sir.'

'How long for?'

'For good sir, she won't be returning.'

'Hmm, I suppose I will have to train someone else now,' with that he turned and went out into the yard to pick my mother's replacement.

I was amazed that no matter how hard you worked or how productive you were, you were just an employee who could be replaced immediately due to the fact that there were so many in need of a job.

The day dragged by and I was relieved when the bell sounded the finish of the day and I was making my way home with the others.

'Well Millie, you tell your Mama I am pleased she has managed to escape the mill work,' Pamela said linking arms with me as usual. 'I will miss her, you tell her that also. See you tomorrow honey.'

As I climbed the stairs up to join my family in Stan's room for our evening meal I wondered how much longer this would continue. I knew that as soon as he could sell his stall he would be going to join Susan in caring for her mother. As I pushed the room door open I was greeted with the sound of laughter and the smell of stew cooking on the hearth. I was home and once again realised that as long as I had my family with me I could endure anything.

On the walk back to our lodging Mama took me by the hand and we slowed to let the others walk ahead.

'Millie, I am sorry how things have worked out, I would do anything to swap places with you at the mill but this was too good an opportunity to miss. Susan has many customers and is earning twelve shillings a week. Just think how much that will help us as a family.'

'I know Mama; you did the right thing in taking it.'

'Listen I am going to work so hard at this and I am going to get new customers so that you can also leave the mill. '

'Mama, don't worry about me, I am fine.'

'Millie, you don't have to pretend with me remember. I know how much you hate it there and I don't blame you, it is a horrible place to work.' Suddenly she stopped walking, turning to me smiling she said, ' In fact I have just thought there is no need for you to go back, I am earning more than twice what we were bringing home so you can stop right now.'

'No Mama, that's not right, you said yourself this is an opportunity for us to better ourselves. I will continue at the mill, I want to help too. Also Tommy will be out of work once Stan sells his stall so he can help you with any new customers.'

'Laundry is not men's work,' Mama said.

'Don't let Danny hear you say that,' I laughed.

'Millie, I don't think you will ever stop surprising me. I give you an opportunity to leave a place I know you hate and you are willing to keep going for the sake of your brothers. I am so proud of the way you have grown. You will make someone a fine wife one day but God help him if he ever tries to dissuade you from doing something in which you believe.'

'I wonder where I get that from.'

Chapter 31

Susan had been gone for three days when Stan shook hands with the tall wiry man who had just agreed to the price Stan wanted for his established fruit and vegetable stall.

'I can have the money with you this afternoon,' said Mr Stone.

'That's grand, it means I can be with my wife by tomorrow evening,' Stan answered. 'There is one more thing I would like your word on before we finalise the deal though.'

'What would that be, I thought we had just agreed the price?'

'Yes we have, but I would like you to keep the lad on, he is a good worker, reliable and honest. His family have struggled and I know they rely on his wage.'

'Why are you so concerned about him that you are prepared to risk this agreement for him?'

'Because I have grown very fond of him and I don't want to see him out of work through no fault of his own.'

'Well I don't know, I would like to choose my own lad.'

'I will vouch for him, he is already familiar with the trade and he is well liked by the customers. I think he will be an asset as you settle in.'

'Very well then, I will agree. Let me see the lad, what's his name?'

'Tommy Rafferty.'

'He's Irish?'

'Yes, he and his family came over to escape the famine. My wife and I have become very friendly with them all and we will miss them greatly.'

Tommy was busy at the back of the stall stacking the empty boxes on to the barrow when Stan called him over.

'Tommy come here and let me introduce you to your new employer. This is Mr Stone and he has just bought my stall from me.'

'Good afternoon sir,' Tommy said looking up at the man who stood before him.

'Stan tells me you are a good worker so I have agreed to keep you in your current position. I will expect you to show me the standards that I have been told you are capable of, is that understood?'

'Yes sir, I will sir. Thank you so much for the opportunity.'

'See you do,' with those words Mr Stone turned and walked away.

Stan looked down at the boy who he had come to love as a son and realised how much he would miss the child. 'Tommy I want to thank you for all your hard work and tell you that I have enjoyed every day that we have spent together here, I have never had a lad who has taken to the task so easily.'

'Thank you Stan, I will miss you and Susan, I hope very much that her mother recovers soon.'

The next morning Tommy reported to work as usual at five thirty only to find the stall empty and no sign of his new employer. He waited for twenty minutes watching as the other stall holders set up ready for the day. At last Mr Stone appeared rushing along the street, fastening the buttons on his shirt as he ran.

'What are you doing just sitting around?' he shouted at Tommy.

'I was waiting for you sir.'

'What do you mean, waiting for me, where is the produce?'

'I don't know sir; Stan always had it here ready for setting up when I arrived.'

'Well you had better go and fetch it from the store; I don't expect to have to do that. From now on that is your job, do you understand?'

'Yes sir.' Tommy ran off and was back after half an hour with the barrow full and began unpacking the groceries. Whilst he did so Mr Stone looked on and made no attempt to help him, then as Tommy walked past him to stack the empty boxes at the back of the stall Mr Stone hit him on the back of the head saying, 'Listen lad Stan told me you were a good worker, so far I am not at all impressed.'

The day continued with Tommy doing all the heavy physical work, whilst Mr Stone took on the task of selling and talking to the customers. At the end of the day Mr Stone left Tommy clearing up on his own as he scooped the day's takings into his pocket reminding him that he expected Tommy to set the stall up each morning before he arrived.

The days that followed took a similar pattern, Tommy doing all the physical work receiving no help from his employer. There was no conversation between the two unless it was Mr Stone giving him instructions or scathing remarks to show his disappointment in the boy. It was also obvious by some of the things he said that he did not approve of the Irish working and living in England. The worse thing that developed over time was the physical abuse that he inflicted more and more on Tommy, all done out of sight of any witnesses.

Tommy came to hate his time on the stall but knew his family needed the money so was determined to stick it out.

Chapter 32

October 1848

It had been five months now since Stan and Susan left to go and care for her sick mother and we all missed them so. Stan managed to sell his grocery stall three days after Susan had left and followed her promising they would return when they could, but so far there had been no sign of them. Stan had also looked after our family once more before he left by ensuring that the new stall holder kept Tommy in employment. At first Tommy had been delighted at this but I could tell that things were not right with him anymore. He was no longer keen to make his way across town with me where I would leave him in the market square in order to continue my journey to the mill, he was quiet on the walk and no amount of my trying to start a conversation would work, he remained silent. He displayed on the outside the feelings I hid on the inside, those of someone who was going to work for the sake of the family and not because they enjoyed it. Finally one day I could stand it no longer, Tommy and I had always been so close and able to share anything.

'Tommy please tell me what is wrong, you used to love working the market with Stan and now you barely speak of it at all. The only time I see you happy is on Sunday's and then that wears off as the day grows older.'

Tommy did not raise his head to look at me but instead looked from under his hair which had fallen across his broad forehead. He was now ten years of age and had begun to fill out a little around his face. His dark brown eyes held mine for a brief moment before once again dropping to the ground as we made our way across the cobbled streets.

'I hate it there now; the new owner is nothing like Stan was, he only keeps me because he gave his word to Stan.'

'Well not everyone can be as kind and generous as Stan was, but I feel there is more than just that. Am I right?'

Tommy said nothing for a few minutes and then suddenly stopped walking. I turned to look at him and realised I had hit a raw nerve. He stood with his shoulders slumped and his head down, he put his hands in his pockets and kicked at a stone on the ground. Then he gave the slightest of nods and said quietly, 'Millie he gives me all the horrible jobs to do, I don't mind that so much. Stan and I used to share them, but I understand that he is the boss and pays my wage so I accept that.'

'Then what is it? Tommy please tell me.'

'He,' Tommy took a deep breath and looked at me briefly before once again breaking eye contact, he told me as tears began to fall, 'he beats me.'

'What?' I asked unable to believe what I had just heard.

'He beats me, he hits me if I am not quick enough to do the tasks he has given me, and he beats me if I drop things or if I can't carry as much as he expects me to. Millie I am scared of him.'

'Have you told Papa about this?'

'No you are the only one I have told. He only does it when there is no one around to see, so who would believe me. Besides if I told Papa he would make me leave and we need the money. Promise you won't tell Papa, please Millie promise me.' Tommy grabbed hold of my hands and looked into my eyes, his own pleading with me to keep his secret.

'I promise,' I said and pulled him to me in a hug. As I squeezed him tight I felt him flinch and he let out a slight gasp. I released him quickly and before he could stop me I lifted his shirt. Across his chest and back were large purple yellow bruises. My hand went to my mouth and I realised that I could not let this go, the man was a bully and I would not let him harm my brother again. I could not believe how I had not noticed this before, I knew Tommy missed Stan but I had failed to notice just how much he had withdrawn into his shell over the last few weeks. We used to be so close and could speak to each other about anything and I had let him down and vowed I would help him.

'Tommy what on earth has he done to you to give you these bruises? Has he punched you also?' I asked, my mind filled with images of the man pummelling my brother with his fists.

'No, the other day I thought he was going to strike me so I jumped out of the way, only I didn't notice the stack of crates and I fell down heavily on top of them.'

'Is that the truth?'

'Why would I lie about that when I have told you the rest?' Tommy reasoned.

By now we had arrived at the market square, I gently took Tommy in my arms and kissed him goodbye, a plan already forming. 'I will see you tonight, don't give him any reason to hit you and make sure you stay in sight of other people at all times.'

Tommy wiped the tears away and squared his shoulders as he approached the stall. The man who now employed him hadn't arrived yet and Tommy began to prepare the stall for the day. When Mr Stone appeared he looked at Tommy and seemed dissatisfied with his progress saying, 'Rafferty I thought I told you I wanted the stall set up by the time I got here, what have you been doing?' I watched as Tommy ran over to the barrow and began stacking the heavy boxes in front of the stall ready for Mr Stone to unpack, but as I continued to observe them Mr Stone walked to a small stool at the side of the wooden table and sat down, folded his arms and lit a pipe, leaving my brother to carry on with the manual labour. Occasionally he would move to speak to a prospective customer but mostly he just sat watching Tommy, his small beady eyes never leaving him.

I had to leave now or I would be late for the mill but as I hurried across town to meet up with the women a plan began to form in my mind. I promised Tommy I would say nothing to our father, but I never mentioned Mama, I could not leave him there another hour working for that bully.

I was a few minutes late and had to run to catch up with the others, 'Pamela wait,' I called out hoping to catch them before we got in view of the mill and possibly Mr Althorpe.

'Ah Millie, there you are, I began to think you weren't coming in today,' Pamela said as I eventually caught up with the group.

'I am not,' I replied.

'Are you ill?'

'No but I have some family business to attend to. Could you please tell Mr Althorpe that I am sick and won't be in today?'

'He won't be happy about it,' Pamela replied as she studied me trying to work out what could be wrong.

'I know but this is something that can't wait another minute, I will be back tomorrow and will work over if needed.'

'Well I know you wouldn't just skive off, so I will tell him for you. Good luck with whatever the problem is, see you in the morning.'

'Thank you Pamela,' I said and without delay and turned and ran all the way back to the house where I hoped to find my mother and brother before they set out to collect the day's laundry.

I ran past Mr Stone's stall keeping over to the other side of the square so Tommy would not see me and noticed that Tommy was nowhere to be seen. Mr Stone was still sitting on the stool smoking but there was no sign of my brother, so I stopped for a moment taking cover behind a large stone column. Eventually after about ten minutes wait Tommy appeared from the other side of the square pushing a heavily laden barrow piled high with boxes. As he neared the stall the barrow wheel hit a rut and the boxes spilled across the cobbles. Immediately Mr Stone leapt from his stool and strode across to my brother who was frantically trying to collect the crates before his employer got to him.

'You stupid Irish idiot,' he yelled, his face bright red with anger, 'can't you do even the easiest task I give you?' Within seconds he was at Tommy's side and he quickly glanced around him, as he did so Tommy ducked down and raised his hands to his head in order to protect himself from the blow he felt must surely be coming his way, but on this occasion he was spared as an elderly woman was approaching, basket in hand.

'Pick them up and be quick about it,' he said to Tommy, turning to the woman giving her an ingratiating smile.

Tommy scurried around and as much as I wanted to go and help him I knew I was best served carrying out my plan.

I rushed into the yard where Mama and Danny were preparing to leave for their daily round, as I ran towards them Mama looked concerned.

'Whatever is the matter child?' she asked, her forehead creased in worry, 'are you ill?'

'No Mama, it's Tommy.'

'Tommy is ill, where is he?'

'No he's not ill, it's worse than that.'

Mama clutched her hand to her chest, her face draining of all colour. 'What has happened, let me see him, where is he?'

Realising my mistake by not having chosen my words carefully enough I hastened to alleviate her worst fears. As I told her what Tommy had told me and the incidents I had witnessed she calmed down a little, but soon her anguish turned to anger. 'He has no business to treat anyone like that, especially my son. Your father must hear of his at once.'

She thought for a moment and then decided what must be done. 'Danny, I want you to take Millie round to all our customers for today and between you collect their laundry and bring it back here. Whilst you are gone I will go and find your father and tell him what has happened. I will be back here by the time you return.'

Danny and I hurried from place to place making the daily collections and I was surprised at how much Danny knew about the people he met at each house. He had obviously listened as the conversations between them and Mama were exchanged and was able to call them by their names and even occasionally ask about a subject that had obviously arisen previously. Everyone seemed very familiar with my brother, some expressing concern as to where our mother was. As we reassured them that all was well and that she was awaiting us back at home they smiled and wished us well.

When we returned Mama was indeed waiting for us.

'Did you find Papa?' I asked.

'Yes and I told him everything you said. He was all for going across there now and sorting the matter out, but I managed to persuade him to stay calm until tonight. We can't afford for him to lose his job over this.'

'But what about Tommy?' I cried, 'we can't leave him there another day.'

'No I agree that is why you are to help me with the laundry and Danny is to go and sit with Tommy at the stall. Danny go to the stall and say that I am not feeling well and you have come to spend the day with him in order to let me rest. Do not let him out of your sight so that that monster cannot lay another finger on him. Do you understand?'

'Yes Mama,' Danny replied nodding his head. 'What if he hits me?'

'He won't, this man is a coward and a bully and only dares to do things when no one is looking.' Mama reassured him.

With that Danny ran off on his mission to save his brother from any more beatings.

I would normally have enjoyed working alongside my mother; just the two of us together again as we used to be back home, but neither of us could stop worrying about Tommy. We worked hard all day to get the laundry washed, dried, ironed and returned to the customers by the end of the day. It was hard work, bending over the steaming tubs, pounding the washing and hanging it out, but I much preferred it to being cooped up in the cotton mill. I hoped it would not be much longer before Mama had enough work to sustain me as well. Finally with the last of the rounds completed we settled down to await my brother's return. Finally they arrived, Mama decided to wait to see if Tommy would tell her what had been going on lately but after about five minutes and he had said nothing she went over and sat next to him. 'Tommy your sister has told me how Mr Stone has been treating you.'

Tommy immediately looked at me, an expression of betrayal etched on his young face. Then he dropped his gaze once more, shaking his head he replied, 'she should not have done that, she promised me she wouldn't.'

'She was right to do so, and her promise to you as I understand it was she wouldn't tell your father and she didn't.'

Tommy looked up at Mama and asked, 'so he doesn't know?'

'Yes he does, I told him.'

'Why did you do that?' Tommy asked in a quiet voice.

'Because what that man is doing is wrong and we cannot stand by and let you be treated in this way by him. When your father gets home we will decide what must be done.'

When Papa returned from work he asked Danny and I to leave him and Mama to speak with Tommy privately for a while so we went and sat on the wall outside the lodging house.

'Did anything happen while you were at the market?' I asked my little brother.

'No, Tommy worked and Mr Stone sat on a stool or served the customers. He never spoke to either of us all day. Then he left to go home and I helped Tommy clear up and we came home.'

Sometime later Mama called us to go in and I helped her prepare the evening meal. Nothing was mentioned about what had been said or what had been decided. Conversation was a little strained and I noticed that Tommy was avoiding speaking to me altogether. This hurt me a great deal because not only had he felt he could not confide in me in the first instance he now blamed me for betraying his trust even though I only had his best interest at heart.

After supper Papa left the lodge for a while returning after around an hour, upon entering the room he nodded almost imperceptibly at Mama before sitting down to smoke his pipe.

The next morning we sat down to breakfast and it was then I found out that Tommy would not be returning to the stall. My parents had decided that he would stay home and help with the laundry work until another position could be found for him. Although his wage would be missed Mama was earning more than she had at the mill and so they could afford this in the short term. I was relieved for my brother but once again found myself thinking selfishly that any new customers she made would be going to support his wage and therefore I would be left at the mill forever. Immediately I felt a great sense of guilt that I should feel this way and only think of myself when my brother had been verbally and physically abused for weeks and said nothing.

As Papa and I left the house to go to work instead of leaving me at the corner to make his way to the dock he continued with me to the market square. Upon reaching the stall where Tommy worked he stopped and said goodbye to me telling me to carry on to the mill.

'What are you going to do Papa?' I asked.

'I am going to tell Mr Stone that Tommy has left and I will get his money he is owed for the days he has worked this week. Nothing more, now run along before you are late.'

'Papa please tell me I did the right thing by telling Mama.'

'Of course you did Millie, you should know better than to have to ask that. We look out for each other and always will.'

'Tommy hates me for it. He thinks I have betrayed him and he may be right.'

'Your brother is hurting right now, he feels foolish, let down by an adult who should know better and a little scared. This is the first time in his young life that he has experienced anything like this and he doesn't know how to handle it. He also feels in some way that he has let us down. He doesn't hate you; he knows you did it for him. Give him a little time and he will come round. You know Tommy has to get things straight in his mind so he can cope with it.'

'Thank you Papa,' I reached up and kissed his cheek before going to join the mill workers on the walk to the mill.

Daniel sat patiently waiting for his son's former employer to make an appearance, finally at ten past six he arrived, as he neared the stall and it registered on him that the lad was not there and nothing had been prepared for the day's trade he began to call out, 'Rafferty where the hell are you?' He rushed to the corner of the street where the store was situated expecting to see him coming with a loaded cart but the street was deserted. He went back to the empty stall and as he stood there trying to work out what had happened he noticed a stocky dark haired man of about forty watching him.

'Can I help you?' he asked of the man.

Daniel put on his best English accent he had picked up during his time spent working on the dock. 'No I doubt it,' the man replied, his bright blue eyes locked on to his. 'You don't seem to have anything to sell me.'

'No sir, you have caught me at a bad time, you see my lad normally sets the stall before I arrive in the morning, but today I can see no sign of him.'

It was obvious to Daniel that the man had no idea he was Tommy's father so he decided to play along with him and see if he could trip the man up about his treatment towards his eldest son.

'That's unfortunate for I was told your produce was the freshest to be found in town.'

'Of that I can assure you, if you wish to come back a little later I will have the stall set up and you will not be disappointed.'

'I am afraid I cannot return until late evening as I have work to occupy me all day, I came at this hour because I was told you would be open for trade.'

'I must again apologise to you, it is only due to the fact that I have been let down by my lad that you have me at a disadvantage.'

'Maybe the lad is ill, is he normally late?'

'No that is one thing I can rely on, he is punctual.'

'Then that can be the only answer, he is unwell and cannot get in today.'

'No I don't think that is the case, he has plenty of brothers and sisters, any one of them could have brought me a message. No I think he is playing tricks with me.'

'Why do you say that?'

'Well only yesterday one of his brothers turned up and sat with him all day long. He said their mother was unwell and needed to rest but I don't believe a word of it.'

'Why would he lie about something like that, what could he gain from it? And without trying to cause you any offence what child would rather spend a day sat here at this stall than being at home with his mother and siblings? And why was he the only one to attend if there are more of them?'

'I have no idea but he was a clear distraction to my lad, I had to keep an eye on the young one in case he stole anything.'

'It must have been trying for you, you can be grateful the rest of the family stayed away. How many brothers and sisters does your lad have?'

'I have no idea, but they are Irish. You know that all the Irish have huge families, then when they had ruined their own country they came over here taking all our jobs and living like rats in sewers.'

It took Daniel all his time not to take the man by the throat and give him a beating. He knew nothing about his family and no right to judge them in this way, but he made his clenched fists relax and drawing a deep breath asked, 'what do you intend to do about it, will you dismiss him?'

'I don't know, you see I gave my word to my predecessor that I would employ the lad, he thought the world of him. I must admit he is normally reliable but I do have to watch him all the time. He is prone to being clumsy and talks to the customers as if he were on a par with them. He addresses them by name instead of title, most insubordinate I must say.'

Daniel had heard enough, he decided it was time to reveal his identity but before he could do so the man added. 'I will make sure he understands that he is lucky to have this job and that he doesn't take advantage of me again.'

Daniel could not resist one last question,' how do you intend to teach him that lesson?'

'There are ways believe me sir, ways that he understands. It won't be the first time I have had to resort to such methods but a little rod never hurt anyone.'

'You sound as if you know how to handle the boy.'

'Yes I do, if only his fornicating parents had the sense to do it, this country would be in a better state.'

Daniel covered the distance between them in an instance and was suddenly standing toe to toe with the man, he was shorter than the other man by about three inches but he looked him in the eye, and snarled, all trace of the affected accent vanished, 'that is my family you are talking about, and the boy you are happy to beat is my eldest son Tommy, who incidentally will not be working for you ever again. Just so you have all your facts straight so that when you tell folk about how the Irish have ruined your precious business, there are five of us, myself, my wife, one daughter and two sons, all of whom are earning a wage and we live in a lodging house and pay rent on time. We only came to your beloved country because if we didn't we would surely have starved and that was through no fault of the common people, it was due to crop failure and the fact that the English continued to buy our crops at a price no Irish man could afford and so compounded the disaster.'

'You have tricked me,' Mr Stone whimpered.

'That may be but it is nothing to what I would like to do to you, now take notice of my son's leaving and pay me his wages to date.'

Mr Stone stepped back a pace and pulled at the front of his jacket as he found the courage to reply, 'the boy gets paid on Saturday, if he is not here to collect he will forfeit them.'

Daniel once again invaded the man's personal space and having backed him into the stall table he had nowhere further to retreat to. 'My son will never come near this place again unless Stan returns so you will pay me his money now or I swear you will regret it. I am not normally a violent man but I am willing to make an exception in your case.'

Mr Stone knew he was beaten and so handed over the money for Tommy's three day's work.

As Daniel turned to leave he looked back at the man and said,' if I hear that you have spoken of my family to anyone the way you have just done to me I swear I will come back and you will regret it. Do I make myself clear?'

The man nodded and Daniel made his way to the docks. When he confirmed his attendance to the foreman he was asked,' Did you sort that bully out Daniel?'

'Yes I believe I did, thank you for letting me deal with it this morning, I will make up my time.'

'You are only ten minutes late Daniel, I will show your time as right. If I can't help a man protect his family I am no better than that stall trader.'

Chapter 33

Between us we were now earning nineteen shillings per week, Mama was paying Tommy six pence each week for his help with the laundry but this was coming from her share of twelve shillings. Our rent in the shared room was four pence each week and our food bill was now ten shillings and ten pence. For that we had fruit, vegetables, butter, milk and bread each day, this was a better variety of food than we ever had whilst back in Ireland, there our diet comprised mainly of potatoes in some form each meal, we only had fruit if we found any in the hedgerows as any crops were sold to England by the landowners. As a result of this healthier diet we were all growing fitter and stronger, my parents and brothers were sporting better complexions due to their physical work outside daily, and only I remained pasty looking because of the work in the cotton mill. The effects of the approaching winter were starting to show themselves a little more each day, mornings and nights were darker for a while longer each day and there was a noticeable dip in the temperature.

One night as we sat in the room we shared in the lodging house Mama spoke in a quiet voice for fear of being overheard by the others in the vicinity, 'Daniel I have been thinking it is time we moved out of this shared room into a single room in a lodge similar to the room Stan and Susan had. We have about eight shillings left over each week and I have been saving this in case anything happens which would mean one of us can't work, but things seem to have settled down and I feel the time is right.'

'Well you are right in that respect, it is far too cramped in here with all the other families and we have no time to ourselves. I know the children get restless and to have a space we did not have to share would be heaven. Are you sure we can afford it?'

'If we can find one for about six shillings a week we would still have a little leftover to use towards the fire and oil for the lamps,' she said in a whisper not wishing to alert anyone to the fact we had savings and a comfortable wage.

'Do you have anywhere in mind?' Papa asked.

'At a matter of fact yes I do, there is a place we pass each day to collect laundry with a notice in the window, it also has a patch of ground at the side of the house where the children could let off steam in the good weather.'

'Well then,' Papa said, 'see if it is still available and secure it tomorrow.'
'Don't you want to see it first?' Mama asked him.
'I trust your judgement; you have never let me down in all the years I have been married to you.'
Mama leant over and kissed him on the cheek, 'Thank you darling.'
I couldn't believe it, finally we were to move out of this cramped room into one of our own, I pictured in my mind Stan and Susan's room on last Christmas day and I grew quite excited. A place where we could once more be a family in the true sense of the word, talking over the evening meal, laughing, being able to come and go as we pleased without having to consider the needs of the others who lived there with us. My brothers showed their enthusiasm for the idea by chattering nonstop making plans for building dens, tree ropes and other sources of entertainment on the ground outside the house. I could not wait and wished I did not have to go to work tomorrow and have to wait until I returned home around half past six to discover whether Mama had been successful.
The following evening I was finally walking home from the mill with the other women wishing they would stop talking and walk a little faster. At last I was alone and I ran the remaining distance and burst into the room. With no thought for any of the other families I cried out, 'Mama what happened?'
Mama smiled in a way I had not seen in a long time and opened her arms wide for me, I ran over and let myself be enveloped in her warm embrace, she pushed me to arms length so she could look into my eyes as she said, 'We have given a weeks' notice here, paid a deposit on the room and a week on Sunday we move to our own room.'
Papa joined us in the embrace and my brothers leapt up and down squealing with delight, I began to weep with joy, I felt as if all we had endured since leaving our home had been worth it. We were to move into a room of our own and we were all earning money, we were healthy and at that moment very happy. The next week seemed to drag by but eventually the day came and we made our way across town to our new home, it was a medium sized room with a fireplace and a stove in one corner, there were two beds pushed in the opposite corner, and a table with six chairs in the centre. The door had a lock to it, something which was lacking in the other place and looking out of the window which faced another row of houses across a narrow cobbled alley I found if I stood on my tiptoes and tilted my head to the side I could see the grassy patch of ground at the end of the row of houses which held so much promise for my brothers. This was the last week in November and I could not wait to

decorate the room the way Susan had done that day last year, I wished our friends could be here to share our new found fortune with us but there had been no word from them since their departure earlier in the year.

Chapter 34

Christmas 1848

Once again we all had two days off work together, Christmas Eve, my fourteenth birthday fell on a Sunday and therefore the work places closed on Saturday evening not reopening until Tuesday. My brothers and I had spent the week leading up to the big event scouring the hedgerows on the outskirts of town for holly and mistletoe with which to decorate the room as befitted our memories of the spectacle we were treated to last year. The room looked resplendent in its red, white and green foliage, Papa had managed to weave some of the branches into a wreath which we hung proudly on the outside of the door. Mama had continued saving each week and had secured a magnificent goose for the celebratory dinner and the smell it gave off as it slowly cooked was delicious, she had roasted some vegetables in the fat and had a pudding steaming on the fire. Papa had spent hours carving a small hand cart in secret for Danny and Tommy to share to use in the collection of the laundry, it was to be their pride and joy, although in truth Danny only pushed it when it was empty, he left the manhandling with a full cart to his elder brother. I received a fine hand stitched shawl Mama had made; it was so warm I couldn't wait to use it on the long walks to the mill.

Just last week though Mama had developed a cough, similar to the one she had protracted whilst at the mill, towards the end of the week. It was not as debilitating but she did worry she would have to take some days off in order to rid herself of it, but after having a day off on the Sunday and resting she was alright to continue the next week. Once again though towards the end of the week she began with an irritating cough which began to worry both Papa and me. I happened to mention this one morning as we were all walking to the mill and Pamela said, 'I know what it is, it will be the same cough she developed at the mill, that is due to the dry humid conditions we are forced to work in. Lots of women get it, some get better, some never return to work.'

'But Mama left a long time ago, why is she still suffering?' I asked not seeing the connection until Pamela pointed it out to me.

'It's the laundry work; she is working in a steamy environment all day, with the washing and the ironing. Now with the cold weather it has triggered it again, with you also saying she is worse at the end of the week and improved after not working on a Sunday I can't see it being anything other than that.'

'What ever are we to do about it?' I worried. 'We can't afford to lose that money; it's the thing that is paying for our room.' Once again I thought just as things seemed to be turning in our favour something came along to try us. I considered whether to tell Papa of this but decided I would watch her to see if it did indeed follow the pattern Pamela had suggested and if so tell him then. With Christmas at the end of the week I felt I could not unduly worry my family if it proved to be a false alarm.

After our sumptuous dinner we all walked through the snow covered streets to the park, it was so beautiful. The grass was covered in a deep white blanket of snow; the branches of the bare trees were covered with the fall overnight and were weighed down with the white powder. The lake was frozen over and the ducks were sliding around on the surface, children were indulging in snowball fights and Danny and Tommy were quick to become involved, their squeals carrying across the chilly air. I pulled my shawl tightly around my shoulders and watched as my parents walked ahead of me, Papa with Mama's arm linked through his as they stood laughing at the antics of the snow fighting warriors. All too soon it was time to return to the warmth and comfort of our room to spend the evening playing parlour games. Some of the houses we passed on the way home had their window curtains open and we could see into their lit rooms, they were nearly all decorated but some had a small tree in the corner of the room decorated with bows and candles. They looked magnificent, this was something that Queen Victoria's husband Albert had introduced to this country, as were most of the Christmas celebrations the country now enjoyed and we vowed next year we would also acquire our own tree.

Chapter 35

I continued to monitor Mama's health and it did in fact turn out that the cough became worse towards the end of the working week and subsided a little after having each Sunday off, I told Papa about this and I knew he was concerned. Although it had not yet reached the severity of the first time she was ill the fact that it was continually present was worrying. As usual Mama did not complain and if she had made the connection to the conditions she was working under doing the laundry day after day she never voiced it.

The snow we had received at Christmas was still with us and as we approached Mama's birthday towards the end of January the country was still wrapped in a white cloak. Although nice to behold from behind a window, once outside the ankle deep snow clawed at your legs making the walk to the mill more tiring than normal, the chill wind biting at any uncovered part of the face, eyes filling with tears and nose red and unfeeling. The relief at arriving inside the mill was short lived as the excruciating pain when the feeling began to return to our extremities had to be withstood.

That morning when I arrived for work Mr Althorpe called me over, 'Miss Rafferty come here.'

I looked at Pamela and wondered what I could have done wrong, she just shrugged and so I walked over to where he stood at his desk near the door.

'Yes Mr Althorpe,' I stammered.

'Miss Rafferty,' he said looking down at me over the spectacles he had taken to wearing recently,' I have been speaking with my brother who works for Mr Edwards up at the big house as a gardener.'

'Sir?' I said not quite understanding why he was telling me this. I knew nothing of his brother or of Mr Edwards.

'He told me yesterday that they are looking to employ a new domestic and wondered if I knew of any young girl who might be interested in the position. I thought of you as you are a hard working lass and I know your family could do with the money.'

'Why are you asking me and not any of the other women, they all need extra money sir?'

'Because the position requires the person to live in and all these ladies have families to care for and would not be able to do so. It pays well and whilst you live there you are provided with your meals also.'

'Oh sir I would have to speak to my parents about this.' I answered.

'Well hurry and do so, they wish to have the position filled as soon as possible, the girl who was there has left with no notice.'

'I will speak with them this evening and tell you of their decision in the morning if that is convenient sir.'

'Very well, now to work Rafferty.'

All day I could think of nothing else, I had no idea how much the position paid or what was expected of me but the thought of being able to leave this place made the job sound appealing. The thought of leaving my family however frightened me somewhat.

When I arrived home I found that Mama had taken to her bed and Papa said that she had fainted in the day and had a slight fever, her cough had also worsened and he was upset in case she was taken as badly as before. I set about making the evening meal, made some broth for my mother and decided to say nothing about the offer I had been made; my family needed me at home. How could they manage if Mama was ill for any length of time and I was living away?

So the next day after having made sure Mama was comfortable and that my brothers would be alright with the laundry details I set off for the mill and told Mr Althorpe that I was very grateful to him for thinking of me but I could not accept the position as I was needed at home.

'Very well, I hope you don't live to regret your decision,' he said. And that was the end of the matter.

When I arrived home that evening Mama was still in bed, she was awake but any sudden movements caused her to begin coughing so she had not been able to assist the boys with the washing at all. They had tried their best but there were still some items waiting to be washed and those that were washed and dried had still to be ironed before being returned in exchange for payment. Papa looked relieved when I walked in, 'Millie, can you give us a hand please. This all needs to be completed this evening ready for return tomorrow morning. The lads have done their best but some of the things are just too large for them to handle on their own.'

'Of course I will, firstly let me set the supper going so we will have a meal ready when we are finished.'

It was half past eleven by the time everything was finished and Papa and I sat down to our meal. Mama was asleep with my brothers alongside her, she had insisted on coming out to help us once she knew what was going on but another spasm had put paid to that. And so that was how the next four days were spent, Papa and I went to our day work and assisted the boys with the laundry upon our return. I had never felt so tired in my life, up at five each morning, the walk to and from work, twelve hours at the mill and then home to prepare the meal and sort the washing, I was getting about five hours sleep a night if I was lucky but the main thing was we managed to keep all Mama's regular customers satisfied and so guarantee the business would still be there upon her return. On Sunday she got up and declared herself fit again, my parents had allowed me to sleep in late and they woke me an hour before our lunch. Although I ate my lunch and went for a walk to the park with my family I could not shake off the feeling of lethargy that had seeped in to my body and found myself nodding off to sleep again after tea at which time Mama said, 'Millie go to bed child, you have done enough and it's time you got some rest.'

I didn't give any argument and fell onto the bed fully dressed and slept for twelve hours.

Things improved as the weather got better and Mama's bouts of illness grew less and by the time May was upon us she was fully fit and the coughs had disappeared. Her and Papa were discussing this one evening and had come to the conclusion it was something to do with the combination of the cold weather and the steamy humid conditions of the laundry work. They were trying to think of a way in which she could continue with the business without sacrificing her health each winter, but try as we may we could not come up with a satisfactory solution.

Chapter 36

June 1849

It was fast approaching Tommy's eleventh birthday and it being Sunday we were all in the local park enjoying an early summers day, the sun was out but there was a cool breeze which was blowing in off the sea and made me glad I had brought my shawl with me. Danny was skimming stones across the surface of the lake and my parents were sat on a bench talking. They did not have much time where they could just indulge in each other's company with the pressures of working and caring for us, so I tried to make sure I kept my brothers occupied in the park so they could have some time to be together and discuss things they may not wish to in front of us.

Tommy had long since forgiven me for speaking to my parents about the bullying he was receiving at the hands of Mr Stone and had admitted he would have done the same if things were reversed so I was not surprised when he whispered to me, 'Millie can I speak with you?'

'Of course,' I replied.

'This is between you and me though,' he stated.

'You know you can trust me, what is troubling you?'

'It's working with Mama on the laundry, I know this will sound ungrateful as she helped me when I left the market stall, but I hate it. I am going to be eleven in a few days and I want to be doing man's work not washing other people's sheets and things. That is not the way it should be.'

I looked at my brother and realised he was right, men do not wash and iron and if we were still back in Ireland he would be working on the farm with Papa and the others.

'I don't mean that in a bad way and it's alright for Danny, he would enjoy anything that kept him close to Mama and Papa. He has always been that way, he is go gentle natured and when we were back home he wanted to grow up and tend animals rather than work the land. He is not lazy I don't mean that, it's just that being the youngest he is more suited to it than I am.'

'Yes I understand what you mean, what do you intend to do about it?' I asked.

'I don't know what to do, I don't want to upset Mama but I can't carry on like this, I have to find something else. I loved working with Stan, it was hard work but we had a good time and he treated me like a man. Mama sees me as her son and always will do. Does that sound ungrateful, for I don't mean to be?'

'No Tommy it sounds perfectly natural.'

'Do you have any ideas what I should do?'

'Well I think the best thing is to be honest and tell them how you feel, our parents have brought us up to be so and I know they will understand your feelings.'

'Yes you are right but I am also worried about leaving Mama shorthanded and what if I can't find some other job, and then we will be short of money.'

'Look just tell them this evening, they will come up with something I know.'

'Thanks Millie, I knew you would set me straight.'

So that evening after supper Tommy told them how he felt. As I predicted my parents were understanding and Mama said, 'I should have thought about it sooner, do you have any idea what you want to do?'

'No I don't, Papa is there anything at the docks?' Tommy asked hopefully. I knew he would love to be working alongside our father once again.

'I don't think so lad, but I will ask tomorrow.'

Mama took a small notebook from the drawer and began to study the figures on the pages. She then took up a pencil and began to make some calculations, after a few minutes she looked up and said, 'Right I have made some workings out and I can say that if Tommy left the laundry and Millie were to take his place, we could manage. The money we would lose from the mill and the sixpence from Tommy means we would have to cut back on the food a little each week but we could keep the room. I manage to save one shilling and eight pence each week at the moment, so if we had to we could use a little of that to help but I would rather not if we can help it in case we need it in the future. What does everyone think to that?'

Papa spoke first, 'Maria I know you would rather not touch our savings but I feel that if we need to for a week or so we should do so, the money is intended for just such a situation as this isn't it? I don't wish to have our family going hungry again, not after all we have been through and how hard working everyone has been. Tommy is a good strong hard working lad and I am sure it won't be long before he finds a new position.'

'Children, what do you say?' Mama asked us.

Tommy and Danny answered immediately that they were in favour of Papa's plan. I had to be asked again by Mama what I thought as I was already dreaming of a life without working in the hot humid conditions of the mill breathing in the fetid cotton laden air.

'Millie, what do you say?' she asked again.

'I agree with the others Mama,' I answered trying to contain my excitement.

'Very well, Tommy can you continue to help me for one further week before you leave?'

'Yes Mama of course.'

'Daniel, you ask tomorrow if there is anything at the docks or if anyone knows of anything. Millie you give Mr Althorpe one week's notice, he has been good to us as a family and God forbid we will ever need to go back there but it is always best to leave on good terms.'

And so that was decided. The next day the walk to the mill was so different to the usual one, I felt as if I were walking on air knowing that after six days I would be free of this place. I would miss the company of the ladies but I could not wait to be working alongside Mama once more, I had missed our time together more than I had realised until now.

Mr Althorpe was very understanding and said he had valued me as a worker, he said I was hard working and honest. On the Saturday as he handed me my final pay he said to me, 'I wish your family well, you seem a decent lot, you would have fitted in well at Mr Edwards house but still you never know maybe another time when you are older.'

I kissed the women goodbye and Pamela wiped a tear from her cheek as she hugged me one last time.

Chapter 37

So at last I was free from the noisy, hot, bone rattling environment of the cotton mill, I could hardly contain my excitement that evening and the following day. It was Sunday but our normal walk to the park after dinner had to be cancelled as the heavens had opened and it had been pouring with rain since first light, the water running in rivers down the window glass. Around three in the afternoon a huge thunderstorm rolled in, the lightning flashes lighting the dark grey sky, and the claps of thunder overhead rattled the window panes. Danny rushed to the window, his face and hands pressed against the glass until Mama pulled him away warning, 'you will be struck if you stand there.'

Danny was fascinated by the natural world and I knew that given a chance he would be outside watching the storm and relishing the force of the wind as it bashed at his small body.

Tommy was interested in manual work, he was happiest when he could work alongside Papa on the farm and would wish for nothing more than to secure a place at the docks.

I always imagined I would marry the boy from the next cottier to us when we were back in Ireland. He was two years older than me and his name was Andrew, he had deep brown eyes and a head of wavy black hair. We used to see one another each Sunday on the way to chapel and I had always liked him, he used to smile at me as I walked with my family and when we sat in the chapel his family were in the pews across the aisle from ours and I would catch him looking at me during the service. I once met him in the town when I had gone in with Papa to sell a goose that we had, we just said hello and smiled but I believed that it was going to lead to more eventually. I wondered what he was doing now, whether he was still in Ireland and if so had he survived the famine, if not where was he, was he in England or further afield?. Still there was no time to think about the past, as Papa used to say, you cannot change the past but you can change the future by the things you do now. I vowed I would do more than just help Mama with the laundry, I would help her expand the business and therefore help our family to enjoy a better quality of life, and it was time I made my mark.

On the Monday I rose early, I was so excited to be helping Mama once again, I helped her prepare Papa's lunch before making the family breakfast. Papa had not managed to find any work for Tommy at the docks but was assured by the foreman that if a suitable position arose he would be first in line for it.

'I think we have been accepted around here that we are hard working honest folk,' Papa said, 'and that counts for a lot. The Rafferty name was respected back home and I am glad it appears to have continued here.'

Tommy was naturally disappointed not to be going to work with Papa but said, 'I managed to find a position for myself before and I shall do so again. I would still be there if it wasn't for that bully!'

'Now Tommy,' Mama said, 'don't go getting all upset about that again, it's past and done with.'

'Sorry, but I did so like working there and I do miss Stan.'

'We all do, but things will work out, you'll see.'

Papa and Tommy left and after clearing away, Mama, Danny and I went to collect the day's laundry. It was a cool day despite the month and so the first day I spent toiling over the steaming tubs was bearable, but the work was hard. By the end of the day my back ached from bending over and pummelling the clothes with the dolly and the muscles in my arms and shoulders were stiff and sore. I knew it was only a matter of time before my body adapted to this new regime but I was glad when the day was done. I had thoroughly enjoyed myself in spite of the hard work, being able to talk to Mama as we had done before was comforting and I realised how much I had missed it. Danny was around all the time but he wasn't at all interested in our conversations, he being quite content to scrub the clothes on the boards, quietly humming to himself, scanning the skies for birds and butterflies. He got quite excited when a large bumble bee landed on a bush nearby and forgot his chores and spent a good five minutes following it as it flitted from blossom to blossom in search of pollen.

'Is Danny always like this?' I asked Mama.

'Yes I am afraid so, you know what he was like back in Ireland, there was always something with more legs than us that attracted his attention. I can't say how pleased I am to have you back here with me, I know how bad the mill work was for you and I just wish it hadn't had to be so long.'

'Mama, don't worry about it, we both worked there but it is behind us now. I wonder how Tommy is getting on, do you think that the fact he is not back yet is a good sign?'

'I hope so, I know he felt obliged to help me but I know he hated the work.'

Tommy had walked into town and was gradually working his way to the centre, enquiring at each place he came to for work; so far he had found nothing. Finally he came to the market square where he had worked the stall previously. He made sure to start at the furthest end from Mr Stone's stall and approached the holders one by one, at his third stall which sold fresh fish, crabs and all varieties of shelled produce, the owner stared at him for a while before saying,' Aren't you the lad who used to work for Stan?'

'Yes sir, Tommy Rafferty.'

'You left shortly after he did, didn't you?'

'Yes sir, I did.'

'Why was that then?'

Tommy did not know what to say, he didn't want to tell the truth about the man who had abused him but neither did he want the man to think he would just walk out on a job.

The man sensed that there was something the boy was reluctant to tell him but decided not to push him on the matter. 'So what are you doing now?'

'Well I had been helping my Mama with her work but my sister has taken over that and I am now seeking another position sir.'

'Really, what do you know about fish lad?'

'I don't know anything; I've never eaten any sir.'

'What, how could you get to your age and never have eaten fish? How old are you?'

'Eleven sir.'

'Well, I liked Stan and I know you got on well with him, he actually spoke well of you. Between you and me I have no time for Mr Stone, there is just something about the man I can't warm to and he can't seem to keep any of the lads who work for him. He says he has to fire them because they are lazy or stealing but it seems a bit rum that every one of them is bad. Too much of a coincidence if you ask me. Look I have been thinking about getting a lad to help me, I can manage on my own but sometimes it would be good to have someone to run errands and such. I can't offer you a permanent position but I can give you a trial on an ad hoc basis and pay you when you work.'

'That's kind of you sir, but I really need some guaranteed work. I am honest and hard working, but I am worried that if I came here and spent all day here but you didn't need me I will have wasted an opportunity.'

'Well ok, good luck with your search Tommy.'

'Thank you sir.'

Tommy walked off and sat on the wall at the edge of the square, his feet kicking back and forth on the brickwork. As he watched the crowds milling around the stalls he noticed a group of four boys leaning against the wall at the far corner. They appeared to be about twelve or thirteen and were dressed in ragged trousers with dirty shirts and flat caps which were pulled down low on their foreheads. They too were busy watching the crowds and after about ten minutes when a tall elderly man passed them they lazily pushed themselves from the wall and slowly walked behind him. Then one of the boys set off running followed a few seconds later by a second, once past the man the second boy caught up with the first and grabbing him by the coat tail pulled him to the ground where they began to wrestle each other. The elderly man stopped and watched as did the rest of the crowd as the fight ensued, then the second two rushed forwards to stop the fight pushing against the man as they past. 'Sorry sir,' one called out as the other lifted the man's wallet from his coat pocket. The fight was stopped and the four boys ran off, Tommy could not believe what he had just witnessed. He had no idea what to do, he thought about pursuing the gang but they were bigger than him and there were four of them, also they had a head start and he had no idea where they may be. Instead he decided on the only course of action left to him, jumping off the wall he ran over to the elderly man. 'Excuse me sir,' he began.

'Yes lad,' the man stopped and looked at him.

'Those boys who just bumped into you, I think they may have taken your wallet.'

The man immediately felt inside his coat pocket, then began frantically patting each pocket in turn, his face turning pale as he came up empty handed. 'Oh my you are right, my wallet has gone. Do you know them, where did they go, what did they look like?'

'No sir, I have never seen them before, they ran round that corner but that's all I can tell you.'

'I must find a policeman, thank you lad.' The man hurried off in search of an officer and Tommy was left alone once more.

Curiosity got the better of him and he made the way across the square and turned the corner into the street the boys had run down earlier, there were a number of alleyways leading off the main walkway and Tommy cast an eye down each one as he passed hoping to catch sight of the thieves. He saw no-one but as he glanced down the last one on his right he noticed something lying on the ground at the end of the alley. He approached cautiously in case the boys were still around, but the alley was deserted apart from the brown leather wallet lying in the dust, Tommy picked it up and noticed it was empty, brushing the dust away from the soft leather he began to walk back to the square hoping to see the owner in order to return his property. He spotted the man talking to the police officer, his face bright red and his arms flailing around wildly as he described the assault and robbery. The policeman was trying to calm the man down and as Tommy drew near he heard the officer say, 'Sir, could you describe these boys to me?'

'No I didn't really see them, they were past me so fast, if it hadn't been for the young lad I was telling you about I wouldn't have even known I had been robbed until later.'

'Was the young lad with them?'

'No I wouldn't think so or he wouldn't have bothered to tell me about it would he?' was the irritated reply.

'How many did you say there were?'

'I don't know that either, five or six maybe,' he hesitated.

Tommy had never had dealings with the police before and was alarmed to hear that he was suspected of being involved in the crime, he had been determined to return the wallet but now was scared to do so. He stopped and weighed up his options, return the wallet and maybe be arrested by the officer or walk away and throw the wallet back where he had found it. He had just made up his mind on the latter course of action when the elderly man saw him, pointing he cried out, 'that's the lad officer, the one who warned me of the theft.'

The police officer turned and cast his gaze upon Tommy, 'is that right young man, did you see what happened to this gentleman earlier?'

Tommy froze on the spot, his mouth and throat turned to dust and he could feel the colour rising in his cheeks as he nodded and whispered, 'Yes sir.'

'Speak up lad,' continued the officer walking closer to where Tommy stood.

Tommy coughed and took a deep swallow in an effort to find his failing voice, 'yes sir, I saw the robbery. I have also found the wallet although it is empty.' Tommy held his arm out towards the elderly man proffering the wallet.

'My my lad,' the man said,' where did you find it?'

'In an alley off the street where the boys ran after they robbed you.'

The policeman moved to within a few inches of Tommy and bending down so his face was on a level with the boy asked, 'how did you know where to look?'

'I saw which way they ran and just went round there to see if I could see them anywhere but they were not around.'

'Good work son, can you show me where you found it?'

'Yes sir, come with me.' Tommy led the police officer to the place where the wallet had been lying and after the officer had examined the area he declared, 'yes it is clear by the tracks in the dust that at least three people have been down here and left the same way. I expect they came here to share out their ill gotten gains and then threw the wallet away as it held no more interest for them. Well boy I need you to give me your name and tell me everything you can remember about the incident and with as much description of the boys as you can.'

Tommy told his tale and by closing his eyes managed to give a very good description of all involved, he was rewarded with praise from the officer for his observational skills. Tommy was about to leave to head home for the day when the officer called him back, 'Tommy, are you going to be back in the square tomorrow?'

'I expect so; I am trying to find some employment.'

'Well do me a favour would you?' he said, 'if you see those boys again please come and find me and let me know, I will be on this beat again all week.'

'Yes sir I will,' with that Tommy turned for home.

When my brother walked in the door I found it hard to determine if he had been successful or not in his quest for work, he looked slightly crest fallen but his eyes shone with an energy I hadn't seen before. As we sat around the table eating supper, Tommy told us of his adventure, I understood the reason behind his mixed emotions, he was disappointed to miss out on work but excited to have witnessed a crime, helped the police and been asked to further assist if possible.

Chapter 38

Tommy woke me early as he was attempting to get dressed quietly ready to walk to the market square to see if he could find the little gang of thieves and help in bringing them to justice. As we lay in bed last night he could talk of nothing else and I think even Danny eventually tired of listening to his older brother's tale.

'Are you going in already?' I asked as he pulled his jacket over his shirt and slapped his cap on his head.

'Yes, I need to get in a good position before they get there.'

'But surely they won't be there this early; there won't be anybody there to rob. They will need to wait for the crowds to build up.'

'They will be there, its easy money for them and I intend to help catch them. The policeman was very pleased with how much I could remember about them.'

'I know, you said so yesterday but surely you can wait for breakfast, you don't know how long you will be gone.'

'Sorry Millie, but I am going now.' With that he quietly opened and closed the room door behind him and was gone. I hoped he would be successful in his mission and laid back down pulling the covers about my shoulders and drifted back to sleep.

Before I knew it, it was time for us all to rise and begin another working day. I explained to my parents where my brother had gone to so early and why.

'He must be really keen if he couldn't wait for his breakfast,' Papa stated.

Soon enough it was time to take to the streets delivering yesterday's laundry and collecting the loads to be dealt with today. We had plenty to keep us busy for the rest of the day but as we were passing one of the larger houses set back from the main street a small girl of about ten called out to us.

'Are you Rafferty's laundry service?'

'Yes dear,' Mama answered. 'Can we help you?'

'The housekeeper sent me to find you, she has been told about you from her friend who works in the mill. She says you are very good and Mrs Jackson had to let the other people go as they weren't very good and last week they lost the master's best shirts. Mrs Jackson says can you go and see her today about taking our work.'

'Of course, I can come with you now, if that's convenient.' Mama told the girl.

'Yes please follow me.'

Mama turned to Danny and me saying, 'Take this load back and start working on it and I will join you as soon as I have spoken to the housekeeper.'

Danny and I wished Mama good luck in securing more business and made our way home to begin the washing. After about an hour Mama walked into the back yard where Danny was stirring the soda flakes into a large tub of boiling water and I was pegging the first of the linen on the line.

'How did you get on?' I asked.

'Very well, 'she said with a smile, 'in fact better than very well. Mrs Jackson wants us to take on all their washing, linen, clothes, everything. They have about three loads a week.'

'That's fantastic Mama,' I said. 'Did you say yes?'

'Of course I did, it's going to mean a lot more work but I know we can manage. Also it will bring in another six shillings each week. I can't wait to tell your father tonight.'

Tommy had been sitting on the wall in the corner of the square for about two hours and he could no longer feel his backside, but he daren't move in case his quarry spotted him and were scared off. So far there had been no sign of the boys despite the fact that the square was now quite busy, neither had he seen the officer from yesterday. He decided to give it another hour before giving up and was beginning to wish he had listened to his sister and had some breakfast before he left home. He looked around the square and his gaze fell on the fruit stall where he had spent happier times with Stan. As he watched, Mr Stone appeared from the back of the table and hefted a large wooden box onto the front of a barrow, he then wheeled this round and began to take the shiny apples from the box and polish them on the tail of his shirt before stacking for sale. He emptied the box and wiped his brow on the back of his shirt sleeve before pushing the barrow around the back once more, picking another box and repeating the process with a box of oranges. Tommy continued to watch enjoying the man's clear discomfort at the manual task he was performing, it was then that Tommy realised there was no sign of an assistant to help him. A woman stopped and bought some potatoes, exchanging a few words before walking away to the baker's stall, as Mr Stone returned to his chores. By now Tommy was bored and sore from sitting on the stone wall for so long and jumping down, stretching his back he walked casually past his former employer. He drew level with the display just at the moment that Mr Stone stooped to collect a stray piece of paper that had dropped on the floor, as he stood up he came face to face with the boy.

Tommy momentarily froze, at once transported back to the days he had worked for him.

'Rafferty,' Mr Stone said as he recognised him. 'What are you doing here, looking for work eh?'

'No sir,' Tommy stammered. 'Well yes sir but not here.'

'If you are looking for work, I have a position.'

'I don't think I want to work for you again thank you,' Tommy said finding his voice.

Mr Stone looked down at the boy and lowering his voice said, 'I was wrong to treat you the way I did. I realise now that Stan was right, you were a good worker. I have struggled to replace you since you left. Would you consider coming back to work for me?'

'I don't think I wish to and even if I did I am sure my Papa would have something to say about it.'

'I was not myself before and I am embarrassed and ashamed at my behaviour. Would you at least speak to your father and see what he thinks?'

Tommy looked at the man and was sure he had aged in the few months since he last saw him, he actually felt sorry for him and left promising to do as the man had requested. With one last circuit of the square completed looking for his quarry, he headed for home and a meal.

Mama and I were loading the sheets from yesterday onto the cart ready for delivery when Tommy returned. For once I could not read him, he went and sat on the stone wall that surrounded the yard where we worked, and watched as Danny pounded the dirt out of a shirt collar.

'Did you find the gang?' I asked for want of anything else to say.

'No, there was no sign of them,' Tommy answered.

'Well maybe you will have better luck tomorrow,' I replied.

Tommy raised his eyes to me and with a slight incline of his head signalled he wanted to speak to me without danger of Mama hearing us.

I told Mama I was going to fetch more soap and walked indoors to our room, I knew by the way she nodded at me that she knew where we were really going, but she had always understood that sometimes we needed to confide in each other before voicing our concerns to our parents. She also knew that any major problem would be encouraged to be discussed with them and so had no issues with it. Since being small children in

Ireland we had formed a strong bond that few brothers and sisters we knew had managed to maintain into their teenage years.

We seated ourselves on the hard wooden chairs each nursing a glass of water and Tommy told me of his encounter with Mr Stone. I waited until he had finished before asking, 'what are you thinking of doing?'

'I don't know, I loved working there when Stan owned it but Mr Stone was a bully and I used to feel so frightened each day wondering what he might do to me that I was relieved when you told Papa about it and he made me leave.'

'Do you want to go back?'

'Part of me does and part of me is scared.'

'Do you think he may have changed?'

'Yes I do, he looks so different to the man who I worked for before.'

'In what way?'

'I don't know,' he hesitated,' he just looks older and tired. He says he wasn't himself before, although I don't know what he means by that.'

'Well if you think you want to go back then you should talk to Mama and Papa, if you don't then just forget about it and say nothing. Only you know how you feel but I think you want to give him another chance.'

Tommy nodded and the conversation was at an end, I rinsed my glass and went back to my duties. Mama smiled at me as I joined her in hanging out the sheets to dry, she knew if it were important she would know soon enough.

Tommy waited until supper was finished before telling our parents of the conversation he had had with Mr Stone. Mama looked at Tommy before saying, 'Son are you sure you want to consider this after the way he treated you?'

Tommy nodded and looked at me for support.

'Tommy thinks that the man was not himself earlier for whatever reason and feels he may be different in the future,' I said.

It was Papa's turn to voice his concerns, 'that's as maybe but there must be a reason why the man cannot keep any workers, and why he is so desperate for you to return.'

'It could be because I was a good worker, better than any of the others,' Tommy snapped.

'Or it could be because none of the others stayed once they found out what he was like,' Papa said.

'What do you mean?' Tommy said.

Mama laid a hand on Papa's arm trying to warn him to think before he answered but it had no effect.

'I mean maybe the others weren't prepared to work for a man who beat them.'

Tommy jumped up and ran to the door, 'you are saying I am a coward and a disgrace to you.' With that he ran from the room slamming the door so hard behind him it rattled the crockery on the dresser.

Papa regretted his words as soon as he had said them but it was too late. I had never witnessed anything like this in our family before and it shocked me, I didn't know what to do. I knew I should not take sides but I knew my brother needed a friend and so without saying a word to anyone I wrapped my shawl around my shoulders and picking up Tommy's jacket went out in search of him.

Daniel immediately wished he could take back the words he had said to his eldest son, he didn't mean it the way it had been taken but he was fiercely protective of his family and could not bear to think of anyone taking advantage of their good nature and naivety. Life back in Ireland was so much simpler but here there were many more unscrupulous characters that would prey on the weak. He looked at Danny who was sitting watching his father with tears in his eyes; he had slipped a little off the pedestal that he usually occupied in the small boy's mind. That hurt as much as the storming out of Tommy, he turned to Maria and said, 'I didn't mean to hurt the lad; I just couldn't bear to see him return to the way he was. He was not the son we used to know when he worked for that man.'

Maria walked over and laid an arm around his shoulders, 'I know that, but he is a proud lad and he has been through a rough time lately. There was the loss of his best friend when Stan moved away, then the bullying by Mr Stone and even when he worked with me I knew he wasn't happy. I prolonged it longer than I should have because I enjoyed having him with me, knowing where he was and that he was safe, but he is a young man now and he needs to be independent from us. He would like nothing better than to be working at your side as he would have been if we were still home but that is not possible here and so he needs to be felt valued as someone who can help provide for his family. I feel that if he is prepared to give the man another chance that we should at least hear him out, after all it was him and not us who suffered at the man's hands.'

Daniel knew she was right and after a few moments leant over and gently kissed her cheek, then feeling he needed to build some bridges with Danny also, asked if he wanted to take a walk with him. Danny hesitated a few seconds before nodding and pulling on his jacket. This one action cut Daniel to the heart, never before had he experienced this situation and he didn't like it at all.

I ran after Tommy and saw him up ahead striding towards the square, I was frightened that he was maybe going to do something he would regret but before I could catch up with him and to my relief he turned to take the path to the park. I finally found him sitting with his back against a large oak tree, his knees drawn up to his chest and his head down, his arms wrapped around his legs. He suddenly looked like a lost and lonely little boy and it was with apprehension that I moved to within three feet of him and stood quietly. If he knew I was there he gave no indication of doing so, and so after another minute or so I moved to the base of the tree and holding out his jacket said quietly, 'Tommy I have bought your jacket so you don't catch a chill.'
He started and looking up at me I could see he had been crying, his eyes were red and wet with unshed tears. He said nothing and I took this as a positive sign and lowered myself to sit beside him waiting for him to make the first move. I knew he was hurting and felt partly responsible for suggesting he speak to our parents on the matter. We must have sat in silence for a good half an hour in which time he had shrugged into his jacket but never once dragged his gaze away from the fowl on the lake to look at me. Just as I was beginning to work out in my mind the best way to approach him he spoke.
'Millie, do you think I am a coward?'
I was taken aback by the question and maybe hesitated slightly before answering, 'No of course I don't.'
'You had to think about it though didn't you?'
'No I just wasn't expecting you to have to ask such a thing.'
'Why not, who else but a coward would let a man beat him and insult him on a daily basis without fighting back.'
'A person who knows right from wrong, a person who was brought up to respect their elders, a person who is prepared to put his own discomfort to one side in order to help provide for his family.'
He turned to face me and asked, 'do you really think so?'
'Yes Tommy I do, we have never lied to each other no matter what and I firmly believe you are no coward, you are a strong person who will go to any lengths for the ones he loves. You remember I was with you on the journey from Ireland and I saw just how much you went through in order to help our mission.'
'You did too.'

'I know, that's what I am saying, we are a family and everything we do is to make sure that the family survives and if that means self sacrifice then that's what we do. Mama worked in the mill for months in appalling conditions for us.' Like my father earlier I regretted the words I had said immediately.

'What do you mean?'

'Nothing, forget it.'

No Millie, I won't. You said Mama worked in appalling conditions but you worked there too, why was it different for her?'

'Tommy I don't want to talk about it, it's behind us.'

'Well then I will ask her when I go home and if she won't say then I will ask Papa.'

'No,' I said, 'you can't, I don't think he knows.'

'What, how can he not know?'

'Because of the same reason you kept Mr Stone to yourself until I found the marks, we are all prepared to suffer for the ones we love. If you promise to tell no-one I will tell you about the mill.'

Tommy nodded his agreement and listened to my description of the mill work without interruption, silently wiping the tears as they fell down his cheeks. At the end of my tale he took me in his arms and hugged me hard.

'Are you ready to go home yet?' I asked as night was beginning to fall and the air was turning chill.

'Yes I am.'

Maria was really starting to worry now, it was approaching ten o'clock and she was still the only member of the Rafferty family sitting in the one room they lived in. She had no idea where any of them may be, but also now had the worry that Danny was out when he should really have been in bed. The family she thought were so strong seemed to have cracked under pressure when she least expected it. Slowly the door to the room opened and Millie and Tommy walked in, she was instantly up on her feet and rushed over taking them both in her arms.

'Where have you been, I have been so worried. Have you seen your father and brother?'

'We went to the park,' her daughter answered, 'we haven't seen the others.'

'Well they left just after you; I thought they were with you.'

Tommy shook his head, 'no we never saw them. Millie and I were talking.'

'Your father didn't mean what he said the way he said it.'

'I know,' Tommy said, but her daughter knew him well enough to know what was coming next. Taking the opportunity that Papa and Danny weren't there he asked her the question.

Maria looked at Millie, silently enquiring why she had told their secret. Millie just shrugged and cast her eyes to the floor in answer.

Maria guided her two children to the chairs near the embers of the fire and answered all the questions that her son asked of her. At the end she somehow felt a great burden leave her and resolved that when the time was right she would tell her husband all about the mill, Danny did not need to know he was too young. Half an hour later Daniel returned with a sleepy Danny on his shoulders, he laid Danny on the bed and whilst Maria undressed the boy and put him under the covers he addressed his eldest son.

'Tommy, please forgive me for the words I said earlier. I did not mean I think you are a coward, I know you are not. I am so proud of you and I wish I could make you see that, I just don't want to let you put yourself at risk again.'

Tommy got up and walked over to where his father stood and looked up at him. He had no words and instead wrapped his arms around him and held on tight.

Maria was relieved to see that harmony had been restored to the family and suggested that tomorrow being Sunday they took a packed lunch to the park and had a family day.

Last night when Tommy and I got home he wasted no time in asking Mama about the working conditions in the cotton mill. Mama looked at me as though I had betrayed the secret we had agreed not to speak of to the others, but she also patiently sat and answered every single question my brother asked her. As we were getting ready for bed I whispered to him, 'I told you not to say anything, why did you?'

'Maybe the same reason you saw fit to tell them about Mr Stone, I don't think our family is any better for secrets. Anything we can do to help and protect each other needs to be done.'

I nodded my agreement and marvelled once again at how mature my brother was despite his age, he would make a good father when his time came.

The morning had dawned sunny and bright and we were rushing around preparing a packed lunch to take with us to the park. By ten o'clock we were sat on the grass under the shade of the very oak tree Tommy and I had spent yesterday evening. The lake was filled with a variety of swans and ducks, some with young in tow. Other families were walking around the meandering pathways, some playing with small children and others picnicking. It was an idyllic scene and a far cry from the daily grind of the working lives most of these people endured. After lunch my brothers were off and chasing each other around the grass, quickly joined by another six or seven young children, their squeals and laughter carrying across the park. I leant back and rested my head on Mama's lap and as she stroked my hair she said, 'Daniel I feel I need to tell you something.'

Papa looked concerned and taking her hand in his said, 'Maria, what is wrong, are you sick?'

'No nothing like that at all, but I was not entirely honest with you when I was working at the mill and you asked what it was like.'

Papa looked at me and then back to Mama,' go on.'

Mama told him of the daily working conditions, which he listened to without comment until she was finished. Then he wiped at his eyes and said to us both, 'my dears why on earth didn't you say? If you had told me I would not have let you spend another hour in that place.'

'That's exactly why we said nothing, we needed to help provide for the family and that was all we could secure at the time.'

'But I can't bear to think of you both in that place.'

I sat up and scooted over to him, wrapping my arms tightly around his neck and kissed him on the cheek. 'Papa it's behind us now, there is no permanent damage done and I am the better for the experience, it has taught me much about myself and how much my family means to me.'

Papa took us both into his arms and said, 'I promise you neither of you will ever have to suffer like that again as long as I draw breath.'

The afternoon was drawing on and we still had some chores to complete before tomorrow and so we began to pack away our basket. A sudden breeze caught up the napkin I was folding and blew it across the grass, it stopped against the back of the legs of a man who was helping a frail woman to seat herself on one of the benches near the lake. Seating the lady he bent down and picked up the item and turning to see me running over extended his hand towards me. As I neared I recognised the man to be Mr Stone from the market stall, I muttered my thanks and ran back to my family.

'Papa, that's Mr Stone.' I said pointing to where he still stood watching us, he started to raise his hand in salute and then thinking better of it let it drop to his side.

'Wait here a moment,' Papa said to us, 'Tommy come with me.'

Mama looked worried and asked, 'Daniel what are you going to do?'

'I just want to speak to the man to see what is going on.'

We stood and watched as the two of them approached the man and began to converse, after some fifteen minutes to my astonishment the three of them shook hands and parted company. Tommy left Papa's side and ran over to us shouting, 'I am starting work tomorrow.'

On the walk home Papa told us that Mrs Stone had been desperately ill of late and her husband was so distraught that he had lost his temper and lashed out at Tommy as he could not give vent to his frustrations at home. He bitterly regretted it and said he was not normally a violent man, his wife was now slowly on the mend and he vowed nothing of the sort would happen again if Tommy were to return. Papa had asked Tommy what he wanted to do and seeing as his son was willing to give the man another chance he also agreed but not before promising that if so much as a hair on his son's head were hurt he would personally see to it that the man suffered at his hands.

'But what of the things he said about us and our heritage?' Mama asked not willing to let it drop so easily.

'He said he was worried his wife had tuberculosis and he knew a lot of Irish were carrying the disease and just said the first things that came into his head, much of which was what he had heard others discussing, in his weakened state of mind he needed someone or something to blame and in us, the Irish, he had plenty of targets.'

'Well I still don't know if I am happy about this.' Mama replied.

'Mama, you always told us to give everyone one more chance before dismissing them as a lost cause,' I said hoping to help Tommy return to a job I knew he enjoyed.

'Well I suppose if your brother and father are willing then so am I but I will be checking the lad each day he comes home,' she stated and none of us doubted this to be true.

Chapter 39

July 1849

Monday morning was a wet and dismal start to the working week, the rain which came down as a fine drizzle none the less soaked us through in minutes. Papa had insisted on accompanying Tommy to the market on the first day to see all was in order and although my brother insisted it was not necessary, I think he was grateful for the show of solidarity and concern. Our job was made more difficult with the weather conditions and we had clothes and linen hanging in every available part of the room and out buildings in an attempt to dry it.

Daniel was pleased to see, as he walked into the square with his son at his side, that Mr Stone was already hard at work unloading the produce and stacking ready for display. He sensed Tommy's apprehension and knew that as willing as Tommy was to give the man another chance he must be nervous.

'Don't worry son, Mr Stone knows what will happen if he steps out of line again, but I really did believe the things he said yesterday. Men can be irrational when it comes to protecting their loved ones. I never told anyone this before but when little Frances died I blamed myself for her death and your mother's illness.'

'But Papa, Mama said there was nothing anyone could have done about it.'

'I know son but it doesn't stop your mind from the way it works under stress and grief. I was ready to leave you all and go away to work.'

'Why Papa?'

'Because I thought you would all hate me for the things I had done, I could not have faced that. You are all I have and I would never hurt a single one of you and I felt I had let you all down. Your mother was so ill and looked so sad and there was nothing I could do to repair that and so I was willing to go, even though it would have broken my heart.'

'But you stayed, why did you change your mind?'

'It was something Danny said one night; I was sitting on the floor next to your mother and pressing a cold compress to her forehead in an attempt to relieve her fever. He was only three and a half when Frances died and he woke up and took my hand in his and looking at me with his wide eyes filled with tears he said, 'Papa why did God take our sister?' I had no answer for him and then he said, 'I think you are better than God, you won't ever let anything happen to any of us will you?' I promised him I wouldn't and suddenly stopped feeling sorry for myself, what good would running away do? I had four other people to take care of and whom I loved so deeply, I could not have survived alone.'

Tommy looked up at his father and felt honoured that he had felt he could trust him with this most intimate of secrets. 'Papa I am so glad you stayed, I would be lost without you.'

'Well enough of this let's go and see Mr Stone.'

At their approach Mr Stone straightened up from picking up a crate of apples, he extended his hand to both in turn and said, 'Mr Rafferty, Tommy, I am so glad you have let me have another chance to prove myself to be a different man to the one you were unfortunate to meet some time ago. You have no worries that such things will occur again, on that you have my word.' Turning to Tommy he said, 'Stan was right about you lad, I found that to be true when I tried to replace you. The others were no way up to your standards, and I look forward to working alongside you.'

'Mr Stone,' Daniel said although with no menace in his voice, 'I made myself clear yesterday and that remains so, but I am entrusting my son to you. Good day,' turning to Tommy he said,' see you tonight son.'

'Bye Papa.'

By the time we returned from our rounds delivering yesterdays laundry and collecting today's bundles the room was quiet and empty and we took this to mean that all had gone well with Mr Stone. We both relaxed a little and began the day's chores, Danny was used as runner and he was kept busy taking the clean clothes from us and finding places to hang them out of the rain. Luckily today we did not have any large items such as bedding so he could manage on his own.

At lunchtime we sat down to eat our bread and fruit when the small girl who had approached us some weeks earlier appeared at the door to our room, she knocked lightly on the open door and stood waiting to be given permission to enter.

'Come in lass,' Mama said.

The girl stepped inside and stood with her hair plastered to her head, small rivers of water tracking down her face.

'Goodness you are soaked child,' Mama said and pointed to a chair near the fire, 'sit yourself down,' and she passed her a towel with which to rub the worst of the water from her hair and face.

The girl accepted it gratefully and began rubbing her hair, casting a quick glance at the bread on the table.

'Are you hungry?' Mama asked.

'Yes mam,' the girl replied from beneath the towel.

Immediately Mama had cut the girl two slices from the loaf and handed them over. Thanking her the girl laid the towel to one side and applied herself to the task of eating. Once she had finished Mama asked, 'what can I do for you today dear?'

'Mrs Jackson wanted to know if you could take any more customers.'

'I don't know, we are quite busy enough. Who wants to know?'

'Mrs Thompson at the big house on the hill. Do you know it?'

'Well I know of it, it belongs to Mr and Mrs Edwards doesn't it?'

'Yes mam, well they need some help with their laundry, the girls who did theirs have left and they can't seem to find suitable replacements. Mrs Jackson says it will pay well, she recommended you on account of how well you have done for us.'

'That's very kind of her, tell her I will call and see her later after we have finished here would you?'

With that the girl rose, handed Mama the towel and thanking her for the bread left as quietly as she had arrived.

So after we had completed our duties the three of us walked over to meet Mrs Jackson in the kitchen to discuss the offer as she knew it.

'Mrs Thompson works up at the house on the hill, she is housekeeper for Mr and Mrs Edwards as you probably know. Anyway they have been let down again by their laundry maid, she left last week and they have not yet found a suitable replacement. Mrs Thompson asked me who we used and I told her about you and what a good job you have done since you took over, always on time, and a good job done to boot.'

'That's very kind, we try our best.'

'Well if you are at all interested you need to go and see her at the house tomorrow morning about ten o'clock.'

'I don't know, I think we have just about as much as we can manage between the three of us,' Mama said.

'Well it's up to you but I know they will be willing to pay at least as much as we do. My thoughts are what do you have to lose?'

'Thank you for thinking of us, I will go and see her tomorrow morning.'

By the time we got home Tommy was waiting for us, sitting at the table drinking a glass of water. He looked up as we entered and I could tell by the look on his face that the day had gone well. Mama however insisted on him removing his shirt so she could examine him for herself, satisfied she listened to his tale of how he had been treated that day by his employer. Mr Stone had not only assisted him with the manual chores, he had given Tommy a full half hour in which to sit and eat his lunch and tried his best to make conversation with him.

'He will never take the place of Stan but I think I will enjoy working for him.' Tommy finished.

'Well that's good, just make sure he continues the way he has started,' Mama warned.

Shortly after Papa returned and Tommy had to repeat the tale again in order to assure him that all had gone well.

Mama told them of the impending visit to the big house tomorrow.

'That sounds like a good customer to take on,' Papa said.

'Yes I know but I am not sure we will be able to manage any more work,' Mama objected.

'Maria, do you want to make something of this business or not?'

'Yes you know I do, it's just ....'

Papa interrupted her, 'it's just nothing. The more large customers you have the better, more money to be had in one place. No running around from house to house collecting two or three garments, this all takes up time, then going back to deliver and get the money, taking yet more time. And you could always take on help, I'm sure Tommy would love to get his arms wet again,' Papa added winking at Danny.

Tommy was about to say something when he saw the wide grin on Papa's face and laughed, adding 'and what if Stan and Susan return as promised, you will have plenty of help then.'

Mama knew they were right and so once Danny and I were organised the next morning she left to walk the half mile or so to the house on the hill.

Maria walked up the long winding drive to the house which was set about half a mile to the north of the outskirts of town. The drive was at least a quarter of a mile long lined on either side with large trees and shrubs, as the house came into view she saw it for the first time and could not help marvel at the building filling the space ahead of her. It was three stories high, built in a light stone, at either end of the house were huge square ramparts that would not have been out of place on a castle. The width of the building was easily as wide as the cotton mill with deep windows looking out over the grounds. Two large wooden doors framed in an arched porch finished off the front, the gravel drive swept majestically up to the porch and around in a circle, thereby aiding the carriages as they arrived at the door. Once Maria reached the door she looked around for the way to the back of the house and the tradesman's entrance, she would no more have dared to ring the front door as she would walk through it. At last to the right of the house she found an archway through the hedge and a pathway leading around the back of the house. As she walked towards the back corner she passed a set of twin French doors set onto a patio, the doors were open and she could not stop herself from taking a quick glance inside. The room was tall and airy, a piano standing just inside the doors, there were two huge green leather sofas facing the fireplace with a leather armchair either side. Above the mantle was a large gilt framed mirror, Maria caught a glimpse of her open mouthed reflection as she stared in. Quickly she proceeded round the back and found the door to the kitchen, it too was open and the delicious smell of baking assailed her nostrils. She raised her fist and knocked on the door.

'Come in won't you, I can't get to the door,' a female voice answered the knock.

Maria walked inside and saw a woman of about five feet with a ruddy complexion and dark brown eyes struggling to pull a tray of tarts from the huge oven. She immediately rushed forward, 'can I help at all?'

'It's alright dear I've got them,' she said placing the tray on the wooden table with a clatter and pushing her grey hair back from her face. She looked at Maria and asked,' what can I do for you?'

'I have come to see Mrs Thompson about the laundry job.'

'Oh right, well take a seat and I will call one of the girls to go and find her.' With that she called out down a passageway off to the left of the room, 'Lizzie, can you please go and find Mrs T. and let her know there is a lady here to see her about the washing.'

A chubby girl of about eighteen appeared from the passageway and exited almost as quickly through the door on the far side of the kitchen.

A few moments later she returned, followed by a tall slim woman of about forty, she was a striking lady with high cheek bones, bright green eyes and a head of light brown hair which was drawn into a loose bun on the top of her head. She carried herself upright and graced Maria with a slight nod of her head and swept her hand towards a high backed chair saying, 'please sit down. Are you the lady Mrs Jackson was speaking of?'

'Yes mam, I am Maria Rafferty.'

'She speaks very highly of you and says you offer a top rate service.'

'Why thank you, we do try to do the best we can for our customers.'

'Who is we?'

'Myself, my daughter Millie and my son Danny.'

'Oh that could be a problem.'

'They are very good workers mam; you have no need to worry there.'

'I am sure but we don't normally take families in, are you married?'

'Yes I am,' Maria answered confused as to what difference that made to the job she was applying for.

'Well is he in service also?'

'No he has a job at the dockyard.'

'Well we couldn't take him in then.'

'I am sorry Mrs Thompson, but I am not following you entirely. I came to enquire about the laundry job, nothing for my husband.'

'You do understand the position is a live in one don't you?'

'No I didn't, all the other jobs we have we take home and then deliver when they are completed. I am sorry I seem to have wasted your time.' With that Maria rose to leave.

'That is indeed most unfortunate, you are the best I have heard of and I was hoping to get the matter resolved today. The last girl had to leave us and we are struggling to find a long term replacement, these young girls come and go so lightly, a more mature woman would be ideal.'

'Well I am sorry but I cannot leave my family.'

The woman thought for a moment and then enquired, 'listen it is most irregular to think of doing it this way, but would you be willing to attend here each week to carry out the laundry. We have all you would need here in the cellar, there would be no need to fetch and deliver.'

'Well yes I think that would be acceptable, how many times a week would you require us?'

'Three times a week, there would be clothes, bed and table linen.'

'Yes that would be fine.'

'The fact that you are not living in means we would be able to pay you five shillings per day, is that acceptable with you?'

Maria tried to do the mental arithmetic but found herself too amazed to be able to concentrate, all she knew was this would be the making of her family's fortunes. 'Yes mam, perfectly acceptable. When would you like us to start?'

'Well I would like you here tomorrow to be honest but I should imagine you have some things to work out so I will expect you the day after. You can work the hours to suit yourself but you must complete the work each day, so you cannot leave until it is done. The staff are always up at five so anytime after that.'

'I will be here by six each day if that is alright, we are all early risers and I value my evenings with my family.'

'Very well Maria, I will see you in the future but Mrs Bowes will be able to see you know where things are when you first arrive,' she cast a look to the cook and raised a questioning eyebrow.

'No problem Mrs Thompson,' she answered smiling at Maria.

Maria left the house and almost ran home to tell of their good fortunes.

Chapter 40

Yesterday had been exceptionally busy as we rushed from house to house collecting the laundry, going home and hastily washing, drying, ironing and returning as much as we could. Luckily the weather today had been in our favour, sunny and warm with a breeze which made drying so much quicker. We had a few items to deliver before we could make a start on the newly acquired customer. Mama had decided that Danny and I could take the returns and receive the payments whilst she went up to the Edwards' house to make ready for the day's work, she would be early but decided it would look good if she were to arrive in order to get the tubs boiling so that we were ready as soon as my brother and I arrived.

As Danny and I approached the house it was every bit as imposing as Mama had described to us and I could not believe I was going to be working in such a place. I thought back to the time I had been offered the chance of working here earlier and wondered if I would have managed to secure the job and what I may be doing now if I had. However as Papa always told us, there was no point dwelling on what might have beens, you have to live in the present with one eye to the future. Nothing could ever change the past no matter how much you may wish for it and so why upset yourself.

We went round to the back door as instructed by Mama earlier and knocked lightly on the open door.

'It's open, come on in,' a voice called out to us and nervously we stepped over the threshold into the large kitchen, which was already a hive of activity. There was a large wooden table in the centre of the room and two girls of around eighteen were busy rolling pastry and filling pie cases, another woman of about fifty was taking a tray of delicious smelling meat from the oven and placing it on the table near the girls. After setting the food on the table she looked over to where we stood and smiled down at us saying, 'well I assume you are Millie and Danny and you have come to help your mother.'

'Yes Mam,' I managed to say. I couldn't remember being so nervous before but she soon put us at our ease.

'Now children,' she said, 'I am Mrs Bowes, I am the cook here and this is Sarah and Lizzie. You don't have to call me Mam, that is only to be used for Mrs Edwards.'

'Sorry Mam,' I said and then remembered what I had just been told and corrected myself, 'Sorry Mrs Bowes.'

'Don't worry dear, you will get used to it,' then she turned to one of the girls saying, 'Sarah show these young 'uns where their mother is, and then hurry back we have pies to make for luncheon.'

'Yes Mrs Bowes,' then she wiped her hands on her apron and asked Danny and I to follow her. Sarah was about five feet six, slim with long blond hair drawn back into to ponytail which fell down her back to six inches or so above her waist. She had striking blue eyes and angular features and when she smiled at us I immediately felt calmed.

We walked down a long narrow passageway off one corner of the kitchen, we past a closed door to our right and Sarah told us that was where all the cleaning supplies were kept including all we would need to complete our work. The passage turned sharp left and I knew we were close as the warm air met us, another turn and then we were standing in a large stone floored room with a low ceiling. Mama was stirring soda into a large metal tub and looked up smiling, 'you found it then, is everything alright?'

'Yes Mama,' I said, 'we have delivered all the clothes and got all we were owed.'

'That's good, well there is no time to waste if we are to get through all the work on time today,' nodding her head to a large pile of bedding in the corner of the room.

'If you need anything you can't find in the stores,' Sarah said, 'ask Mrs Bowes.' With that she turned and left the room.

With no windows in the room and three large tubs boiling away it was not long before the sweat was rolling off us, my hair and clothes stuck to my body, my throat parched. Although it lacked the noise and the vibrations the heat was every bit as much as the cotton mill, this was going to be money well earned and I could see why others had left. After about an hour Lizzie appeared at the door and said, 'Mrs Bowes says if you would like a drink come to the kitchen.'

The three of us gratefully left the heat of the laundry and walked down the cool passageway into kitchen, although it was warm in here from the ovens, there was a welcome breeze coming in through the open door and the high ceiling made it feel bearable. We drank thirstily from the glasses handed to us and gave our thanks to the cook before returning to work.

'Anytime you need a glass of water, just come up. I know how hot it gets down there,' Mrs Bowes told us smiling and taking in the dishevelled state of us, compared to the three people who reported for work some two hours earlier. 'I will send one of the girls for you when lunch is ready.'

'We have brought our lunch with us,' Mama told her.

'Well that's up to you but I have made enough for you all. Whilst you work here you are no different to the live in staff and your lunch is provided.'

'Thank you, that is most kind. We would be honoured to accept your hospitality,' Mama answered.

Sometime later Lizzie returned and told us lunch was ready and we followed her back to the kitchen where we found Mrs Bowes and Sarah placing plates of food on the table. Seated around the large wooden table were three men and a woman who I had not previously met.

The woman at the head of the table looked at Mama and asked, 'have you everything you need Mrs Rafferty?'

'Yes thank you Mrs Thompson, everything is fine.'

'I take it these are the two children you spoke of.'

'Yes, this is Millie and my youngest son Danny.'

'Well please be seated and we can eat,' she said.

We moved along to the end of the table where three vacant chairs were placed and sat down. I could not believe my eyes when I saw the food that had been placed in front of us. There were meat pies, poultry, potatoes, bread, fish and eggs. Mrs Bowes explained that any food that was not eaten by the family was alright for the staff to enjoy. The family did not wish to eat the same food on any two consecutive days and also the mistress had a tendency to throw impromptu dinner parties when she would suddenly decide to change the menu entirely, so rather than wasting the food it was served up each lunch time in the kitchen.

'Well help yourselves, we don't stand on ceremony here,' Mrs Bowes instructed, 'we only have half an hour and then the table must be cleared so we can begin on the evening's dinner. Also let me introduce you to the rest of the staff, there's Mr Morgan and he is the butler, next to him is Bernie the gardener and lastly Peter the stable boy.' Each nodded in turn to us and then concentrated on eating. Danny immediately looked over at the slim young man with light brown hair and grey eyes sat opposite him, his interest sparked by the two words, stable boy.

I wasn't sure what to choose and so waited and followed Mama's lead, selecting a slice of meat pie, some roasted potatoes and a slice of bread covered with a rich creamy butter. I had never tasted anything like it before. Mama was a good enough cook but she had to work to a budget at all times, here only the best of everything was good enough for the

Edwards' and it showed. The pastry on the steak and ale pie was so light it melted in my mouth and the meat was soft and succulent in its rich gravy, the potatoes had been roasted in goose fat and were brown and crispy on the outside and yet soft and fluffy inside. I glanced at Danny who was watching as one of the men used a thick slice of bread to mop up the remains of the gravy from his plate, my brother quickly did the same and then sat back with a contented smile on his face.

All too soon the meal was over and we had to return to our chores after having thanked Mrs Bowes once again.

'It's no problem dear, you are welcome to eat with us every time you are here, unless of course you prefer to bring your own,' she said winking at Danny.

We made our way down the passage back to the hot atmosphere of the laundry room but not before Danny had waited and watched which direction Peter headed off after leaving the kitchen. I whispered to Mama, 'shall we take bets on how long it will be before Danny has managed to get himself invited to the stables?'

'Well if I know anything about my son it won't be long.'

The afternoon passed quickly enough and by three thirty all the laundry had been completed and we walked back through the kitchen and said goodbye to the three women who were busy with the evening meal preparations, making arrangements to return in two days time.

As we walked back towards our humble accommodation in the warm afternoon sun we chatted about the day, the magnificent meal we had eaten and how friendly everyone had been to us.

'I cannot help but feel slightly guilty at the meal I am about to give your father and brother after the banquet we have eaten today,' Mama said.

'Do you think we should tell them about it or not?' I asked.

'Well if we don't I know someone who will,' Mama answered nodding towards my younger brother who was skipping on ahead of us, no doubt his head filled with plans to get friendly with Peter as soon as possible.

That evening over supper as usual we all talked about the events of the day. Things still seemed to be going well for Tommy with Mr Stone and although it was early days my brother was getting back to the happy confident boy we used to know. He chatted happily about the fact that Mr Stone had left him in charge of the stall whilst he nipped home to check on his wife at lunch time and how he had been praised by the man upon his return. Papa was still fully occupied at the dock yard and if he felt in anyway aggrieved that Mama was earning more money through the laundry work he never said anything, the main thing was the welfare of the family and I finally felt that the Raffertys had made it. The pain and desperation of two years ago was becoming a distant memory and I almost felt it had happened to five people I no longer knew, people who had been left on the farm back in Ireland.

My father, who had only known the farm work he had been brought up on by his father and grandfather, had made a momentous decision to uproot his family and set out on a perilous journey to a foreign country in order to ensure we survived and prospered, who had risked leaving with nothing and had made sure upon arriving in England that as soon as possible he found employment and began to do what he lived for, which was to provide for us all.

Mama, who had stood by his side throughout and accepted his judgement and in spite of her fears had been strong when needed and the gentle voice of reason when she felt he was maybe pushing his children a little too hard, a woman who in spite of her instincts to protect her own, also helped others where she could. She endured the terrible conditions of the mill in order to get the family back on its feet as quickly as possible. Now she was a woman who had taken over the healthy business that Susan had handed over and grown it successfully, whilst still looking after the family and making sure she kept an eye on the money in order that we could move into better living quarters.

Tommy, who had gone from an eight year old boy who also only knew farming to the eleven year old who had the maturity to give a man who had treated him dreadfully another chance and was reaping the rewards. A boy, who like his parents, was willing to suffer in order to help the cause. Just lately he had put on a sudden growth spurt and his legs appeared too long for him, he reminded me of the colt we used to pass each Sunday on our way to Chapel, he had become somewhat clumsy of late as if trying to adjust to his new stature, tripping over unseen obstacles. He was still infinitely patient and slow to lose his temper, taking time to sort through any problems he may have by getting things straight in his mind so he could move on in his own way, forgiving others where needed and accepting his errors readily.

Danny, still somewhat an innocent to the ways of the outside world, who worshipped Papa but despite that he had decided at an early age that he did not want to farm crops he wanted to work with animals. With his gentle easy going nature he went along with whatever he was asked as long as he could be close to his family, I admired his constant optimism.

I hoped I had also changed for the better and knew I would never be able to repay my parents for the sacrifices they had made for us, but I would do whatever I could to make them proud of me. I was content; the only regret was not having my little sister with me.

Chapter 41

After a couple of weeks life once again settled into a routine. On Tuesday, Thursday and Saturday of each week the three of us worked at the Edwards' house from six in the morning until around three thirty, depending on how quickly we managed to get done. The other three days were spent on the regular customers we had had since taking the business over from Susan plus the work that Mrs Jackson provided. It was hard work but the financial gains were more than anything we had ever known before. The total income for the family now was one pound seventeen shillings and three pence, our out goings including rent, food, fuel and laundry supplies were one pound and two shillings. Our diet continued to improve and so too did our health, we were now eating meat regularly and the benefits were evident. Sundays were still given over to the family day and we continued to take picnics to the park, that place would always be dear to us as the first green space we had found in this bustling overcrowded grey scenery.

One morning when we arrived at the Edwards' to begin our usual task, we were greeted at the door by Mrs Bowes, who looked quite flustered.

'Maria, Millie, thank goodness you have arrived. I need your help if you can see your way clear.'

'Of course, what do you require?' Mama asked.

'Well the master and mistress are entertaining this weekend and Sarah has taken sick today. She has a bad stomach and cannot leave her bed. Lizzie and I cannot cope with the catering without some assistance. If you could help in any way I would be so grateful.'

Mama didn't hesitate, 'Of course, tell us what you need us to do and we will be happy to help.'

'Well if you could both help with the cooking that would be a god send, Lizzie and I have managed to get the breakfast cooked and served but there are pots to be washed and lunch and dinner to be prepared and served. Also I am afraid that there is still the laundry to be done; heaven knows how we will cope.' With that she sank herself down onto one of the kitchen chairs and began to wring her hands.

Mama took charge and it was decided that once we had set up the laundry, Danny and I would manage as much as we could on our own, whilst Mama helped with the food and oversaw us. When we all met at the table for lunch' things seemed to be under control and Mrs Bowes was her normal jovial self, chatting and laughing as she passed around the plates.

'How is Sarah?' I asked.

Mrs Bowes glanced across at Mama and told me, 'she is to stay in bed today, she has been sick all morning and although she feels somewhat better now it's best she stay where she is with all that's going on today. How are you getting on with the washing dear?'

'We are all done but could do with a hand to carry it out into the yard after lunch.'

'Peter, could you give them a hand with that?'

'Yes Mrs Bowes, the horses are not required to be saddled until three and I have already groomed and fed them and cleaned all the tackle.'

Danny sat up suddenly taking an interest in the conversation around the table and I could not help but feel a little sorry for unsuspecting Peter as this was just the opportunity my brother had been waiting for. My amusement was short lived however by the next part of the conversation.

'Maria,' Mrs Bowes said and then hesitated.

'What is it?'

'I was wondering if I could impose on your good nature further?'

'Yes if I can help.'

She glanced over at Mrs Thompson who nodded her agreement. 'Well you have been a tremendous help today, you truly have but there is still a matter if the evening meal to be cooked and served. I have spoken about the matter to Mrs Thompson and if you and your daughter could stay on this evening to assist we would be most grateful, you will be paid for your time of course.'

'What did you have in mind?'

'Well we thought you could help me with the meal and Millie could help Lizzie serve.'

'Oh I don't know about that, we need to get home to my son and husband, they will be worried about us.'

'Millie and Danny could go home as normal after the laundry is completed and tell your husband what is happening, you will both be able to leave after the meal has been served, Lizzie and I can cope with the dishes with some help from the others. What do you say?'

Mama looked over at me, knowing that I was terrified of the idea, but also not wanting to let her down, so she said, 'let me speak to Millie privately first.'

'Of course, take your time.'

We walked outside into the kitchen garden and Mama turned to me, taking each of my hands in hers.

'Mama, I can't possibly do it, I have no idea what to do and I certainly have no idea what to say to these people.'

'I didn't think you would want to do it, but I feel obliged to stay and help with the meal.'

'Well that's ok; Danny and I will go home as normal and I will make them their supper.'

'Thank you Millie.'

We returned to the kitchen to give our answer and I could tell that Mrs Bowes and Mrs Thompson were disappointed in me.

'I have no idea how to serve the gentry,' I blurted out trying to justify my decision, it's then that I let my defences down, they had spotted a weakness that said I would do it if only I knew how.

'It's nothing dear, Lizzie will show you what to do this afternoon when she sets up the table and you don't have to worry about speaking to them, only Mrs Thompson and Mr Morgan are expected to do so.'

It was then I knew I had no way out without making myself look a coward and so with a heavy heart and feeling of trepidation I agreed. All the time that Danny and I were hanging the washing with the help of Peter I worried about the forthcoming evening more and more and found myself on more than one occasion digging my nails into the palms of my hands. Even all of Danny's questioning of Peter passed by me somehow and I left him to his inquisition without interruption.

As we walked home to give Papa and Tommy the news and make their meal I found out that Danny had learnt there were eight horses, four for the Edwards family members and four spare for whenever guests were staying and fancied a ride. Although Danny had not seen them today, due to the fact that everyone was so busy, Peter had promised him that he would show him the stables and horses when we were next there on Tuesday.

Once we arrived home, Papa and Tommy were already at work scraping the vegetables, they looked up at us concerned that Mama was not with us. I explained all that had happened that day and that I was to return this evening to help in the dining room.

'What time will you be finished?' Papa asked.

'I am not sure, whenever the meal is finished,' was my reply.

'Well then the boys and I will walk you back and I will find out more. I am not having you both walk home unaccompanied tonight.'

So after the supper things had been cleared we walked back to the house, Danny busy telling his brother all about Peter, the horses and how he wanted to be a stable boy just as soon as he was old enough.

Arriving at the bottom of the drive that lead up to the house Papa and Tommy stood for a moment taking in the view, the splendour of the home and the sweeping grounds of lush green grass, beds of flowers and shrubs, trees and a lake with two fountains. They had heard much about the property from us all over the past few weeks but as yet had not seen it for themselves. I knew just exactly what they were thinking, having had the same experience myself when I first approached the imposing estate. Although I was still overawed by the property I had become more comfortable in my immediate surroundings and felt at home in the company of the staff, tonight however would be totally different. I had never even set eyes on any member of the family and yet shortly I was to be serving them and their guests their dinner.

We entered the kitchen and were met by a frenzy of activity. Mama and Mrs Bowes were busy at the cooker and Lizzie was occupied with rolling out pastry. Bernie and Peter were polishing glasses and Mr Thompson was wiping the dust from some bottles of wine with a damp cloth. Although it looked chaotic it seemed they were all pleased with their progress and everyone knew exactly what needed to be done, everyone except me.

'Daniel, what are you doing here?' Mama asked looking up.

'I just came to see what time you will be finishing this evening so I can meet you both, I don't like the idea of you walking home alone late at night.'

'Mrs Bowes, this is my husband Daniel and my eldest son Tommy,' Mama said. 'Do you have any idea when we will be finished?'

'Well dinner starts at seven sharp and they should be served the last course by nine, once that is done you can both go. As I said we can manage the dishes between us and Mr Morgan serves the cigars, ports and coffees.'

Promising to return by nine my father and brothers left us to continue our work. At half past six Mrs Thompson came into the room carrying a uniform which she passed to me, it consisted of a black dress, white cap and apron and a pair of black shoes and stockings.

'I think that should fit you, go down to the laundry room and try it on, and then come back here.'

Nervously I did as I was told, I managed everything but the cap, which try as I might I could not get to stay on my head, after about five minutes I gave up and went back to the kitchen.

Lizzie rushed forward and with a few deft movements and plenty of grips she had plaited my hair and then twisted it up and set the cap on the top. I felt most awkward; I had never worn anything like this before, even the shoes felt heavy and cumbersome on my feet. Mama turned and looked at me, nodding her head approvingly.

'Millie, don't forget what Lizzie showed you this afternoon,' Mrs Thompson said, 'you always serve the ladies first, Lizzie will serve Mrs Edwards, she will be seated at the end of the table and you will serve Mrs Fraser, then you will serve the men, Lizzie will serve Mr Edwards and you will serve Mr Fraser, then you will serve Arthur whilst Lizzie serves Charles, you always serve from the right and take the empty plates from the right. You do not speak to any of the diners and if you are asked a question, step back a pace and either Mr Morgan or myself will answer. Once the course has been served you are to stand one on each side of the table looking at me, upon my cue you will remove the dishes and take them to the kitchen for the next course. Also I must state that any conversations you may hear during the meal are not to be repeated to anyone outside this house. Do you understand?'

'Yes mam,' I said. I felt sick and butterflies were dancing in my stomach. I had helped Lizzie and Mr Morgan set up the table for dinner in the afternoon and the dining room looked magnificent, fresh flowers adorning the dressers, the long oak table polished to a perfect shine, then covered with a crisp white linen cloth which Mrs Thompson smoothed with a flat iron before we laid the silver cutlery and crystal glasses, all of which were lined up precisely by Mr Morgan using a ruler.

'Very well, Mr Morgan will now ring the dinner bell and as soon as they are all seated I will come and fetch you both and you will begin service.' With that she left the room to attend to her duties. Within minutes she was back and Lizzie and I wheeled the large soup tureen to the dining room, we ladled the soup into bowls and served the diners as instructed, my hands were shaking and I feared I would spill the contents over any one of them but somehow I managed. Once everyone was served I took my place at the wall and waited for Mrs Thompson's signal to clear the table. After a few moments it was obvious she would not be doing so until the course was eaten so I took the opportunity to take a quick glance at the people seated around the room. I had worked out who was who by the fact that I had been told who I was to serve. I kept my head slightly bowed but my eyes up and this way I thought I was able to view the dinner party without being observed but also keep an eye for my signal to start clearing.

Mr Edwards sat at the head of the table to my right, he looked to be in his middle fifties and was broad shouldered and appeared to be tall, his dark brown hair was receding and at the temples it was turning grey, he looked out at the guests from behind hazel eyes and his voice was deep and commanding when he spoke with an upper class accent, he was also carrying the beginnings of a paunch.

His wife sat at the far end opposite him and she was slim and willowy, I thought she was either late forties or early fifties with long blond hair piled high on her head and piercing blue eyes. Her movements were calm and relaxed and she had an elegant poise about her that I thought could only come with breeding. In comparison to her husband she was very quietly spoken and appeared somewhat too eager to agree with her husband's point of view.

Then from the corner of my eye I noticed Mrs Thompson bring her arms up from her sides and brought her hands together in front of her, Lizzie moved away from the wall and I took this as the signal to clear the dishes. We left the dining room and trundled back to the kitchen where covered dishes were waiting for us, once loaded we returned and began serving the fish course, then again taking my position against the wall, I observed the people seated at the table.

My gaze was drawn to Mr Fraser as he was facing me sat to the left of Mrs Edwards, he was a plump man of around sixty with a florid complexion and narrow eyes which made it difficult to determine the colour other than pale, his head was almost bald but with a narrow band of white hair around the back of his head level with his ears. When he spoke he seemed to find it impossible to do so without moving his hands.

Mrs Fraser sat with her back to me, she was a small woman with hair that was predominantly grey, her hands were very tiny and she sat very erect in her chair as if trying to make herself as tall as possible.

Next to her and also with his back to me, sitting to the left of his father was Charles Edwards, his thick wavy hair was dirty blond, he had a tall broad frame and he appeared confident when he spoke, completely at ease in joining in on whatever the chosen topic. Occasionally he would lean into Mrs Fraser and whisper some remark that only she could hear and she would respond by giggling girlishly and bringing her hand to her face in mock indignation.

The last member of the party was Arthur Edwards, youngest son, he was in his early twenties with mousy hair and almond shaped hazel eyes, he did not appear to have the confidence of his elder brother, on the occasions that he spoke he did so quietly, almost nervous to voice his opinions. Also in contrast to his brother he was thin and wiry, his pale delicate hands ending in long slim fingers. He did not seem at all interested in the utterances of his father but hung on every word his mother said.

When we returned with the meat course I stole a quick glance at Charles Edwards as I entered the room, I immediately averted my eyes when I found he was also looking at me. He had a strong face with a square jaw and piercing blue eyes, he gave me a slight smile and I found I was quite taken by his handsome looks.

The rest of the meal went smoothly enough and I was more than pleased with myself with the way I had managed to get through the evening without any major mishaps, the occasional lapse when I forgot which side I should serve from but nothing too drastic. It wasn't until we were clearing the dessert plates when Charles said loudly, 'well who is this new girl we have tonight and where is Sarah?'

Mrs Thompson replied, 'Sarah is under the weather today and has taken to her bed, this is Millie.'

'Millie eh, and where did you come from?'

I nearly answered, but I caught the look from Lizzie in time and remembered my position.

'Millie is the daughter of our laundry maid and is helping today in Sarah's absence.' With that she ushered Lizzie and I from the room and back to the kitchen.

'You have both done very well this evening and I thank you on behalf of Mr and Mrs Edwards for making the dinner a success, you may return home now and I will see you are both paid accordingly at the end of the week,' Mrs Thompson told us and then she swept out of the room to return to the others.

'Yes thank you both so much,' Mrs Bowes added, 'it would have been a real struggle without you. Goodnight and a safe journey home.'

Papa was waiting for us outside and as we walked home I found myself slightly envious of Sarah and Lizzie of their positions.

Chapter 42

The next day being Sunday, Daniel decided to let his wife and daughter have a bit of a lie in after the late finish last night. He could see they were tired when he met them at the house and escorted them home. As soon as the boys were awake he managed to get them dressed and out of the room without disturbing the others.

'Is something wrong Papa?' Tommy asked.

'No son, but your mother and sister were late finishing last night and are very tired so I thought the three of us would go to the park for a while and let them rest.'

After an hour they returned home to find the two of them up and busy preparing Sunday lunch.

Maria looked up, 'ah there you are, we were wondering where you had got to.'

'I just thought you might appreciate a bit of extra shut eye after last night.'

'That's very thoughtful of you all; I must say I feel better for it. Even though it was nonstop last night and hard work I must admit to actually enjoying myself. How about you Millie, how did you get on? I was too tired to talk much when we got home.'

'Me too Mama, I didn't think just serving food could be tiring but we were backwards and forwards to the kitchen all evening and just standing still makes you tired in a strange sort of way, but like you once I lost some of my nerves, I thoroughly enjoyed it. I especially liked Mrs Edwards, she is so pretty and she seemed to make sure that no-one was left out of the conversation for long, a proper lady.'

'I wish I could have seen them all, tell me what were the ladies wearing?'

Daniel sighed, Maria took the hint, 'tell me later when we are alone, we have hungry men to feed.'

Lunch over, the family went to the park and whilst the boys played and Daniel dozed, Millie told her mother everything about the previous evening, from the ladies attire, to her observations about the family and their guests. She lingered some time when describing Charles and Maria smiled to herself, understanding how a young girl's head could be turned by a handsome young man.

On the walk home, Danny not wishing to be outdone chattered on about the promise of being able to see the stables on Tuesday.

'Tommy, do you think we will be good enough for these three soon?' Daniel joked.

'No Papa not unless we talk proper and wear posh frocks or grow another two legs in Danny's case.'

Maria realised that maybe they had been a little too enthusiastic about the Edwards and was upset in case she had hurt her husband's feelings. She slipped her arm through his and kissed him lightly on the cheek saying, 'they may have money and a big house but they don't have what I have and I would never wish to trade places for a moment.'

Chapter 43

I walked up the long drive to the house with my mother and brother to take on the laundry once again. Saturday still lingered in my mind and for some reason I had butterflies in my stomach as the house came into view, I had no idea why, we had been coming here three times a week for some time now and felt comfortable and relaxed around the staff. There was something else today that I could not identify but I was excited, I didn't have to worry about conversation as it was monopolised by an excited eight year old boy who today would be fulfilling his dream of being allowed to visit the stables, I couldn't imagine what the journey home would be like once he had done so.

Sarah was back to work and although she looked a little pale she assured Mama it had just been a bug when she had enquired as to her health. So with a full complement of staff it was back to the hot, damp confines of the laundry for us.

The feeling of anticipation from earlier soon disappeared once the task of washing had begun, although as I was sorting through the clothes putting them into the correct piles ready for the tubs I found myself holding a man's white linen shirt and fleetingly wondered if it might belong to Charles, I had to resist the urge to hold it to my face and smell it. Suddenly embarrassed by this alien impulse I looked around to see if anyone had seen me, but they were busy and I got back to the task in hand.

Lunch time arrived at last without any further lapses and we took our places at the kitchen table, Sarah picked at her food and after a few moments excused herself and went outside to the kitchen garden. Peter came in and grabbed a plate which he piled high with food and then looking at my brother said, 'well Danny bring your plate, and we will eat in the stables.'

Danny scooped another piece of pie onto his plate, and jumped up to go.

'Danny Rafferty,' Mama scolded him, 'where are your manners?'

Quickly he sat back down, 'sorry Mama, 'may I be excused?'

' Anything else to say?'

'Thank you for the food Mrs Bowes.'

'You're welcome lad.'

'Very well, you may go, do not be late back,' Mama said smiling.

Danny grabbed his plate and rushed after Peter who was already striding out across the yard.

Watching my brother as he left I turned to Mama and said, 'Do you think he will be back before we finish?'

'Not a chance, we've seen the last of him today, we will most likely have to go and find him when it's time to go home.'

Laughing I helped to clear the table before returning to the washing.

Danny rushed out of the kitchen in time to see Peter turn a corner up ahead, by the time he caught him up Peter was opening a side gate that led into the stable courtyard. Upon entering Danny saw that the courtyard was a square, on three sides were the stables, three stalls to each side, the fourth side was open with a drive which led to pastures and the open countryside beyond that. One of the stables was completely closed and locked; the other eight were open but all empty.

Seeing the look of disappointment on his young companions face Peter explained, 'All the horses are out in the meadow at the moment, I need to finish cleaning out their stalls and then I can bring them in, before making sure they all have food and water to see them through until tomorrow. Would you like to help me?' Peter wanted to see how Danny would react to having to do some work before he could see the horses.

'Yes please, what do you want me to do?' Danny enthused.

They went to the tackle room which was set slightly back from the stables and Peter loaded forks and brooms onto a barrow, walking past the first five stables, Peter dropped the barrow at the entrance to the sixth explaining that he had already done those this morning. Danny looked in as they passed and saw all were indeed clean and furnished with fresh straw bedding. He was understandably upset at not seeing the horses straightaway as he had been expecting, but just the prospect of seeing them shortly was enough and he threw himself into the task in hand, raking the old bedding and loading it onto the barrow, Peter would then push this around the back of the stables where he explained it was used for compost in the kitchen garden. Danny was sweating and his arms were aching by the time they finally finished the last stall, and he felt a certain pride when Peter praised him for his hard work and told him he had worked well.

'Right then Danny, let's go and find the fellas shall we?'

Danny could hardly contain himself and fell into step alongside Peter as they made their way out of the courtyard towards the pastures. Then he heard his name being called and turned to see his mother standing at the side gate by which they had entered some three hours earlier. He suddenly realised he should have been helping in the laundry and asked

Peter if he would wait a minute while he went to speak with his mother. Peter nodded and Danny ran over to join her, 'Mama I'm sorry I forgot the time, I will come back and finish my work now. Could I just go and look at the horses before I do as I haven't seen them yet.'

'Why what have you been doing all this time?'

'Helping Peter to clean the stalls out.'

It was then that Maria noticed the state of him; covered head to toe in dust and bits of straw sticking in his hair and clothing, his face was red and sweaty.

'I came to find you because it's time to go home; we've finished for the day.'

Danny could not believe he had spent the whole afternoon without a single thought for his mother and sister, 'I'm sorry Mama, I didn't realise the time.'

'It's alright son, I didn't expect you back today and we managed fine, but I am sorry you haven't seen the horses. Look I will go and fetch Millie while you look at the horses and then we must set off to get a meal ready for your father and brother.'

Danny raced off and explained the situation to Peter, his face a picture of fresh disappointment.

'I'm sorry Danny; I didn't think you would have to go so soon, otherwise I would have at least brought one of them in for you.'

'Can I still see them before we have to go?' Danny asked, frightened he would have to wait a few more days for this to happen.

'Yes of course, let's go before they return.' Peter picked up a bucket of horse feed and began to rattle it as they walked to the gate to the pasture. Over at the far side Danny caught sight of the horses, their heads lifting when they heard the bucket and they began to trot over towards them.

'Right, watch this,' Peter said, 'you see the pure white one, well she's the boss around here. The others always let her get the oats first.'

Peter passed the bucket to Danny and told him how to hold it and Danny held his breath as the white mare came over and after looking at him briefly as though summing him up, bent her head to eat. Peter waited for a few moments and then slipped a halter around her neck, telling Danny to put the bucket down out of reach of the others.

'We'll take her back and then see if you can stay a little longer.'

'What's her name?'

'This is Phantom and she belongs to the mistress, she is really gentle natured and a pleasure to handle, here take the rein.'

Danny did as instructed and led the horse to the first of the stalls, his body shaking with excitement as the horse trotted obediently at his side, his head coming to just below her shoulder. Peter showed him how to remove the halter and where to fetch the food and water to fill her troughs, then they closed the bottom half of the stable door and bolted it, Peter telling him he didn't lock them in until dusk. He then walked with Danny over to where his mother and sister were waiting and apologised for keeping them.

Maria said she understood but they needed to get home in order to prepare the family evening meal, she looked down at her son and saw in his eyes a fire and excitement she had never seen before, it was as if he was consumed by a passion and she realised he was fulfilling part of his dream since being a very small boy back in Ireland, the desire to work with animals. Danny turned and held his hand out to Peter, the young man took it and they shook hands, 'Peter I must thank you for your time this afternoon, I have enjoyed myself so much and I hope I did not hinder you.'

'Nonsense you have been a big help and I have enjoyed your company, normally it's just me and the shovel most of the time. Come back anytime you like and I will make sure you get to see more of the horses.'

Maria was quite taken aback at her young son's maturity and manners, making her mind up suddenly she said, 'If everyone is in agreement, Danny can stay another hour but then he must come straight home. Millie would you mind waiting here for him and walking him home?'

'No Mama, of course not.'

Danny rushed to his mother's side and hugged her tightly, placing a kiss on her cheek, 'Thank you Mama.'

'Good day Mrs Rafferty, I will make sure they leave on time,' Peter said raising his cap and then to Danny, 'well let's not waste time eh? Horses to bed down.'

The three of them walked over to the meadow and Millie watched as Danny confidently picked up a halter and approached a large chestnut stallion. Peter informed them his name was Flame and he belonged to Master Arthur.

I was so pleased to see how much my little brother was enjoying himself, horses had never really held any fascination for me, I could admire their grace and elegance but quite honestly I found them a bit intimidating. They always seemed to regard me as if I were not worthy of their attention as they looked down on me, I was also very wary of the strength they harboured and was worried about receiving a kick or bite. However witnessing how at ease Danny was around them in spite of his size I relaxed a little, hearing Peter declare that Flame was Master Arthur's mount I suddenly found myself asking, ' which one does Master Charles ride?'

'His horse is the one standing by himself, his name is Ebony,' he replied pointing to a jet black stallion with one white sock. The creature looked to me as if he knew how handsome he was and held himself with a dignity I had never witnessed in an animal before. Peter and Danny took a horse each and I followed and watched as they bedded them down, supplying their food and water for the evening, this they repeated until there were only three remaining in the field.

'Time is getting on,' Peter announced,' Millie would you like to lead a horse in?'

Flustered I said, 'Oh I don't know what to do.'

'Don't worry, I'll halter them, you only have to lead it and they know there is food waiting in the stall so they are always quite happy to come in.'

'Very well, can I take Ebony?'

And so I found myself leading the powerful stallion into his stall, I felt a thrill I couldn't explain as he followed me back to the yard.

When they were all settled we once again expressed our gratitude and took our leave to join our family for supper. 'A pleasure,' said Peter, 'young Danny is a natural; he has no fear and the horses know they can trust him, that's rare in one so young.'

Danny beamed at this and I remembered the comment of Roy when he had fed the horses on the towpath. Obviously Danny's obsession with animals was more than just that, it was a calling. The walk home was filled with the tales of everything that Danny had experienced that afternoon and I knew that I would be hearing this again once he saw the rest of the family and found my thoughts drifting off, picturing a black stallion running across the meadow with a handsome man on his back.

Chapter 44

October 1849

By the time Danny reached his eighth birthday he was spending every afternoon that we were at the Edwards' house over at the stables. Mama had instilled into him that he had duties to perform helping us with the laundry and if he did not pull his weight he would not be allowed to go. She had confided in me that really we could have managed but she wanted to teach him that he had responsibilities to his family and that hard work brought its rewards. Not once did he complain and he threw himself into the work with a vigour I would not have believed him capable of a few months ago. Just like his elder brother he had accepted his role in helping towards the welfare of the family. He had developed a confidence I had not possessed at his age and wasn't sure I even did now, Peter had taught him so much about the care of the horses, their individual personalities and idiosyncrasies, which helped to spot any signs of illness before it developed too far.

Tommy was thriving on the market and Mr Stone had given him a wage rise of a penny a week, along with the responsibility of running the stall on his own on a Monday afternoon, closing it down and taking the money round to his house before coming home. There had been no reoccurrence of the ill treatment and Tommy told me that he had totally forgiven the man for his previous behaviour.

Papa continued to work on the docks and came home one day to tell us that he had been promised that he would be promoted to foreman as soon as a vacancy became available.

Mama had suffered a couple of recurrences of the cough she had developed at the cotton mill, but nothing as bad as before and had not even had to take to her bed. I made a mental note to keep an eye on her when the cold weather returned.

We had managed to find a chapel in the town and had returned to attending each Sunday morning after a long lapse. I admit I felt quite guilty at not having given much thought to worship after such an absence and also thought it odd that now that times were good we were praying, when we were struggling, we were so busy surviving that worship fell by the wayside. Mama said we were worshipping now to thank God for getting us through the bad times and that he understood, I supposed that made sense and made sure I thanked him myself.

We had not been called upon to serve dinner at the house anymore but I had noticed that Sarah was beginning to put some weight on and she was complaining of back ache and tiredness. Mrs Bowes did not seem very sympathetic towards her which I found a little out of character but Mama said it was none of our business and so I kept quiet but continued to watch and listen at lunch times, something was not right.

Then one day we went to the house and upon entering the kitchen saw a young girl of about seventeen standing at the side of Mrs Bowes watching her as she showed her how to roll the dough out for the bread loaves. She was small with light brown hair tied up in a plait which fell across her left shoulder, when she smiled she displayed a row of very tiny teeth, her grey eyes were wide and her nose was upturned slightly.

'Ah this is Patsy,' said Mrs Bowes, 'Patsy meet Maria, Millie and Danny. Patsy has taken over from Sarah.'

'Has Sarah left?' I asked.

'Yes she left at the weekend.'

I found this a little strange, Sarah had not mentioned anything over the previous week, not that she confided in me, but most things seemed to be discussed at the kitchen table during lunch and her departure had never been a topic of conversation on the days we were there.

Chapter 45

December 1849

Christmas and my fifteenth birthday were only one week away. I was excited today because Mama had arranged that when we had finished the laundry we would walk to meet Tommy from the stall where Mr Stone had promised he would have a Christmas tree waiting for us to take home. The past two Sundays my brothers and I had spent the afternoons making decorations to hang from the branches, many of these were stars cut from newspaper and coloured; Mama had sewn some old rags together in the shapes of angels and bells and stuffed with any pieces of paper we had not yet got our hands on.

Finally when the last garments had been delivered we turned for the market square. Pushing the barrow into town was not too difficult as the snow which had been falling steadily for the past three days now was packed down by the many feet passing over it. The afternoon light was fading fast as we reached the square and the sky was still heavy with grey snow clouds. Tommy and Mr Stone were busy packing away the last of the produce as we arrived. Even after all this time Mama had not truly forgiven Mr Stone for the way he had treated Tommy, but as her son was content again and there had been no relapses she was prepared to be civil to the man.

'Good afternoon Mrs Rafferty,' he said, touching his hat, 'I trust you are all well.'

'Yes thank you Mr Stone, and you and your wife also?'

'Yes, yes quite healthy thank you.' Then looking at Danny he said,' I bet you want to see the tree I have picked out for you don't you?'

'Yes please sir,' Danny replied.

Mr Stone went to the back of the stall and bent to lift the tree from where it had been laying.

'It's truly magnificent,' Tommy said.

And indeed it was, it stood about four feet tall and was thick with pine needles, the scent it gave off was heady.

Danny clapped his hands together and squealed with delight.

'Mr Stone, it's wonderful,' I said, 'isn't it Mama?'

Mama nodded and answered, 'yes it certainly is. It will look a picture in our room once we have decorated it. Thank you very much Mr Stone, how much do I owe you?'

'Nothing at all Mrs Rafferty, think of it as a gift.'

'No we couldn't possibly do that, please tell me how much it costs.'

'Mrs Rafferty, it's the least I can do after the way you and your family had the good grace to give me another chance. Tommy is a good lad and I should never have let my frustrations take over my actions. I will be offended if you do not accept my gift.'

I looked at Mama and could see she was struggling with her feelings towards the man, eventually she smiled and said, 'Mr Stone we would be honoured to accept, thank you so much. '

'Well that's settled then; let's get it loaded on your cart so you can get it home before its dark.'

Once back at home we began to decorate the tree whilst Mama prepared supper, we wanted to have it finished before Papa returned.

Daniel and three other men had been unloading the crates from the ship's hold for the past hour. It was growing dark outside and they were grateful to be out of the wind as it whipped the snow around the dock yard. The only drawback from being down here was the smell that was pervading the space. They had thought at first that maybe some of the produce had turned rotten but now that the last of the crates had been lifted out the smell still persisted.

'Must be a dead rat or something,' said one of the men.

'Well it's not our problem, we've done our job,' said another, let's get off home boys.'

'Wait, let's have a quick look and see if we can find it,' Daniel said.

'You can if you want, but I'm off, rats aren't my problem.'

Two of the men picked up their caps, coats and scarves and bidding the others good afternoon, climbed the ladder and disappeared.

'I'll give you a hand Daniel,' Bobby said. He was a young lad of about eighteen and had only been working there for two months. Daniel had taken to the young man immediately and had shown him the ropes and generally looked out for him.

'Thanks Bobby, it shouldn't take long now the hold is empty. Bring that lantern over this way; it seems to be coming from behind those sacks in the corner.'

Bobby did as he was asked and the two men walked forward to the corner Daniel had indicated.

'Wow that's ripe,' Bobby exclaimed, pulling his handkerchief from his pocket and covering his face.

'Stand there and hold the lantern up, I'll just move these sacks out of the way,' Daniel said also covering his nose and mouth with his scarf. He pulled at the sacks and put them to the back of him in order to see what was in the corner. Then as he grabbed at the next sack his hand brushed against something hot and clammy, Daniel jumped back and took the lamp from Bobby. Walking forward slowly he peered behind the remaining sacks and let out a gasp.

'What is it?'

'It's a man,' Daniel said, 'he's half dead.'

'Oh my God.'

'Go and get the foreman quickly.'

Bobby turned and scuttled up the ladder and out of sight.

Daniel crept closer to inspect the man, who looked to be about thirty and was painfully thin, his ragged clothes hung loosely on his thin frame, and his complexion was pale apart from the dark circles under his closed eyes. His left hand was curled up like a claw, dirt was caked under his fingernails and in his hand was a dirty rag covered in blood, and blood was crusted around his mouth and nose. The source of the terrible stench was due to the fact that the man lay in his own blood stained vomit. Daniel knew enough to know that this man had tuberculosis and stepped back.

Bobby returned with the foreman and Daniel called up to them not to come down, 'the man has tb. Send down some ropes and planks and I will get him out.'

The foreman threw down the items Daniel had requested along with a pair of gloves. 'Make sure you don't touch him Daniel,' he warned.

Too late, thought Daniel and set about getting the man ready for removal. As Daniel tried to drag the man over to the make shift stretcher the man began to cough uncontrollably, bloody phlegm trickling from his mouth. Daniel retreated and waited until the coughing had subsided before approaching again and manhandling him onto the wooden planks. The man reached out to Daniel and gasped something Daniel could not hear, natural instinct took over and Daniel bent his head down to place his ear next to the man's mouth in order to make out the words.

'Am I in America yet?' he gasped. Daniel did not have the heart to disappoint him although he knew the man would be lucky if he lived to see England fully. 'Yes,' he told him, 'you're in New York.'

'Praise the Lord, I didn't think I would …….' the man coughed again, more violently this time, his whole body racked with convulsions. He wiped his mouth with the back of his hand and took Daniel by surprise by suddenly grasping him by the hand. Daniel could feel the warm sticky mucus on his palm and tried to pull his hand away but the man's grip was surprisingly strong. Then just as soon he released him, his eyes rolled up into the back of his head until only the whites could be seen, a long last breath hitting Daniel in the face. By the time he had finished his task and the man's body had been removed, the ship's captain had been called.

'He must have stowed away when we were in Ireland,' he stated, 'didn't know he was there.'

Daniel watched as the covered body was wheeled towards the river to be disposed off and set off for home. He stopped at the drinking fountain on the way and washed his face and hands in the freezing water, but the smell lingered, even if only in his imagination.

He wearily climbed the stairs to their room, worrying about seeing his family. He knew they were collecting the Christmas tree today and that they were bound to be excited, most likely ambushing him and covering his eyes before the great unveil. He could not let them near him before he had changed and bathed, he would take no chances with his precious wife and children.

When he reached the door he stopped and listened and could hear the excited voices inside, sighing he raised his hand and knocked on the door. 'Maria, would you please come out here a moment, I need to speak with you.'

Maria looked nervously at the children wondering what could have brought on this strange behaviour from her husband. 'Stay here children, I will go and see what's going on.' She left the room closing the door behind her and finding Daniel pushed up against the far wall.

'Stay there,' he ordered and proceeded to tell her all that had happened. 'I can't risk that I may have contracted something and pass it on to you all.'

Maria stood with her hand to her mouth, 'Daniel are you sure you touched him?'

'Yes he grabbed me by the hand,' Daniel found he could not bring himself to tell Maria the full extent of his contact with the dead man. He did not want to worry her unnecessarily.

'Wait here, I will boil water and fill the tin bath outside, when you are done I will bring you your other clothes and we will have to burn those I am afraid.'

'What will you tell the children?'

'I will tell them you have managed to get yourself covered in tar and must clean up before you can come in.'

Papa was later than usual returning from work but we were grateful for it gave us a chance to finish decorating the tree before he arrived. It looked splendid stood in its pot in the corner of the room, bedecked with our homemade decorations. The room was warm and cosy and filled with the delicious smell of stew and dumplings simmering on the hearth. The snow was still falling outside in the dark night and settling on the pavements below. At last we heard Papa's tread on the stairs but instead of the door opening there was a knock and he called out for Mama to join him. Mama looked concerned but left closing the door behind her and instructing us to remain where we were. We strained to hear what was happening but could make nothing out from the hushed voices outside. Presently she returned and instructed us to boil enough water to fill the tin bath outside, telling us Papa had accidentally got covered in tar and needed to bathe and change before coming in.

'I must see this,' Tommy said heading for the door.

'No Tommy, stay here and help!' Mama snapped.

Tommy stopped dead in his tracks, Mama had never spoken that way before and we busied ourselves as instructed. Once she had taken all the water and clothes downstairs we began to discuss what we thought could be the matter.

'Maybe he has some presents for us and he wants to hide them,' Danny suggested optimistically.

'If so, why the water and clothes?' Tommy asked.

'I don't know,' he admitted.

'Maybe he's been in a fight and they don't want us to know,' Tommy offered.

'No Papa didn't even fight Mr Stone when he had good reason,' I answered.

Danny looked out of the window but could not see round into the yard, although he did say it looked as though someone had lit a fire. Having exhausted our ideas as to the issue we sat down and waited for our parents return.

Papa came in, his hair still wet from the bath, dressed in his Sunday afternoon clothes. He smiled at us and said, 'I bet you can't believe how silly your father is to get covered in tar can you? Wow the tree looks fantastic, you've really done it proud.'

The evening passed in the usual manner but my parents seemed a little withdrawn and I was reminded of the night two years ago when they had decided to leave Ireland and I found sleep difficult to come by that night. I determined to get Mama by herself tomorrow and find out the truth to this strange behaviour.

No amount of my questioning the next day could glean any information about the previous day other than the story we had been told and so believing that if it were anything important we would have been made aware of it I gave up and put it to the back of my mind. Papa went to the dockyard the next day wearing his Sunday best clothes promising Mama that he would go into town as soon as he got a break in the day to buy some suitable work attire. After that the incident was not mentioned anymore and plans for the upcoming Christmas celebrations occupied everyone's minds.

Chapter 46

Christmas 1849

Christmas day fell on a Tuesday this year and so for the first time since we had arrived in England we would only have one day for the celebrations.

As we sat having lunch in the Edwards' kitchen on the Tuesday before Mrs Thompson turned to Mama asking, 'Maria, I just need to check that you understand the arrangements we have previously discussed about the duties coming up to Christmas?'

Mama nodded answering, 'yes Mrs Thompson, you have said the master and his wife are entertaining over the holiday and you will require us here on Christmas Eve in order that everything is in order and up to date.'

'Yes I trust you have managed to rearrange your other commitments accordingly?'

'Yes, we are to work on our other jobs on Sunday so we are free to be here the following day.'

'Very well, that is splendid; there will be much to do.'

We carried on eating for a while before she continued,' if you were all live in staff you would obviously spend Christmas day here and eat with us, however this is not the case.'

Mama jumped in quickly saying, 'Mrs Thompson, we ………'

Mrs Thompson held up her hand for silence, indicating she had not finished speaking yet. 'Although that is not the case, Mrs Edwards has asked me to extend the same hospitality to you and your family for the festivities as if you were live in staff. She has been most impressed with your service and my reports of you.'

Mama was taken aback as I was, 'Mrs Thompson please pass on my gratitude to the mistress for her kind gesture but we could not possibly leave my husband and other son alone on Christmas day so I am afraid we must decline the offer.'

'No Maria, you don't understand, the invitation is for you and all of your family.'

'Oh my, I am sure I don't know what to say. May I speak with my husband first and let you know?'

'Of course, but please do so by tomorrow.'

'Yes indeed I will.'

As we walked home that afternoon Mama and I chatted excitedly, trying to imagine what dinner at the house would be like. Danny kept interrupting as he wondered if he may be asked to help with the horses. Then I suddenly said, 'Mama whatever will we wear?'

'Good heavens, our Sunday clothes I should imagine, we have nothing else, and we can't go like this,' she said looking down at our everyday work clothes.

I realised we were already planning the day and we had not even spoken to Papa yet, I truly hoped he would agree.

Tommy was home when we arrived and Danny wasted no time in telling his brother about the invitation. I was surprised to see that in no way was Tommy as excited as the three of us were, his reaction was a shrug of the shoulders.

'What is wrong Tommy?' Mama said.

'I thought we were having our own Christmas here, with our tree.'

'We will still have that, we will only be there for dinner,' she tried to reassure him.

'I don't know any of the people there.'

'You will like them,' I said,' they are all very friendly.'

'They may be but they are different to us.'

'In what way are they different,' Mama asked.

'They are rich.'

'Tommy we wouldn't be eating with the family, just the staff and they are workers just like us.'

Tommy said nothing, and I was worried that this may also be the reaction of my father. I hadn't thought of it from their point of view.

'Danny, when your father comes home please let me talk to him alright?' Mama said.

'Yes Mama,' Danny answered, slightly deflated.

Finally Papa returned home and Mama waited until he had settled himself on his chair by the fire before she broached the subject. Once she had finished speaking she asked, 'well Daniel, what is your opinion?' I could hear the anticipation in her voice.

'Well it is indeed a very generous invitation, but I am not sure. Tommy and I don't know them as you three do. Also the children have gone to so much trouble with the tree and the decorations. You have already made the pudding, and ordered the goose. If you cancel that it won't be very fair on the butcher and he may not be so happy to take our order next year.'

'We could cook the goose when we get home on the Christmas Eve and have it cold for our tea the next day and the pudding would only need steaming. We could have our family Christmas when we get back in the afternoon. You will like the staff Daniel, they are very friendly.'

Papa looked at Tommy, I knew he was aware how much we wanted to go but was concerned for my brother, 'Tommy what do you think? I want you to be truthful.'

Tommy looked around the room at the faces of us all, he took a while before answering finally saying, 'well as long as we can have our own celebrations when we get home, I will go.'

Danny hugged his brother, saying 'I will ask Peter to show you the horses.'

Mama stopped him by saying, 'Danny your father hasn't told us yet what he wants to do.'

Danny let go of Tommy and looked at our father.

Papa smiled at him and said, 'don't worry son I will go.'

Danny leapt around the room squealing with delight and giving everyone a hug.

So the run up to Christmas was extremely busy, we worked at the Edwards' on the Saturday, then from home on Sunday, Papa helped us that day as Tommy was working on the stall, customers buying their fruit and vegetables early as most would be working the following day. Still the extra money would be welcome.

Papa had said he would collect the goose when he finished work on Monday and Tommy was bringing the rest of the things from the stall. So with everything in place we set off to the Edwards' early on the morning of my fifteenth birthday. Mama had even left instructions with Papa so that he could put the goose on to begin cooking when he got home.

There was a fresh covering of snow shrouding the trees and bushes; everything looked beautiful in the early morning sunlight. Although it was early the streets were busy, people going to work and others to market to collect their provisions. Tommy had said that they had been extremely busy the day before and Mr Stone was expecting it to be even more so today. Many people had placed orders with him last week and the goods had to be ready for collection today, he was hoping to be home on time but said he would stay until all the jobs had been completed. Mr Stone wasn't leaving him alone today even though it was a Monday.

We arrived at the house at six o'clock and already the kitchen was a hive of activity, Mrs Bowes was making pastry and the two girls were peeling vegetables. Mr Morgan appeared from the wine cellar with a selection of bottles and began to wipe the dust from them, placing the white wines to one side to be chilled ready for the dinner tomorrow.

Bernie came in from the garden, stamping his feet on the door scrape to remove the snow from his boots, his arms full of holly and mistletoe which he placed on a small table in the corner, ready to be made into displays for the table.

As we were removing our coats Mrs Thompson swept into the room, she seemed to move so effortlessly, gliding across the floor so gracefully. Although she was very busy making sure all was going according to plan and everyone knew what they were doing she did not appear in the least bit flustered.

'Mrs Bowes,' she began, 'the butcher says he will be delivering the poultry and meat at ten this morning, the fruit and vegetables will be here at eleven. I trust you have everything else you need?'

'Yes everything is in hand Mrs Thompson; the larder is full and the fishmonger delivered just before six this morning, we are up to date with our preparations.'

'Good,' turning to Bernie she said, 'as soon as you have finished what you are doing you need to speak to Mr Morgan and he will instruct you what to do next.'

'Yes mam.'

Happy that things were all in hand she left.

Mrs Bowes looked at us and said with a smile, 'I have worked here for twenty six years now but still she checks on me every Christmas.'

Mama smiled back and we left them to their chores and went to begin our day. Today the main tasks were starching, pressing and ironing, all the washing having been done previously. The Edwards' had their friends Mr and Mrs Fraser coming today and staying overnight and then they had another eight guests coming for Christmas day, all ten would then be staying and leaving on Saturday. We had already been asked to go in on the following Sunday again to make a start on all the bed linen and such like. Although it was eating into our family time, my parents had agreed that as it was only once a year it was worth the sacrifice for the extra money it would bring in.

When we went for our lunch we could hardly believe our eyes, every available surface was filled with cooling pies, breads, cakes and other delights. There were trays of others waiting to go in the ovens, the smells were amazing and I wondered what on earth it would be like tomorrow. Bernie was busy peeling potatoes and looked pleased to leave the job in order to eat. We were joined by two girls and a young man who Mrs Bowes explained were hired waiting staff who they employed whenever the Edwards' had a large gathering.

Peter came in from the stables and asked my mother if there was any chance that she could spare Danny for a while this afternoon as he had to prepare extra stabling for the Frasers carriage horses and Mr Edwards and Charles had been out riding this morning unexpectedly, which meant he had to groom Duke and Ebony. Mama was about to answer when Mrs Thompson said, 'Maria before you commit to anything I will be bringing the mistresses dresses this afternoon for you to press.'

'How many will there be?' my mother asked.

'Well there are three for each day, so twelve in total.'

I couldn't not imagine owning so many dresses; I had two, one for work and one for best. I was eager to see these garments up close, the one I had seen her wearing that evening was absolutely beautiful.

'I will see how we get on Peter, if we can spare him I will send him over,' Mama told him. I could see both Peter and Danny were disappointed by this but my mother was right, we had to make sure we had everything done before we left.

Lunch finished we returned to work and Mrs Thompson delivered the dresses, they were amazing. Made from silks and cotton, with long sleeves, narrow waists and frilled shoulders and necklines, three had huge bustles at the back. Three were a deep blue, one purple, two green, four were blood red and the other two snow white. Along with the dresses there were petticoats to fill out the skirts, I would have loved to wear any of the dresses but I wasn't sure of the huge heavy petticoats and wondered how someone as delicate as Mrs Edwards managed it.

In a little over an hour the three of us had finished everything apart from the gowns, Mama decided that it was best if she kept Danny away from such lavish garments and told him he could go and help Peter until we were ready to go home.

We finally finished work at about four o'clock and we collected our coats ready to go and find my brother. The kitchen was still a hive of activity and I wondered what time they would get finished tonight, everyone was busy, even Mr Morgan and Mrs Thompson were now engaged in the food preparation.

Mrs Thompson looked up at us both, 'thank you for all your hard work this morning, and we will see you tomorrow for dinner at three o'clock.'

We walked over to the stables and found Danny with Peter brushing down Duke, the large grey stallion that belonged to Mr Edwards, he was a huge muscular animal but Danny handled him with confidence, the horse standing patiently as Danny pulled a huge comb through his tail.

'Come on now Danny, we have to leave, your father and brother will be waiting for us.'

'Thank you for the loan of your son Mrs Rafferty,' Peter said, 'I look forward to seeing you all tomorrow and meeting the rest of your family.'

'Is it right that dinner will not be until three tomorrow?' Mama asked.

'Yes, we have to wait until everyone upstairs has finished before we can sit down, but I guarantee it's worth the wait.'

'Of course,' Mama replied, 'I should have thought about it.'

By the time we got back to our room, Papa and Tommy were home and Papa had followed Mama's instructions and the goose was roasting in the oven.

'Mr Stone sends his best wishes to us all for Christmas Mama and he has given me these oranges that were left over,' Tommy said.

Mama admitted she had been wrong about the man and regretted her cold treatment towards him but said she still would never forgive him.

After greeting us all Papa flopped his body down into his chair by the fire, sighing and rubbing his face with his hands.

'Are you alright Daniel?' Mama asked him.

'Yes just a little weary today.'

'Well put your feet up and we will take care of you this evening.'

'No I'm fine, you have been working just as hard, if not harder, I am just tired. Nothing a good night's sleep won't cure I'm sure.'

After supper we sat around the fire chatting for a while, excitement mounting at the thought of tomorrow. I looked across to Papa and he was asleep, his chin resting on his chest.

'That's not a bad idea,' Mama said, 'let's call it a day. Danny seems to be waking us up earlier each year, at this rate we won't be getting to bed at all in the future.'

Christmas day arrived with a clear bright sky and a watery sun reflecting off the newly fallen covering of snow overnight. Danny was the first to awaken and soon made sure the rest of us were also awake. Because we were not due to eat dinner until three o'clock we decided to have some of the cold goose for breakfast, thinking we wouldn't be too hungry in the evening when we returned.

Then we went for a brisk walk around the park, returning home to warm up near the fire. After that we exchanged our gifts, I received a pair of delicate lace gloves that Mama had made, which I felt sure would not look out of place up at the big house.

Having washed and changed into our Sunday clothes we left the house to walk to the Edwards' for our dinner. Mama had spoken to me and

Danny before we left telling us to make sure that Papa and Tommy did not feel out of place there.

'Don't forget,' she warned us, 'they don't know these people as we do and so it is up to us to put them at their ease.'

'We will,' we promised.

As we arrived at the door to the kitchen, Papa stopped, straightened his collar and tie, removed his cap and smoothed down his hair, my two brothers copying his actions, then he nodded to Mama that he was ready and we walked in.

Mrs Thompson walked over and kissed Mama and I on the cheek, then she held out her hand to my father and brothers wishing us all seasons' greetings. I was quite taken aback, never having witnessed such emotions from her before. Then she introduced all the staff by their given name, Mama carrying out our introductions. The hired staff were Rosie, Jean and George.

Once the formalities were over we took our places at the table, it was laid out with a pure white table cloth, and in the centre was a decoration of holly and mistletoe. I looked at the cutlery in front of me, I had three knives and forks to either side and a spoon and fork at the top of the placing, and there was a linen napkin on my left and three glasses also.

Mr Morgan went around the table pouring white wine into all the glasses apart from mine and my brothers, these he filled with water. Then once he had taken his place at the head of the table, Mrs Thompson, Rosie and Jean began to serve us, placing a plate of fish in a white sauce in front of us. It smelt delicious, grace was said and then I watched as Mr Morgan picked up the knife and fork on the outside of his plate, looking around quickly I saw that's what everyone else had done and so I followed suit. As I cut into the fish it separated with no effort at all, but it was the taste I couldn't believe, the fish melted in my mouth and the sauce was rich and creamy with a slight salty taste. The fish course was cleared away and once again Mrs Thompson and the two others began to load the table with dishes. My mother started to rise from her seat to help but was told by Mrs Bowes to sit down.

'It's the tradition in this house at Christmas that the housekeeper and butler serve the staff, also Mrs Edwards insists that we eat as they do on this one day.'

With that Mr Morgan rose and began to refill the wine glasses, this time with a deep red liquid, when he reached me he asked, 'Millie would you like to try some wine?'

I had never drunk wine before in my life and looked to my parents for guidance, finding none from my father who looked as bemused as I did I turned to Mama.

'Well my dear, you were fifteen yesterday so I think you could try a little, but be careful, don't rush it.'

Mrs Bowes suddenly looked up, 'Oh my dear girl, I had no idea, a very happy birthday for yesterday.' She came round to me and placed a kiss on my cheek, blushing I accepted the hearty cheers from everyone else. By then the meal was laid out, dishes of crispy roasted potatoes and parsnips, carrots, onions, green beans, bread and cranberry sauce. Mrs Thompson placed a huge silver plate in front of Mr Morgan upon which rested a huge turkey, it's skin brown and crispy and when he pushed the fork in, the skin crackled and juices flooded the platter. He carved expertly and soon we all had a portion each, then dishes were passed around and we began to eat. I took a sip of the red wine and I was amazed by the smooth taste of it, as I swallowed I could feel the warmth of it as it slipped down my throat. The potatoes were crispy on the outside and soft and fluffy inside, the turkey tasted so different to the goose we had eaten earlier, it was not at all greasy but altogether drier.

More wine flowed as the table was cleared and the sound level rose as we talked and laughed, looking across at Tommy who was sat in between Danny and Patsy I could see he was overwhelmed by it all but more importantly he was happily chatting to each of them. Papa was sat in between Mama and I and he seemed to have relaxed also, he bent his head to me and said, 'if this is how their staff eat I can see why you like coming here so much.'

'Are you glad you came Papa?'

'Yes I am, they are good folk as you said.'

Next we were presented with a plate of roasted beef with a creamy mashed potato, covered in rich onion gravy. The buttery potatoes were a hit with Tommy who had a second helping. I had no idea how he managed it as I was feeling decidedly full by now. I took another sip of my wine, feeling relief that we had come to the end of the fare, and then I remembered the fork and spoon at the top of my placing.

Sure enough a huge fruit pudding was brought to the table, Mr Morgan then called for quiet, when every head turned to him he placed a match to the pudding and it caught alight, blue flames licking the edges, he managed to make sure each person received a slice of the still flaming dessert, bowls of rich brandy cream were handed round.

Once the meal was over, Rosie, Jean and George began the dishes and I went to help them, I felt it was the least I could do, also I was glad of an excuse to move from my seat, Mama coming over to join us.

Peter said he must go and attend to the horses for the evening and asked Danny to go and help him. 'Can my father and brother come please?' Danny asked.

'Of course, if they would like to,' Peter answered.

Both nodded, my father adding, 'I need to see these horses I hear so much about for myself.'

It was now five o'clock and suddenly a bell hanging high up on the kitchen wall rang, there was a sign underneath saying parlour. Mr Morgan rose and left to see what his employers wanted.

He returned a short while later telling Mrs Bowes they would like some sandwiches and tea. The celebrations appeared to be over with duties again to be performed.

At last the final dishes were cleaned and away and Mama thanked Mrs Bowes for the wonderful meal and Mrs Thompson for the invitation.

'None of us will ever forget this day I know.'

'Surely you are not leaving so soon,' Mrs Bowes said aghast.

'Well yes.'

'Nonsense, it's too early, you don't want to miss all the fun do you?'

'What do you mean?'

'Well we play parlour games and sing carols just like they do upstairs, the only thing they do that we don't is the dancing' she said.

I was reminded of our first Christmas with Stan and Susan and hoped very much that we could stay. Mama said she would see what my father wanted to do when he returned from the stables. When the four of them returned, pink faced from the cold and brushing the snow from their coats, Mama asked the question, amazingly Papa did not hesitate at all before answering positively, 'yes I would love to stay.'

And so we spent the next three hours, playing games, singing carols, laughing and telling stories. Occasionally the bell would ring and some refreshments would have to be taken up, but the intrusion was brief. We could hear music drifting down from upstairs; apparently they had hired some musicians and were holding a dance with more guests from the town, Mr Morgan and George were kept busy taking wine and spirits from the cellar.

When Mrs Bowes drifted off to sleep in a chair by the fire Mama decided it was time we took our leave.

'Thank you so much once again for a wonderful day,' she said, 'I know none of us will ever forget today. Also would you please express our sincere gratitude to the master and mistress for their hospitality?'

'Of course, it was so nice to meet your family today, they are a credit to you both,' Mrs Thompson said.

As we walked round the side of the house towards the drive we passed the ballroom windows, the curtains were open and I cast a glance in. The room was a swirl of colour, men and women were whirling around the floor, the men elegant in their dress suits, but it was the women in their beautiful colourful gowns, long lace gloves, hair piled high on their heads, their hands held lightly in the backs of their partners that took my breath away. As the couples swept past the window I suddenly saw Mr Charles as he spun a dainty girl across the floor, he looked so handsome in his crisp white shirt and high collar, smiling at something she had said to him, and then he had gone.

We walked home through the quiet snow covered streets, again catching glimpses of other people's celebrations; I doubted anyone would have had a better day than us.

The room was cold when we entered, the fire having gone out some time ago, so we set about building it up once again and once the room was warm we sat for an hour reliving our evening before going to bed.

Last year as we had made our plans we had never thought it would turn out like this, I drifted off to sleep trying to imagine what it must be like to live like that every day.

Chapter 47

It was now the second of January and Papa had developed a cough that left him short of breath, although he refused to take any time off work. Mama had tried to persuade him to take at least one day in bed, saying that working outside in the cold would only prolong his recovery. I hadn't remembered her being so concerned over a cough before and wondered what it could be that was worrying her but she did not confide in me.

Sunday arrived and Papa was no better and said he would spend the day in bed in order to take some rest. We tried to keep the noise to a minimum whilst we prepared the lunch and he slept soundly all morning, woken only by the clatter of plates as we prepared the table. He propped himself up on his pillow saying he felt better for the lay in but did not feel up to eating anything. Mama told him he must have something and prepared a sort of broth from the meat stock which she seasoned and served him with a large slice of bread. He did manage the broth but could not eat the bread saying it made him cough to chew.

After lunch Mama told the three of us to go to the park for a while and so we left her sitting on the side of the bed, Papa's hand in hers. Upon our return about an hour later she had not moved although her patient was once again asleep. She looked anxious and I asked her if I could do anything to help, she shook her head and tears began to fall from her eyes. I ran to her and gathered her in my arms, 'please Mama tell me what's wrong,'

She looked up into my face and I knew she was ready to tell me what was wrong but her glance at my brothers as they removed their outer garments told me she wished for privacy.

'Boys,' I said, 'could you please fetch some more fuel for the fire, we need to keep the room warm for Papa.'

Without a word of protest they donned caps and jackets once again and trudged out to the yard.

'Oh Millie, your father and I agreed we would not worry you all unduly but I fear the worst for him.' She pulled me to her and squeezed me tightly, 'you can't repeat this to your brothers. Do you promise me?'

'Of course,' I answered immediately with a deep sense of foreboding.

Mama then told me of Papa's encounter with the stowaway who ultimately died from tuberculosis. I sat still and quiet, trying to make sense of what she had just told me, Papa was always so fit and healthy, nothing like this could be happening to him, but then I looked at him as he lay back on the bed, his eyes shut and his hair wet at the scalp as if in a fever.

'We will take care of him, he will be alright you'll see.'

With that Tommy and Danny returned hauling a basket of wood across to the hearth.

All evening we kept the fire build up to keep the room warm, Mama saying she was sweating it out of him. My brothers went to bed but we stayed up all night to tend to him, taking cat naps on and off.

The next morning Papa said he felt better but after the day in bed he was weak and Mama persuaded him to take a day off in order to fully recover. I ran down to the docks to report his absence and to say he would be back tomorrow, then after picking up Danny we went around collecting the washing for that day and taking it back to the house. Mama came down to help us, returning upstairs at regular intervals to check on Papa. By the end of the day he looked better, some colour returning to his face, he sat near the fire eating soup Mama had made especially.

Tuesday morning dawned and Papa declared himself fit to return to the docks, although I could tell Mama was not happy with the idea but as we would be at the Edwards' house all day she let him go making him promise to come home if he relapsed.

'I cannot afford to take any more time off,' he said, 'I am losing pay and I fear for my position if I stay away for too long. There are more than enough people waiting for permanent work as it is.'

The weather today was wet and cold, which did not make conditions very good for either Papa working outside or for us trying to get all the linen dried inside the humid room. By lunchtime we were drenched in sweat and water from the dripping ceiling as the clothes dried in the steam.

Sitting at the kitchen table eating leftover meat from the Sunday roast Mama spoke to Mrs Thompson. 'Excuse me Mrs Thompson but may I ask you something?'

'Of course Mrs Rafferty.'

'Well, I have been told that one of our other customers died of tuberculosis recently.'

'Oh dear that is sad to hear, I thought the worst of those days were over. What is it you want to know?'

'I wondered if you knew whether we could have caught it from her, by touching her clothes.'

Mrs Thompson replied, 'No Mrs Rafferty, the only way you can contract the disease is either by breathing the air in which they are, this has to be over a long period of time. It is rare to contract it from casual contact, or if they cough or sneeze on you, you could get it that way. Have you done any of those things?'

'No Mrs Thompson I haven't.'

'Well then you are perfectly safe.'

Mama looked over at me and I could see the relief flood her face.

As we walked round to the stables that afternoon to collect Danny to go home Mama said, 'I have just realised, we burnt a perfectly good set of your fathers work clothes for nothing.'

We both laughed, the tension leaving us.

When Papa returned from the docks he was clearly still suffering from the effects of his cough, but Mama took him to one side and told him what Mrs Thompson had said about contracting TB and I could see he was relieved.

'Thank God,' he said, 'I would never forgive myself if I had caused any of you ill health by my own stupidity.'

Over the next few days Papa gradually shook off the cough and returned to full health; however it wasn't to be long before we experienced another family health issue.

Chapter 48

January 1850

We had been experiencing a strange mixture of weather during the early part of January, ranging from days of heavy rain to a thick heavy fog that shrouded the town for days, its damp tendrils clinging to everything and seeping into your very core. As we approached Mama's thirty sixth birthday, on the twenty fifth, she was taken ill, she once again fell victim to the hacking cough she had contracted whilst working at the cotton mill. I was not surprised as we were constantly working in hot steamy rooms trying to keep on top of the laundry that paid for so many things for us. We were beginning to fall behind with the work as we could not get things dried quickly enough. Mama had said we may have to let some of our customers go if we were to survive and keep those that paid the best. She felt bad about this, as these people had kept us going in the early days when times were tough, but we had to do the best for us. She had not made the final decision before she was taken ill.

It started on the Tuesday the twenty second as we were walking up to the Edwards' house; she was finding it difficult to get her breath as we trudged through the early morning mist.

'Are you alright?' I asked concerned as she stopped for a moment to catch her breath, her hand clutched to her chest.

'Yes,' she wheezed, 'just a little breathless.'

'Maybe you should go home,' I suggested.

'No we are nearly there now, I will be alright.'

We continued onwards and at last reached the warm sanctuary of the kitchen, she took a glass of water from the tap and we went off to our room to begin our day's work. I tried to keep my eye on her but she told me to stop fussing and we carried on.

I pulled Danny to one side and said to him, 'Danny would you mind terribly staying and helping us this afternoon, I want to get Mama home and to bed as soon as possible.'

Danny was obviously also concerned as he didn't hesitate in his reply, 'no I will tell Peter at lunchtime that I have to help here.'

Finally we completed the task and made the walk back to our room, the fog had not lifted all day and by the time we arrived home our hair and clothes were covered in moisture. Once inside I built up the fire and insisted Mama get out of her damp clothes and into bed, she did not resist me and within minutes was tucked up with the blankets pulled up to her chin, by now she had begun to shiver and complained that she could not seem to get warm. I was relieved when Papa and Tommy arrived home shortly after us. I set about making supper whilst Papa tended to my mother; eventually she fell into a fitful sleep. During the night she developed a fever and became delirious, mumbling in her sleep and throwing the blankets off in an effort to cool down. Papa and I kept soaking rags in cold water and laying them on her hot brow, and trying to get her to sip water, but she could not swallow it and so we gave up in the end.

By the time morning broke none of us must have had much more that a couple of hours sleep, Mama's coughing and fevered ramblings having kept us awake, not to mention the concern. Once again as before we tried to work out a plan whereby we could look after Mama and also earn money, we knew Mama had some put by but did not want to use that until we had to, we had already experienced Papa losing a day's wage due to unforeseen circumstances.

Luckily today was a day when we would have been working in the yard outside, so after making sure Mama was comfortable, Danny and I rushed around collecting the washing and raced back home. I ran upstairs to check on her, and finding her asleep went downstairs to help my brother. Constant visits upstairs by the two of us meant that we were falling behind in our work and by the time Papa and Tommy came home we were nowhere near finished. As with the last time she was ill, I went upstairs to put the supper on and then back down, the four of us working until the jobs were completed and we trudged back to our room to eat and then collapse into bed. The next day would pose a problem if she were no better as we were supposed to be at the Edwards' and there was no way she could be left in her present state. She in fact was worse than the previous night, alternating between fever and delirium to chills, her whole body shaking as she tried to get warm. There was also the shortness of breath and the violent hacking cough during which she was coughing up mucus. We were all deeply worried about her and I began to wonder if maybe Mrs Thompson was incorrect when she said that Papa could not have contracted tuberculosis and had in fact passed this on to Mama, I could see that this was on his mind also.

The next day Papa and I sat down to work out what we would do and it was decided that Papa would walk to the Edwards' house early before attending the docks to inform them of the situation and see if we could rearrange the days this week, whilst Danny and I looked after Mama.

Daniel walked up to the kitchen door as he had been told to do by his daughter; he knocked lightly and stepped inside. The kitchen was warm and inviting after the cold outside.

'Is Mrs Thompson available, I need to speak to her, I am Daniel Rafferty, Maria's husband?'

'Yes, just a moment, I remember you from Christmas,' Mrs Bowes said to him, then turning to one of the girls said, 'Patsy please go and find Mrs Thompson and ask if she will come and speak with Mr Rafferty.'

The girl nodded and left the room returning moments later followed by Mrs Thompson.

'What can I do for you Mr Rafferty?'

'It's my wife Maria, she is very sick at the moment and I am afraid she will not be able to attend today, I have had to leave Millie to look after her so that I can go to work. Would it be acceptable if they were to come tomorrow instead?'

'Oh dear, I am sorry your wife is ill, but this is most inconvenient. Are you sure they will be here tomorrow if she is as ill as you say?'

'Yes, they do not want to let you down and so they will definitely be here tomorrow,' Daniel answered although he was not at all sure that would be the case, but he knew how much they depended on the money this one contract alone brought into the house and he did not want to risk losing the work.

'Very well, I will accept the inconvenience today, but I will expect them to attend work tomorrow and Saturday to make sure they do not fall behind. The Edwards' have many guests here this weekend and everything needs to be in order. If they let us down I am afraid I will have to look elsewhere.'

'Thank you Mrs Thompson, I will pass the message on.' With that he left and worried how they were going to work this one out.

Papa called in on his way to the dock yard to tell me what Mrs Thompson had said, I was grateful she had accepted the change of arrangement, but I had no idea how we were going to fulfil all the work without letting somebody down. Mama had worked so hard to build up the business and it was my duty to keep it running smoothly.

'Danny, I want you to sit with Mama for a while, I am going to go and collect the washing that we would normally do on Fridays and bring it back here, that way we will be free to go to the Edwards' tomorrow. Can you do that?'

'Yes Millie, you won't be long though will you?'

'No I will be as quick as I can, if you need any help get the lady who lives across the landing.'

With that I went out and hurried as quickly as I could around the houses, precious time was eaten up by having to explain to each customer why we were forced to change their day, but all understood and as they were very fond of Mama they wished her well and handed over the loads. The only issue with this arrangement was that all expected to have to pay on Friday and so they said they would not have the money available for my return. I assured them that I would collect the money tomorrow as normal after I had finished at the Edwards'.

Rushing back I ran upstairs, Danny said Mama had been coughing a lot and was still sweating from the fever but he had not needed to call for help. Once again the day's labours took longer than usual and after the four of us had finished supper we were ready for bed, but before we could do that Papa and I had to work out how we were going to sort out tomorrow as it was obvious Mama would not be fit by then. It was decided that Papa would take the day off tomorrow and Tommy would ask for Saturday off, with any luck she would be back on her feet by Monday, if she wasn't Danny and I could manage the work from home again that day, Tuesday would pose another problem altogether, but we hoped it wouldn't come to that.

Danny and I walked up to the Edwards', upon entering the kitchen Mrs Bowes looked up from her pastry and frowned, 'where is your mother?'

'She is still poorly,' I replied.

'I hoped she would be better, what is wrong with her?'

I explained about the recurring cough she had suffered since working at the cotton mill.

'Oh I have heard about that, they can certainly take it out of a person, I hope she gets back on her feet soon. But how are you two going to manage on your own?'

'We know what we are doing.'

'I know that, I didn't mean to imply otherwise, I just know how long it takes the three of you.'

'Well we will just have to work later if needs be,' I replied defiantly.

'Millie, I didn't mean to upset you; I just don't know how you will get finished.'

Danny and I slogged all morning and I was concerned that we would not actually get finished no matter how long we stayed. We were grateful to sit down at lunchtime, although we encountered our next problem when Mrs Thompson walked in to join us.

Looking around she asked, 'where is your mother?'

'At home in bed, she is still very poorly.'

'Well I am not sure this is what I agreed with your father yesterday.'

I was not sure what to say to the formidable lady, but Mrs Bowes came to my rescue.

'Begging your pardon Mrs Thompson, you and Mr Rafferty agreed to change the day from Thursday to Friday. They are here and working and have said they will stay until they are finished, so no harm is done.'

Mrs Thompson looked at Mrs Bowes and then at us, ' I concede that was our agreement, but I must insist that after lunch I come and inspect your work to date to make sure it comes up to your mothers high standards.'

She was true to her word and followed us to the room and inspected many garments before declaring, 'although I am not sure this is at all proper, you are doing a good job, carry on.' Just before she left she added, 'don't forget to be here tomorrow as usual, will we see your mother?'

I had to be honest, 'I really don't know, but previously she has recovered after the weekend.'

Mrs Thompson seemed satisfied and nodded her head leaving us to continue our work. I ran after her, 'Mrs Thompson,'

'Yes?'

'The other day when Mama asked you about her customer who had died of tuberculosis.'

'Oh my goodness is that what's wrong with her?'

'No, well I hope not. She asked you if she could have caught it off their clothes.'

'Yes.'

'Well could she?'

'No dear, I told you how you can contract it.'

'Are you entirely sure?'

'Girl, do you doubt me?'

'No mam.' I went on to explain the situation with my father and the dying man.

'Look dear, you have nothing to worry about if what you tell me is true. Listen I like your mother and if she is no better by Monday, call round and let me know and I will see if I can persuade the family doctor to call and see her.'

'Thank you so much Mrs Thompson, you are indeed very kind, but I don't know if we will be able to afford to pay him.'

'He is a very good friend of mine,' she said smiling,' I may be able to get him to waive any fee for a consultation; however any treatment would have to be paid for.'

I thanked her once again and feeling more relieved I rejoined Danny and set to the mountain of work we still had to complete.

Our normal finish time of three thirty had been passed some hour and a half ago and just when I was wondering what time we would ever get back home, knowing I also had payments to collect yet, we heard footsteps approaching down the passageway.

Looking up I saw Peter standing in the doorway, 'Hey little fella,' he said to Danny,' I am missing you.'

Danny sighed and replied, 'me too but I have to help Millie, Mama is very ill and we have to get all this done before we can go home.'

'Can I help?'

'No it's not your work,' I said.

'Look your brother has helped me for some time now and it wasn't his work either, the least I can do is pay back the favour. I have finished my work for the day, besides I can bring Danny up to date with the horses.'

Thanking him and accepting his generous offer we managed to get everything done within the next hour and left for home at six o'clock.

I dropped Danny off at home, checking with Papa on mother's condition before I went out collecting the money. She was pretty much as before and still had not managed to eat anything. I told him what Mrs Thompson had said and about her offer of the doctor.

'Your mother told you about the man who died then,' he stated flatly.

'Yes she was worried about you.'

'I was foolish to risk such a thing.'

'Well no harm has come of it, I am going to get the money and then I will prepare our supper.'

'I have done that,' Papa said, pointing to a pan of vegetables boiling on the stove, 'it may not be up to the standards of you or your mother but it will be edible.'

Kissing him, I thanked him and walked out into the cold dark evening.

It took me about forty minutes to walk to all the houses we serviced and collect the money, everyone asked how Mama was and I was quite cold by the time I got back home. Gratefully I flopped in a chair near to the fire and stretched out my legs to warm my feet.

Papa served up the supper and afterwards we all took to our beds, the long hours and the worry were taking their toll on us all.

The man watched the young girl as she entered a door off the street and disappeared from view, he waited a while but she did not reappear so he presumed she must live there. He had caught sight of her some twenty minutes ago as she stood shivering talking to an elderly woman in her kitchen doorway, the woman then passed the girl some money. The girl then left waving and walked to another house and followed the same routine. He had seen her collect money from at least six houses now and wondered how many she may have called at before he noticed her.

He then went to the tavern to join his brother and friend, taking a note of the time as he entered the building.

'You're late, I thought you weren't coming,' his brother said.

'I've just been doing a bit of research,' he replied.

'What do you mean?' the other man asked.

'I have been watching a young lass collecting money from houses.'

'What and you let her keep it? You're slipping, how old was she?'

'I don't know, about thirteen, the reason I let her keep it this time was I only spotted her after a while, I don't know how many places she had been to beforehand. The thing was she went into a house and didn't come out.'

'Ok so you know where she lives, so what. You can hardly walk in there and demand the money, I doubt she will be on her own.'

'I sometimes wonder if you are really my brother, you are so stupid. I now know where she lives and where the last house she collects from is, plus the way she goes home.'

'And?'

'So I know the best place to wait for her before she gets home and I can relieve her of her money.'

'Oh yes,' his mind finally catching up with that of his brother.

'Are you in Robbie? I don't know how much there will be between the three of us.'

'Well even if it only pays for a couple of ales each it will be easy money, yes I'm in.'

'Right, we will sort out what we are doing when we meet next week. Now whose round is it?'

Chapter 49

Monday morning came and there had been no improvement in Mama at all. She still had a fever combined with a rattling cough; she had not eaten for five days now and was only taking sips of water. Her breathing was laboured and when she was not coughing, she slept.

I ran all the way to the Edwards' and rushing in, gasped out, 'please Mrs Bowes could you ask Mrs Thompson to send her doctor friend round to us as soon as possible. Mama is still very poorly and we are all so worried about her. We will find the money if we have to, just please help us.'

'Of course child.'

I gave her our address and ran all the way back home, when I got back Papa was sat on the side of the bed, his hand tightly holding Mama's.

'Millie, what did she say?'

'She is going to get the doctor to call today.'

'When?'

'I don't know, as soon as she can. You must go to work now, there is nothing you can do here and you have already lost two days this month. You don't want to risk losing your job or that promotion you have been promised.'

'Yes but I shouldn't be leaving this to you.'

'Papa, I am alright. I have Danny with me; we can't afford to lose money, we may have to pay for treatment. Mama doesn't know who is here anyway. Danny and I are the only ones who have a bit of flexibility in our work. If we need you we know where you are.'

Reluctantly Papa left, after making us promise to let him know as soon as the doctor had left.

Danny and I were washing in the yard when the doctor finally arrived at about ten o'clock. We led him up to the room where Mama lay in her bed, pale and drawn, her auburn hair spread on the pillow, and wet at the scalp due to the fever.

I told the man her symptoms and how we were worried it could be tuberculosis. He reassured me at once that wasn't what she was suffering from. So then I told him all about the cough she had contracted at the cotton mill and that she had never fully shaken it off.

'Well dear, that may well have contributed to her present condition,' he said after thoroughly examining her, 'but your mother has bronchial pneumonia.'

'Is that bad?' I asked, feeling rather stupid as soon as I had said it; it was obvious by her condition that it was bad.

'Yes dear, it can be very serious. The fever should go after about a week, but she may continue to have chest pain for about four weeks. The breathlessness and cough can last up to six weeks.'

'But she will get better won't she?' I could feel my nails pressing into my palms as I held my breath waiting for his reply.

'She should do, but even after these symptoms have gone she will not have the energy she used to have for maybe as much as three months, it could be six months before she is fully recovered.'

'What can we do for her?'

'Continue to keep her warm and make sure she has plenty to drink, as soon as she is able get her to eat. Then it's just a question of time. Good day to you.'

With that he left the house, I told Danny to run and tell Papa and Tommy what he had said as I knew they were both worried. I then sat down near the fire and wondered how much longer we could manage to keep the laundry business going without her. So much depended on that income, I looked at my mother and promised her I would work until I dropped to keep the family in food and housing, I owed her nothing less.

Chapter 50

Our mother had been ill for one week now, and although we had all managed to keep our jobs and all of the laundry customers serviced, the extra workload was beginning to tell on us all. The laundry paid the most money but it took the most time, especially when the weather was against us. Papa and Tommy were helping us when they came home, but we were not sitting down to eat until around eight o'clock at the earliest. The combination of the worry along with the fitful sleep we were getting was also having an adverse impact on our health. The knowledge that it could be some weeks at the least before she was fully fit made matters worse.

I felt close to exhaustion and could see in my families faces that I was not alone in this, and as I walked with Danny to the Edwards' house I found it took all my effort to place one foot in front of the other. I looked at my little brother plodding at my side and decided I could not expect him to carry on without a rest.

'Danny, why don't you go home today and have a rest?'

'No Millie, you need my help,' Danny said wearily.

'Look, I can manage today, go and stay with Mama and Mrs Johnson.'

Mrs Johnson was the woman who lived in the room across from us and once we had established for definite that Mama was not suffering from tuberculosis, Papa had asked her if she wouldn't mind sitting with mother while we were away. The lady lived by herself and I think she was glad of the company.

'Mama might come out of her fever today and it would be nice if one of us was there when she does.'

I knew this would hit the spot, Danny wanted to help me but he wanted to be there for Mama even more.

He looked at me questioningly once more and I shoed him away. 'Go and make sure you get some rest and some food.'

With that he turned and headed back home, how I wished I were going with him.

Arriving at the house, Mrs Bowes said, 'where is Danny?'

'I have sent him home; he is out on his feet.'

'Yes but how are you going to manage on your own, they had guests at the weekend as you may recall, and there is more than usual today.'

My heart sank, I had forgotten that and when I walked into the laundry room I felt like crying. Clothes, bed and table linen were arranged in piles and it would have been enough for the three of us, on my own I had no idea when I would get this done.

At lunchtime Patsy appeared in the doorway, 'Mrs Bowes says lunch is on the table.'

'Tell her thank you but I can't afford the time.'

Patsy looked at me but did not answer, instead leaving the room and heading back to the kitchen. A few minutes later I heard footsteps once again in the corridor, followed by Mrs Bowes.

'Now look Millie, I know you have a lot to do, but if you don't eat and take a break you are not going to be any good to anyone. Now come with me.'

'I can't Mrs Bowes,' I said, 'I have all this to do, we must keep this job. My family depends on it.' It was too much for me suddenly and I burst into tears.

She rushed over to me and took me in her arms, 'hush now Millie, we will sort it out. Look there are only two for dinner tonight, Mr and Mrs Edwards are out. The girls will be able to cope so I can come and help you this afternoon.'

Normally I would not have even entertained any thoughts of help, but I was desperate and so I asked, 'are you sure?'

'Never more so, now come and eat.'

It was a relief to sit down and although I didn't feel in the least bit hungry I ate well knowing I needed the energy. Mrs Thompson looked at me a couple of times over lunch but said nothing other than to enquire after Mama's condition.

I told her what the doctor had said and thanked her again for her help in the matter.

After lunch as Mrs Bowes and I were folding sheets I plucked up courage to voice my confusion over the housekeeper.

'She seems like she isn't interested in us, that she is only concerned that we get the job done, but then she sends her friend the doctor round for no charge.'

'Millie, remember that the sole function of her job is to make sure that all the jobs in the house are carried out to a certain standard and on time, if not it's her who takes the hassle. She is still a caring woman and recognises the commitment you are showing.'

Even with help it was half past seven when I left for home. When I walked in my spirits were lifted by the sight of Mama sat up in bed, Danny sleeping soundly at her side.

'Mrs Johnson said her fever broke about three o'clock,' Papa said smiling. 'Now come and sit down and get your supper, you look exhausted, I was just about to come and find you.'

'I had a lot to do but Mrs Bowes helped me, otherwise I would still be there.'

Crossing over and giving Mama a hug and kiss, I ate my supper and then fell asleep it the chair near the fire, waking up later to find a blanket over me and a pillow placed behind my head.

The next day I felt as if I were walking through quicksand, my legs felt so heavy and everything seemed to be taking me so long. I was struggling to lift the heavy wet washing and peg it on the line. My head was spinning and I felt nauseous, I could not face eating even though I knew I should and I was so relieved when we finished for the day and I climbed the stairs. Mama was now free of the fever that had gripped her for eight days but she had a long way to go before she would be fully fit. She was hoping to be back at work by Monday, but we had insisted she was not to return until her breathing was back to normal.

We had planned that if she felt up to it, on Sunday we would celebrate the birthday she had missed due to her illness, nothing too strenuous, just a family day.

Chapter 51

Today was the first day of February and Mama had managed to get out of bed, she wasn't fit to return to work, but she was alright to not have to have a sitter, although I think Mrs Johnson was enjoying the company and the feel of being needed, so she came over anyway. The two of them promised to prepare the days meals which left Danny and I all day to concentrate on our work which was a blessing.

The day was another damp day and made our job more difficult. We had washing hanging all over the yard, but little was drying due to the mist that persisted. We dare not take it to our room to dry in case it set off another of Mama's coughing fits, they were becoming less frequent but there was no point taking any chances.

When we went upstairs for a break, Mrs Johnson, on hearing off our problem kindly let us use her room for drying. We built the fire up in there and could see an improvement immediately. By the time Papa and Tommy came home we were nearly finished with the work but still had to return all the garments and take the payments.

As I struggled to load the last of the deliveries onto the cart Papa came down into the yard.

'Millie, you need to rest.'

'Papa, I am fine, we have only got to deliver these and then we are finished.'

'Yes but tomorrow you are at the house. Go upstairs, I will take these back and get the money. Danny can come with me and show me where we need to go.'

I had to admit that I was so tired and I could see that Danny was keen to spend some time with Papa, even if it was delivering laundry, so I agreed.

'Thank you Papa, I love you. Hurry back and then we can eat.'

Papa kissed my cheek and turning to Danny said, 'come on then son, let's see how quickly we can get this done.'

I climbed the stairs and sat down next to Mama, who had taken to bed again after having spent all morning helping make supper. I dozed in the chair whilst waiting for the return of my father and brother.

Danny led his father around the streets, keeping to the route that he used with Millie to ensure he didn't miss any of the houses. They had done this so many times they now knew the quickest way to complete the job. He chatted to his father, telling him all about the horses up at the

Edwards' house and how much he was looking forward to being able to return to help Peter.

'You really make me proud son,' Daniel said, 'I know how much you like to be at the stables but you have put the family first, just as your sister and brother do, and stepped up to help out while your mother has been ill.'

'You and Mama taught me that,' Danny said, accepting the praise from his father. 'She will get better won't she?'

'Yes Danny, she is improving every day. She must take her time that's all, it's going to take a while, but you should be able to get back to your horses soon enough. How many more houses left?'

'Just three Papa, we go down here, then cut through the alley and home.'

'Good, I'm ready for my supper.'

As they turned the corner they passed three men sitting on a wall smoking.

Robbie turned to his companion, 'I thought you said it was a young girl on her own Ben.'

'It was last week.'

'Well it ain't this week.'

'No kidding, I am glad you pointed that out otherwise I might not have noticed,' Ben said sarcastically.

'Both of you be quiet,' the third said, 'okay so it's a man and a boy. There are three of us and the boy won't be a problem.'

'What, you still want to do it?' Robbie said staring at him.

'Well I have been counting on that money and I need it.'

Ben came to the defence of his brother, 'Mo's right, we can take them.'

'Well are you in Robbie?'

'I don't know,' Robbie said.

'Robbie, don't forget we have our friend with us as well,' Mo laughed patting his jacket pocket.

Robbie cast a glance at Mo and decided it was best not to cross him, so nodding his head he said, 'alright but we only use the knife to frighten them.'

'Of course,' Mo smiled.

The last of the money had been collected and Danny sat on the cart as his father pushed him towards home. Turning into the street which ran parallel to their own he saw two men leaning up against the wall, Daniel hesitated unsure of himself for a moment.

'Why have you stopped Papa?' Danny asked.

'I thought maybe I had taken a wrong turn.'

'No this is right,' Danny answered.

Daniel picked up the handles to the cart again and began to walk slowly forwards, the men pushed themselves from the wall. Daniel turned the cart to retrace his steps, only to be confronted by another man who had followed him in. Daniel made to charge the man with the cart, when he produced a large knife from his jacket pocket saying, 'now don't do anything silly, we won't hurt you if you give us the money.'

Daniel glanced over his shoulder and saw the two others closing in, 'I'll give you the money, just let my son go.'

'We have no quarrel with either of you, we just want the cash,' one of the men at his back said.

Daniel lowered the cart saying, 'Danny climb off the cart slowly and go home.'

'Are you coming?' Danny asked, his wide eyes staring at the blade in the man's hand.

'Yes in a minute, but I need you to go first.'

Danny climbed off the cart and went to stand beside his father.

'Kid, go home!' one of the men shouted.

Danny flinched as the man shouted at him as if he had been struck, he was terrified.

'Very well, if the boy doesn't want to go, just give us the money and we can all go home.' Mo said walking closer to the pair, the knife held tightly in his right hand.

Daniel had no choice and slowly reached into his jacket pocket and pulled the bag of coins out, holding out his hand for the man to take it.

One of the men leaned in and grabbed the bag, 'there that wasn't so hard was it?'

'It's a shame the young girl wasn't here tonight,' Mo said, an evil grin spreading across his face as he twisted the knife in the moonlight, light dancing from the polished blade.

Daniel lunged at the man, but his companions saw what he intended to do and covered the distance between them before Daniel could reach his target, pulling him back and pinning his arms behind his back.

Mo stepped back and walked up to Daniel, his face inches away. 'Now that's not playing nicely is it?' he bought his fist back and punched Daniel in the stomach. Daniel doubled over and Danny screamed.

'Shut up kid,' one man said, 'we don't want to attract a crowd.'

'Come on Robbie, let's get out of here.'

Mo punched Daniel on his jaw and Daniel dropped to the ground, stunned.

'If I see you again, I'll have you,' Daniel said spitting blood onto the ground.

'Oh you think you're a big man do you? We know where you and your daughter live so I should be careful what you say.'

Daniel pushed himself up onto one knee and said, 'you are nothing but cowards, and if you come near my family I will kill you.'

Mo slapped Daniel across the face with the bag containing the coins, knocking him unconscious. Then pulling his leg back he kicked Daniel in the stomach.

Danny was frozen to the spot; he could not move and watched as the man attacked his father.

The man turned and saw Danny watching him, 'this is what you get for trying to be a hero,' approaching the boy and pushing him roughly to the ground. Then he proceeded to kick Daniel about the head and stomach, one kick catching Danny on the side of his jaw, before the others dragged him away and they fled into the night.

I was awakened by Tommy shaking me gently by the shoulder, 'Millie wake up.'

Stretching I roused myself, looking at Tommy I could see something was worrying him. Mama was also agitated and standing by his side said, 'your father and Danny aren't back yet.'

'How long have they been gone?'

'About an hour and a half,' Tommy told me.

That was too long I knew, picking up my shawl I said, 'I'll go and find them. I bet they are just talking.'

'I'll come with you,' Tommy said, 'its dark out there now.'

We stepped out into the dark street and started to walk the route in reverse going to the last drops first. As we turned into the alley we could see two figures laid on the ground up ahead.

'Oh no please don't let it be them,' I screamed, running as fast as I could towards the prone bodies.

'Papa, Danny!' Tommy shouted. No movement, no response.

Papa lay on his side, blood covering his face and coating his mouth and lips, he was curled up in a ball his hands clutching his stomach. Danny was face down next to him, his left arm flung out towards my father, a large bruise already forming on the side of his chin, blood trickling from a cut on his forehead where he had hit the pavement.

'Tommy go and get help.'

Tommy just stood there, taking in the sight of our father and brother.

'Go to the nearest house and get them to help us, we can't go for Mama, she isn't well enough.'

'Are they alright?' he asked.

'I don't know, please hurry.'

Tommy ran off and disappeared round the corner, returning a few moments later with two men.

One of the men gently moved me aside and knelt down beside my brother, he turned him over and felt at his neck, 'He's alive,' he said. Then he moved to my father, doing the same, he then held his face close to my father's mouth, then back again to feel at his neck. He looked at the other man and shook his head.

'No!' I shouted, 'he can't be.'

'I'm sorry love, he's dead.'

Tommy sank to his knees at the side of me and put his arms around me. We sat there for a few moments, still and quiet trying to make sense of it all. Tears streamed down our faces, our father, the man who had protected us, provided for us and loved us unconditionally was dead. After all we had gone through, the harrowing journey, the homelessness, lack of food, had ended in a dark alley.

'The lad is alive and in need of attention,' one of the men said, 'we can't do anything for the man I'm afraid, but if you want to help the boy we must move him now. Where do you live?'

Tommy rose up and pointed towards home saying weakly, 'just round that corner.'

The men lifted Papa onto the cart, one took up the handles and began to wheel him home, the other picked Danny in his arms and they set off. Suddenly I thought of Mama, she would be distraught and I had to break the news to her before they carried the body of my father into the room.

'Tommy stay with the men and show them the way, I must tell Mama before she sees Papa.'

Tommy looked at me blankly and nodded as I ran on ahead.

I rushed up the stairs knowing I did not have much time before they would be there. I pushed the door open and ran across to Mama, wrapping my arms around her tightly.

'Millie whatever has happened? '

'It's Papa,' was all I could say and then I burst into tears once more.

She waited, although I think she knew, she needed to hear it from me.

'He's dead Mama, he's dead, he's been beaten badly, and he's dead.' I could feel myself reaching a point close to hysteria, I began to shake and the tears continued unabated.

She clutched her hand to her chest, 'and Danny, where is he?'

'He's hurt, but alive,' I sobbed, 'some men are helping Tommy bring them home.'

Mama fell into a chair, her face as white as a sheet. Then we heard slow steps on the stairs and a man appeared carrying the limp form of my brother in his arms and laying him on the bed the three of us shared. Then without a word he left the room. My mother ran over and took Danny's head in her hands, examining the cut and the bruising. She set about cleaning and dressing the wound, and then she put a cold compress on his forehead. I could do nothing to help; I stood and watched, shaking from head to toe. All too soon we heard slow heavy footsteps on the stairs once again; Mama rose from the bed and stood to face the door preparing to receive father's body.

The two men came silently into the room and nodded at us, then laid my father on the bed beside the wall he shared with my mother. They touched their caps and said, 'Mam we are so sorry, but we were too late. We will go and find a policeman for you.'

'Thank you,' she replied, not taking her eyes off my father.

The men left and Tommy walked in, his legs giving out on him as soon as he got into the room and he collapsed onto the floor. I managed to stir myself enough to walk over and raise him up, leading him to a chair by the fire.

We sat there in silence for some moments, we had no idea what had happened that evening only that Papa was dead and Danny injured and still unconscious.

A policeman arrived presently and began to ask questions, but we had no answers to give him, he left promising he would see if he could find any witnesses and inform a doctor.

I had a sudden urge to get out, I knew my mother and brothers needed me but I just felt I had to get out or I would suffocate. My vision had become restricted, all I could see was what was directly in front of me, I had no periphery vision at all, and my heart was pounding in my chest so hard I felt it would burst out at any moment, my breathing was coming in huge gasps and I was sweating, the room spinning. I felt sick and my mouth was dry, my fists were clenched, I saw my mother look over at me, her mouth was moving but I couldn't hear anything she was saying.

'Sorry Mama,' I said and ran from the room and hurtled down the stairs and out into the cold night, drawing in the cool air in great heaving gulps.

Tommy struggled to get to his feet and headed to the door to follow his sister.

Maria shook her head, 'leave her Tommy, she needs some time on her own.'

'But will she be alright, what if they come back?'

'They won't be around now and the police will be out there, she will be alright. Help me look after Danny,' she said trying to keep him occupied.

Maria went over and helped Tommy to his feet and over to a chair, she was trying desperately hard to keep it together for the sake of her children, but her whole world had just fallen apart. Her husband had been murdered, he was the only man she had ever loved, and he had been her best friend on whom she knew she could rely at all times. He had never let her down and had been a fantastic father to their three children. Now she would have to face the rest of her life without him, she had no idea what she was going to do, but right now she had to look after her children. She took Tommy in her arms, rocking him gently, and held him as he cried, his body shaking from head to foot. After a while he stopped and she felt him relax a little, she looked over at Danny knowing she should be with him also, she was torn. Millie was out somewhere, she knew not where and despite saying she would be alright she was worried sick about her. Just then Danny began to stir, he moaned and his eyes flickered open. She rushed over to his side and took hold of his hand, his eyes appeared unfocused and she was not sure he could see her properly.

'Danny, it's alright, you're safe now.'

Danny did not respond, he continued to stare at the far wall, his breathing was shallow and his skin was cold to the touch.

'Danny, can you hear me?'

Again no reply from him, he did not even shift his gaze from the wall to her. She was frightened now that maybe he had suffered some damage to his head in the attack, she was already missing being able to talk to Daniel about her fears.

Tommy rose slowly from the chair and came over and lay alongside his brother, putting his arms around him. Eventually they both drifted off to sleep.

Seeing her sons were both asleep and Millie not yet back Maria walked over to where her husband lay, she kissed him gently on the lips and took his hand in hers, he was still warm to the touch and it made it more difficult for her to accept his death. She felt the tears began to fall and heard a low keening noise, realising it was herself, she laid her head on Daniel's chest and let herself give in to her grief.

    I walked around the dark streets of the town and found myself at the entrance to the park, the gates were locked and I stood, my hands clutching the iron railings, my face leant against the cool metal. It all looked so peaceful in the light of the moon, the lake reflecting the white light as it shone down. I knew I should go home but I couldn't, not yet. I walked round the perimeter and was startled by a sound behind me, turning I was confronted with a small girl of about nine.
    She smiled at me saying,' it's nice isn't it?'
'Yes very nice,' I answered her.
'Do you want to go in?'
'It's closed.'
    'I know a way, follow me,' she said. She held out her hand and I took it in mine, suddenly she pulled away and looked down at her palm which was covered in blood, my blood I realised as I opened my hands to see the damage my nails had done.
    'I fell,' I said by way of explanation.
    She shrugged and wiping her hands on her skirt led me to a small gap in the railings obscured from the path by bushes. We pushed through and were in the park, it was quiet and still and we walked towards the lake, causing the ducks to waddle off to the safety of the water and swim off protesting loudly.
    I saw the place where we usually picnicked on Sundays and lowered myself to the grass leaning against the tree where Tommy and I had sat before when we confided in each other. The tears trickled down my face and I sobbed, great heaving sobs that came from somewhere deep inside. The girl sat quietly by my side, saying nothing, she did not seem startled in any way by my behaviour and I felt some comfort in the presence of this silent companion. Gradually my sobs subsided and I knew I must go home, without a word she rose as if sensing my decision. I stood also and we walked in silence back to the gap in the rails, slipping through. I turned to her, not knowing what to say, but she hugged me and then without a word walked away.
    I stood for a few moments watching her until she was out of sight and then turned for home.

I slowly climbed the stairs, each step was a physical effort, opening the door, I opened my mouth to apologise, but Mama just took me in her arms saying, 'Millie it's alright I understand.'

Apparently Danny had regained consciousness and was now asleep, he had not spoken and Mama had not pushed him, she felt it best he rest.

I looked over to where my father lay under the sheet my mother had placed over him, hardly believing I would never hear his voice again or feel his touch.

I stood at the open grave of my father with my mother and Tommy; we had left Danny with Mrs Johnson. Danny was not well enough to come with us, he had not spoken a word since he had come round, and he just lay in bed staring into space, not acknowledging our presence. We tried to talk to him, but it was as if he was in a different place to us altogether. He was not eating, but Mama managed to get him to take soup, by placing the spoon to his lips and tilting his head, the swallowing a reflex reaction only.

There were no other mourners, we had no other family in England, our only friends had left some time ago and we had not heard from them since. I wondered where they were now and hoped Susan hadn't had to bury her mother. The day was cool, a stiff breeze blowing across the cemetery, the priest finished his prayer and Mama bent down and picked up a handful of soft dirt and threw it into the hole, crossing herself as she did so, Tommy and I followed suit and then we turned and left the grave side, leaving my father alone. Mama was trying so hard to keep herself together for the sake of the three of us; I knew she felt she had to. I also heard her crying in the darkness of the lonely nights. She had once told me that she had known as soon as she had first seen Papa all those years ago back in Ireland that she would marry him. I had asked how she could have been so certain, and she just said I would understand for myself one day.

The funeral had taken all of our savings and we had to earn some money urgently, we had no idea what awaited us in the way of employment, having abandoned everyone so suddenly. Tommy and I had spoken to Mr Stone and Mrs Thompson but we were not up to speaking to each individual customer and so unless they had heard what had happened they would think we had just let them down, plus there was Danny to consider and Mama was still not fully recovered.

Chapter 52

We had buried Papa yesterday, and now we had to pick up the pieces of our shattered lives. I knew we were still all in denial, expecting him to walk through the door any minute. There was nothing that could prepare you for such a tragedy, it was so unexpected. When Mama was really ill, although I did not want her to die, I couldn't help but think about it, it was at the back of my mind all the time, as much as I tried not to acknowledge it and I felt guilty for even considering it, as if I were betraying her somehow. However I did not have time to prepare for this, one minute they were there with you, and then they were gone. No time for goodbyes, no time to say, 'I love you,' just a vacuum that could not be filled and I didn't think ever would be. Next came the self recrimination, the 'what if's'. What if I had gone to collect the money, what if I hadn't fallen asleep, I knew how long it took to collect the payments, and I might have gone looking for them sooner. I knew Mama was going through the same pain, what if she had not become ill, none of this may have happened. We hadn't yet spoken these thoughts out loud, the pain was still too raw, but I did not doubt that day would come eventually.

So the three of us sat at the kitchen table on the Tuesday morning to try and work out what we were going to do. Danny was sleeping soundly; he had still not uttered a word and was surviving totally on soup and water.

'Well, as we know the job that brings in the most money is the Edwards',' Mama said. 'I think that is the one we should try and concentrate on.'

'But that took three of us all day to carry out,' I said, 'and you are not strong enough yet to walk there and back and then work all day. The humid conditions are likely to make your cough worse again; you haven't lost it yet and are still short of breath. You nearly collapsed yesterday walking home.'

Mama's eyes dropped when she remembered the walk back from the cemetery, she had to sit for a while to get her breath back. As much as she wanted to pretend she had recovered, the outward signs were there and all the denials in the world were in vain.

'Maybe we should contact all the other customers and see how many are still willing to use us,' she said, 'at least that way we would not be working in that room and we wouldn't have to make Danny walk all that way, I don't think he is capable.'

Tommy had listened to all of this and I could see him struggling to work out his place, what his best option was. At last he said, 'do you think I should go to the docks and see if I can take Papa's place? He earned more than I do.'

Mama reached out and gently stroked his cheek, 'Tommy I don't know if it will still be there.'

Finally we reached an agreement that today Tommy and I would walk round the local customers and see if we had enough to make it worthwhile, if not then we would have to see if the Edwards still wanted us and if so fathom out a way to make it work.

Once outside Tommy and I set off towards the first house, walking the route that we would have done to collect the payments, I realised we were following in my father's last footsteps and tried desperately to see if I could feel some of his spirit out there in the streets.

Tommy broke the silence, 'Millie, do you think they will have replaced Papa already?'

'I don't know Tommy,' I said, suddenly realising we had not informed them of Papa's death.

He lifted his head up to look at me, he eyes silently pleading with me and I knew my brother too well to deny him. 'Tommy go to the docks now and see the foreman, tell him what has happened and then come back to find me. I don't want to walk the last part on my own.'

Tommy nodded his head and slowly walked towards the yard, I watched him go, a lump building in my throat. He was eleven and a half and found himself at the head of the family; I knew he felt it was up to him to provide security and income for us all.

Firstly I called at the Jackson's and they had heard the news, I was invited in and condolences were offered. They had hoped we would return and were happy to resume with the arrangement so that was six shillings a week, of the other local jobs we had lost all but two. I tried explaining why we hadn't contacted them but they all said they had to make alternative arrangements and so now we had six shillings and three pence per week. I sat and waited for Tommy and before too long he appeared, I could tell by the way he was walking it was not good news.

'I'm sorry Tommy,' I said when he joined me.

'They said they were very sorry about Papa but they had heard what had happened and they had filled his position.'

We decided we could not face walking past the place where Papa had died and so took the long way back home.

Once we had told Mama how we had got on she said, 'right so we have six shillings and three pence, if Tommy goes back to Mr Stone we have another seven pence. The rent is six shillings a week and fuel and laundry supplies another shilling. That means we cannot cover those costs, let alone buy any food.'

'What about if we went back to a shared room?' I asked, although I didn't think I could bear to return to that situation.

'Well if we did , we wouldn't have anywhere to do the laundry and so we would be worse off, also I wouldn't like to think how Danny would cope in his present state.'

I looked over at my brother who was awake but lay staring at the ceiling, his eyes vacant and seeing nothing. I had no idea what was wrong with him and worried he had suffered some damage from the blow to his head.

Then suddenly Mama slapped her hand on the table, 'I've got it,' she said. 'How about if one of us does the Jackson's and the other two customers from home for five days and the other one goes to the Edwards' for five days. We would be short handed but doing the same amount of work over a longer period.'

'It could work,' I said excitedly, 'I will go and see the Edwards now. Who shall I say is going to go there?'

'Well until Danny is any better I don't want to leave him, I'm sorry,' Mama replied, 'I know it's a lot to ask of you but would you mind going?'

'No of course not, I will go and see what they say.'

'And I will go and see Mr Stone,' said Tommy, 'and make sure I still have a job there.'

As I walked up the long drive I hoped desperately that Mrs Thompson would accept our proposal. I knocked nervously on the kitchen door and stepped over the threshold, I had only been away a matter of days but I felt as if it were a life time ago. Before I could speak Mrs Bowes rushed over and pulled me to her, hugging me so tightly I found it hard to breathe.

'How are you dear? And how is Maria? We were all so sorry to hear your sad news.'

I choked back my tears and answered, 'we still can't believe it.'

'No dear, it will take some time but it will get easier.'

At that moment I very much doubted it 'is Mrs Thompson available?'

'Patsy, go and tell Mrs T. that Millie is here to see her.'

The girl smiled at me and left the room, returning minutes later saying, 'she is busy at the moment but asks you wait for her, she will only be about ten minutes.'

Mrs Bowes placed a glass of water in front of me and a slice of apple pie with cream. 'I bet you aren't eating properly, so get that down you.'

'Thank you,' I said, not wishing to offend her, but it was the last thing I felt like. I sipped the water and hoped she would not notice I hadn't touched the pastry.

Eventually Mrs Thompson came in, 'Millie please accept my condolences and pass them onto your mother. I presume you have come to inform me what is happening as regards your employment.'

'Yes Mam,' I said, 'firstly may I thank you for being so understanding.' I then proceeded to lay out our plan and hoped that she would accept it. I also told her the state of health of my mother and of our worries for Danny.

'Just one moment Millie,' she said and rising she left the kitchen.

I looked at Mrs Bowes, 'what have I done wrong?'

'Nothing as far as I know.'

She returned after a few moments, 'I am sorry about that, but the family doctor is in the house today and I have asked him if he would call in and speak to you about your brother. He is the one who visited your mother if you remember.'

'Yes I do, he was very helpful, and I liked him.'

'While we wait I must admit I do have concerns about the proposal you have put forward. I am worried about the fact that you will be working totally on your own; however I do admire the commitment you made to hold the position whilst your mother was ill. Therefore I am prepared to try it out, I will give you two weeks trial, but if it doesn't work out I must warn you I will have to let you go, no matter how much I would hate to do so. Also you have missed two days already so I would expect you back tomorrow and would ask that you work whatever it takes to catch up, even if that means you work on Sunday this week. What do you say?'

'Thank you Mam, I am very grateful to you. I will be back tomorrow.'

Deal done I sat and waited for the doctor. Once he entered the kitchen he asked me how my mother was, nodding when I told him.

'Yes she is very much where I would expect her to be at this moment in time, she still has some way to go and you must make sure she does not try to overdo it or she will suffer a relapse, mark my words and with the circumstances you presently find yourselves in and what Mrs Thompson has told me about her character and also that of yourself I believe she may do so.'

'Doctor I appreciate your warning and I promise to keep my eye on her.'

'Good, now tell me about your brother.'

I told him in detail what had happened to Danny as far as I knew and how he had behaved since.

'Your brother is suffering from shock I am afraid.'

'What can we do for him?' I asked.

'You have to make sure he is not put in any stressful situations, also you must ensure he stays in places and with people he knows and feels comfortable with. Do not try to force him at all in anything, you must have patience which you will find frustrating sometimes but if you push him he could retreat deeper. '

'We don't even know if he knows Papa is dead yet.'

'Well you definitely can't speak to him about that until he is better, that will do more damage, and he will not be able to process that in his present condition. Once he is better you should wait to see how much he can remember, let him instigate the conversation.'

Returning home, I told Mama what the doctor had said about Danny, and she was like me relieved to find out he had not sustained any damage in the attack. Tommy also had good news in that Mr Stone was happy to keep him on. Things would never be the same for us, but at least it looked as if we could hold on to all we had worked so hard for.

Chapter 53

I was up early on Wednesday in order to be able to collect the washing that Mama would be doing at home that day. She was not up to walking that far herself and also did not want to drag Danny out. She knew she could leave him with Mrs Johnson but wanted things to be as normal as they possibly could in the hope he would recover quicker. After seeing her settled I walked alone to the Edwards' house, it felt strange knowing that I would be working on my own permanently from now on.

Many times during the day I wondered how Mama would be getting on, I hoped she wouldn't push herself too hard. Peter called in to see how Danny was, I told him of his condition and what the doctor had said.

'I hope he gets better soon, I miss having him about the place, he was so good with the animals and I know they liked him.'

'That is kind of you to say so, I will tell him, although I don't know how much he is taking in at the moment.'

Although I had not fully caught up with the back log of work I felt I had made enough progress to be able to go home. I would be returning tomorrow and was confident I would be able to complete the job. It was six o'clock when I finally climbed the stairs to our room, Mama was sitting near the fire and Tommy was stirring the supper on the hearth.

'Is everything alright?' I asked.

'Yes, I just felt a little dizzy and so Tommy took over.'

Tommy looked at me, and I thought I saw something else in his eyes.

'How did you get on at the house?' Mama asked.

'I made some headway but there is quite a lot still to do. How was your day? Is Danny any better?'

'He is the same, I managed but I am certainly not back to full strength yet.'

For my mother to admit this I knew things weren't right.

'Well I'll take the things back tomorrow and collect the other jobs before I go to work,' I said. 'I will also get some shopping on the way home; we are nearly out of food.'

'I can do that Millie, I am in town anyway so it saves you a walk,' Tommy said.

As we sat at the table we talked about our day, but the conversation was stilted and difficult, the absence of our father still so prominent.

Danny sat quietly at the table and I remembered the conversation earlier with Peter, so I said to him, 'Danny, Peter came to see me today and he says the horses and he miss you and he hopes you will be back soon.'

If I hadn't been looking at him when I said it I don't think I would have noticed it, but for a brief second Danny raised his eyes from the table where he had been staring since we had sat down.

'Did you see that?' I asked the other two.

'See what?' Tommy asked.

'Danny seemed to come out of his trance for a minute,' I whispered. We all watched but there was no further sign.

'It was when I mentioned Peter and the horses,' I said quietly.

'Say something else Millie,' Mama encouraged.

Thinking hard I added, 'Peter says he can tell the horses like and trust you.'

This time we all saw it, a flicker of something in his eyes, some brief spark of life we hadn't seen since the attack. All too soon it was gone again but there was definite hope to be had.

Mama went to bed after supper saying she needed to rest as she was tired after the day's work and Tommy and I sat watching the fire. When we heard Mama's breathing change indicating she was asleep Tommy said quietly, 'Millie, I am worried about Mama, when I came home today she was sitting on the back step fighting for breath, I had to help her up the stairs and I had to finish the laundry.'

'I was afraid this would happen,' I said, 'it's too early for her to start back to work.'

'What are we going to do?' Tommy asked concern etched on his face.

'Maybe we should get her to take the day off tomorrow,' I said.

'But what about the laundry?'

'I will do it when I come home,' I said, wondering how on earth I would fit it all in.

'I'll help you; we can get it done between us.'

'Thanks, well we had better get some sleep; we are going to be busy tomorrow.'

The next morning Mama was complaining of chest pains and her breathing was once again laboured, 'Millie I'm sorry, but I don't think I can manage today.'

'That's alright Mama, you stay in bed, will you be alright if Tommy and I go to work?'

'Yes dear, you both go.'

'I will send Mrs Johnson to sit with you,' I said.

When we were having our lunch break I plucked up the courage to speak to Mrs Thompson and told her about my mother's relapse.

'She obviously hasn't recovered sufficiently to begin work yet, these things can take weeks or months to get over.'

I nodded, wondering how long Tommy and I would be able to cover the chores.

When I got home, Tommy had already made a start and I left him to it a moment to go upstairs and prepare a meal, so we could eat when we were finished. On hearing me climb the stairs Mrs Johnson came across the hall, 'your mother hasn't been well at all today dear; she has had trouble breathing and been complaining of a headache.'

'What about Danny?'

'Much the same.'

I went in and Mama was dozing in bed, Danny crooked in her arm. He didn't even look at me as I walked over to the bed; it was as if he were somewhere else entirely. His face was pale apart from the ugly bruising on his chin. Mama stirred and opened her eyes, 'Millie, how are you?'

'I am fine Mama, how are you feeling now?'

'I am alright when I lay down but as soon as I try to get up I start coughing again.'

'Mrs Johnson says you have been short of breath again and complaining of a headache.'

Mama glanced at the elderly woman as if she felt betrayed by her, 'well yes, but I am sure I will be better tomorrow.'

'Mama, I don't think you will, I spoke again with Mrs Thompson and she said it could be weeks before you are fully recovered.'

'Well as much as I like and respect the woman, she is no doctor.'

'No but her friend is, and it was him who came to see you when you were ill.'

I could see I would get no further with the conversation at the moment so I put some vegetables on the stove, we hadn't much in the way of food in the house at the moment, and Mrs Johnson said she would call us when they were ready, then I went and joined Tommy in the yard.

We left our chores to quickly eat the vegetables and then returned, it was nine o'clock by the time we had got it all washed but by no means was it dry and there was little chance of it drying overnight in the cool February air. We dare not take it indoors for fear of upsetting mother's chest and so we left it hanging in the yard. Tommy and I slumped in chairs by the fire in order to warm up for about half an hour before going to bed. Mama and Danny were sleeping so we kept our voices down.

'I don't think we can do this,' I said, voicing the concerns I was already having about how we would manage all the work, look after two invalids and also shop for food and any other chores we had to do. 'If we take on too much I know Mama will try and help us. She is not ready yet and I couldn't cope if anything happened to her.'

Tommy looked distraught; he was still coming to terms with Papa's death, as we all were, 'what will become of us?'

'As much as I hate to do it, I think we need to let the home customers go and I will continue to work at the Edwards', as that pays the best.'

'Would if help if I left the stall and did the home customers?' Tommy offered.

'No, there is too much for one person to manage, we will just have to hope we can get them back when Mama and Danny are fit again.'

'Well shall I help you at the Edwards'?'

'I think I will be able to manage by going there all week, and I know Mrs Johnson will sit with Mama and Danny. We will let the others know we can't service them at the moment, I hope they will understand.'

So with that decision made we went off to bed, even though I was shattered, I didn't sleep too well. I was worried whether we had made the right choices. We had always had our parents to make the important decisions, but with Papa gone and not wanting to worry Mama with it, we felt we had no other option.

The next morning I crept out of the room quietly to go and see whether any of the washing was dry enough to return yet. As I pushed open the door to the yard I was rooted to the spot by the sight before me. There wasn't a single item of clothing to be seen, hoping Tommy had been down and collected them up I ran back upstairs, he was just finishing dressing and although I thought I already knew the answer I asked the question anyway, 'Tommy have you been down and brought the washing in?'

'No Millie, I have just woken up, why what's happened?'

'It's all gone; someone must have stolen it during the night.'

'They can't have, why would they do that?'

'I have no idea, but it's all gone. What are we going to do?'

I sat down heavily in a chair, my head in my hands, I had no idea.

Tommy sat down and put his arm around my shoulders, and I leant against him, tears falling from my eyes. 'We will have to tell them all tonight when we get back.'

So that's what we did, we called at each house and told them we had lost their clothes, some were sympathetic, most were angry, all wanted paying in order to replace the items. We explained that we didn't have any money until we got paid on Saturday. Most of them accepted this knowing what we had been through lately, but some wanted their money now, threatening to call the police if we didn't return with it tonight.

'Now what do we do?' Tommy asked.

'I have no idea,' I answered truthfully. We needed eight shillings and sixpence in order to pay the compensation, of which three shillings were needed tonight, and we wouldn't receive payment for the work we had done. We would earn one pound one shilling and ten pence this week and the rent was six shillings, after taking out fuel and laundry materials that would leave us twelve shillings and four pence to live on, that would buy us some food this week but not up to the standard we had been used to of late, but at least Mama could still eat reasonably well in order to assist in her recovery.

'I am going to see Mrs Thompson and ask her if she will advance me the three shillings today,' I said. 'You may as well go home and wait there.'

'No way I am leaving you to walk around the streets in the dark alone Millie, I'll come with you.'

I didn't protest, I was grateful for his company.

Mrs Bowes looked up when we knocked and entered the warm kitchen. 'Whatever are you two doing here at this time of night?' she asked concerned. 'It's not Maria or Danny is it?'

'No Mrs Bowes, I need to ask Mrs Thompson if she can help me with a problem we have.'

'Sit down; I'll get one of the girls to fetch her.'

After a few minutes Mrs Thompson swept into the room, 'what can I do for you this evening?'

I explained the dilemma we found ourselves in and asked if she could pay me some money in advance to help us out.

'This is most improper,' she said, 'I am not at liberty to do such a thing without Mrs Edwards' approval.'

Although I had expected this may have been the answer, hearing it said brought my barely controlled emotions crashing down around me. I grasped the edge of the table and only just managed to catch myself before I fell, my head was spinning and I felt so hot all of a sudden.

'I'm sorry Millie, but Mrs Edwards is out at the moment with her husband and will not be back until late, there is nothing I can do to help.'

'Thank you for listening to us,' I said barely keeping the tears back.

'Wait there a minute,' Mrs Bowes said and bustled off. She returned some minutes later and held out her hand to me, the hand holding three shillings. 'Here take this,' she said smiling.

'What is this?' I asked.

'The money you said you needed tonight.'

'But I don't understand how you can get it if Mrs Thompson can't.'

'It's mine,' she answered.

'No we can't take it,'

'If you don't, I shall be offended, I know you will pay me back on Saturday, I can't bear to think of you in trouble after all you have all been through.'

'Mrs Bowes, you have a big heart,' I said and I took the money after giving her a hug and a kiss. 'I will pay you back I promise.'

'I know, now get home and the two of you get some rest, you both look terrible.'

We turned to go when she called us back, 'here take this as well, I was only going to throw it out,' she said wrapping four slices of pie in a towel.

Payments made we climbed the stairs, we had agreed not to tell Mama yet so she didn't worry, but we knew it was only a matter of time before we would have to. Mama was sat in a chair by the fire with Danny curled up on her lap, she looked up as we entered the room.

'My goodness you're both late, I was really beginning to worry.'

'Sorry Mama,' I said, 'we had quite a lot to do this evening.'

'Well please let me know in future, after all that has happened I was fearing the worst.' She clutched at her chest again and took shallow breaths.

'Look what we have got for supper tonight,' I said unwrapping the pie slices.

'My they do look good,'

'Mrs Bowes sent them along with her best wishes.'

We all moved to the table and sat down, my mother tried to interest Danny in the food, but he paid little attention, staring off as usual, saying not a word.

'I have another message for you Danny,' I tried hoping to see the spark I had seen before. 'Peter says he will be shoeing the horses soon and wants to know if you will be able to help him.'

I watched in anticipation for some sign of him understanding what I was saying, and then there was a slight side wards movement of his eyes as they found my face. Then very slowly he reached across the table and picked up a slice of the pie and began to nibble it.

After all that I happened today this was a huge relief, maybe Danny was returning to us.

Chapter 54

Tommy and I had agreed that we would tell Mama the bad news about the stolen washing and the loss of customers on Sunday, that way we could keep her company as she came to terms with the impact of the loss. She would have noticed all too soon when we were reduced to eating basic meals again, but this way we could make sure she didn't go off trying to win back the customers and suffering another setback.

She surprised us both by the way she accepted the news, ' Well it's not good that we lost the clothing and had to pay out extra money, but I know I am not ready to return to what I was doing. It was placing an unfair burden on you two and I worried that you would both make yourselves ill, you are working hard enough as it is. I will see if I can find something else I can do from home that is not so strenuous, we still have Danny to consider.'

'Maybe you could take in some sewing or something,' I said, 'you were very good with a needle back on the farm.'

In the afternoon a watery sun made an appearance, and after our meagre lunch Mama suggested we take a slow walk around the park. 'I think it will do us all good to get out of the house for a while.'

So we donned our outer coats and descended the stairs, Danny was at the back of us with Mama, neither were up to rushing about yet. Tommy and I stepped out into the yard followed by our mother, but instead of joining us Danny stopped at the threshold, his eyes wide and staring, his tiny body was rigid and his breath was coming sharp and fast.

'Come on Danny,' Tommy said, 'we're going to the park.'

Nothing, no reaction, it was as if he had not spoken, Danny just stood rock still. Mama rushed back to his side, 'he is terrified of going outside,' she said. 'We must get him back upstairs.'

Taking him by the hand she said softly, 'come back upstairs Danny.'

Still he didn't move, in the end Mama scooped him up in her arms and carried him back, laying him gently on the bed and covering him with a blanket, before breaking out into a spasm of coughs.

'This is going to take a lot longer than we thought,' she said, 'God only knows what he went through at the hands of those thugs.'

Things seemed to be going from bad to worse, and I couldn't see a way out of it at the moment.

Chapter 55

Two weeks had passed since we had attempted to get Danny to leave the house, we dare not try again for we didn't want to frighten him any more than we had to. Mama was continuing to improve but it was a slow process, so there was only Tommy and me bringing in any money. We were not eating quite as well as we had been when we were all earning but we had eight shillings and sixpence at the end of each week and so we could afford a reasonably healthy diet once again. Also Mrs Bowes kept giving parcels of left over's to take home as often as she could, I had tried to refuse them at first but had now given up and accepted them in the nature they were meant.

Each day I would ask Peter for any news on the horses that I could pass onto my brother as we had all noticed that this was the only time he appeared to come out of his trance like state. He was once again managing to feed himself but he did not eat a great deal and he had still not spoken. We did not know whether he actually knew our father was dead, and we certainly dare not mention it in his presence in case he didn't. How we would tell him we had no idea, worried as to what further harm we may cause him.

When I was recounting this one lunchtime, Mrs Thompson suggested that I told Danny that Peter wanted him to come and help him with the horses. 'If as you say that is the only thing that seems to snap him out of his trance, it may be the incentive he needs to give him the courage to leave the house.'

'I don't know, 'I said, 'what if it makes him worse?'

'Well as long as you don't force him and let him make up his own mind, I think it will be alright, I will ask the doctor what he thinks.' With that she left the table to return to her duties, lunch time over.

'Is the doctor here all the time?' I asked Mrs Bowes.

'No dear, why do you ask?'

'Well Mrs Thompson seems to be able to speak with him a great deal.'

'They are courting, my dear, have been for about three years now.'

'Oh, I thought she was married.'

'No, she is a widow like me.'

I returned to my hot steamy cell and thought about what Mrs Thompson had said. I would wait to see what the doctor said, but I would definitely mention it tonight when I got home and see what Mama thought.

If we could get Danny to leave the house, Mama would be able to seek some home work. She had tried to leave Danny with Mrs Johnson in order to do so but he began to react in the way he had when we were leaving for the park and so she had now been confined to home.

I was finding the work hard on my own, but so far I had managed to get it all completed over the six days, however I welcomed the arrival of each Sunday to get some respite and enjoy my family's company.

Today I was washing the bed linen and as I carried the last armful outside to hang to dry, I slipped on the wet floor. My legs just slipped out from under me and I began to fall, instinctively I put my free hand out to try and break my fall, in doing so my left hand slipped into the gap between the sink and the table. As I fell my wrist snapped back, I heard a loud crack and I felt the most excruciating pain I had ever experienced, a red hot feeling travelled up my arm and I felt suddenly hot, sweat beading on my forehead. As I lay on the wet floor I thought I was going to pass out, the room was spinning so fast. Finally the pain subsided long enough for me to be able to attempt to rise to my feet, I put my hand to the floor to try and push myself up only for the pain to return. I screamed out loud and collapsed back to the floor, my breathing laboured.

I heard running footsteps and Patsy and Lizzie burst into the room.

Lizzie knelt beside me and looked at my wrist, covering her mouth with her hand, 'Patsy fetch Mrs B.'

Patsy ran from the room, bumping in to Mrs Bowes as she rushed into the room.

'It's her wrist,' Lizzie said.

'Let me see,' Mrs Bowes said.

I raised my arm slowly, looking down at my wrist which was already swelling but more worryingly was twisted out of shape, the bone at an odd angle.

'Oh Millie, you've broken your wrist.'

I broke down in tears, not just from the pain, but also at the realisation that I could no longer continue to work here. I had let everyone who was depending on me down.

Mrs Thompson called on her friend, and the doctor came and confirmed that I had broken my wrist.

'I will reset it for you,' he said, 'afterwards you must rest it.'

Looking at my wrist and knowing how intense the pain had been when I broke it, I was terrified.

'How long will it take to heal?' I asked, 'I need to work.'

'A few weeks, depending how much you can rest it.'

'Can I still work and sort it out later?'

'No, if you leave it the bone will fuse and then it will have to be broken again before it can be set. I will give you something for the pain whilst I perform the procedure.'

'Can I just ask you something before you do it?' I said.

'Yes what do you want to know?'

I told him about what Mrs Thompson had said about getting Danny to come and see the horses in order to speed up his recovery.

'Well, it could work, if he is showing interest when you mention them, it may be the stimulus he needs.'

Then he poured some liquid into a cloth and placed it over my nose and mouth and I drifted off, when I came round, my wrist had been reset and bandaged and was resting in a sling.

Mrs Thompson arranged for Peter to take me home in the carriage, and I returned to my family utterly defeated.

I burst into tears when I tried to tell them what had happened, both Mama and Tommy were totally sympathetic, not one word of recrimination, but I knew that like me they knew that was the end of life as we knew it. We could no longer afford our accommodation and food would be an issue. We had no savings to tide us over until we were all fit to work, and Tommy's wage would not be sufficient. In Danny's current condition he could not possibly live on the streets, we sat long into the night talking over our options and as we saw it we only had one chance of survival. We were desperate to stay together.

The next morning Tommy walked to work and told Mr Stone of the family's decision and thanked him for all his help, he then went to the Edwards' house and informed them.

'Come back on Saturday and I will give you Millie's wages,' Mrs Thompson said. 'I am so sorry but we obviously have to replace her.'

'Thank you Mam,' Tommy said and left the kitchen to return home.

Mrs Bowes looked at Mrs Thompson, a frown on her face, 'not many leave there once they have gone in.'

'That's true and it is a shame, they tried so hard to make it work, my heart goes out to them.'

Saturday came round and we had decided to see if we could get Danny to leave the house, knowing that once our plans had been put into place, we would have little opportunity to do this.

We were hoping to walk to the Edwards' house to collect my part week wages, say our goodbyes to everyone and take Danny to the stables.

Danny sat at the table slowly chewing on a piece of bread, we had some food in the house and once I had collected my money we would have enough to pay last week's rent and just enough food to last us until Monday evening. After that we would have nothing left, we could not live on Tommy's wages.

'Danny,' I said, there was no answer, 'I spoke to Peter the other day and he said he would like you to go and see the horses today, he needs your help.'

Very slowly Danny turned his head towards me and actually held my gaze.

'Would you like to do that?' Mama asked him.

Danny sat for a few moments before slowly nodding his head once.

'Right let's go now,' Mama said, before Danny had time to think about it too much and change his mind.

Having engaged him I tried to keep the interest going and racked my mind for anything I could remember about the horses.

'Which one is your favourite? I think mine is Ebony.'

He didn't reply but he continued to look at me and seemed quite happy as we put on our outdoor clothes and walked down to the door. Mama took his hand in hers and Tommy opened the door, stepping out into the yard. Danny hesitated, so I tried to coax him further. Joining Tommy outside I began to talk to him once again.

'Peter has really missed having you around and he is looking forward to seeing you again very much. Come on let's go.' I held out my good hand for him and after a brief hesitation Danny stepped across the threshold and took hold of me.

We walked slowly because not only was Danny anxious but Mama was still not up to walking far. Once it appeared as if Danny was a little more relaxed Mama said to me,' Millie I need to rest, you carry on with Danny, for I don't want to break the spell. Tommy can walk with me and we will join you as soon as we can.'

So I kept Danny moving, not giving him the chance to look back and see that our mother had stopped walking. I kept talking about the horses and felt his hand relax in mine even further. At last we reached the driveway and Danny actually increased his pace, we went straight around to the courtyard, I was hoping Peter would already be at work.

One of the stable doors opened as we approached and Peter emerged leading a grey horse behind him, he saw us and dropped the rein, rushing over.

'Danny, my friend,' he said, 'I am so pleased to see you. How are you lad?'

Danny did not answer, but I thought I saw a slight smile flit across his face, his eyes then shifting to take in the horse standing quietly behind Peter.

'I hope you don't mind us turning up like this,' I said explaining why we were there.

'Of course not, anything I can do to help. You only have to ask.'

Peter was amazing, he didn't push Danny at all, he just went over and took hold of the reins once more saying, 'Danny please would you hold Duke while I go and fetch Phantom?'

Danny let go of my hand and walked over taking the rein from Peter and waited patiently as Peter went to fetch the other mount. He didn't speak but his hand went up and he gently stroked the animal's neck. The horse nuzzled my brother and as I watched this I could see that Danny was responding positively.

We spent half an hour at the stables, Danny becoming more animated as the time went on. Mama and Tommy joined us and I went over to stand with them.

'I think it's doing him good,' Mama said, tears rolling down her face. 'I would love to let him stay longer but I don't want him to tire himself out. Hopefully when we get sorted out he may be able to return.'

We collected Danny, thanked Peter and went to the kitchen to collect my money and say our goodbyes.

I hadn't realised until that moment just how much I would miss them all. Mrs Bowes came over and wrapped her arms tightly around me, 'Millie, I hope everything works out for you all. If ever there is anything I can do to help you please come and see me.' She kissed me and then pulled away wiping away her tears.

Mrs Thompson took my mother to one side, talking quietly to her. I could not hear what they were saying.

'Maria, are you entirely sure that this is the only option left to you all?' Mrs Thompson gently enquired.

'Yes, we only have Tommy's wage now that Millie is injured. Danny is not fit to be left without me and unfortunately I am still not capable of any physical work. I was hoping to take in some work from home but I have not yet had a chance to look for any. We can't even afford the rent let alone any food and Danny won't survive in a strange environment. At least we will have food and shelter until we are once again fit to work.'

'Yes dear, but the workhouse.'

'It will be alright; at least we will all be together.'

Mrs Thompson looked at her uncertainly, she had heard tales but had no firsthand knowledge and so decided to keep her concerns to herself rather than upset the woman standing in front of her who was only trying to do the best for her family. She hoped it was not as bad as she had heard and that things worked out well for them, she was nothing but full of admiration for everyone of them.

We walked back to our room, all deep in thought, everything was about to change once again.

On Tuesday March the fifth, my broken family walked through the gates of the workhouse; we left the house early whilst the streets were quieter. We hoped with less people about Danny would not be too stressed. He was hesitant but did follow us out without any recurrence of his panic attack.

In just under three years our good luck had finally been outweighed by bad.

Chapter 56

March 1850

Joining the steady queue of people walking through the gates of the workhouse and in the huge doors I wondered what had happened to them to bring them to this decision. Ours was forced on us by the downward turn in our fortunes. Thinking back to only a few months ago we had experienced our happiest time ever, last Christmas. Now Papa was dead, Mama still suffering the effects of the bronchial pneumonia and Danny unable to speak and frightened to leave our home due to the shock of being beaten and witnessing the attack on our father.

We had decided to come in for a short time, so that we could remain together and recover. Once fully fit we intended to leave and find work and housing. We had done it once, successfully, so we could do it again.

Looking around us, the others were mainly families; I found out later that if an able bodied man came in, his whole family had to come in also. If it hadn't been for me breaking my wrist I believed we would have survived but it wasn't to be.

We reached the head of the queue and Mama gave our names to the two men sat at a large table in the entrance hall, they made a note of our names and dates of birth.

Then the harsh reality of the situation we had put ourselves in dawned on us with these words, 'Women go through the door on the left, girls to the right and boys straight down that hallway.'

We stood there as the instructions sank in.

Mama was the first to collect her thoughts, saying, 'No, we all want to be together.'

'I'm sure you do, but that's not the way things are run here.'

'My son is ill and I can't leave him.'

'Is he diseased?'

'No but he has had a bad experience and is suffering from shock. He can't speak at the moment and is scared to go outside.'

The men looked at each other, trying to decide what to do about this. Meanwhile the queue of people waiting to come in was building, eventually one said, 'alright he can stay with you, but the rest must go where they have been told.'

We moved away from the table and watched as others did exactly that, families being split up.

Seeing our hesitation a large woman of about forty walked over to us, 'come on hurry up, and go to your rooms.'

Once again Mama tried to explain, but received the reply, 'sorry but if you are coming in you have to abide by the rules.'

'I can't leave my children.'

'It will all be explained to you properly in your dorms, but you will see your children, now if you are staying, move along.'

Danny had not been too fretful on the walk over and we had taken our time walking through the darkened streets, but now in the confines of the building with all the noise and confusion, he stood and watched with terror in his eyes as dozens of people pushed and jostled their way around us, he made no sound but his body was tense and he turned and buried his face in our mother's skirts.

'We had better do as they say,' Mama said looking at Danny. We all knew we would not survive outside with no means of income, even if we managed to find shelter, what would we do for food? Visions of the deported flashed through my mind, we may become separated permanently.

We clung to each other for some minutes before pulling away and walking in the direction we had all been previously instructed.

I watched as my mother and younger brother walked away, Mama talking gently to Danny all the time trying to reassure him and him walking rigidly beside her, his face pale and his eyes wide. Tommy stopped at the entrance to the corridor and raised his hand, giving me a feeble wave and a tight smile. We had never spent any time apart before and I worried I would ever see them again.

On the other side of the doors, the room was full of girls with ages ranging from eight to sixteen. I fell into line with them and as I reached the head of the queue a woman briefly looked me up and down. Behind her were piles of clothing, she walked over to one of the piles and taking one from the top she handed it to me.

'This is your uniform, follow the rest through there to your dormitory.'

I did so, my hand feeling the coarse material of the dress she had given me.

Another woman was waiting a little further along the passageway at an open door, as I approached she asked my name, wrote it down on a paper and said, 'this is your dormitory, when you are not working or eating you will be in here. Find yourself a bed and get changed, leave your other clothes on the bed.'

'When will I see my family?' I asked.

'I haven't time to talk to you, ask one of the other girls.'

I stepped into the room and was overwhelmed to see the amount of girls who were milling around. There looked to be around sixty, I had no idea. Some were changing from their own clothes into a uniform; these I assumed like me were new. Others were pulling on shoes and rearranging their clothing, they looked as if they had just got out of bed, their hair messy, some of them yawning. A bell rang somewhere out in the corridor and they filed out, leaving myself and the other new girls looking at each other in bewilderment, were we to follow? We continued changing and then stood hugging our old clothes to our bodies unsure of the next step. After some thirty minutes or so, the other girls returned and the woman who had been at the door came in.

'Stand still girls,' she called out, and then she began to count us all, satisfied she said, 'right this dorm is full. Those of you who are here for the first time need to find yourselves a bed, the others will show you where there is a space, once you have sorted that out you need to be ready to go to work. Just do as the others show you,' with that she left the room.

I watched as the others milled around, either being told there was no room or finding a space. I shuffled along the room, a girl was watching me, she was small with dark eyes. 'I'm Irene and this is my sister Heather, we have a space in this bunk if you want to share with us,' she pointed to another girl who just nodded at me.

'Yes thank you,' I answered, 'my name is Millie.'

'Well Millie, put your clothes there, we will be going to work soon.'

'Will I be seeing the rest of my family then?' I asked hopefully.

'No, we all get to see each other for about an hour on a Sunday and maybe a few minutes each day.'

I felt as if I had been physically punched in the chest, my heart was pounding and I could hear the blood rushing in my ears. We had not been prepared for this, we came in here for sanctuary, food, and shelter, a time to heal and to remain together and we were alone in a world of strangers. I felt responsible and vowed there and then that as soon as my wrist had healed; I would find a way to get us out of there.

A woman walked past the open doorway, loudly ringing a bell.

'That's the bell for work,' Irene said, 'come with me.' I placed my clothes on the bunk as I had been told and followed Irene and her sister. Another girl joined us and Irene told me it was her other sister Marjorie. We walked down a long corridor and entered a huge room which was full of tables upon which were huge coils of ropes, they smelt of tar and I was reminded of our journey across the sea all that time ago, shuddering at the thought of the cramped hold.

'Right,' Irene said, 'we have to pick these apart so that they can be used again for other things.' She suddenly noticed my wrist, 'what have you done to that?'

'I broke it last week.'

'Oh my, I don't know how you will manage to work with that, shall I call someone for you?'

'What will happen if I can't work?' I asked, already worried that I may be thrown out.

'I think you have to go and stay in the sick rooms with the others.'

The thought of this terrified me; I had seen some of the people outside with disease and sickness and did not wish to spend any time with them.

'No I will try and do it, if you show me how.'

Irene and Heather took a length of rope and working between them they picked at the coarse material, slowly picking it apart. By leaning my forearm on the rope in order to pin it down I managed very slowly to unravel some of the threads, but it was slow and awkward. Eventually Irene came up with an idea and we sat in a line, the one in the middle holding an end of a rope in each hand and the outer two picked at the cord. Although not ideal we managed better this way.

Sometime later another bell sounded and we all filed out of the room and into a huge hallway filled with tables and benches, at the far end of the room, one either side, stood two women behind huge pots from which steam was rising. The girls formed a queue either side of the room and slowly filed past the servers and then went to sit and eat at the tables. I was given a plate on which was a slice of beef and mutton pudding with some soggy vegetables. It was not too bad but it was nothing as good as Mama would have made.

My thoughts went immediately to my family and I wondered where they were and what they were doing. After dinner we went back to the rope room and worked all afternoon, another bell rang sounding supper which was a slice of bread and butter with a glass of milk. Then we went back to our dormitory and climbed between the rough blankets hoping to find sleep. I found sleep hard to come by despite my fatigue, I could not stop worrying about the others and as I lay there in the dark I felt the tears begin to trickle softly down my face. Even in a room full of other girls, I had never felt so alone.

Tommy walked as far as the door and turned to see his sister standing across the hallway from him, he slowly raised his hand and gave her a slight wave of farewell, and he hoped he was smiling but he didn't feel inside as if he was. They were both reluctant to leave first but a queue of girls pushed Millie through the door and out of his sight. This wasn't what they had been expecting, they had heard of the workhouse, and as far as they knew it was a place where families could go and they would be given food and shelter in return for work. None of them were afraid of hard work and so it had been decided to be the best option for the short term.

He had been given a uniform and then had found a bed in a room absolutely packed with boys aged between eight and thirteen; after a bell had rung he had followed the others outside where they had spent the rest of the day, apart from a break for dinner, breaking stones. After supper he had gratefully climbed onto the hard bunk and pulled the thin blanket over him, his back ached and his hands were cut and bleeding, on his left palm he had a huge angry red blister. He wondered whether his Papa could see him now and if so whether he was disappointed in the way he had taken care of his family since his death. Turning over on his stomach he buried his face in the hard pillow and sobbed.

Maria turned to watch her two elder children leave her for the first time since they had been born and it tore her heart in two. She took Danny by the hand and led him through the door indicated, trying to keep him away from the crowds as much as possible, worried about the effect it would have on him. They had been given uniforms and sent to a room filled with other women, some had children with them, and others were alone. Of all the children there, none of them looked to be above the age of eight. She was grateful to have been allowed to keep Danny with her, but worried about Millie and Tommy. She had to undress Danny and put the uniform on him as he had just stood in the centre of the room, not moving, apart from his eyes which flitted all around trying to make sense of his surroundings. A loud bell had rung, which set off a fierce trembling in her son, and she followed the others to the work room and sitting Danny at her feet began to labour all day. At dinner she could not get Danny to eat a single bite, she was already concerned how he was going to cope with all of this and wished she had paid more heed to Mrs Thompson, but she truly thought this would be the salvation they all needed to allow them time to heal.

She turned to the woman seated next to her and asked, 'have you been in here long?'

'Yes, about a year.'

'Have you any family here?'

'Yes, my husband and my son.'

'Do you get to see them?' Maria wasn't sure whether she wanted to hear the answer.

'Well we are supposed to see our children for about ten minutes every day and on Sundays we all meet for an hour or so.'

'Why didn't that happen today?'

'Well it's up to the guardians, and if they are too busy to supervise it, then we don't get to see them as we should.'

'What makes them so busy?'

'Well, if there are a lot of new folk to attend to, or any accidents or sickness, anything like that.'

At night as she lay in the bed with her son trembling beside her, she quietly prayed to the Lord to give them all the strength and courage to survive this latest ordeal. Maybe tomorrow she would be able to see her precious children, and she hoped it would help Danny, he had lost his father and now as far as he knew he had also lost his brother and sister.

The next morning as I ate my breakfast of bread, butter and gruel I listened to two girls who were seated behind me talking, they were both about my age.

'I am fed up of not being able to see my parents, we should see them every day but it's been three days now.'

'So am I but, what can we do about it?'

'Well nothing whilst we are in here, but we are free to go if we can find local work outside, so I am going to ask if there is anything to be had outside.'

'I'll come with you.'

So there was a way out to be had, I just had to wait for my wrist to heal, as we worked that day, another without seeing any of my family; a plan began to form in my head.

If you have enjoyed this book, follow Millie's story in Millie Rafferty – The Workhouse Years.

Chapter 1

Saturday 9th March 1850

The bell sounded outside in the corridor, I slid out from beneath the thin blanket and stepped onto the cold stone floor. I quickly pulled on my shoes and dragged my fingers through my hair in an effort to remove some of the knots. I was about to begin my fifth day in the workhouse, my family had entered here on Tuesday to seek sanctuary, shelter, food and a time to heal before once more seeking work and a place to live. We hadn't realised that we would be housed separately from each other. Although I had been told that normally we would be allowed to see the other members of our family for about ten minutes each day and an hour on Sunday, so far I had only seen the girls I shared the large dormitory with; we ate, slept and worked together. Irene, the young girl who had offered me a place to sleep alongside her and one of her sisters, had also told me that we received three hours of tuition each day but again this had not happened, we had learnt that it was due to a number of the guardians being ill and they were short of staff to carry out all of the duties. So until they were fully staffed we made do, I desperately hoped that the situation would improve by Sunday and I would get to see my mother and brothers.

The circumstances which had brought us to this desolate place were tragic, we had fled Ireland, the country of our birth, three years ago in order to escape the potato famine which claimed thousands of lives due to starvation and disease, emigrating to England and settling in Liverpool. Through determination, hard work and some good fortune we had managed to secure work and find acceptable accommodation. Then in January my mother had been taken ill with bronchial pneumonia, whilst she was ill my father had gone out with my youngest brother Danny to collect money owed to us from our laundry work. He had been robbed and attacked and died of his injuries. Danny had also suffered injury and due to having witnessed the attack on Papa he was now suffering from shock, which had resulted in him not talking and being terrified of leaving the house. My other brother Tommy and I had tried to keep things going but when I had fallen at work and broken my wrist we had to admit defeat. My brother's wage was not enough to feed us let alone pay for the rent on our furnished room and so we had come here in order that we did not have to sleep rough and beg on the streets, neither Mama or Danny's health were up to this at the moment.

I followed the other girls into the large kitchen and lined up to receive my plate of bread and gruel, walking over to take my seat at one of the long wooden tables to eat my breakfast. I walked slowly trying to catch a glimpse of two girls who I had overheard talking yesterday about leaving this place, I wanted to know more, I had already decided that if we could not be housed together then the whole purpose of us coming here was pointless. We had, naively perhaps, thought we would live together as a family unit but men, women, girls and boys were all housed apart. The only exceptions were young children, under seven, who stayed with their mothers; although Danny was eight and a half he had been allowed to stay with Mama due to his condition.

I had spotted the girls and seeing an empty space upon their table I quickly made my way over and sat down opposite them. I listened as they chatted but no reference to their conversation of the previous day was made so I decided to take matters into my own hands.

'Excuse me,' I said looking over at them both, 'I didn't mean to eavesdrop on you yesterday but I thought I heard you talking about leaving here.'

They looked at each other and then back at me; they seemed to be deciding whether or not to answer me.

'What if you did?' the fair haired girl eventually said defensively.

'Well I would like to know how you set about doing it,' I said hoping they felt they could trust me.

'Why?' was the abrupt reply.

'Because I very much want to leave here as soon as I possibly can.'

The dark haired girl who as yet had not spoken touched her friend on the arm and said, 'Come on Nancy, let's go.'

Nancy pulled her arm away and asked me, 'what have you done to your wrist?'

'I broke it last week at work.'

'Where were you working?'

'At the Edwards' house, doing their laundry. Do you know it?'

'No I don't think so.'

I pushed my plate away, the gruel had now gone cold and I was more interested in keeping Nancy talking than eating.

'Have you been in here long?' I asked, I knew I didn't have long left before the bell would ring instructing us to go to our various work rooms.

'Two months, I came in with my parents after my father lost his job due to illness, we couldn't afford to pay the rent anymore and we were told that we all had to come with him even though we were not ill. At least until this week I had seen them both briefly every day and we get to be together each Sunday, but this week because the staff are ill I haven't seen them at all. I might as well take my chances outside.'

'Can you just leave then?'

'Well no, but if you can prove you have found some work you can. We also were receiving lessons every day so now I can read, write and add up a little.'

'How do you find work when you are in here?' I asked as the bell sounded.

Nancy rose from her seat and said, 'many of the town's folk let the guardians know if they have employment, so you ask at the matron's office.'

'Thank you so much,' I said as I carried my plate over to the sink area. I knew my wrist had some way to go before it was healed but at least I had hope.

The morning was spent as every other day since I had entered this place, painstakingly unpicking ropes, but after dinner of stew and potatoes we were told to report to the classroom for tuition. We spent the next three hours being taught reading and writing. I was ecstatic because not only was I learning, which I knew would help me to secure employment, but I also hoped that this meant the staff were returning to their duties and I would see my beloved family tomorrow.

That night sleep didn't come easily, I was excited at the prospect of seeing my family once again but I also couldn't stop thinking about my dear Papa who we had lost only a few short weeks ago. I could picture his face so clearly in my mind, his clear blue eyes and thick curly dark hair, his lopsided smile that was never far from his lips. He was a very loving father and was quick to praise and slow to scold, I had never thought that he would not be around to see me get married and give him grandchildren. I knew they would have doted on him and he on them, I felt that I had grown even closer to him during the time we had spent making the perilous journey from our small holding in Ireland, across the Irish sea to England. We had had to start a new life from scratch, landing in Liverpool with only three pennies and the clothes we were wearing, but we had done it and even when times were tough never once did my father waiver in his belief that we would survive. As I lay in the darkness, the tears falling from my eyes I vowed to bring our family back together and provide for them once again.

Printed in Great Britain
by Amazon